ALSO BY TOM McCARTHY

Remainder
Tintin and the Secret of Literature

Tom McCarthy

ALFRED A. KNOPF NEW YORK 2010

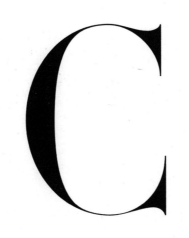

THIS IS A BORZOI BOOK
PUBLISHED BY ALFRED A. KNOPF

Copyright © 2010 by Tom McCarthy

www.aaknopf.com

Knopf, Borzoi Books, and the colophon are registered trademarks of
Random House, Inc.

Originally published in Great Britain by Jonathan Cape,
the Random House Group Ltd., London.
A portion of this work previously appeared in *Granta*.

Library of Congress Cataloging-in-Publication Data
McCarthy, Tom, [date]
C / by Tom McCarthy.—1st ed.
p.   cm.
ISBN 978-0-307-59333-7
1. Technology—Fiction.   2. Self-actualization (Psychology)—Fiction.   I. Title.
PR6113.C369C3   2010   823'.92—dc22   2010004071

Designed by M. Kristen Bearse

Manufactured in the United States of America
First United States Edition

FOR EVA STENRAM

Ourselves must we beneath the Couch of Earth
Descend, ourselves to make a Couch—for whom?

—OMAR KHAYYÁM

ONE

Caul

I

i

D r. Learmont, newly appointed general practitioner for the districts of West Masedown and New Eliry, rocks and jolts on the front seat of a trap as it descends the lightly sloping path of Versoie House. He has sore buttocks: the seat's hard and uncushioned. His companion, Mr. Dean of Hudson and Dean Deliveries (Lydium and Environs Since 1868), doesn't seem to feel any discomfort. His glazed eyes stare vaguely ahead; his leathery hands, reins woven through their fingers, hover just above his knees. The rattle of glass bottles and the fricative rasp of copper wire against more copper wire rise from the trap's back and, mixing with the click and shuffle of the horse's hooves on gravel, hang undisturbed about the still September air. Above the vehicle tall conifers rise straight and inert as columns. Higher, much further out, black birds whirr silently beneath a concave vault of sky.

Between the doctor's legs are wedged a brown case and a black inhaling apparatus. In his hand he holds a yellow piece of paper. He's scrutinising this, perplexed, as best he can. From time to time he glances up from it to peer through the curtain of conifers, which reveal, then quickly conceal again, glimpses of mown grass and rows of smaller trees with white fruit and green and red foliage. There's movement around these: small limbs reaching, touching and separating in a semi-regular pattern, as though practising a butterfly or breaststroke.

The trap rolls through a hanging pall of wood smoke, then turns, clearing the conifers. Now Learmont can see that the limbs belong to children, four or five of them, playing some kind of game. They stand in a loose circle, raising their arms and patting their hands together. Their lips are moving, but no sound's emerging from them. Occasionally a squawk of laughter ricochets around the orchard, but it's hard to tell which child it's coming from. Besides, the laughter doesn't sound quite right. It sounds distorted, slightly warped—ventriloquised almost, as though piped in from somewhere else. None of the children seem to notice his arrival; none of them, in fact, seem to be aware of their own individual presence outside and beyond that of the moving circle, their separateness given over to its fleshy choreography of multiplied, entwining bodies.

Without jerking the reins or speaking to the horse, Mr. Dean pulls the trap to a halt. Beside it, to its right, a narrow, still stream lies in front of a tall garden wall over which, from the far side, ferns and wisteria are spilling. To the trap's left, a veined set of rose-bush stems and branches, flowers gone, clings to another wall. The wood-smoke pall comes from beyond this. So, too, does an old man with a rake, emerging from a doorway in the wall to shunt a wheelbarrow across the gravel.

"Hello!" Learmont calls out to him. "Hello?"

The old man stops, sets down his wheelbarrow and looks back at Learmont.

"Can you tell me where to find the main house? The entrance?"

The old man gestures with his free hand: *over there.* Then, taking up the handle of his wheelbarrow once more, he shuffles past the trap towards the orchard. Learmont listens as his footsteps die away. Eventually he turns to Mr. Dean and says:

"Silent as a tomb."

Mr. Dean shrugs. Dr. Learmont climbs down onto the gravel, shakes his legs and looks around. The old man seemed to be pointing beyond the overspilling garden wall. This, too, has a small doorway in it.

"Why don't you wait here?" Learmont suggests to Mr. Dean. "I'll go and find—" he holds his yellow paper up and scrutinises it again— "this Mr. Carrefax."

Mr. Dean nods. Dr. Learmont takes his case and inhaler, steps onto a strip of grass and crosses a small wooden bridge above the moat-like stream. Then, lowering his head beneath wisteria that manage to brush it nonetheless, he walks through the doorway.

Inside the garden are chrysanthemums, irises, tulips and anemones, all stacked and tumbling over one another on both sides of a path of uneven mosaic paving stones. Learmont follows the path towards a passageway formed by hedges and a roof of trellis strung with poisonberries and some kind of wiry, light-brown vine whose strands lead off to what look

4

like stables. As he nears the passageway, he can hear a buzzing sound. He stops and listens. It seems to be coming from the stables: an intermittent, mechanical buzz. Learmont thinks of going in and asking the people operating the machinery for more directions, but, reasoning that it might be running on its own, decides instead to continue following the path. This forks to the right and, after passing through a doorway in another wall, splits into a maze-pattern that unfolds across a lawn on whose far side stands another wall containing yet another doorway. Learmont strides across the lawn and steps through this third doorway, which deposits him onto the edge of the orchard he saw as he first arrived. The large, lightly sloping gravel path he descended with Mr. Dean is now on the orchard's far side, half-hidden by the conifers; a smaller footpath, on which he's now standing, lies perpendicular to this, between the garden's outer wall and the orchard's lower edge. The children are still there, wrapped up in their mute pantomime. Learmont runs his eye beyond them: the rows of small, white-fruited trees give over to an unkempt lawn that, after sixty yards or so, turns into a field on which the odd sheep grazes. The field rises to a ridge; a telegraph line runs across this, then falls down the far side, away from view.

Learmont glances at his paper once again, then turns to his left and follows the footpath along the garden's outer wall—until he eventually finds, at the end of this, the house.

ii

He rings the bell, then steps back and looks up at the building. Its front is overgrown with ivy that has started to turn red. He rings the bell again, bringing his ear up to the door. This time someone's heard it: he can hear footsteps approaching. A maid opens for him. She looks flustered: her hair is dishevelled, her sleeves rolled up and her hands and brow wet. A girl of three or four stands behind her, holding a towel. Both maid and girl look at Learmont's case and inhaler.

"Delivery?" the maid asks.

"Well, I . . . yes," he answers, holding up his paper. "I've come to—"

A man appears from within the house and pushes his way past the maid and child.

"Zinc and selenium?" he barks out.

"That's in the trap," Learmont replies. "But I came with it to—"

"And acid? And the reels of copper?" the man interrupts. He's portly and his voice is booming. He must be forty, forty-four. "Came to—what?"

"I came to deliver the baby."

"Came to—ah, yes! Deliver: of course! Splendid! You can . . . Yes, let's see . . . Maureen can show you where . . . You say the copper's in the drive?"

"Beyond the . . ." Dr. Learmont tries to point back past the gardens, but he can't remember which direction he's just come from.

"And there's a man there with it? Perhaps you could help us to—"

"Sir . . ." the maid says.

"Maureen—what?" the man replies. Maureen gasps at him exasperatedly. He stares at her for a few seconds and then slaps his thigh and tells her: "No, of course: you take the doctor to her. Is everything . . . ?"

"Fine, sir," Maureen informs him. "Thanks for your concern."

"Splendid!" he booms. "Well, you just carry on. Maureen will see to it that you have everything you . . . Is that the telegram?"

He's looking at Learmont's yellow paper, his eyes glowing with excitement.

"I was a little confused . . ." Learmont begins, but the man grabs the paper off him and begins to read aloud:

" '. . . expected next twenty-four hours' . . . good . . . 'parturient in labour since last night . . .' Excellent! 'Parturient,' each letter crystal clear!"

"We weren't quite sure as to the provenance . . ."

"What—provenance? Hang on: what's this? 'Doctor refuested as soon as . . .'? 'Refuested'? What's that for a damn word?"

"Sir!" Maureen says.

"She's heard much worse," he barks. " 'Refuested'? I've been . . . That blasted key!"

"Sweet Jesus!" says Maureen. She turns to the child and takes the towel from her. Another woman appears from the hallway, carrying a tray of biscuits out towards the orchard and trailing in her wake a cat. "Go with Miss Hubbard," Maureen tells the child.

". . . F . . . Q . . ." the man mumbles, then, barking again: "Provenance?"

"We weren't quite sure of the telegram's provenance," Learmont explains. "It didn't originate in the post office down the road in Lydium, yet it seemed to come down the same line which—"

"Miss Hubbard," the man says, "wait."

The second woman pauses in the doorway. "Yes, Mr. Carrefax?" she asks.

"Miss Hubbard, I can't hear the children speaking," he tells her.

"They're playing, Mr. Carrefax," she replies.

"Are you sure they're not signing?"

"I told them that's not allowed. I think they—"

"What? Told them? Telling them won't do it on its own! You have to *make* them speak. All the time!"

The child is reaching her arm up to the tray of biscuits. The cat is watching the child's efforts closely, still and tense. Maureen takes Learmont's sleeve and starts to pull him into the house.

"The provenance, good doctor, is right here!" Mr. Carrefax booms at him as he squeezes past. "*F* and *Q* notwithstanding. Disappointing. Fixable. The copper! In the drive, you say?"

"There's a man waiting in a—"

"Splendid! Miss Hubbard, if I can't hear them I'll think they're signing."

"I'll do what I can, Mr. Carrefax," Miss Hubbard tells him.

"At all times!" he barks at her. "I want to hear them *speak*!"

He strides out with her, heading for the drive. The child follows the biscuits, and the cat follows the child. Maureen leads Dr. Learmont in the other direction, up the staircase. There's a tapestry hanging above this, a silk weaving that depicts either this same staircase or one very similar to it. They cross the landing at the top and step into a room. A second tapestry hangs on the wall of this: another picture woven in silk, this time of an Oriental scene in which pony-tailed peasants reach up into trees full of the same white fruit as the ones in the orchard. Lower down the tapestry, beneath the trees, more peasants are unravelling dark balls. Beneath them, in the room itself, a woman lies supine on a bed. A bearing-down sheet has been tied around the mattress, but the woman isn't clutching this. She's lying back quite peacefully, although her thick brown hair is wet with sweat. A second maid sits beside her on a chair, holding her hand. The woman in the bed smiles vaguely at Learmont.

"Mrs. Carrefax?" he asks her.

She nods. Dr. Learmont sets down his canister and, opening his case across the bed, asks:

"How far apart are your contractions?"

"Three minutes," she tells him. Her voice is soft and grainy. There's something slightly unusual about it, something beyond fatigue, that Learmont can't quite place: it's not a foreign voice, but not quite native, either. He takes her blood pressure. As he removes the strap her body is seized by a new contraction. Her face scrunches, her mouth opens, but no scream or shout comes from it: just a low, barely perceptible growling. The contraction lasts for ten or fifteen seconds.

"Painful?" Learmont asks her when it's over.

"It is as though I had been poisoned," she replies. She turns her head away from him and gazes through the window at the sky.

"Have you been taking any painkillers?" he asks.

She doesn't answer. He repeats the question.

"She has to see you speaking," the bedside maid tells him.

"What?"

"She has to see your lips move, sir. She's deaf."

He leans over the bed and waves his hand in front of Mrs. Carrefax's face; she turns her head towards him. He repeats his question once more. She seems to understand it, but just smiles vaguely back at him again.

"Small doses of laudanum, sir," the bedside maid says.

"I prefer chloroform," Learmont says.

Mrs. Carrefax's eyes light up. Her soft, grainy, strange voice utters the word "Chlorodyne?"

"No, chloro*form*," Learmont tells her, pronouncing the name clearly and emphatically. He takes a gauze mask from his case and, fixing this to the end of his inhaler's tube, straps it round Mrs. Carrefax's face. He opens a valve on the canister's neck; a long, slow hissing seeps out as the gas makes its way along the canvas corridor towards her mouth and nose. The muscles in Mrs. Carrefax's cheeks slacken; her pupils dilate. After half a minute Learmont closes the valve and unstraps the mask. A second contraction soon follows; again the woman's body seizes up, but her face registers less pain. He refixes the mask, administers more chloroform and watches the silent features further slacken and dilate beneath their gag. When he removes it again, she begins to murmur:

". . . un fleuve . . . un serpent d'eau noir . . ."

"What's that?" he asks.

"It is like a fall of velvet," she tells him. "Black velvet . . . covering a camera . . ."

"That's the chloroform," he says.

". . . a camera," she tells him, "looking in the dark . . . There is a river with a water snake, swimming towards me . . . More." Her hand releases the bedside maid's and gestures to the canister.

"I don't want to knock you out completely," Dr. Learmont says. "I'll let you—"

"Sophie!" Maureen gasps. Learmont follows her eyes towards the doorway. The child is standing in it, watching. Maureen walks over and plants herself in front of her, blocking her view of the room. "You shouldn't be here!" she scolds—then, softening, scoops her up into her arms and says: "We'll go and help Frieda make the kenno." As Learmont listens to her heavy footsteps descending the staircase, another contraction takes hold of Mrs. Carrefax. He takes from his case a bottle of carbolic acid and tells the bedside maid to go and fetch him olive oil.

"Olive oil, sir?" she repeats.

"Yes," he answers, rolling up his sleeves. "Not long to wait now."

But there is long to wait: all afternoon, and more. He leaves the room twice: once to stretch his legs in the hallway, from whose window he watches Mr. Carrefax and Mr. Dean carrying the coils of copper wire and crates of bottles through the walled-in garden to the stables; once to eat some sandwiches the maids have knocked up for him. He administers more chloroform and hears, above the hiss, the sound of Mr. Dean's trap making its way up the gravel path, departing. The contractions continue; Mrs. Carrefax dips into and out of her twilight sleep. Dusk turns into evening, then night.

The final pushes come at half past two. The bedside maid holds Mrs. Carrefax's shoulders, Mrs. Carrefax grips the bearing-down sheet and the baby's head appears between her legs—or rather, half-appears behind a glistening film of plasma, a skin-membrane. Learmont has heard of this phenomenon but never witnessed it before: the baby has a caul. The amniotic bag envelops the entire head, a silky hood. As soon as the baby's fully out, Learmont pinches this away from its skin and peels it upwards from the neck, removing it. He washes off the green-and-red mess covering the rest of the body, ties and cuts the cord, wraps the baby in a sheet and hands it to the mother.

"A boy," he tells her. "Now we need to get your afterbirth out."

He starts filling a syringe with epithemalodine. When it's ready, he takes the baby back from her and places him in the maid's hands. The baby starts to cry.

"This will sting a little," Learmont says, tapping the air bubbles out. He straps the gauze mask to the mother's face again and turns the chloroform back on, then shoots the epithemalodine into the folds of her vagina. Her body flinches; her back arches, then relaxes into the bed again. The placenta follows shortly afterwards. Learmont turns the valve off, looks down at the muffled woman and tells her:

"I'll get rid of this—unless you want to bury it. Some people do. Some people even fry it up and eat it. And the caul is meant to be a sign of—"

But she cuts him short with a gesture of her hand towards the canister.

"It can't hurt, I suppose," he says. "We'll give it a couple more minutes." He turns the valve back on. Mrs. Carrefax's eyes warm and widen. The baby stops crying. For a long while the room is silent but for the hiss of the chloroform and, quieter than this, the intermittent mechanical buzzing he heard earlier, floating in from outside, from the stables.

iii

At dawn he's fed a breakfast of kippers, eggs and bread. When he's finished Maureen tells him that Mr. Carrefax would like to see him.

"Where is he?" Learmont asks her.

She snorts and answers: "In his workshop, of course. Follow the house round to the left and you'll find it, through a doorway in the garden wall."

There's dew on the grass and snakes of mist about the tree trunks in the orchard where the children were playing yesterday. Following the perimeter of the house as instructed, Learmont turns away from the orchard and, walking towards a part of the estate he didn't cross on his way in, passes some kind of enclosed park. A gate is set in its tall wall, its columns topped with obelisk-shaped carvings. Behind the wall, taller, conker trees loom, their leaves all big and yellow. The park drops away as the ivy-coated house wall turns and leads him across a neat lawn held in by low walls, then onwards through a further wall of hedge onto a smaller, unmown lawn around whose far side lime trees stand. He picks a very quiet buzzing sound up as he moves across this, but it's not the same as the buzzing he heard coming from the stables: this one seems less agitated, less electrical. He understands why as he comes to the lawn's far side: beehives are set among the limes. He skirts these and passes through a second hedge-wall to emerge into a sub-section of garden in which a rectangular trough-pond sits absolutely still, covered in pea-green slime. At the far end of this sub-section, a door leads back into the walled-in garden he arrived through yesterday. He tries it, but it's locked. He can hear a metallic snipping sound on the other side.

"Mr. Carrefax?" he calls.

The metallic snipping stops and Mr. Carrefax's voice booms back: "What? Who's that?"

"The doctor," Learmont calls back. "The baby's fine and well."

"Fine and—what? I've misplaced the key to this door, I'm afraid. You'll have to come in through the far side. Follow the wall round."

It's not apparent how to do this: the wall's so overgrown with ivy and with bushes extending outwards like buttresses that it's hard to tell where it leads. Learmont detours away from it into a long avenue of conker trees behind which lies an apple orchard. The avenue takes him towards a set of smaller houses, but before he reaches these he picks the wall up again, emerging from still swirls of tangled hedge to turn and run beside the narrow, moat-like stream that he crossed yesterday; eventually it passes the same wooden bridge and presents to him, once he's re-crossed this, the same small doorway. He's come full circle. He bows his head again, steps back through the wisteria onto uneven mosaic paving and moves once more between the rows of stacked-up tulips and chrysanthemums.

The purple of the irises seems stronger, more intense that it did yesterday. The passageway formed by the hedges and trellis seems more closed-in, more laced-over. The wiry, light-brown vines that split from the poisonberries and run off towards the stables seem to have multiplied. When he arrives beneath them he sees that they're not vines at all: they're strands of copper wire, and more have been strung up since yesterday. The coils that came with him in Hudson and Dean's trap are spilling unravelled from the stables' entrances. Mr. Carrefax is standing over one with metal cutters, measuring a length.

"Hold this," he tells Learmont, handing him one end.

Dr. Learmont obeys. Mr. Carrefax paces from the stable to a point on the trellis, paying out the length as he goes.

"Twelve feet, I'd say. Remember that. You hungry?"

"I've had eggs and kippers and—"

"Kippers and—what? Take kenno with me. There's some groaning malt as well. Splendid stuff!"

He leads Learmont into one of the stables. Benches of machinery lie under shelves on which sit rows of instruments: telegraph tappers, telephone receivers, large phonograph machines with strips of paper hanging from them, wax cylinders, bottles, objects and instruments whose name and function he can only guess at. On a work table, among metal shavings, are a jug of dark brown liquid, two mugs and some cheesecake. Wiping his hands on a cloth whose surface looks no cleaner than they are, Mr. Carrefax cuts two slices of the cheesecake with a knife, hands one to the doctor, then pours out two mugs of malt.

"Breakfast, lunch, dinner—who knows? Haven't slept all night," he tells Learmont. "Your health, Doctor!"

The malt's refreshing; the cheesecake is rich and sharp. The two men eat and drink in silence for a moment.

"I've fixed it," Mr. Carrefax tells Dr. Learmont after a while.

"Fixed what?" Learmont asks.

"The F and Q firk—quirk, I mean. It wouldn't have happened if I'd run the wire all the way from here up to the public lines uninterrupted."

"I'm not sure I understand," Learmont says.

"Aha!" booms Mr. Carrefax. He places a firm hand on Learmont's back and marches him out to the workshop's entrance. "Look!" he says, pointing up at the trails of copper running over their heads to merge with the curling poisonberries on the trellis. "Where do you think they end?"

Learmont's eyes follow the trellis to the wall and the locked door on whose far side he stood five minutes ago. Among the billowing mesh of ivy and bushes stands a kind of metal weathercock. The wires are wound around the base of this like serpents.

"They end there?" he asks.

"Aha!" booms Carrefax again. "Yes—and no! The wires end, but the *signal* jumps onwards! Five feet, for the moment. With this copper I'll be able to increase it to ten—fifteen even. It's been jumped further, mind you. That Italian is out on Salisbury Plain right now, with all his towers and masts and kites . . . He's in with the Post Office, you see? Got all the funding. Always the way! A mentor—nod, wink here and there: probably a Freemason. The new birth will bear his name no doubt, when it comes. Boy or girl?"

"The baby? A boy."

"Splendid! Splendid! Have some more malt and kenno. Came out smoothly? The girl had to be dragged out. Virtually needed toys set at the foot of the bed before she'd show."

"It took a while, but he came calmly in the end. He had a caul."

"Had a—what? A cold?"

"A caul. A veil around his head: a kind of web. It's meant to bring good luck—especially to sailors."

"Sailors? I tell you, Doctor: get this damn thing working and they won't need luck. There'll be a web around the world for them to send their signals down. You came with the delivery trap?"

"Yes. The telegraph company's woman had taken both your messages, so she knew Hudson and Dean were sending a man down."

"Splendid! You need transport back, though."

"Lydium's not far. I can walk there and take a train."

"No need to walk!" booms Mr. Carrefax. "I'll telegraph for a new trap to come and fetch you."

"Oh, that won't be necessary," Dr. Learmont tells him. "The walk will clear my head."

"Will clear your—what? I wouldn't hear of it! Go back into the house. Rest while I jump your orders clear over the wall."

Dr. Learmont obeys. He's too tired not to. He walks back through the irises and chrysanthemums, across the narrow stream, along the avenue of conker trees. The black birds are still whirring high above them; Learmont can't tell if they've multiplied or if it's just his tiredness breaking the sky's dome into slow-moving dots. Inside the house, he gathers his possessions back into his case. He can't find the phials of epithemalodine or the codeine pills, but it's not important: there are plenty more back in the surgery.

The baby's feeding; its mother sits up in the bed, calm and contented, while the bedside maid combs her hair, unravelling it like the Chinese women pulling at their strange dark balls in the silk tapestry above them. Maureen stands at the foot of the bed; in front of her, enfolded in her arms, the girl watches her brother silently. They all watch silently: the room is silent but for the clicking lips of the sucking baby and the copper buzzing rising from the garden.

2

---

i

I n the beginning," says Simeon Carrefax, standing on a small raised podium in Schoolroom One, "—in the beginning, ladies and gentlemen, was the Word."

His audience, a gaggle of the parents of prospective pupils at the Versoie Day School for the Deaf, sit squeezed into the schoolroom's child-size chairs. Miss Hubbard stands behind them at the back of the room, her gaze darting nervously between Carrefax and a box full of small pieces of lead piping lying by her feet.

"The Word was with God," Carrefax continues, "and the Word *was* God. Which is to say: speech is divine. Speech itself breathed the earth into being—and breathed life into it, that it in turn may breathe and speak. What, I ask you, are the rising and falling of its mountains and its valleys or the constant heaving of its seas but breath? What are the winds that rush and swirl around it, now one way, now another? What are the jets of steam that gush from geysers or the spray that issues from the blow-holes of whales? And which man who has stood beside the torrent of a waterfall or, pausing in a wood, has heard the whisper of the leaves, the chirp and clamour of the birds, can deny that he has heard earth speaking?"

His eyes sweep the room intently. As they fall on individual parents, the latter cast their own eyes to the floor, or fix them on a wall-mounted whiteboard behind Carrefax. Here, drawn in charcoal across cotton-backed ground glass, a diagram shows plates, hinges, corridors and levers locked together in an intricate formation that suggests an irrigation system or the mechanism of a crane.

"And we, ladies and gentlemen: do we not also move to the same gasping and exhaling rhythm? Is not our spirit, truly named, *suspirio*? Breathing, we live; speaking, we partake of the sublime. In our conversing each one with the other—listening, responding—we form our attachments: friendships, enmities and loves. It is through our participation in the realm of speech that we become moral, learn to respect the law, to understand another's pain, and to expand and fortify our faculties through the great edifices of the arts and sciences: poetry, reason, argument, discourse. Speech is the method and the measure of our flowering into bloom. It is the currency and current of our congress in the world and all the crackling wonders of its institutions and exchanges."

He pauses, and the parents grow aware of their own breathing, suddenly loud and ponderous in the quiet of the schoolroom. He draws his head and shoulders back and continues:

"Ladies and gentlemen, I am proud to call myself an oralist. I count among my intellectual forebears Deschamps, Heinicke, Gérando and the great Alexander Bell. The human body," he says, turning half-round to tap his knuckles on the whiteboard's glass, "is a mechanism. When its engine-room, the thorax, a bone-girt vault for heart and lungs whose very floor and walls are constantly in motion—when this chamber exerts pressure sufficient to force open the trap-door set into its ceiling and send air rushing outwards through the windpipe, sound ensues. It's as simple as that. Children!" He turns to face a row of three boys and a girl who have been sitting quietly on the side of the podium, opens the palm of his right hand and raises it firmly. "Up!"

The children rise from their chairs. Like a conductor Carrefax holds his hands out and then shoves them forwards, quivering in the air in front of him—and all four children break into a chorus made up of a single word:

"*Haaaaaaa.*"

The sound is long, drawn out and without harmony or intonation. A few seconds into it several prospective parents shift in their small seats, adjusting their positions. The children's eyes stare straight ahead, vacant, as though entranced, or taken over by a set of ghosts; their shoulders, drawn back as they launched into their utterance, slowly crumple and deflate as it fades out. Carrefax draws his hands back again, then once more shoves them quivering forwards and the children moan again:

"*Haaaaaaa.*"

The sound, the second time round, seems like a response, a weary, empty answer to a hollow question. Carrefax's hands draw it out for as long as they can, all the while trembling from the effort. Eventually, though, the children's voices start to shudder, then to break down into groans, which die away as the inarticulate spirits that have seized their bodies give up and relinquish them again.

"Children," says Carrefax, turning his palms to face the podium's boards, "down!"

The children sit back in their chairs. Carrefax points at them and announces:

"When these four children came to my school, each of them was held to be not only deaf but also mute. What? Yes, *mute:* doubly afflicted. And yet how erroneous the diagnosis! Are you, sir, considered mute due to your lack of proficiency in the Mandarin tongue? Or you, madam, because you never speak Estonian and, beyond that, remain entirely ignorant of the very existence of Quichua, the language of the remote Inca people of the Andean cordillera?"

He fixes two prospective parents with his gaze. They look slightly alarmed and shake their heads.

"Of course not! No human born with thorax, throat and mouth is incapable of speaking these or any other languages! Yet how would you come to speak a tongue that you had never been exposed to, tried on, tested? So is it for the deaf child with English. Speech is not a given: it must be wrung from him, wrenched out. The body's motor must be set to work, its engine-parts aligned, fine-tuned to one another. Miss Hubbard."

Blushing, Miss Hubbard crouches down beside her box and, picking up the short lengths of lead piping, starts distributing these around the room.

"Gentlemen and ladies," Carrefax instructs the prospective parents, "press your lips firmly together and blow air between them."

The prospective parents look at one another.

"Do it!" Carrefax commands. "Compress your lips, like so—*hmmm*—and blow air through them."

He half-raises his hands in front of him again. Slowly, the prospective parents purse their lips, take deep breaths, then expel these through them like so many toddlers making farting sounds at table. As the sounds fill the room, the parents' faces redden with the strain, or with embarrassment, or both.

"It is a far-from-pleasant sound, I think you'll all agree," announces Carrefax above the tuneless rasping. "A fly trapped in a glass sounds no less gracious. But now take the length of pipe you each have in your hand and, making once again your buzz, bring the tube firmly to your lips. Go on."

The prospective parents obey. As each one presses the tube to their mouth, the flatulent rasps give over to clear, trumpet-like notes.

"Splendid!" booms Carrefax. "Now tighten your lips further." The prospective parents do this and the notes rise in pitch. "Wonderful! Now you, sir, and you, madam, loosen yours two notches while the others hold them tight." They comply; the high-pitched notes become offset by deeper ones. "Magnificent!" roars Carrefax. "We have a brass band here, no less! What symphonies we could compose! Miss Hubbard."

Miss Hubbard moves around the classroom gathering the instruments back from their players.

"Were we to pay a visit to the finest opera singer," Carrefax announces, "and, secreting ourselves among the curtains and décor of the opera house armed with a sword, rush out onto the stage right in the middle of her most enchanting aria to cut her head off in mid-song with one sharp, well-aimed blow—Splendid! Yes, what? Were we to do this, her headless neck, while air still rushed through it, would issue forth a sound just like your buzzing lips denuded of their pipes. Well, in the same way, deaf children . . . deaf children are like headless opera singers inasmuch as, inasmuch as . . ."

There's a pause while he searches for his next words; then a clang as Miss Hubbard drops a length of lead pipe to the floor. Prospective parents turn to look at her. She curtsies to pick it up; Carrefax clears his throat and continues:

"Our job here is to restore to the deaf child the function of his pipes and all their stops: the larynx with its valves; the timbre-moulding pharynx; the pillar-supported palate which, depressed, hangs like a veil before the nares; and so on. Speech, like song, is but the mechanical result of certain adjustments of the vocal organs. If we explain to deaf children the correct adjustments of the organs they possess, *they will speak*. Timothy, Samuel and Felicity—" he points to three of his four protégés, opens his palm and resolutely raises it towards the ceiling—"up!"

The two boys and the girl rise once more. Carrefax conducts them with one hand this time, using it to sculpt precise shapes and positions in the air in front of him, repeating a sequence which is mirrored in the looping series of sounds that spill from the children in unison:

"*Ah ee o ee, ah ee o ee, ah ee o ee . . .*"

He lets the sequence run through several times, then brings it to a halt with a decapitating slice.

"Here, with the mere sinking and lifting of the palate, we already have the base for a range of words. Timothy." He singles out a boy with freckles and, pinching his own ear between his fingers, draws from the boy the utterance:

"*Ee-ah.*"

"Splendid! Good lad!" he booms. Then, taking a piece of charcoal, he writes on the board the word *area* before pointing to the girl. "Felicity."

Felicity pronounces the progression "*aih-ree-ah.*" Its second syllable is expelled with a heavy breath.

"Splendid again!" booms Carrefax. He turns back to the board, wipes out *area* and writes in its place *eerie*. "Samuel."

The round, blond Samuel reads the word aloud. Again a heavy exhalation flushes out the "*rie.*" Carrefax nods at him contentedly, turns to his audience and tells them:

"*Ear, area, eerie:* the slightest command of our vocal apparatus opens up for us the wherewithal to indicate the body's organs, to conceive of blocks of space, to name the southernmost of North America's Great Lakes and to express the air of mystery that clouds our dreams. How much more of a blossoming of our verbal powers arises when we bring into play the tongue, which flicks against the palate's ceiling like the brush of Michelangelo against the Sistine Chapel's still-wet plaster, or the lips which frame the masterpieces crafted in our throats and mouths—and, in so doing, attract, as temples to the pilgrims of our eyes. How right is Romeo, upon his first meeting with Juliet, to shun her palmistry! Our lips communicate, not our hands. Watch this profoundly deaf child read mine—and listen as this supposedly mute child uses the full range of her own vocal apparatus to respond." He turns to Felicity and, fixing her with an intense stare, says to her slowly: "Felicity, what part of England were you born in?"

There's a pause, then Felicity replies: "Talesbury, Mr. Carrefax." She pronounces the *T* and *b* of "Talesbury" with utter precision, but its vowels drag and stretch out, as though snagged on the consonants. The *f* and *x* of "Carrefax" hiss like a punctured football.

"Splendid! Now ask Timothy how many brothers he has."

Felicity turns to the freckled boy and says, slowly and diligently:

"Timothy: how many brothers have you?"

Timothy eventually responds: "I have two brothers." His voice is slightly deeper than hers; his final *s* resembles more a buzz than a hiss. His hands twitch slightly by his sides as he intones the words, then cling to the fabric of his shorts, as though tethering themselves down.

"Splendid! And now, Felicity and Timothy both: tell me, what poem have you been committing to heart of late?"

The children reply together but slightly off-kilter: " 'The Shepheardes Calender.' "

"Recite the first few stanzas for our friends here," Carrefax instructs them. The children turn away from one another; Carrefax cues Felicity with a nod and she declaims:

> *Cuddie, for shame hold up thy heavy head,*
> *And let us cast with what delight to chase,*
> *And weary this long lingering Phoebus race.*
> *Whilhom thou wont the shepherd's lads to lead,*
> *In rhymes, in riddles, and in bidding base . . .*

She speaks slowly and deliberately; the words snag and stretch and drag and hiss again. Prospective parents lean forward in their undersize chairs, straining to catch the meaning of her phrases. These give the strange effect of coming from some other speaker lurking out of view— off to the podium's side, or under it. A couple of prospective parents glance around the room, disoriented. When Felicity's finished, Carrefax nods at Timothy and he begins:

> *Piers, I have pipéd erst so long with pain,*
> *That all mine Oten reeds be rent and wore:*
> *And my poor Muse hath spent her sparéd store,*
> *Yet little good hath got, and much less gain.*
> *Such pleasance makes the Grasshopper so poor,*
> *And lie so laid, when Winter doth her strain . . .*

His words, like Felicity's, seem to issue not from him but rather to divert *through* him—as though his mouth, once it formed and held the correct shape for long enough, received a sound spirited in from another spot, some other area, eerie, ear.

In a room to the side of this one, Schoolroom Two, Simeon's son Serge spends what he has been told in passing, although only by the maid, is his second-and-a-half birthday playing with wooden blocks. He sits on a floor which, unlike the bare wooden floor of Schoolroom One, is muffled by a rug. Morning sunshine falls in a long beam through the bow-window, vaults the cosy recess seat that runs along the inside of the window's curve and comfortably lands among the rug's curling hairs; rising from these, it hovers in jars and bottles in which labelled toys—horses, cars, clowns and acrobats—are stashed. More labels, unattached to objects, spill from a low table to spread a debris of words across the floor.

The wooden blocks have geometric figures painted on them, like numbers on dice: squares, triangles, circles and other, more complex forms. On a single side of each block (the side that, were they dice, would bear the number six), several of these figures have been combined so as to form a picture—of a cyclist, a house, a hippopotamus or a magician pulling a rabbit from his hat, for instance. Serge has stacked the magician above the cyclist and, above that, a butcher who clutches a knife in one hand and a string of sausages in the other, holding them up for inspection much as the magician does his rabbit. The figures all appear in profile, flat; the landscape across which the cyclist rides, made up of rectangles and segments, is as shallow as the round wheels above which his trapezoid body sits—as though, even within the painted world of the block's surface, he were no more than a cardboard cut-out posed in front of a piece of stage-scenery. Serge ponders the combination for a while, then, holding cyclist and magician in place, removes the butcher and replaces him with the large, round hippopotamus, who wallows, again in profile, in an elliptic pool of mud. Serge holds this new vertical line-up together while he contemplates it; then, deciding it's satisfactory, he removes his hands from the stack. As soon as he does, it starts to wobble, the combined weight of hippo, mud, rabbit and magician proving too much for the beleaguered cyclist, who's further let down by the soft, uneven surface underneath his wheels. As the blocks tumble, rhombi, trapezia and deltoids flash and disappear in a frantic progression, spreading out across the rug.

Serge looks up at the window, then at a whiteboard on whose surface more geometry is displayed: rows of round shapes with lines inside them have been drawn on it. The shapes modulate as they repeat, their curves narrowing or widening, their lines arcing and flexing as they process across the glass. Looking down again, Serge turns his attention to a toy soldier who's been resting until now against his thigh. Picking the soldier up, he holds him to his face. The soldier's eyes are neutral, gazing off into the middle distance; his mouth is set in a calm, still expression that contains the tiniest hint of a smile. Serge lays the soldier front-up on the rug, smoothing its hairs aside to form an enclave for the back to nestle in. The thick fibres thread and wrap around the soldier's sides. Serge reaches for one of the wooden blocks and, lifting it up above the soldier, slams it down hard onto his face. The soldier's legs and feet jolt upwards as the comparatively huge slab hits him. Serge draws the block back, then slams it down onto the soldier's face again; then again, several times. When he's done smashing him he holds the soldier up to inspect the damage. His eyes are unaffected, still vague and distant, but his mouth has been deformed, its plaster dented and chipped away. Serge scrapes at the ground-down surface with his thumbnail, lifting off more flakes of plaster. Then, to no one but himself since he's alone, he says:

"Bodner."

He sets the soldier down gently on the rug, propping him up in a sitting position against the wooden block that's just mutilated him. Serge is reaching out towards another block when his attention is distracted by the hurried entrance of the family cat and, close on its tail, his older sister Sophie. Sophie is half running, half skipping, with clenched hands held out in front of her. Placing herself between the cat and the door, she thrusts her hands towards the cat and sings:

"Spitalfield! Oh, Spitalfield!"

The cat retreats beneath the recess seat. Sophie stoops low and creeps towards it, opening her palms to reveal four or five small white larval balls nestled warmly in them.

"Just try one, Spitalfield," she purrs, holding the balls temptingly up to the cat's face. The cat turns its head away, then, ducking beneath her hands, breaks cover and darts out of the room. Sophie lets out a sigh and, setting the larvae on the recess seat's cushion, turns her attention to Serge. Scooping three or four of the wooden blocks up from the carpet, she starts laying them out in front of him. Then, kneeling behind them and pulling the front of her skirt forwards so that it covers the figures on their surface, she says: "If you can remember which one is which I'll give you my pocket money. If not, forfeit."

But Serge doesn't want to play her game. He reaches between her legs, pushing through the pleated fabric. She grabs his wrist and pulls it out again. "Forfeit!" she cackles. "Take your trousers down."

"No!" Serge snaps. But she's stronger than him. She wraps her arm around him, pulls him to his feet and, still kneeling beside him, yanks his trousers down his legs. He wriggles as she pulls the pants beneath these down as well.

"Aha!" she shouts in triumph. "Now to telegraph the Admiralty." Holding him in place, she begins tapping his little penis with her index finger. " 'Dear Sir: Please send reinforcements,' *tap-tap-tap*. 'Enemy quite outnumber us,' *tap-tap*. 'Are holding out but fear total submission if not soon relieved,' *tap-tip tap-tip*."

"Stop it!" Serge shouts.

"Why? I've seen Miss Hubbard do it. She did it with the man from Lydium. 'Dear Man from Lydium,' *tap-tap,* 'please send more charcoal and wipers for our school class,' *tip-tip-tip*. 'Weather here fine but rain is forecast for tomorrow.' *Tippety-tap*. See? You're laughing."

"No I'm not!" Serge shouts, straining to get away. Eventually he manages to break loose. Sophie half-heartedly grabs after him, but he pushes her hands away. Moving a safe distance from her, he pulls his pants and trousers up, then gathers the wooden blocks up in his cradled arm and shuffles through the door through which the cat's just made its own escape.

Sophie watches him go, then shrugs, sits back and tilts her head to one side as she looks up at the whiteboard. As she runs her eyes along the rows of round, lined shapes, her mouth forms positions, holding each in place for several seconds before morphing to strike up the next one: her jaw lowering and lifting, cheeks tautening then slackening, fattening, rising to form pregnant mounds while her lips stretch back in terror or jut forwards to pucker into silent kisses.

iii

Out in the warm March sunlight, Serge totters with his blocks towards a wooden trolley. It's a small trolley with a large handlebar at one end: it's been his for a year now, ever since he started walking. He stoops over it and, loosening the cradle of his left arm, lets the blocks fall into it. Grabbing the handle with both hands, he starts pushing the trolley along the gravel footpath. To his right, women are moving among mulberry trees, climbing and descending ladders, carrying baskets to and from the spinning houses. One of them stops and waves at him but he ignores her, pushing on. To his left is the wall between the Mulberry Orchard and the Maze Garden; coming to the doorway in this, he steers his trolley through and pushes it into the corridor formed by the paving laid into the lawn. When the corridor forks, cutting at right angles in opposite directions, he chooses a branch and follows it until, after performing several more right-angled turns and forking twice more, it comes to a dead end. He doubles back to the last fork, advances down another branch and follows it until it, too, runs out—at which point he doubles two forks back and takes a new branch. There's no need to stick to the paved section—the maze is wall-less, two-dimensional as the figures on the blocks, and the grass is short and wouldn't slow his trolley down—but he continues working his way along the abruptly turning corridors, held by their pattern, until they deliver him back out, through the same doorway, to the footpath once more.

The same woman waves at him; again he ignores her and, pushing his trolley past the house's main entrance, turns into the Low Lawn, crosses it and passes through the hedge into the Lime Garden. Leaving his trolley at the edge of this, he walks to its centre and pauses there. The lime trees are flowering; little white and yellow petals teeter on the ends of branches. The bees are active: Serge can see a blur of movement around the openings to their hives at the garden's far end. He tilts his head to one side, then the other; then he slowly rotates his whole body above the spot on which he's standing. The bees' hum first grows and then recedes, changing pitch as his ears turn through the air. As trees, grass and hedge run together, the bees seem to relocate, and hum from a new spot within his head, their pitch and volume being modulated from inside him now, not outside. He rotates several more times, relishing the acoustic effect, its repetition.

Eventually he returns to his trolley, swings it round and pushes it back across the Low Lawn, steering it off the path after he rounds the house's edge. A swathe has been mown through the longer grass, leading up to and through a large metal gate set in tall stone walls. The gate is open. Serge follows the swathe between the gate's obelisk-topped supporting columns and enters the Crypt Park.

It's darker in here. Tall hedges wall him in; the obelisks cast shadows on the ground. Trees and bushes sprout up willy-nilly, closing off most lines of view. Serge pushes onwards, following the mown swathe until, beside an empty bench, it suddenly gives out. He continues, but from here on in the going's harder: grass-strands twine themselves around the trolley's wheels; the blocks slide and jump across its floor. Serge rests beside a tree stump and, looking up, catches sight of his mother. She's sitting on another bench, leaning her back against the Crypt. On the bench beside her a teapot, a cup, a jar of honey and a little phial are laid out.

Serge pushes his trolley over to the bench, pulls to a halt in front of it and leans into his mother's knees. These give a little but not much. He looks up at her face: it's staring at some point beyond the trees and bushes. He climbs onto the bench beside her and tugs at her shoulders. She looks down at him and her eyes look like honey, warm and murky. She smiles through him, at the ground, or something underneath it. Serge dips his finger in her honey jar, pulls it out again and sticks it in his mouth, rolling and smearing it around the inside of his cheeks. The bench's surface has a sticky patch on it between the jar and the cup. A wasp has landed in this and is drawing off the syrup with its needle-like mandible. Its legs have broken through the honey's surface; they tread slightly, trying to free themselves, but they're already immersed; its mandible, meanwhile, continues drawing. Serge watches it for a while, then takes the phial and presses it down across the insect's body, using its rim to slice apart the bridge where thorax meets abdomen. The wasp's legs continue their treading and its mandible its drawing even after they're no longer joined. Its thorax throbs, then stiffens and is still. Serge takes his trolley's handle up again and pushes on.

Light dapples his shoulders as he passes beneath budding conker trees. Eventually he arrives at the stream that hems in the Crypt Park on the side furthest from the house. Beyond the stream, he can see sheep grazing on Arcady Field, diminishing in size as the field rises into Telegraph Hill. Serge gathers up the blocks and, cradling them once more in his left arm, edges towards the stream. He crouches down close to it and sees the slope of Telegraph Hill and the bright sky above it reflected in the water. He leans forward and catches sight of the top of his own head, his eyes, his nose and mouth. Then he takes a block from his left arm and places it gently on the surface of the water. The block floats. He prods it with his finger and it sinks, then bobs back to the surface again. Its upper face has a flat, in-profile football player on it. He prods it off-centre so as to spin it in the water; the block sinks and bobs, tumbling; when it comes to rest, a lone triangle is uppermost. Serge floats a second block, then a third. As he prods them they drift further from the bank. He leans out after them, so far that he can see his whole torso reflected in the water, right down to his knees, with the blue sky revolving above it like a turning lid . . .

And then he's in, tumbling and turning like the blocks as water rushes up his nose and burns his throat. His hands push muddy slime and he bobs up again, his face back in the air, his legs beneath him. He grabs at the blocks but these spin and sink away from his splashing hands. He tries to breathe in but the passageway is blocked: it makes a kind of elongated gasp that turns into a splutter, then a gulping as his head goes under again. Beneath the surface of the stream, he opens his eyes. The water is bright and murky at the same time, like honey. Snake-like fronds wave and dance in its lit-up darkness; particles of mud hang between these, stirred up into canopies of blossom. The water's right inside him; it's not nasty anymore, just cold. And he's no longer sinking: if anything, he's been lifted up, by strong arms coiled round him, hugging him . . .

Then he's being pushed, right in his chest, and spurts of stream are shooting from his mouth into the air before cascading back onto the muddy grass. He's lying on the bank, and Maureen's kneeling above him, pumping him. He vomits water, gasps, coughs, vomits more and gasps again; then, once he can breathe properly, just lies there quietly, breathing. Between him and the sky hangs Maureen's face; it stares straight at him, sobbing. He stares back, perplexed: her mouth and eyes look funny from this angle. They're red and fat. The eyes close and she shrieks; then she grabs him in her arms and holds him to her breast so tightly he can hardly breathe again. He slips out of her grasp, scrambles to his feet and wanders back towards his trolley—but she sweeps him up again before he reaches this and, trussing him up between her arm and waist, starts striding with him through the Crypt Park, back towards the gate.

"Incapable!" she sobs as they pass the Crypt. On the bench in front of it the teapot, cup and jar of honey have been left. "Incapable and arrogant! Can't even bother to look after what they're lucky enough to still have . . ."

She stops between the obelisk-topped columns of the Crypt Park's metal gate, sets him down on the grass and, holding him by the shoulders, kisses him on both cheeks. Serge squirms and tries to escape but she's got him trapped.

"I'll never let you from my sight again until you're . . ." she begins, but her voice trails away. She kisses him once more, then sweeps him up into her arms again and strides decisively towards the house. Women look over at them from the Mulberry Orchard. Behind the women, shapes and pictures drift flat and unnoticed on the stream as it emerges from behind the Crypt Park's walls and oozes silently along its course.

3

i

Under the central staircase of the main house, the one above which the tapestry that shows a staircase hangs, there's a photograph of Jacques Surin. It's an early daguerreotype—one of the very first. If visitors enquire about it, either out of politeness or from genuine curiosity, they're fed a tale that Versoie's residents have heard so many times it's taken on the aspect of a biblical fable involving plagues, exoduses, and long lines of "begot"s.

It goes something like this: When, in November 1796, Surin received from his recently deceased cousin—the baron de Saint-Surin, a resident of Lower Saxony whom he had never met but who, like him, was a second-generation *réfugié*—a chrysoprase ring, a round Dresden china box, a gold medal of Prince Henry of Prussia and a significant amount of money, he upped sticks from London and, acquiring a large plot of land in West Masedown, named it Versoie. He brought with him an entourage at once human, animal, vegetable and mechanical: spinners and dyers who had worked for him in Shoreditch, canaries whose chirping had drowned out the sounds of the machines but annoyed his English neighbours no less for that, worms and mulberry trees descended unadulteratedly from larvae and seeds smuggled out of La Rochelle one hundred and nine years earlier and a loom whose dis- and reassembly had presented a challenge no less daunting than that facing the architects of acropolises and mausoleums. To accommodate them all, Surin, who liked to style himself as a latter-day Noah despite the fact that all his offspring, and his offspring's offspring, were female, built on the south-west corner of his new estate a complex of houses and workshops linked by doors, corridors and yards. It is into the outermost of these, the Hatching Room, that Surin's several-times-great-grandson Serge, seven and sprightly, has just bounded from the garden.

Here, he finds two women kneeling over boxes. The boxes are small and shallow: the size of writing-table trays or vanity cases. Their lids have been removed, and the women are peering inside to watch moths laying eggs. The moths are females of the phylum Arthropoda: *Bombyx mori*. They have creamy white, scale-covered wings, the upper two of which are threaded with brownish patterns. Their bodies are hairy. They crawl slowly and groggily around each box's paper-lined floor, stopping intermittently to let more tiny black baubles fall from their genital region. From their rudimentary mouthparts they dribble a gummy substance, which they smear onto the paper with their legs: as the eggs fall they stick to this, dotting the white with black. Scattered and sparse at first, the dots grow into small constellations, then whole galaxies made up of thousands of black stars. When these dark clusters have become so thick that they threaten to eclipse the space between them, the women pick the moths up one by one and, pinching their wings between their thumb and middle finger, deposit them inside another open box to continue their laying there. As the intermittent flow and drop of eggs from each individual moth dries up, the moth is picked up for a final time and cast onto the floor to die while a new moth is introduced into the box to begin laying in her place.

Serge was loud and panting when he cleared the threshold but, after adjusting both his pace and breathing to the room's quiet, steady rhythm, is now standing still behind the kneeling women, watching them. Their faces, turned away from him and propped up on their forearms, are held just above the boxes, which makes the skirted waists that they present his way ride up into the air. The skirts' fabric folds and pleats around their thighs but smoothly hugs their bottoms' curves. Serge focuses on these, shifting his gaze from one woman's haunches to the other's. After a while he turns around and watches a third kneeling woman, bent over like the others but occupied instead with placing hatched larvae on a mat. This woman is facing him. Her arms are spread, her shoulders pulled back as she manoeuvres the slug-like creatures into place. She lays them out in rows, her hand returning to each row to neaten it the way a baker's hand returns to rows of unbaked pastries on a tray. Each time she does this the top of her blouse falls half an inch or so, giving Serge a glimpse of breast. The larvae stir and wriggle slightly, their greyish-brown flesh soft and wrinkled, like the trunks of miniature elephants.

He's come here looking for his mother, carrying a message from his father: something about costumes for the chorus, for the Cronos, children, Saturn, Saturday. It can wait, though. Two more women step into the Hatching Room with baskets slung across their backs. When they set these on the floor the woman kneeling by the mat pulls from them handfuls of mulberry leaves which she starts tearing up and scattering onto the larvae. The silkworms recoil and contract as the leaves hit them, then expand again, their oral cavities opening as they close in on the leaf-shards. The woman covers the mat in a gauze sheet, then turns to a second mat across which larger larvae have been spread and scatters torn-up leaves over these too. The women who have just walked in pick up empty baskets from beside the two mats and walk back towards the Mulberry Orchard, weaving around Serge on their way out.

A kind of clicking sound pervades the air: a fidgety, unsatisfying, low-level chafe. It's doesn't seem to be the laying moths who are making it: it's coming from the far side of the room, from a large pit. Serge walks over to this, kneels beside it and sees something he's not paid much attention to on previous visits to this room. Walled in by wooden planks, scores of white moths are coupling. Some are crawling around, their antennae twitching as they seek out partners; some are bumping blindly into one another, wrestling a little before moving on; but most are slotted into other moths. The males crouch over the females, thorax stacked above thorax, wings resting over wings. Once joined, they frot around, vibrating, as though trying to unhook themselves again, or to travel somewhere in this new formation. Serge reaches in and prods a couple with his finger; the stack of legs and wings topples onto its side and separates, leaving each half to stagger around in circles before beginning the slow process of reassembly. Once they've managed this, Serge scoops them up into his palm and, raising his hand into the air, says:

"You can do it, Orville and Wilbur!"

He jerks his palm upwards, propelling them towards the ceiling, but they arc leadenly, fall straight down to the floor and separate again. He picks the male, or perhaps female, moth up and, pinching its thorax in the fingers of one hand, plucks first one and then the other of its wings off. He sets the denuded torso back inside the pit to stagger around as it did before while he holds the wings up for inspection. Their markings, seen from close up, look like anaemic reproductions of the ones on the mulberry leaves. Thin, brown skeins run in lines through softer white tissue—straight, parallel lines all leading to a jagged, perpendicular main skein like spokes joining a central axis, breaking the creamy white into compartments. The pattern reminds Serge of the stained-glass windows of St. Alfege's in Lydium—only these windows are without colour, void of scenes or characters: a set of empty, white, elongated boxes. He holds one right up to his eye, a moth-wing monocle: the Hatching Room, its wooden beams and kneeling women all sink behind gauze. They look like a daguerreotype, pale and sepiad. Serge, seven and splenetic, thinks: this is how this scene would look in years from now, if someone were to see it printed onto photographic paper—anaemic, faded, halfway dead.

ii

A ghost's heading towards him, looming white and large behind the veil. The ghost lacks decorum: far from being awash with ghoulish dread, its face wears an expression of bemused derision.

"You look stupid," Sophie tells him.

Serge drops the wing and tells her:

"So do you."

He's got a point: she's all togged up in long white silks. The strips hang awkwardly about her almost-adolescent body, pinned around her shoulders and ungathered at the waist.

"It's not finished yet," she says. "It's got to have stars spilling from it. You'll look worse. Papa says you have to hold a scythe. Where's Mama?"

"Through here somewhere." Serge jerks his head in the direction of the Hatching Room's inner door. Sophie picks up her trailing hem and steps through it; he follows. They cross a small courtyard and enter the Rearing House. Trellises rise from floor to ceiling: bamboo frames that cut the room up into grids which, half-filled by cocoons, veil this room like the wing-prism veiled the other. Some of the cocoons are thick, barely translucent; others are fine and transparent: through their incomplete white carapaces Serge can see worms moving their heads in slow figures of eight inside, the repetitive movement pulsing through the thin shells like dark heartbeats. They pass through to the Reeling Yard, in which a woman tends a pot from which wispy smoke is rising.

"Master Serge, Miss Sophie."

"Where's our mama?" Sophie asks.

The woman prods at the cocoons that bob in the pot's boiling water, dunking and turning them as though she were cooking gnocchi. "With a buyer," she says. She bends down towards a bowl of cooler water and picks at a pre-cooked cocoon with a needle, pulling its loosened filament out and attaching it to the reeling wheel. The cocoon spins in the water as she turns the wheel, unravelling completely until only the withered black body of the chrysalis inside is left, to float on the surface for a few seconds before sinking to the bottom of the bowl.

"Maureen's baby," Sophie mumbles to Serge.

"What?" the woman asks.

"You have to kill them or they rip the thread when they come out."

The woman frowns: she knows that's not what Sophie said. She unhooks the newly reeled bobbin, gives it to Serge and tells him to carry it through to the Throwing Room. Here, he and Sophie find three women standing several feet apart, the first twisting individual threads together, the second paying out the combined organzine across the room, the third cutting it when it reaches a certain length. Serge rests his reel above a stack of other reels at the first woman's feet; the woman glances at him and nods without breaking her rhythm. The children move through to the Dyeing Room, about whose air an acrid smell hangs, borne on vapour rising from a large cauldron over which an older woman hovers like a witch, pushing with a stick at the mass inside it, as though trying to drown a kitten. As the children pass, she sets her stick down, plunges her arms elbow-deep into the cauldron and pulls out a soaked, crimson bundle of silk threads which she swings red-dripping through the air and hoists up to hang from wooden poles.

"Yuk," says Sophie, skirting the room's edges to avoid the splashes bouncing to a regular rain-drumbeat off the floor. Another rhythmic noise mingles with this: the repetitive whirring and clanking of a machine in the next room, laced which the higher, shriller sound of bird-song. A third sound weaves its way into the mesh: footsteps, growing louder as they near the door the children have just come through. Bodner enters, holding a bucket full of crimson berries which he sets down beside the cauldron before continuing towards the Weaving Room. As they follow him through, Sophie reaches down to scoop up a small handful of the berries.

"Open wide," she tells Serge, holding one above his mouth: "Medicine."

He opens with an "*Aaaaa*"; she pops it in; he closes, chews. It's bitter; the taste stays with him as he moves past the large loom that fills most of the room, its piston-levers shoving a huge comb through warp into which weft-silk is fed from a bobbin that unwinds jerkily at the loom's edge. The comb's teeth move again and again through the same stretch of warp, as though obsessively brushing and rebrushing the same clump of hair. Bobbin-side of it lies tight, finished fabric; piston-side, the weft's strands run adjacent but unjoined, like the strings of some strange, tuneless piano. There's music in the air, though, coming from canaries perched in hanging cages. Orange-brown or brown-grey, spangled by regular, symmetrical markings that run down their breast and back, they chirp and tweet shrilly and decisively in overlapping relay, as though issuing instructions to the loom, machine-code. The woman moves around the loom making sure that it complies with these instructions, lining up new bobbins, picking fluff from the woven fabric's surface, checking that the loose parallel strands are evenly spaced out: a human go-between.

Serge and Sophie follow Bodner through to the Store Room. Finished silks lie in piles here, folded and pleated, leaning against walls as they rise halfway to the ceiling. Silk tapestries hang between these piles: large, patterned weavings. One shows, in red and gold against a background of black moiré, a throned king being handed a baby by his queen, or perhaps one of the palace servants, while courtiers whisper to one another in the background. Another, on the facing wall, depicts a woman holding what appears to be a lion's head as she runs after a man who seems to be dressed as a woman, while shepherds and their very human-looking sheep gaze on smilingly. Others have ciphers in place of pictures: flowing, dancing signs that suggest Chinese or Indian script, or else some kind of musical notation. A woman moves around beneath these, selecting sample fabrics from the piles and carrying them towards Serge and Sophie's mother, who's seated on cushions. Her legs are folded away beneath a low table across which several samples have been laid out for inspection by a man who's kneeling awkwardly on the table's far side. Facing away from Serge, Sophie and Bodner, she's unaware of their presence in the room.

"... two hundred yards of crêpe ... two hundred of Jacquard ... three hundred thrown singles ..." the man reads from a notebook; "organzine and tram, two hundred and fifty ..."

"Versoie originals," she tells him.

"Naturally, Mrs. Carrefax," he answers. "Finest around. If you produced five times as much we'd buy it just as fast."

"Five times? You want five times more?" she asks him.

"I said *if* you made five times as much we'd buy it."

"Why would I want to make five times as much?" she asks him.

"You'd make more money."

She stares at him quizzically, not having understood his last phrase.

"Mo-ney." He mouths the word slowly, raising his voice—then, realising that this second action makes no difference, drops it right down and continues: "And what with technology leaping forwards as it is, new century and all that, you might consider—"

"We have no need of more money here. We are not poor," she tells him.

"Maybe so, maybe so. But your methods are somewhat antiquated, it must be admitted. The loom, for example, must be more than—"

"It is a Huguenot loom. Its craftsmanship has never been surpassed. Where else can you find silks like these?" Her arm sweeps round the room, past the piles and hanging tapestries—and as her eyes trail after it she catches sight of Bodner and the children, interlopers on this small business colloquium. Her face drops—though the look she gives them isn't unkind. "The costumes," she says wearily.

"Papa says because I'm Rhea I should have stars coming from mine," Sophie tells her.

"Tears?"

"*Stars,*" Sophie repeats.

"Stars," she repeats back. "And you, Serge?"

Serge. He always relishes the way she says his name: where his father gives it as an electrical "Surge" rounded by an abrupt *j*, her version takes the form of a light and lofty "Sairge" that tails off in a whispered *shh*.

"I'm Cronos. That's Saturn. I need sheets around my head. But Papa says to tell you that he also must have streams of nectar which must be gold and eleven feet long. And the other children will be Curetes. These are shepherds, Mr. Clair says. And they must have clashing spears."

"And Papa says to tell you Serge must have a scythe," says Sophie.

"Nathaniel is Poseidon," Serge adds, "and he must be disguised like a sheep so he can hide among the real sheep."

"Tell your father to send Nathaniel and the other children to me in the morning to be measured. The sheep too if he wants—but in the morning." As his mother speaks these words, her hands dance with one another, the fingers of one tripping along the palm of the other before rising to tap her chest. Bodner signs back. His twisted upper lip rises and falls slightly as he does this, as though he were slowly chewing something.

"He's saying 'poppies,' " Sophie says to Serge.

"You don't know that," Serge tells her.

"Yes I do."

Their mother tells the buyer: "I must leave you now. My tea awaits."

"A pleasure, as always, Mrs. Carrefax," he tells her, rising to his feet. "And do think about what I . . ."

But she's turned away from him; his words, redundant, shrivel in the air. She follows Bodner, who has left the room, passing her hand lightly over Serge's hair as she brushes past him. Serge and Sophie stand abandoned by the doorway for a while, quiet, floor-gazing. Then Sophie chirps, more shrilly than the birds in the next room:

"Let's do some chemistry!"

iii

They run out to the stables. As they cross the Maze and Mosaic gardens they can hear the Day School children chanting their lines in preparation for the Pageant:

Then streams ran milk, then streams ran wine, and yellow honey flowed
From each green tree whereon the rays of fiery Phoebus glowed . . .

The lines loop and repeat, obeying commands barked by their father's voice, which occasionally comes in, succinct and loud, over the blurred and uncertain infant voices for one or two words before retreating into the background again. The chanting fades as they pass beneath the trellises, muffled by thick poisonberry bushes.

The workshop door, window impastoed with a film of grease and dust, is unlocked; Sophie pushes it creaking open. An array of instruments greets them, strewn across shelves and benches: manometric flame and typesetting machines, phonautographs, rheotomes, old hotel annunciators and telegraph station switches—most of them opened, disgorged, their inner wiring spilling tangled, trailing from one level to another. Sophie selects a low-lying table and, pushing her right arm from her long silk robe and moving it across the table in a slow, broad sweep, indiscriminately slides the objects from its surface to the floor. Serge, meanwhile, starts opening cupboards.

"Where's the set?" he asks.

"Above the work table," she tells him.

He clambers onto this and retrieves, from a glass-fronted cupboard on the wall, a large boxed chemistry set. His father gave it to him for his seventh birthday, but Sophie's made it more hers than his. She grabs it keenly as he passes it down, and tells him:

"Get the book as well."

His hand feels its way around the cupboard and pulls out a heavy hard-bound tome: *The Boy's Playbook of Science*. She grabs this from him too. By the time he's climbed back to the floor she's opened the box's lid and is flipping through the book, looking for an experiment to carry out. Her eyes dart from it to the glassed, coloured liquids with a kind of avarice. Serge kneels on a stool beside her, peering over her shoulder. Her hair smells fresh and alive amidst the workshop's must.

"Sulphur," she says. "Yes, we've got that. Potash . . . yes. Nitre?" Her finger runs up and down the rows of bottle-stoppers as though playing a glockenspiel. Serge feels a chemical reaction in his stomach, a kind of effervescent coupling and expanding of juices and elements. "Right," Sophie announces. "We'll do this one. Read me the recipe. Page eighty-four."

She thrusts the book at him and starts laying out tubes, bottles, retorts and a gas burner. The *Playbook*'s cover has a flowery pyramid embossed on it. Serge flips it open, flips past "Properties of Matter," "Adhesive Attraction," "Impenetrability," arrives at "Chemistry." Hermes or Mercurius Trismegistus, minister of Osiris . . . alchemy . . . chemical combination, one or more substances uniting and producing third or other body different in nature from . . . Page 84: To return to . . .

" 'To return to our first experiment with the gunpowder,' " he reads, " 'take sulphur, place some in an iron ladle, heat it over a—' "

"Iron ladle?" Sophie says. "We can use a cup." She roots around the work table, tips a bunch of fuses from a metal cup and, after wiping its interior with her fingers, decants clear liquid into it from a bottle. A sharp smell burns Serge's nose, inside the bridge. Wrinkling her own, Sophie sets the bottle down, sparks up the Bunsen burner and holds the cup over it. "What next?"

" '. . . over a gas flame till it—' "

"I'm doing that already, stupid. Till it what?"

" '—catches fire,' " Serge reads.

On cue, the cup starts burning. "Oh, wow!" says Sophie. The flames are blue, not orange; they make her eyes, already blue, glow bluer and her teeth flare bluey-white, like patterned marble.

"We're meant to pour it into a bucket of water," Serge says, "but the room should be blacked out."

"Well, we'll skip that," Sophie tells him. "What's next?"

Next is an experiment with sulphur and dissolved nitre; then one with sulphates of potash and baryta; then another with nitrate of baryta and metal potassium. Serge reads directions from the *Playbook;* Sophie executes them, her face running red, orange, grey and blue again as each compound lights, flares or fizzles. When they come to heat up charcoal Sophie blows into the cup and they watch sparks fly out, the powder turning from black to red, then fiery white, before falling back grey and ashen, consumed by its own heat. As Sophie prods the ashes, Serge feels the reaction in his stomach again: a liquid flaring eating his own insides.

"Pearl-ash next," says Sophie. "Read out the next passage."

" 'If some more nitre be heated in a ladle, and charcoal added,' " Serge begins, " 'a brilliant deflagration (*deflagro*) occurs, and the charcoal, instead of passing—' "

"It's *'day-flag-row,'* stupid, not *'der-flower-grow,'* " she says as she holds the new concoction over the Bunsen flame. "Carry on."

" '—instead of passing away in the air . . . passing, passing away as . . .' "

The queasiness is spreading to his head as his own stomach deflagrates, something sour and crimson blossoming, expanding. He looks up. Sophie's staring at him, static. Her whole face seems to have slowed down—slowed down and expanded too. Her hair has expanded outwards from her head, rising to stand straight up in the air. His gaze follows it upwards and he sees instruments rise and hover above shelves. They do this incredibly slowly, as though willing themselves upwards, through excruciating effort, millimetre by millimetre. A window breaks, with the same slowness; he watches each of its glass fragments separate from the plane around it. There's no crash or tinkle; there's no sound at all. Serge tries to ask Sophie how she can make her hair stand up like that, but finds that his words, instead of travelling out into the air, push back into his mouth and on towards his stomach. Now sound and speed return, first as an after-rush of air, then, emerging from within this, a high-pitched hum that seems to have been going for some time but of which he's only now become aware. Sophie's still staring at him. Her hair's tangled and her eyes are wild. A gasp comes from her mouth; then another, then a shriek of pleasure. She shouts something to him.

"What?" he shouts back. The hum's filling his ears.

"Expl—" she begins—but he throws up right then, on the floor. His puke is red, laced with a briny, effervescent silver the same colour as potassium. Sophie looks at it, then back at him, then shrieks again, her shoulders shaking as the shrieks turn into sobbing laughs that judder her whole body.

Their father opines later that there must have been some contaminant in the cup to cause such a violent explosion. He ventures, further, that Serge and Sophie's extreme proximity to the point of detonation kept them from harm: had they been standing three feet from it, the force of the expanding air would have been enough to kill, or at least seriously injure, them. He plots diagrams showing the explosion's vectors through the room—table to work table, to shelf, to window—and tries for several days to ascertain the exact nature of the compound inadvertently concocted by his children. Serge and Sophie, for their part, spend weeks, then months, trying to reproduce the blast. They use means more intuitive than their father's—mixing elements together at random, heating, cooling and remixing them—but have no more success than he did. All they ever get are small-fry *phutt*s and *phizz*es, unsatisfying placebos.

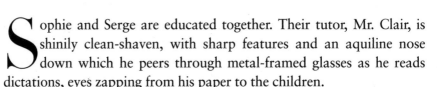

4

i

Sophie and Serge are educated together. Their tutor, Mr. Clair, is shinily clean-shaven, with sharp features and an aquiline nose down which he peers through metal-framed glasses as he reads dictations, eyes zapping from his paper to the children.

" 'Amund-sen's last ven-ture, through the Northwest Pass-age, yielded little joy. It is to be hoped, by those that value con-quest of the earth, that his current one, to the anti-po-dean regions, will prove for-tui-tous. For those whose daily tra-vels take them no fur-ther than the slums of Man-chester and Glas-gow, it will be of scant conse-quence. The forth-coming coro-nation, simi-larly, will do little to put bread on ta-bles of the poor.' "

Serge gets stuck on words like "antipodean" and "fortuitous," and even ones like "tables." He keeps switching letters round. It's not delib-erate, just something that he does. He sees letters streaming through the air, whole blocks of them, borne on currents occupying a zone beneath the threshold of the comprehensible, and tries to pluck and stick them to the page as best he can, but it's an imprecise science: by the time he's got a few pinned down, the others have floated on ahead or changed their meaning, and "Manchester" 's "chest" has turned into an old oak coffer, the king's "coronation" into a flower, a carnation. While Sophie scrib-bles neatly and assiduously, and always faultlessly, inscribing each word as it emerges from Mr. Clair's mouth, Serge, bathing in the phrases' after-glow, usually gives up after a few lines and just lets the words billow around him, losing himself in their shapes and patterns, bright and alive in front of Clair's grey skin.

When Mr. Clair arrived at Versoie House, one of the first things he unpacked from his trunk, alongside volumes by the likes of Morris, Bastiat and Weber, was a painting, which he hung carefully on the wall of his small room. Under interrogation from Serge and Sophie, who spent so much time curiously perching on his bed and window-sill that Maureen had to come and turf them out, he admitted having painted it himself. It showed, he told them, Venice: the intersection of two canals, a mooring jetty being approached by a small boat. Painting's a big thing for him; he's made it a large part of their curriculum. Here too, though, Serge is wanting. He's a steady brushman, and has a good feel for line and movement, but he just can't do perspective: everything he paints is flat. Mr. Clair's explained the principle of it to him, its history, and what he calls its "use-value"; he's shown him its mechanics, how to scale figures and objects so as to make them appear distant, how to make lines converge towards a vanishing point set within or just beyond the picture's border and so on. But Serge just can't do it: his perceptual apparatuses refuse point-blank to be twisted into the requisite configuration. He sees things flat; he paints things flat. Objects, figures, landscapes: flat. Even when Clair sits him down in front of reproductions of Giottos, Constables and Vermeers and orders him to copy them, the scenes accordion down into two dimensions, sideways-facing characters stuck straight onto squashed backdrops. On Tuesday afternoons, the slot Clair's assigned to landscape painting, the children invariably head up to the attic, and Serge paints the estate from above: its paths, corridors and avenues all laid out in plan view. Sophie, meanwhile, takes a leaf or branch with her and copies it in photographic detail.

Sophie's so advanced in natural science that Mr. Clair makes no pretence of knowing anything she doesn't, or even half of what she does. When the three of them collect pollen samples from around the Crypt Park or Mosaic Garden, Sophie whisks the jars off to her "lab," the smaller stable workshop (ceiling-beams stained by a burn-mark that the years have faded but not wiped away) she's now made her own and from which Serge is more or less excluded, and emerges two days later with drawings of magnified slides and diagrams showing varying rates of cross-pollination which she's correlated with her analysis of the constituent mixture of this season's honey. It is she, not Clair, who leads the trio on walks through Bodner's Kitchen Garden. While the mute servant trundles around shunting wheelbarrows of dead stems to the compost corner, she reels off the names of plants:

"Portal Ruby, Jonker Van Tet, Symphony, Haphill, Royal Sovereign . . ."

"A tautologism," Mr. Clair says. "All sovereigns are royal."

"This one is Boskoop Giant," Sophie continues. "And this, blackcurrant Ben Sarek."

"And most of them are illegitimate."

"Cherries: Stella, Morello. Pear: Doyenne du Comice. And here are apples: Charles Ross, Lord Lambourne, King of Pippin . . ."

"A cavalier named all our fruits. Come the new Commonwealth we'll name them after tradesmen: cobblers, bakers—"

"Shh!" hisses Sophie. "Look." She juts her finger at a stalk two or three inches from the ground, where a small spider clings almost vertically to its web. "A walnut orb-weaver," she tells them. "And this," she says, pointing at a tiny dark thing navigating its way over clumps of earth below the spider's eyrie, "is a bloody-nosed beetle. It dribbles bright red fluid from its mouth . . ."

Behind them, a fountain more than dribbles as its centrepiece, a wrought-iron swan, gurgles and vomits as though it had over-gorged itself on the garden's aristocratic fruit. Sophie leads them round this, towards the lilies. As they pass the enormous poppy bed she exchanges finger-signs with Bodner, who's half-lost among the swollen, bulbous heads.

"Don't ever let your father catch you doing that," Clair warns her.

Sophie shrugs. "These lilies," she continues lecturing them as they arrive beside swathes of deep maroon, "are Sun Gods. Here—" she digs her hand into the ground to scoop and scrape earth away from the bulb—"is the basal plate, this round pyramid thing. At the top, the flowers: three outer sepals and three inner petals." As her fingers gently separate the flower-parts, Serge gazes at the earth wedged beneath their nails, stark half-moon hemispheres of dark against pale white. "Six anthers and a three-lobed stigma." She caresses the stamen, running her fingers right up to the end where white pistils stick out like antennae. "These ones are seventh generation, from a single parent flower."

"They can't be from just one flower," Clair says. "You need two to make baby flowers."

"Not with lilies," Sophie corrects him. "They can fertilise themselves. And then their offspring fertilise each other."

"Endogamy," tuts Clair. "Perversion of royal houses."

"What's mahogany?" asks Serge.

"You're as bad as Mama," Sophie tells him.

"No I'm not!" he snaps back. She flicks small flecks of earth at him.

"I think this conversation has gone far enough," says Mr. Clair. "Back to the classroom."

Their tutor's not averse to games. He even schedules in a "ludic session" every week. Excitedly unwrapping a parcel which arrives from London via Lydium several months into his tenure, he presents to them the Realtor's Game, in which contestants must move object-avatars (a car, a ship, a dog) round squares which represent the city of Chicago, amassing wealth and influence as they progress.

"R.R.: I own that. Fare, one hundred dollars!" Sophie gleefully announces as Serge's near-destitute mutt pitches on her territory. She has a knack of snapping up prime squares, leaving Serge to mop up dregs of real estate: Rickety Row, Shab Street and the like—although he's always keen to buy the Ting-a-Ling Telephone Company, despite its poor yield, sold on visions of humming wires and buzzing switchboards, of connections.

"Public transport should be gratis," Clair announces as he lends Serge the hundred. "And that loan is interest free: I don't need a pound of dog-flesh thrown into the bargain. I hope this game adequately impresses upon you the iniquities of capital."

It doesn't: they both love it. They play extra rounds during free sessions and at weekends. One warm early-summer morning they decide to play outside, but, finding the board won't sit flat on the Mulberry Lawn's grass and being so familiar with the layout of the grid that its actual presence before them has become unnecessary, they assign one of the estate's landmarks to each of its squares—Crypt Park's second bench for George Street, beehives for Soakum Lighting System and so on—and conduct their game by moving physically from one spot to another. To determine the number of places to advance on any go, they throw a handful of sycamore leaves up in the air and see how many fall within the circumference of a skipping-rope laid on the grass around the thrower's body. As the outdoor version takes over from the original, additions creep into the rules, modifications: if two players find themselves in the Maze Garden at the same time, one may challenge the other to a "rolling duel" in which two tennis balls are rolled by hand along the maze path, the goal of each roller being to knock the other's ball out of the maze, the winner subsequently commandeering from the loser a property of his or her (usually her) choice; or if a player finds him- or herself short of rent when lodged beside the beehives, he or she (usually he) may place his hand against a hive and hold it there, braving stings, for half a minute in lieu of making payment—a full minute if the rent's above five hundred dollars. At first, games advance slowly as both players have to travel to their opponent's game-location on each move, to check that the other doesn't cheat when counting sycamore-leaf numbers. After a while, though, Serge has the idea of expanding the Ting-a-Ling Telephone Company out into real space, and they rig up, with the help of poles that feed them over garden walls and around hedges, a primitive web of strings and soup-can mouth- and earpieces through which they can communicate their positions and report the outcomes of each sycamore-throw, for some reason trusting each other to tell the truth when being overheard live. The network can't cover the whole estate; they have to come to speaking-listening hubs that, in reality, are close enough to one another that they could simply shout. So as not to blow the fantasy of telecommunication, they conduct their business in hushed voices, almost whispers. After a few days they're spending whole sessions not trudging from spot to spot but rather sitting at their tele-posts, quietly agreeing their positions and negotiating sub-clauses for each now-imaginary move . . .

The attic draws them back again and again. On rainy days they go to play the estate-wide version of The Realtor's Game at its window, shunting their imaginary doubles from park to garden, avenue to path to lawn. While doing this, they fiddle with their father's archive. He has stacks of old recordings: lamp-blackened glass phonautograph plates and rolls of paper bearing scratch marks laid down by voices moaning from deaf bodies before either of them was born; zinc master discs that, cut in the final years of the last century and the first few of this, appear to Serge like coins of some exotic currency gone out of circulation— miniature, round islands of arrested time. The surfaces of the zinc discs give off a faint smell of beeswax—beeswax overlaid with some sharp chemical. ("Chromic acid," Sophie tells him when she sees him wrinkling his nose at one. "I've got a whole phial of it in my lab.") The cylinders they find beside these are formed entirely of wax: solid brown columns of the stuff whose smooth, moulded surfaces have been defaced by networks of engravings—strange, meshed graffiti. Sophie and Serge can play these back, thanks to an old Edison phonograph they find gathering dust among them. Selecting recordings at random (some are in labeled cardboard tubes, others are loose and unmarked), they slide the cylinder onto its mandrel and wait for the sound to trickle out. Most of the cylinders contain sequences of letters, spoken out aloud, repeatedly:

"B. B-ee. B-b-b-b-b-ee. T. T-ee. T-t-t-t-ee. S-s-s-s-s, S-s-s-s-s. B-ee . . ."

The voices, those of Day School pupils (now alumni), manifest varying degrees of distortedness and atonality; the letters warp and morph as they progress. They gather certain rhythms, patterns of repetition or half-repetition, then, just when it seems that there's a logic to their sequences, break and relinquish them again. Serge and Sophie fall into the habit of putting on these recordings each time they're in the attic, a mechanical background chorus to their various antics up there. Sometimes they play, on a newer Berliner gramophone, not cylinders but discs: exhibition plates their father's had printed to showcase his students' ability to enunciate whole phrases or manage entire conversations. After setting the disc gently on its turntable and cranking the Berliner's handle, they lead the needle down towards the narrow groove with the assiduousness of surgeons guiding knives back to incisions made on previous occasions, then return to their tasks while random dialogues (model exchanges between infant shopkeepers and customers or passengers and train guards) waft around them. Often, when a disc's come to its end, they let it run on, playing and replaying the same stretch of silence—silence which in fact is anything but silent, bursting as it is with a crackle and snap that conjures up for Serge the image of Bodner's deformed mouth opening and closing: many Bodners' mouths, repeated side by side in rows that fill the attic's air and extend out beyond its roof and walls. Sometimes, while Sophie's busy copying plants, he props his head right up against the gramophone and watches the needle running through its trench, snagging and jumping constantly as though locked in constant hostile struggle with the furrow. The disc's made of a thick black material.

"It's shellac," Sophie informs him when he asks her one overcast Monday. "Made from secretions of the lac bug."

"The lack bug? What's it lacking?"

"Lac, no *k*. I've got one of those in my lab as well. That's Rainer's voice."

She's right: the disc he's come across this morning contains not phrases but a passage of verse which, spoken in a child's unbroken voice, seems strangely fitting for its newfound auditorium:

Be not afeard; the isle is full of noises,
Sounds and sweet airs that give delight and hurt not.
Sometimes a thousand twangling instruments
Will hum about mine ears, and sometime voices
That, if I then had waked after long sleep,
Will make me sleep again . . .

The speaker, Rainer, spent a year or so at Versoie: a half-German boy who lost his hearing, then his life, to a cancer that developed in his ear. Serge saw the cancer one day: it was bulbous, like a set of roots buckling the organ's inner chamber, upsetting the delicate architecture of its whorls and plateaus from beneath the skin's surface while a moss-like coat overgrew it from above. Serge moves his head round and looks down into the reproducing horn. Its brass has turned slightly green with time. The tube darkens as it narrows, then disappears into the sound box. Listening to Rainer, Serge thinks of entrances to caves and wells, of worm- and foxholes, rabbits' burrows, and all things that lead into the earth.

ii

Towards the middle of June, Simeon Carrefax's old university associate Samuel Widsun pitches up, by car, from London. His arrival, in the middle of a rehearsal for this year's Pageant, causes some commotion: few of Versoie's residents, child or adult, have ever seen a motor car. Even before it's turned off the road into the lightly sloping path that leads down past the Mulberry Lawn towards the house, the pupils have picked up the vibrations of its engines, choppy waves ruffling the ground they're standing on. As it hauls into partial view through the conifers they run out and skip along beside it, almost tripping on the hems of their long robes. This year's theme is Persephone: the Pageant is to represent her rapture by and marriage to Hades, and subsequent coronation as Queen of the Underworld.

"Better a Greek than a German!" Widsun quips heartily to Simeon when his host explains the set-up to him as strangely dressed pupils unpack his bags. "Can you believe we're crowning another of those blasted cabbage-eaters?"

"That bastard Korn's just pipped me on the phototelegraphic patent," Carrefax replies.

"The children can lip-read that word as well as any other, sir," Maureen warns Carrefax as she takes Widsun's cap and gloves.

"We must have been working neck and neck the whole time, he and I. Another week and I'd have had the application in. I've a wealth of new projects to show you. A damn cornucopia!"

"And that one too," adds Maureen.

"What, 'cornucopia'?"

"No, the other one. You'll turn out gangs of thugs: deaf thugs."

"The Krauts are gearing up to let loose at us, make no mistake," says Widsun. "Hey: watch out with that one!" he shouts at two Day School pupils dragging and bumping a heavy case across the gravel—boys who, facing away from him, remain oblivious to his concern. "It's delicate," he explains to Carrefax by way of compensation for being ignored by the boys. "A present for you and your family."

The present's a really good one: a Projecting Kinetoscope. On his first evening in Versoie, after supper, Widsun sets it up on the Mulberry Lawn and projects onto a bedsheet strung between two trees moving images of fire crews riding through the streets of London on their engines' sideboards, then of clothes jumping from laundry baskets, snaking across the floor and throwing themselves into laundry machines which then start churning them around and washing them, all without any human interference. The whole household turns out to watch the spectacle. Mr. and Mrs. Carrefax recline in large armchairs; Miss Hubbard and Mr. Clair sit on wooden seats beside them; Serge and Sophie sprawl belly-down on the grass; Maureen and the other servants stand in a huddle to the side. Only Bodner's absent: he glances in at the film's outset but seems unimpressed, as though he'd seen it all before, and wanders off towards his garden. Widsun stands at the back, beside the projector, announcing each of the reels he threads between its cogs and sprockets.

"This one's called *Caught by Wireless*," he explains as the flickers steady to reveal a domestic setting that seems to involve a compromised wife and a not unreasonably suspicious husband. "And this one, a tribute to our hostess's French ancestry: the *artiste* Méliès's *Voyage dans la Lune*."

"It's funny they have titles," Mr. Clair says as a pockmarked and unhappy moon gets it in the eye from some misguided scientist's rocketship. "Shouldn't the children be in bed?"

"Fiddlesticks!" scoffs Carrefax. "It's not every night they get to observe interplanetary transit."

But every night they get to watch Kinetoscope projections. It becomes a ritual: as soon as supper's over the bedsheet's hauled up, chairs laid out and reel after reel fed into the mechanism. Serge carries the sounds of the celluloid strip running through its gate to bed with him, clicking and shuffling in his ears long after the machine's been put to sleep, more real and present than the trickle of the stream or chirping grasshoppers. Each time Widsun racks up a new spool and starts running it, Serge feels a rush of anticipation run through the cogs and sprockets of his body; his mind merges with the bright bedsheet, lit up with the possibilities of what might dance across it in the next few seconds, its outrageous meta-morphoses as moths' and mosquitoes' shadows on the screen turn into jumping hairs and speckles, then the first unsteady pictures, empty linen springing into artificial life.

Widsun stays at Versoie for more than a week. Each morning, over eggs and kippers, he peruses the *Times*'s personal notices.

"It's amazing that these fools still think they're safe conducting their illicit business in rail-fence cipher. Break it before my egg goes cold, what?"

"What are they saying?" asks Sophie.

"Hmm, let's see. It's a three-line rail-fence, *a, d, g* . . . *d-a-r-l* . . . Got it: 'Darling Hepzibah'—Hepzibah? What kind of name is that?—'Will meet you Reading Sunday 15.25 train Didcot–Reading.' Reading you all right, you idiots."

"Do you think they're eloping?" Sophie says.

"Ladies don't ask those kinds of questions," Maureen tells her as she clears her plate. "Or drink three cups of coffee."

"This one's using atbash, at least," Widsun continues.

"Tell me what he's saying!" Sophie chirps, creaming her dark cup and sliding from her chair to wander over to his.

"*V* for *e* . . ." Widsun mumbles. "*Q* as null-sign . . . Give me one tick . . ." Sophie leans on his broad shoulder, peering over him into the page as his pencil flicks between the encrypted text and a row of letters scrawled in hangman-style beneath it, adding, crossing out. "Righty-ho: 'Rose. Smell of your bosom lingers on my clothes and spirit. Must meet again next week. Advise when Piers away using this channel.' The saucy scoundrel! I've a mind to give him a reply."

"Oh, let's!" she squeals, patting her hands across his back. "You can teach me the code."

"My delightful child, nothing would give me greater pleasure."

He whisks her away to his room and they spend the whole morning there, poring over lines of Scytale, Caesar shift and Vigenère. Widsun hovers over her, his chin above her hair, correcting the odd letter here and there. Serge tries to join in, but the sequences, their transpositions and substitutions, are too convoluted for him to keep track of. After an hour he's reduced to sitting at the escritoire in Widsun's room and playing with Widsun's personal seal and ink set, stamping the man's signature across the sheets of headed government paper that he's brought with him from London, and then, when these give out, his own forearm.

"Leave us alone," says Sophie. "Go and do something else."

"You can't tell me what to do," Serge snaps back. "And besides, Papa wouldn't let you do this if he knew."

It's true. Carrefax hates the notion of codes, ciphers and encryption. "Goes against the whole principle of communication," he harrumphs to Widsun over post-lunch brandy and cigars one afternoon.

"Secure communication," Widsun replies, stabbing his cigar precisely as though plugging its lit point into some invisible telephone exchange socket in the library's air.

"Secure—what? Secure from whom?"

"Your enemies."

"Are hearing people deaf ones' enemies?"

"Ah, yes," taking a puff. "Your muted flock. In a way, that's what I—"

"Muted no longer once they've been here for a stretch."

Widsun mouths silent acknowledgment of this, blowing a smoke-ring from his lips. "You know I'm working for Room 40 now?"

"Room 40?"

"At the Ministry. Signals."

"Ah: they got you, did they? *Consummatum est,* and *Homo fuge* branded on your body. I wondered what the secretive tone in your letters was about."

"Carrefax, listen: things have changed since I was last here."

"Too damn right they have! When you were last here I was beavering away at wireless, only to get pipped at the post. When was it? 'Ninety-seven? 'Ninety-eight? Best part of a year before the boy was born, at any rate." He gestures vaguely at Serge, who's sitting quietly in the corner holding the guillotine with which the men have allowed him to cut their cigars. "Now we've got seven RX stations in Masedown alone."

"No, I mean that—"

"Happens every bloody time. You work on it, prepare its way into the world, then some other bastard sneaks into the nest and steals your egg."

"Politically, old friend: I mean politically. There'll be a war."

"Be a—what? War? Nonsense! The more we can all chatter with one another, the less likely that sort of thing becomes."

"If only that were true," sighs Widsun dolefully. He sips his brandy, lets out a measured, spirit-heavy breath and continues: "We were hop-ing—my colleagues and I—we thought we might pick your brains about the sign language your pupils use when—"

"You've come to the wrong place, old chap! It's banned here from day one. We teach them language here, not secrecy and silence. *That's* what leads to wars!"

"I've seen old Bounder doing it . . ."

"Bounder?"

"Your gardener."

"Oh, Bodner! Blast that fellow. My damn wife insists on keeping him around. He came with the estate; been with her since she was born. Spe-cial connection, you see, what with his mouth . . ."

"That kind of communication will become important when—"

"When I first came down here to teach her to speak I tried to get him to do it too—but he was having none of it, the stubborn ox."

Serge, still fiddling with his guillotine, pictures Bodner's mouth again: the undulating lips, the shrivelled trunk of tongue. He thinks of ox-tongue, sliced and laid out on a plate. It makes him swallow, and his spit taste bitter.

Sophie prances into the library and straight up to Widsun.

"I've found seven of them!" she sings, thrusting a spread palm and two fingers from her other hand right up against his face.

"Seven of what?" her father asks.

"He puts messages in the papers every day, and I have to crack them and reply in the same code," she announces in a voice that's guilty and defiant at the same time.

Carrefax looks daggers at his guest.

"I'm training her up as a spy," Widsun confesses. "Good mental exer-cise, you must admit, if nothing else . . ."

"I'll be a double agent," Sophie purrs, bunching up her hair, "a double-double agent. If I'm caught, I'll poison myself before the enemy can make me spill the code. I'm even working on the potion. Before you leave—" to Widsun, this, snaking her arm along his broad shoulder again—"I'll give you a whole bunch of different poisons to take back to your Ministry. And in two years, when all your other spies are dead, I'll come and be the greatest spy of all. Oh: apples!"

"Apples—what?" her father asks her.

"From the garden; Bodner; don't you worry; need the pips, Papa; pip-pip!"

And she's off again. She spends the next few days scurrying between her lab and Widsun's room, clutching pages filled with columns of letters, numbers and other, indeterminate ciphers scrawled and crossed out in her own hand, not to mention lighter pages hand-torn from the *Daily Sketch* and *Daily Herald,* from the *Globe, Manchester Guardian* and *Times,* the *Star,* the *Western Mail* and *Evening News.* Serge, no longer allowed into Widsun's room with her, hears shrieks and squeals each time she finds or breaks a cipher, mixed with Widsun's deep roars of approval. Occasionally she passes him in the corridor as she emerges with her hair messed up and ink spattered and smudged across her face.

iii

Pageant Day starts out unsettled. Clouds scud by swiftly; Carrefax monitors them anxiously, his head cranked back to watch them slide out from behind the house's ivy-covered chimneys, elongating and unravelling as they drag patches of shade across the Mulberry Lawn—patches that wrinkle as they dip into the stream, then shorten as they make their way up Arcady Field, contracting right down to thin lines that slip away over the brim of Telegraph Hill. Staff and pupils lighten and darken as they move through these, hurrying from spinning sheds to schoolrooms, schoolrooms to Mulberry Lawn, house to spinning sheds and back again. The décor is being finished; women balance on the top rungs of stepladders, hanging leaf-tresses over wooden posts. In front of these, children lay out chairs in rows across the grass. Off to the side, Maureen and Frieda set up tea and coffee urns on trestle tables while their girls carry out plates laden with pyramids of cucumber and chopped-egg sandwiches, moving over lawn and gravel in an unbroken ant-like chain. Spitalfield slinks around among them, hoping for scraps. At the top of the lightly sloping path, Mr. Clair ties to the open gate a sign which bears, in both conventional and phonetic script, the text that most of Lydium's tradesmen, clergy, civil servants, farmers, housewives, shop-keepers and misc. have already found slipped through their letter boxes in leaflet form during the past two weeks:

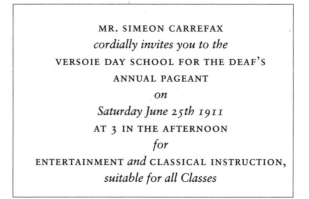

MR. SIMEON CARREFAX
cordially invites you to the
VERSOIE DAY SCHOOL FOR THE DEAF'S
ANNUAL PAGEANT
on
Saturday June 25th 1911
AT 3 IN THE AFTERNOON
for
ENTERTAINMENT *and* CLASSICAL INSTRUCTION,
suitable for all Classes

"Damn weather gods!" Carrefax snaps to Widsun. "Toying with us. Like wanton flies, in shambles—no, like wanton boys in sport. What was it . . . ?"

" 'As flies to wanton boys are—' " Widsun begins, but Carrefax cuts him off:

"I'm working on a patent for a way of using radio to sense the weather in advance. The waves travel through it, after all. Why aren't you in your costume?"—this to Serge, who's come to ask him something.

"I don't put my mask on till later. But Miss Hubbard wants to know what volume to set the amplification to."

"Amplification—what?"

"Who's this one meant to be, then?" Widsun asks.

"Ascalaphus," says Serge.

"He's the witness, isn't he? Sees her eating grapefruit or something . . ."

"Witness indeed," Carrefax replies. "Pomegranate. Tell her to set it to medium and watch out for my signals. Go!"

Serge scuttles back to Schoolroom One, where discarded clothes are strewn across a floor stripped of all its chairs save one, in which his mother sits stitching last-minute pleats and scales and feathers into costumes, turning their placid wearers one way, then another. Miss Hubbard stands beside the window, running the chorus through their lines, conducting them in unison while simultaneously getting individual actors to recite their phrases, the resulting cacophony flustering her into mixing up the words herself.

" 'Near Enna walls—this damsel to—Pergusa is—' No, start again. Where's your owl head?" she asks Serge.

Serge points to a corner. The mask is staring at him with large golden eyes whose centres are pierced by holes, like gramophone discs.

"Father says to play it medium, and to watch for his—"

"Not now, Serge. Take the mask out to the Mulberry Lawn. Set it with the other props behind the sheet. Don't stop! 'Near Enna walls . . .' " She leads the chant again. Behind her, through the window, Serge catches a glimpse of Bodner pushing a wheelbarrow full of flowers and foliage towards the stage.

At two o'clock small specks of rain dot Maureen and Frieda's tablecloth. It holds off, though: by quarter to three the air is blustery and slightly chill but dry. The path's gravel crunches with arrivals; murmurs of greeting grow into a loud mesh of general chatter punctuated by clinks of cups on saucers and the odd peal of women's laughter. At five to, Miss Hubbard leads the players from the schoolrooms to the Mulberry Lawn to "aahh!"s of appreciation and gasped "Oh, look!"s as parents recognise their disguised sons and daughters—exclamations which prompt her to throw her arms out in an attempt to shield the actors from being gazed upon before their time. She blushes as she bustles them behind the sheet which, strung between the same two trees as it was when serving as a screen for Widsun's films, makes for a larger back-, or, rather, side-, stage area than the free-standing folding screens used in previous years' Pageants.

An electric crackle whips the assembled crowd into attentiveness. It repeats, twice, then gives over to music that starts out loud but almost immediately drops in volume until it's barely audible, then climbs back to the same level as the general conversation. Miss Hubbard peers out nervously from behind the sheet, scanning the crowd for Carrefax. He, meanwhile, ushers people to their seats. Once they're all settled in, he raises his hands and stands before them on a grass stage across whose floor lie variously coloured strips of silk; the music stops abruptly and he says:

"Ladies and gentlemen: our classical cycle—*The Versoie Mysteries*—

enters another phase, just as our human cycles do. Today's story is Persephone's—but is it not also our own? Are we not the stuff of dreams, such dreams as . . . aren't we all—?"

Another crackle interrupts his speech. Electric birdsong spills through the sheet and fills the air. Carrefax waits for it to stop; it doesn't; he creeps over to the chair that's been kept for him in the audience's front row. Beside him sits his wife; beside her, Widsun. Standing behind the sheet, Serge watches Miss Hubbard send onto the stage first the chorus, then, hot on their tails, the non-speaking extras. Not quite under her jurisdiction since she's not his teacher, he creeps round to the sheet's side and watches them take up their positions: the chorus in a line at stage left, the extras moving from stage left to right mock-hacking at the ground with cardboard pitchforks. Miss Hubbard then nudges into this scene the slightly older Amelia, who moves about it slowly carrying a large handful of poppies. On a cue from Serge's father, the chorus begin chanting:

Dame Ceres first to break the earth with plough the manner found;
She first made corn and stover soft to grow upon the ground;
She first made laws . . .

Their eyes dart nervously from side to side. Their strange voices, imperfectly synchronised, are buffeted by the breeze; words blow and slip away. Carrefax conducts them from his seat, urging them to speak louder. Ceres/Amelia waves her hand vaguely in the direction of the pitchfork-wielding extras and they pull from their farmers' robes golden confetti which they toss into the air; it billows up and flashes brightly, carrying far across the lawn. The audience "aahh!"s.

"Melissas," Carrefax explains, to no one in particular. "Honey-silk harvest."

"Dame Ceres looks like Mrs. Carrefax," a random lady murmurs.

It's true: Amelia's hair is thick and brown. She has a languid look. Serge turns his head towards his mother, but his eye is caught by Widsun next to her, who's making hand signs. He's not using the vigorous language that his mother and Bodner sign in, but more surreptitious signals formed by simply opening and closing the fist that rests across his lap in bursts either long or short. His eyes are pointed at the stage, but his hand is facing Sophie, who's kneeling six or seven yards away from him at her own post just off stage left, behind an array of phials and bottles lined up in a box (she gave up playing on-stage roles two years ago to take up the post of stage and special-effects manager), and using the same barely perceptible Morse to signal back at him.

Little round Giles is sent out from behind the sheet now, as a chubby Cupid whose bow-free hand is held firmly by his stage-mother Venus, in reality his older sister Charity. In a weird voice that seems to buzz, she starts charitably goading him, suggesting that while the powers on earth obey his "mighty hand" (chuckles from audience), he should expand his sphere of influence into the underworld and thus "advance thy empire."

"That's Bismarck talking to the Kaiser," Widsun mumbles to Carrefax without breaking off his signals to his daughter.

Giles/Cupid takes a wooden, rubber-suction-pad-tipped arrow from a quiver slung across his shoulder; his sister/mother helps him place it in his bow and draw the string back. His hands fall away but hers have got the object firmly: with an elastic *pyongg* the arrow flies out, arcing above the Mulberry Lawn's far edge and dropping out of sight among the undergrowth beside the stream.

"Now death itself's infected by desire," Carrefax explains.

There's a pause. Performers and audience both look in the direction of the arrow, as though expecting something to emerge from where it fell. After a few seconds' silence a sheep's bleat carries to the lawn from Arcady Field. Everyone laughs.

"Let's hope it didn't hit one," a man jokes, unnecessarily.

The extras have ditched their pitchforks behind the screen-sheet and returned carrying posts strung with twigs and foliage; they plant these in a semi-circle, then, unfolding a round, green silk lying at their feet, create the semblance of a pond. Sophie creeps in to give the pond some shape, smoothing its edges into place before slinking back to her post. The chorus chant:

Near Enna walls there stands a lake; Pergusa is the name.
Caïster heareth not more songs of swans than doth the same.
A wood environs every side the water round about
And with his leaves as with a veil doth keep the sun-heat out.

"I'd rather he let it in," says the same man mock-shivering, emboldened by, or perhaps trying to make amends for, his last interjection.

"How does a wood shade 'as without fail'?" asks Widsun.

"No: 'with a veil,' " Carrefax tells him. "The leaves are like a veil."

Now it's the heroine's turn to enter. Bethany, a year younger than Serge, emerges from behind the sheet and glides around the stage gathering flowers from beneath other silks. The chorus continue:

While in this garden Proserpine was taking her pastime
In gathering either violets blue or lilies white as lime,
And while of maidenly desire she filled her maund and lap,
Endeavouring to outgather . . .

"Proserpine?" asks a lady in the second or third row.

"Persephone: her Latin name," explains Carrefax.

Sophie's hidden so many flowers among the silks that Bethany's filled maund, lap and both underarms and is basically pretty outgathered.

"Should've kept Bodger's wheelbarrow at hand," Widsun says to Carrefax.

"Dis is about to enter in his chariot," Carrefax warns him, turning towards the second-or-third-row lady as he adds: "That's Pluto. Hades."

The chorus, echoing Carrefax in more metered language, announce Dis's imminent arrival. But no Dis arrives. Tense whispers leak out from behind the sheet. The audience shuffles.

"That's the problem with chariots," Widsun comments to the gathering at large. "You have to crank the buggers up for ages."

Sophie giggles, then disappears behind the sheet to see what's happening. A few seconds later Dis is drawn out onto the lawn by human horses in a chariot whose gramophone-disc wheels and wooden pistons float above the ground as though borne on cushions of air.

"Dis must be the fellow!" Widsun announces.

Sophie squeals with laughter. Dis drives his chariot past Bethany/Proserpine and wraps his arm around her waist. She throws her flowers away, lets slip an elastic girdle she's wearing and climbs on board, taking care to step over the pistons.

"Not all that reluctant," another random lady, or perhaps the previous one, ventures.

Dis drives Proserpine around the stage two or three times until they come to a new silk-lake that, with a little help, emerges from the floor. This one's bright blue and made of strips that, shaken from both ends by extras, give a passable impression of rippling water. A nymph surfaces from among these; the chorus explain that this is Cyan, and that her lake is an agglomeration of other bodies of water known as

. . . the Palick pools, the which from broken ground do boil
And smell of brimstone very rank . . .

This is Sophie's cue to uncork one of the test tubes lying at her feet and pour its contents into a large conical flask resting beside it. Almost immediately, vapour fills the flask and oozes from its neck into the air, where the breeze catches it and paints a thin trail above the grass. Sophie picks the flask up and runs to the far side of the stage so as to be upwind of the audience. The vapour threads its way among them; it's rank all right. They start to cough; handkerchiefs and gloves come up to noses. Gasps of "Poo!" and "Christ!" waft from the chairs. But Sophie's not done yet. She scurries back to her effects box, uncorks another phial and pours another batch of liquid into a large crucible. Smoke pours from this. Carrying it to the centre of the stage, she sets it down in the middle of Cyan's lake. It billows and gushes smoke, as though it had a fake bottom and concealed below it, underneath the lawn, were a whole factory of stoves and ovens. Dis, Proserpine, Cyan and the lake-rippling extras screw their eyes and wave their arms, overwhelmed. The chorus wince and stare on in alarm.

"Carry on!" shouts Carrefax. " 'The ground . . .' "

The ground straight yielded to his stroke and made him way to hell,
And down the open gap both—

Two or three of the chorus break off, coughing. The others pause, then try to continue:

. . . down the open gap both horse and chariot—

But they start coughing too. The smoke's blowing everywhere now, swirling around stage and audience. The chorus disappear beneath it; a solitary voice heroically chants from its depths the words

headlong fell

then gives up. People rise from their seats and head for safer, upwind ground; Miss Hubbard and her behind-sheet helpers abandon their post too, eyes streaming. Serge does the same. Only Sophie remains in position, completely unperturbed, beaming out at them from veils of smoke.

"We'll have the interval here," booms Carrefax.

Prevented by brimstone from reaching the trestle tables on the lawn to the house-side of the stage, the audience and players hover around stream-side, hemmed in by the water, cheeks wet with tears. Conversation is stifled: topics include the aesthetic merits and demerits of the telegraph line on the hill; the improvement in voice quality of the children year on year; ditto that of the staging; how Sophie has a bright future in armaments and explosives; the extent of Germany's military ambitions; how tea would be nice if only they could get to it. The smoke dwindles, then peters out until the crucible sits on the grass innocuous and empty. Sophie removes it; Miss Hubbard and the players return and start moving props around; Carrefax orders the audience to retake their seats; they do so.

They find the stage transformed. Where Pergusa's trees stood is a bed of upright reeds; beside these, two trellises covered with white asphodels. The round, cyan-coloured lake has given way to two rivers, one fiery red, one black, both undulating thanks to extras who've now donned shadowy robes. Two adamantine columns have appeared; between them, a winged Fury brandishes a whip above a dog two of whose three fierce papier-mâché heads loll about his shoulders. The audience make appreciative murmurs; Carrefax acknowledges these, turning back to grin one way then another.

"Hades' realm, you see. That's Phlegeton, and Styx."

"Is this in the original?" asks Widsun.

"Poetic licence," Carrefax replies. "The Versoie Folio variant. Malone. Music, Miss Hubbard!"

From behind the sheet jumps the now-familiar scratch and crackle of the gramophone, followed by loud music full of pomp. Borne on this music, Dis and Proserpine re-emerge arm in arm. Dis wears a tall arched crown with a border of what looks like genuine ermine; in his hand he holds a staff topped with a stuffed bird that Serge knows is real because he watched his sister gut and stuff it just two days ago. Proserpine wears a small diadem formed by a wreath of laced dried flowers. They advance slowly, ceremoniously, towards the audience; the extras fall into line behind them, Fury, dog, river-undulators and all, their collective gaze focused firmly on the middle of the front row. Drawing the whole train to a halt just inches from the audience, Proserpine slowly removes her diadem and places it on Mrs. Carrefax's head. Then Dis removes his crown and places it on Widsun's.

"No!" says Carrefax. "The crown goes on *my* head!"

But Dis isn't looking at him and, consequently, can't read his lips' instructions. He shoves his bird-staff out to Widsun too; Widsun receives it, smiling.

"Why, thank you."

"That was a mix-up." Carrefax turns left and right to explain the mistake to those behind him. "Must've told them I'd be sitting on her other side. No matter: carry on!" he calls out, rolling his hands redundantly at the actors, who have turned round and are heading back towards the sheet. As they pass Sophie, she snaps her box shut, rises to her feet and strides off decisively towards the Maze Garden. The smoke's caught up with her at last: as she brushes by Serge he notices her face is red and flushed.

The underworld disappears as suddenly as it appeared, whisked off by its own undulating shadows, who replace it with dull brown and grey silks around which they plant sticks strung with dried-out vines and rotten husks of corn. The chorus shuffle back out to explain that this agricultural blight is Ceres' doing; Ceres/Amelia re-appears to confirm this by languidly waving her hand towards the barren earth.

"Her way of mourning," Carrefax adds.

Cyan the nymph re-appears and tries to say something to Ceres, but seems unable to recite her lines: her mouth moves falteringly, emitting gurgles. The audience shuffle awkwardly, embarrassed for the girl—but the chorus reassure them that this is part of the act: Cyan has lost the powers of speech, and

mouth and tongue for utterance now would serve her turn no more. Howbeit,

they continue,

*a token manifest she gave for her to know
What was become of Proserpine. Her girdle she did show
Still hovering on her holy pool . . .*

On cue, Cyan shows Ceres the girdle Proserpine let slip earlier, and the two girls nod conspiratorially at one another.

"Aha!" says Widsun to Carrefax, in an equally conspiratorial tone. "Mute signals serve their purpose after all!"

Carrefax snorts. On stage, a new character appears: the portly Ivan, sitting at a table sporting a long crude-wool beard. In front of him, on the table top, the extras have placed a mechanical object with turbine and handle.

"Zeus," Carrefax announces proudly. "Now watch out for his thunderbolts . . ."

When Amelia approaches Ivan and informs him that she's less than happy about their daughter's ravishment by her own uncle, he responds by cranking the handle of his turbine round and round. The thing whirrs; the whirrs rise in pitch as the cylinder accelerates until, eventually, sparks fly from its end. The audience purr, impressed.

"Pretty good, no?" beams Carrefax.

The sparks have the effect of summoning back little round Giles, who's kept his wings but traded his bow and quiver for a telegram boy's cap.

"Isn't that Cupid?" asks the second-or-third-row lady.

"No, he's Hermes now," Carrefax corrects her. "Zeus's special envoy."

The next few scenes are confusing. Their gist seems to be that Hermes has to run around carrying messages between Pluto and Ceres; but the content of these messages, although read out aloud by their recipients, is lost amid the whirring and cracking of the turbine, which Ivan continues cranking throughout, as though its sparks alone guaranteed the network's operation. Serge slinks back behind the sheet in preparation for his scene, which involves him snitching on Proserpine by testifying that he saw her suck seven seeds from a pomegranate while sojourning in the underworld, an act which for some reason makes her ineligible for revivification. Despite his semi-villainous role, his entrance is greeted with "hurrah!"s—a tradition dating back as long as he can remember, the locals' vicarious way of paying tribute to his father. The cheers continue as he snitches; they turn to boos as Ceres—becoming what the chorus describe as "wrought with anger," despite the fact that Amelia seems as unwrought by his skulduggery as she's been by everything else that's happened over the last forty minutes—waves her hand vaguely at him and decrees that he be turned into an owl. Sympathetic cries accompany his head's disappearance beneath the huge feathered mask, followed by applause as he flaps his arms to reveal intricately webbed sleeves.

The Pageant's almost over now. Ascalaphus's transformation heralds that of most of the other characters as Ceres goes on a bird-producing rampage. Harvesters, undulators, shadows are all rendered avian, disappearing like Serge beneath beaks and feathers. Some, robbed of speech, are condemned to be "sluggish, screeching"; others are allowed to retain human voices and ordered to take to the skies above the oceans,

> *of purpose that your thought*
> *Might also to the seas be known . . .*

Even the chorus who pronounce these lines are transformed into birds. Since there's no one left to put their masks on, they transform each other, the last remaining one pulling the feathered head onto his own shoulders with the resigned look of the final participant in some mass suicide. The stage now full of birds, the same recording that started the whole Pageant off is now replayed from behind the screen, growing louder and louder until birdsong fills the whole lawn. Sophie's meant to repeat her smoke-trick at this point, to produce clouds for all these newly generated birds to soar through, but she's nowhere to be seen.

"Where is that blasted girl?" Carrefax barks. He scours the lawn eagle-eyed for a few moments, then booms out: "No matter: curtain call, everyone!"

The masked children can't really see him, and continue soaring around, bumping into one another. A couple of them fall over. Carrefax steps out onto the stage to haul them into line. He pokes his head behind the sheet and the music stops abruptly. There's silence for a moment; then the audience break into loud applause.

"Thank you, thank you!" shouts Carrefax above it. "Tea, coffee, light refreshments on the lawn. And if . . ."

But his sentence is lost amidst the bustle of people rising from seats, stretching limbs, straightening skirts and waistcoats. Parents make their way towards the sheet for reunions with their children. The volume of general chatter rises as people vie to outdo each other in their praise for the production, for Mrs. Carrefax's costumes, for Miss Hubbard, Serge, the chorus, Maureen and Frieda's sandwiches, the gramophone for providing such ambience, the skies for holding off. Carrefax works the crowd:

"The coronation scene? I thought that this year, of all years . . . What? The crown was meant for my head . . . No, quite funny really: honoured guest and all that . . . Perfectly safe: water and glycerine combination; she was going to make clouds, but I don't think we could have withstood any more brimstone . . ."

Shadows grow longer. Children grow tired. They tug at parents' sleeves, or sit beneath the trestle table unpicking cucumber slices from sandwiches' entrails and mining seams of chocolate from the ruins of layered cakes. Cupid/Hermes dozes in a chair. Sophie remains as absent as Persephone. Eventually people slink off, their footsteps dwindling up the path's gravel. Urns, tables and chairs are brought back in; the props are returned to the schoolrooms. Only flattened grass, the odd discarded feather or crushed flower, Sophie's box of chemicals and the tautly strung-up sheet still bear witness to the fact that something has happened on the lawn when Serge comes out after dark to fetch his bird mask.

The wind's died down by now; clouds hug the ground more closely, warming the night air. It's quiet: the only sounds Serge hears are the slow oozing of the stream and a kind of rustling that he thinks at first must be a badger or hedgehog in the undergrowth beside it. It's a rhythmic scratching, a rubbing chafe that carries on its back a higher sound, a squeak like the noise of an unoiled gate being opened and closed repeatedly. As Serge moves across the lawn he realises that the sound's coming not from the undergrowth but from somewhere much closer. He looks around; although there's no moon to light up the lawn a small glow is spilling from a lantern someone's left behind the sheet. When he comes face-on to the sheet he sees what's making the noise—or, rather, sees its shadow, cast on the sheet's far side by the lantern so as to be visible from this side, like a film made up of only silhouettes. It's some kind of moving thing made of articulated parts. One of the parts is horizontal, propped up on four stick legs like a low table; the other is vertical, slotted into the underside of the table's rear end but rising above it, its spine wobbling as the whole contraption rocks back and forth. The thing pulses like a insect's thorax, and with each pulse comes the rustle, scratch and chafe; with each pulse the horizontal, low part squeaks, and the vertical part now starts emitting a deep grunt, a gruff, hog-like snort.

The grunts grow more intense as Serge comes closer to the sheet; the squeaks grow louder. The front part has a head; the back part too—Serge can make this out now, rising from broad shoulders. The thing's rocking and wobbling faster and faster, squeaking and grunting more with every pulse.

Serge has started moving round to the sheet's side so he can find out what the source of this strange shadow display is when a scream comes from some way behind him. He turns round. A second scream follows the first: the voice is Maureen's, and it's coming from the house. He runs back across the lawn towards it. The door's open; in the hall, Maureen's crouching down in front of Spitalfield, who's lying immobile on the floorboards. Spitalfield is stiff: his legs are sticking straight out at an odd angle to the ground; his mouth is frozen in a gaping rictus; foam sits hard-set on its lips.

"The little bitch!" shrieks Maureen. "Where's your sister?"

"I don't know," replies Serge. "Is he dead?"

He's dead alright. Sophie, when she eventually emerges, denies having fed the poison to him deliberately.

"He must have sneaked into my lab," she whines. "It's not my fault."

Maureen thinks otherwise. She tries to get her employer to punish his daughter, but Carrefax takes Sophie's word on this one.

"We're British, not Napoleonic. Innocent till proven guilty."

Sophie assuages whatever guilt she might feel by deciding to accord Spitalfield proper funeral rites. To Maureen's further horror she persuades her father to allow her to stuff the cat. This takes her two days of uninterrupted labour: Serge, perched on a chair in her lab's corner, watches her empty out his stomach of its organs, guts and juices, then peel the skin back from the skull towards the spine and ribs. The innards, gathered in a bucket, exude a rancid, sour smell; Serge moves closer to Sophie to block it out by breathing in the odour of her hair.

"Now you're distracting me," she says. "Clear off."

She calls him back, though, some hours later, to show him a trick of which she seems extremely proud. Sticking two electric wires into the cat's left hind leg, she throws a switch on to complete the circuit—and the leg, galvanised by the current, twitches and then flexes, as though Spitalfield were trying to walk. She switches the current off, and the leg reverts to its rigid, straight position. She throws the switch again; again the leg twitches and flexes. As she animates the leg over and over again, she shakes with a laughter that's sparked up afresh with each new quickening—as though she were also animated by the current, which was somehow running through her body too. Serge, watching the leg move with the angular stiffness of a clockwork mechanism, thinks of semaphore machines, their angles and positions, then of the strange, moving shapes he saw played out across the sheet. After a while, he starts to wonder if perhaps the morbid and hypnotic sequences being executed by the dead cat's limb contain some kind of information—"contain" in the sense of enclosing, locking in, repeating in a code for which no key's available, at least not to him . . .

On the third day after Spitalfield's demise, Sophie emerges with the reconstituted cat mounted on a board and, gathering a small crowd in the Crypt Park, has them squeeze into the Crypt itself, whose door her father opens with a large, rusty key. Here, among cobwebs undisturbed for who knows how long and dust-residues whose origins must lie in the last century if not the one before that, she installs her trophy on top of a tomb whose upper surface is so strewn with dead insects that she has to clear a swathe for it with her sleeve.

"He's the wrong shape," says Serge.

He's right: Spitalfield's surface has gone corrugated, with stiff ripples running down his fur; his neck juts out aggressively, like a tiger's or leopard's; his face is dented and irregular, with unmatching marble eyes.

"Gives him more character," their father says. "Good job! Any words?"

There's a pause while they all wait for her to say something: Serge, their father, Bodner, Miss Hubbard and Mr. Clair. Widsun's not with them anymore: he left the day after the Pageant. After a few seconds Sophie brushes her hands and replies:

"No. Let's go."

But after they've stepped out and locked the door behind them she seems to change her mind. She stops, turns to her father and, pointing to the Crypt, smiles as she asks:

"You know what this is now?"

"No," he answers. "What?"

"A catacomb."

"A cat a—what? 'Catacomb'? Ah, yes," says Carrefax, "a catacomb: that's good. Very good."

5

---

i

The static's like the sound of thinking. Not of any single person thinking, nor even a group thinking, collectively. It's bigger than that, wider—and more direct. It's like the sound of thought itself, its hum and rush. Each night, when Serge drops in on it, it recoils with a wail, then rolls back in crackling waves that carry him away, all rudderless, until his finger, nudging at the dial, can get some traction on it all, some sort of leeway. The first stretches are angry, plaintive, sad—and always mute. It's not until, hunched over the potentiometer among fraying cords and soldered wires, his controlled breathing an extension of the frequency of air he's riding on, he gets the first quiet clicks that words start forming: first he jots down the signals as straight graphite lines, long ones and short ones, then, below these, he begins to transcribe curling letters, dim and grainy in the arc light of his desktop . . .

He's got two masts set up. There's a twenty-two-foot pine one topped with fifteen more feet of bamboo, all bolted to an oak-stump base half-buried in the Mosaic Garden. Tent pegs circle the stump round; steel guy wires, double-insulated, climb from these to tether the mast down. On the chimney of the main house, a pole three feet long reaches the same height as the bamboo. Between the masts are strung four eighteen-gage manganese copper wires threaded through oak-lath crosses. In Serge's bedroom, there's a boxed tuning coil containing twenty feet of silk-covered platinoid, shellacked and scraped. Two dials are mounted on the box's lid: a large, clock-handed one dead in the centre and, to its right, a smaller disc made from ash-wood recessed at the back and dotted at the front by twenty little screws with turned-down heads set in a circle to form switch-studs. The detector's brass with an adjusting knob of ebonite; the condenser's Murdock; the crystal, Chilean gelina quartz, a Mighty Atom mail-ordered from Gamage of Holborn. For the telephone, he tried a normal household one but found it wasn't any use unless he replaced the diaphragms, and moved on to a watch-receiver-pattern headset wound to a resistance of eight and a half thousand ohms. The transmitter itself is made of standard brass, a four-inch tapper arm keeping Serge's finger a safe distance from the spark gap. The spark gap flashes blue each time he taps; it makes a spitting noise, so loud he's had to build a silence box around the desk to isolate his little RX station from the sleeping household—or, as it becomes more obvious to him with every session, to maintain the little household's fantasy of isolation from the vast sea of transmission roaring all around it.

Tonight, as on most nights, he starts out local, sweeping from two hundred and fifty to four hundred metres. It's the usual traffic: CQ signals from experimental wireless stations in Masedown and Eliry, tapping out their call signs and then slipping into Q-code once another bug's responded. They exchange signal quality reports, compare equipment, enquire about variations in the weather and degrees of atmospheric interference. The sequence *QTC*, which Serge, like any other *Wireless World* subscriber, knows means "Have you anything to transmit?", is usually met with a short, negative burst before both questioner and responder move on to fish for other signals. Serge used to answer all CQs, noting each station's details in his call-book; lately, though, he's become more selective in the signals he'll acknowledge, preferring to let the small-fry click away as background chatter, only picking up the pencil to transcribe the dots and dashes when their basic *QRN*s and *QRA*s unfold into longer sequences. This is happening right now: an RXer in Lydium who calls himself "Wireworm" is tapping out his thoughts about the Postmaster General's plans to charge one guinea per station for all amateurs.

". . . tht bedsteads n gas pipes cn b used as rcving aerials is well-kn0n I mslf hv dn this," Wireworm's boasting, "als0 I cn trn pian0 wire in2 tuning coil fashion dtctrs from wshing s0da n a needle mst I obtain lcnses 4 ths wll we gt inspctrs chcking r pots n pans 2 C tht they cnfrm 2 rgulatns I sgst cmpaign cvl ds0bdns agnst such impsitions . . ."

Transcribing his clicks, Serge senses that Wireworm's not so young: no operator under twenty would bother to tap out the whole word "fashion." The spacing's a little awkward also: too studied, too self-conscious. Besides, most bugs can improvise equipment: he once made Bodner's spade conduct a signal and the house's pipes vibrate and resonate, sending Frieda running in panic from her bath . . .

Serge moves up to five hundred metres. Here are stronger, more decisive signals: coastal stations' call signs, flung from towering masts. Poldhu's transmitting its weather report; a few nudges away, Malin, Cleethorpes, Nordeich send out theirs. Liverpool's exchanging messages with tugboats in the Mersey: Serge transcribes a rota of towing duties for tomorrow. Further out, the lightship *Tongue*'s reporting a derelict's position: the coordinates click their way in to the Seaforth station, then flash out again, to be acknowledged by Marconi operators of commercial liners, one after the other. The ships' names reel off in litany: *Falaba, British Sun, Scania, Morea, Carmania,* each name appendaged by its church: Cunard Line, Allen, Aberdeen Direct, Canadian Pacific Railway, Holland-America. The clicks peter out, and Serge glances at the clock: it's half a minute before one. A few seconds later, Paris's call-sign comes on: *FL* for Eiffel. Serge taps his finger on the desktop to the rhythm of the huge tower's stand-by clicks, then holds it still and erect for the silent lull that always comes just before the time-code. All the operators have gone silent: boats, coastal stations, bugs—all waiting, like him, for the quarter-second dots to set the air, the world, time itself back in motion as they chime the hour.

They sound, and then the headphones really come to life. The press digest goes out from Niton, Poldhu, Malin, Cadiz: *Diario del Atlántico, Journal de l'Atlantique, Atlantic Daily News* . . . "Madero and Suárez Shot in Mexico While Trying to Escape" . . . "Trade Pact Between" . . . "Entretien de" . . . "Shocking Domestic Tragedy in Bow" . . . "Il Fundatore" . . . "Husband Unable to Prevent" . . . The stories blur together: Serge sees a man clutching a kitchen knife chasing a politician across parched earth, past cacti and armadillos, while ambassadors wave papers around fugitive and pursuer, negotiating terms. "Grain Up Five, Lloyds Down Two" . . . "Australia All Out for Four Hundred and Twenty-one, England Sixty-two for Three in Reply" . . . Malin's got ten private messages for *Lusitania,* seven for *Campania,* two for *Olympic: request instructions how to proceed with . . . the honour of your company on the occasion of . . . weighing seven and a half pounds, a girl . . .* The operators stay on after the Marconigrams have gone through, chatting to one another: Carrigan's moved to *President Lincoln,* Borstable to

Malwa; the Company Football Team drew two–all against the *Evening Standard* Eleven; old Allsop, wireless instructor at Marconi House, is getting married on the twenty-second . . . *His tapper-finger firing up her spark gap . . . Short, then long . . . Olympic* and *Campania* are playing a game of chess: *K4 to Q7 . . . K4 to K5 . . .* They always start *K4 . . .* Serge transcribes for a while, then lays his pencil down and lets the sequences run through the space between his ears, sounding his skull: there's a fluency to them, a rhythm that's spontaneous, as though the clicks were somehow speaking on their own and didn't need the detectors, keys or finger-twitching men who cling to them like afterthoughts . . .

He climbs to six hundred, and picks up ice reports sent out from whalers: FLOEBERG/GROWLER 51N 10' 45.63" lat 36W 12' 39.37 long . . . FIELD ICE 59N 42' 43.54" lat 14W 45' 56.25" long . . . Compagnie de Télégraphie sans Fil reports occasional light snow off Friesland. Paris comes on again; again the cycle pauses and restarts. Then Bergen, Crookhaven, Tarifa, Malaga, Gibraltar. Serge pictures gardenias tucked behind girls' ears, red dresses and the blood of bulls. He hears news forwarded, via Port Said and Rome, from Abyssinia, and sees an African girl strumming on some kind of mandolin, jet-black breasts glowing darkly through light silk. Suez is issuing warnings of Somali raiders further down the coast. More names process by: Isle of Perim, Zanzibar, Isle of Socotra, Persian Gulf. Parades of tents line themselves up for him: inside them, dancers serving sherbet; outside, camels saddled with rich carpets, deserts opening up beneath red skies. The air is rich tonight: still and cold, high pressure, the best time of year. He lets a fart slip from his buttocks, and waits for its vapour to reach his nostrils: it, too, carries signals, odour-messages from distant, unseen bowels. When it arrives, he slips the headphones off, opens the silence cabin's door to let some air in and hears a goods train passing half a mile away. The pulsing of its carriage-joins above the steel rails carries to him cleanly. He looks down at his desk: the half-worn pencil, the light's edge across the paper sheet, the tuning box, the tapper. These things—here, solid, tangible—are somehow made more present by the tinny sound still spilling from the headphones lying beside them. The sound's present too, material: Serge sees its ripples snaking through the sky, pleats in its fabric, joins pulsing as they make their way down corridors of air and moisture, rock and metal, oak, pine and bamboo . . .

Above six hundred and fifty, the clicks dissipate into a thin, pervasive noise, like dust. Discharges break across this: distant lightning, Aurora Borealis, meteorites. Their crashes and eruptions sound like handfuls of buckshot thrown into a tin bucket, or a bucketful of grain-rich gravy dashed against a wash-boiler. Wireless ghosts come and go, moving in arpeggios that loop, repeat, mutate, then disappear. Serge spends the last half hour or so of each night up here among these pitches, nestling in their contours as his head nods towards the desktop and lights flash across the inside of his eyelids, pushing them outwards from the centre of his brain, so far out that the distance to their screen seems infinite: they seem to contain all distances, envelop space itself, curving around it like a patina, a mould . . .

Once, he picked up a CQD: a distress signal. It came from the Atlantic, two hundred or so miles off Greenland. The *Pachitea,* merchant vessel of the Peruvian Steamship Company, had hit an object—maybe whale, maybe iceberg—and was breaking up. The nearest vessel was another South American, *Acania,* but it was fifty miles away. Galway had picked the call up; so had Le Havre, Malin, Poldhu and just about every ship between Southampton and New York. Fifteen minutes after Serge had locked onto the signal half the radio bugs in Europe had tuned into it as well. The Admiralty put a message out instructing amateurs to stop blocking the air. Serge ignored the order, but lost the signal beneath general interference: the atmospherics were atrocious that night. He listened to the whine and crackle, though, right through till morning—and heard, or thought he heard, among its breaks and flecks, the sound of people treading cold, black water, their hands beating small disturbances into waves that had come to bury them.

ii

One night, at about half past two, Serge looks out of his bedroom window and sees a white figure gliding over the Mulberry Lawn, skirting the Orchard's border as it heads towards the Crypt Park's gates. It looks like Sophie; he leans out further but the figure disappears from view before he can identify it. The experience startles him—not least because it plays out in the real and close-up space around the house an aspect of some scenes that he occasionally intuits but never quite pins down when riding the dial's highest reaches: vague impressions of bodies hovering just beyond the threshold of the visible, and corresponding signals not quite separable from the noise around them—important ones, their recalcitrance all the more frustrating for that reason. He sees these things, and hears, or half-hears, them as well, quite frequently—usually as he's straddling the wavelength-border between consciousness and sleep. This white figure tonight's no somnolent vision, though: it's a real person, of the size and shape of Sophie, and dressed the way she dresses when she goes to bed each night, to boot. The next day, he visits her in her lab and asks if she was wandering about in night-skirts last night.

"What's it to you?" she asks. "Who said you could come in here?"

"Can I come in?" he asks.

Sophie shrugs, and turns back to her work desk. She's stayed in this room pretty much non-stop since arriving back from London, where she's been studying natural sciences at Imperial College for two terms now. In front of her, on the desk's surface, microscope slides smeared with variously tinted substances fan out like card-hands; dotted around these, like tokens wagered by invisible opponents, or perhaps the miniature opponents themselves, are insects, dead ones: beetles, grasshoppers and dragonflies, rigid as the dog-avatar in the Realtor's Game. Above these, pinned to the wall, are charts, diagrams and passages written in Sophie's hand. She doesn't seem to object as Serge leans over her and scans a couple of them:

I placed a specimen of the Helochara family inside a jar,

one reads,

and introduced into its cell a mixture of potassium and ether until it turned onto its back and appeared dead; however, when a little ammonium was sprinkled over it, it effected a complete recovery.

Another states:

Aphrophora spumaria entomb themselves within a frothy coat of viscid cells. The bubbles not only surround the insect and the stem upon which it rests, but flow in a continuous sheet between the ventral plates and abdomen.

Beside the text, an annotated sketch shows some kind of tick embedded in a mass of spawn-like foam. Serge runs his eyes across to one of the charts. Beneath the heading "Poisonous Qualities of" a complex set of lines—straight, curving and dotted—threads disparate Latin words and letter sequences together. To Serge's mind, cluttered with RX traffic, the sequences appear like call-signs. It's not just the compounds on the chart that make him think this way; Sophie has highlighted certain letters of the wall's various texts, making them stand out by drawing over them in yellow, blue or purple crayon, as though tracing from one to the other a kind of continuum, a grander alphabetic sequence slowly emerging from the general eclectic mesh. Most intriguingly of all, a study of the Emperor moth, complete with illustration demonstrating the vibratory capacities of its antennae, carries the word, written in brackets in the margin, "Morse."

"Morse?" asks Serge. "Do moths know that?"

"What?" she murmurs—then, following his eye towards the wall, scoffs: "No, stupid; no connection. Professor Morse, an entomologist from Nanterre, France."

She doesn't venture any more, and turns back to the slide in front of her. She seems preoccupied—full not of the eager energy with which she used to throw herself into their chemistry experiments, but with a more concerned and troubled set of mental compounds. She looks haggard, much older than she did six months ago; staring at her cheeks, Serge can see worry-lines snaking their way down from her eyes towards the corners of her mouth.

"What are you looking at?" she snaps. "Go now; I've got to work."

She works the next day, and the next night too, and the day after that. Serge starts to wonder when—or if—she ever sleeps. By the time he wanders down for breakfast late each morning, she's already gone, a few scattered breadcrumbs and a buttered knife the only evidence of her having passed through the kitchen—those, and the eviscerated newspapers she leaves on the table after tearing from them headlines that, for whatever reason, catch her eye. With their father away at a conference on deaf education up in London ("His train will have passed yours," Serge commented to Sophie's pronounced indifference when she first arrived back) and Mr. Clair home on leave, they've got the run of the place. Maureen's given up trying to stage meals in single sittings, and leaves out bread, meats, cheeses, pies and stews for them to help themselves to when they like. As far as Serge can tell, Sophie only takes breakfast, and doesn't even seem to eat that: each time he visits her lab over the next few days he sees sandwiches piled up virtually untouched beside glasses of lemonade that, no more than sipped at, are growing viscid bubbles on their surface like *Aphrophora spumaria*. Above these, on the wall, the texts, charts and diagrams are growing, spreading. Serge reads, for example, a report on the *branchiae* of *Cercopidida,* which are, apparently, "extremely tenuous, appearing like clusters of filaments forming lamellate appendages," and scrutinises the architecture of *Vespa germanica* nests: their subterranean shafts and alleyways, their space-filled envelopes and *alveolae* . . .

Bizarrely, Sophie's started interspersing among these texts and images the headlines she's torn from each day's newspapers. These clippings seem to be caught up in her strange associative web: they, too, have certain words and letters highlighted and joined to ones among the scientific notes that, Serge presumes, must correspond to them in some way or another. One of these reads "Serbia Unsatisfied by London Treaty"; another, "Riot at Paris Ballet." Serge can see no logical connection between these events and Sophie's studies; yet colours and lines connect them. Arching over all of these in giant letters, each one occupying a whole sheet of paper, crayon-shaded and conjoined by lines that run over the wall itself to other terms and letter-sequences among the sprawling mesh, is the word *Hymenoptera.*

"*Hymenoptera?*" Serge reads. "What's that? It sounds quite rude."

"Sting in the tail," she answers somewhat cryptically. "The groups contain the common ancestor, but not all the descendants. Paraphyletic: it's all connected." She stares at her expanded chart for a long while, lost in its vectors and relays—then, registering his continued presence with a slight twitch of her head, tells him to leave once more.

Three or four nights after his first sighting of the white figure on the Mulberry Lawn, Serge sees it again. This time he sees her face: it is Sophie, most definitely. She glides past the Orchard like she did the other night, then disappears from view again. Serge shuts his RX station down, throws on a jumper and heads down the stairs and out of the front door. He catches up with her inside the Crypt Park, where she's moving through the long grass slowly, hesitantly.

"Sophie," he calls out as he approaches her from behind.

Sophie takes two more steps, then stops and slightly turns her head in his direction.

"What are you doing?" he asks.

She stays there with her head half-turned, as though preferring to sense him rather than face him—through the skin on her cheek, perhaps, or the small hairs on her neck. He repeats his question. After a while she answers:

"Looking for the Balkan beetle."

"What's that?" he asks.

"A type of flying insect, made by Pilcher," she answers absently. Her eyes turn down, towards the grass—then sharpen, as though catching sight of something couched within it. "There are all these segments," she murmurs. "Broken bodies."

"Where?" asks Serge.

"Everywhere," she replies. "When one antolie colony attacks another, they cut the victims up, and leave their limbs and torsos lying around the battlefield."

"What's an antolie colony?" asks Serge.

Slowly, her head turns fully away from him again, and she moves onwards through the long grass—ponderously, her exposed legs angling sharply at the knees, like an insect's articulated limbs.

"You'll catch cold," he calls after her, then heads back to his radio set.

The next day, sure enough, she does look ill—although not colded: more ravaged, as though worn down by fatigue yet at the same time fired up by a manic sense of purpose. When Serge slinks into her lab, she's scribbling away, furiously sketching the anatomy of flowers that, culled from Bodner's garden, lie dissected on the desk in front of her.

"The ovaries," she mumbles over her shoulder to him. "Here's where the pollen grains and utricles get into them, into their cavity."

He peers forwards, and sees where her scalpel has sliced through the corolla, pegged back its flesh and let the pistil stand out stiff and long. She scrapes the prostrate membrane, gathering its secreted essence on the blade's side, then smears this onto a slide-plate. She looks up to the wall; Serge follows her eyes, and sees spelt out above the dissection table the word *uterus*. Above it, ripped from today's *Daily Herald*, the headline "Young Turks Target Armenians." Beside the printed text, Sophie has written, in brackets, *Anatolia*.

"Anatolia," Serge reads aloud. "Is that what you were—"

"Shh!" Sophie holds her hand up, and the two of them freeze for a few moments: she sitting with the scalpel in her hand, mouth open and ears pricked up as though listening for something; he standing behind her, head above her shoulder, breathing in the sleepless odour wafting from her hair and body. After a while she turns to him and says: "Come find me tonight."

"Here?" Serge asks. "Or in the Crypt Park?"

She waves her hand across her giant diagram, as though to say "Wherever," then signals for him to leave again.

That night, as he trawls through the ether, he pictures spiracles and stamen rising upwards, prodding at the sky like hungry aerials, and shellacked setae wound like tuning-coils around segmented abdomens. From time to time he looks out of the window, hoping to catch a glimpse of Sophie drifting silkily across the Mulberry Lawn, but never does. At three or so he makes his way towards her lab. It's empty, and now smells of stale sandwiches, old lemonade and flower- and insect-secretions overlaid with the odour of the chemicals stored on the shelves' jars. Serge half-recognises this last odour from the days when he and Sophie would mix compounds in this very room—but only half: these chemicals are more sophisticated, *real* ones, loaned from cupboards at Imperial, cases guarded by white-coated men who commune with Sophie in a language too complex for him to follow. *They*'d understand her chart, Serge thinks, looking at the wall whose web of lines and vectors has grown still larger and more complex since this afternoon: they'd look at it and know immediately what the letters meant, the links, all the associations . . .

He finds her outside, in the Mosaic Garden. She's moving among the flowers, pacing from one spot to another, back again, then onwards to a third spot, a fourth one, as though following a strict set of instructions. As he comes near, she leaves the path and starts moving around the flower bed itself, her lower body lost among tall iris-stems, like some giant grasshopper.

"What are you doing?" Serge asks.

She motions to him to be quiet. He treads softly as he walks across to join her. She takes two steps forwards, then one back, then one to the side, then stops, her whole body tensed up. She seems, once more, to be listening out for something. With each hand clasped around an iris stem, she looks like a tethered radio mast.

"Why did you want me to come out here?" he asks.

She's silent for a while, then turns to him and says:

"I wanted to tell you something."

"Tell me, then," he tells her.

She stands in silence for what seems like an age—then, just when he's about to turn away and give up in frustration, says:

"I've got a lover."

Serge is overtaken by a sudden sense of vertigo—as though the surface of the path he's standing on, and of the lawn and flower beds around it, had all turned to glass, affording him a glimpse into a subterranean world of which he's been completely unaware till now although it has been right beneath his feet: a kind of human wasp-nest world with air-filled corridors and halls and hatching rooms. More to regain his bearings than for any other reason, he asks Sophie:

"Who is he?"

"He's my instructor in—" she begins; then, cutting herself short, says: "He's secret; it's all secret. But he's made me sensitive. He's done stuff to me. I can see things that . . ."

"That what?"

"See things. What's coming. When the bodies meet and separate, and more bodies come out, the parts all lie around in segments."

"What bodies? Where?" asks Serge.

"In London, Stamboul, Belgrade, everywhere," she says. "It's all connected. I feel it inside me. Look."

She takes his hand and lays it on her stomach. Her skin, through the cotton of her thin white dress, is soft and pliant. Serge can feel a rumbling beneath it. She must feel it too, because she adds:

"It's not the same as hunger."

He takes his hand away again. He knows what lovers do: he's seen photographs, in a magazine he found lying on a bench in Lydium. There was a woman kneeling on a sofa, in front of creased curtains, and a man standing beside her on a carpet, sliding down her dress with one hand while in the other he held his own huge fleshy mast, which rose from the open fly-gap in his trousers; the woman was looking at it, smiling in a fiery, complicit way, as though she belonged to that subterranean world as well, was intimate with its cells, its *alveolae,* and could look out at the normal world from inside, mocking and unobserved. Does Sophie kneel on sofas in front of curtains? Does her face have that look? Right now, she's looking straight ahead of her, but her eyes have emptied—or, rather, seem in the process of being filled from somewhere else. She's muttering:

". . . when the bodies . . . and more bodies come, the parts . . . a bug massacre in Badsack, Juno Archipelago . . . above Buc, France: Pegonde—Reuters . . ."

She looks as though she were tuning into something—as though she had somehow turned *herself* into a receiver. Is that possible, Serge wonders—like Bodner's spade, the house's pipes? He's read in *Wireless World* of a girl in America who picked up experimental stations on a filling in her tooth—but via insects and news headlines, flowers? The notion seems ridiculous. And yet *some* kind of transmission seems to be coursing through her body. As he watches her, her eyes grow brighter, which makes the sunken parts around them, their ridge-shadowed sockets, darken and become more cavernous.

"You really should sleep," Serge tells her. "Why don't we go back to—"

"He's coming soon," she interrupts him.

"Who?" Serge asks.

"Tomorrow, or the next day, he'll come back."

"Oh, Father. Day after tomorrow, yes. Why don't—"

"Father!" she snorts. "He's not your . . . It's the other one. Monarch. Didn't use paraphylectic." She pauses, then continues: "He taught me the transpositions. Then he'll slink into my dormitory, and wreak carnage."

Serge feels a chill. The air is cold, but it's not that that makes him shiver: it's the sense that Sophie's talking about things he's simply not equipped to understand, an apprehension that gulfs as wide as frozen interstellar distances are opening within her words, expanding beyond measure the gap between her and him. He asks her:

"What dormitory? The one where you sleep in London?" She stays in a boarding house for young ladies in South Kensington, just opposite the Science Museum.

"No," she answers. "That's not where. I'll have to kill him in me, or there'll be more bodies: segments, on the battlefield."

"You're crazy," Serge says. "I'm not listening to this rubbish. Go to bed, or I'll wake up Maureen and she'll haul you inside."

Sophie looks at him bewilderedly, then around the garden. Dawn is breaking. Birds are singing in the bushes and the trees over the wall. A couple are hopping in the grass's dew. To his surprise, she releases the iris stems, acquiesces with his order and walks slowly beside him to the house. When they arrive there, she goes to her room, he to his. He sleeps all day. He dreams of Sophie's innards, her stuffing: of organs sensitised by passion while, on the outside, hinged limbs twitch and fletch and signal, current-galvanised, against creased backdrops, both inner and outer body shaken by transmissions. In his dream, the divan turns into a dissecting board; Sophie becomes a bird, cat or insect whose stomach has been opened; heart, gizzard and other nameless parts are spilling outwards in a long, unbroken tapestry, a silken shawl—and spilling up into the air, sticking to wires. He wakes up sticky himself, and ashamed.

"What kind of time is this?" Maureen asks him when he finally makes his way down to the kitchen. "And where's your sister?"

"Still sleeping," he tells her. "We were both up late."

"The hours in this house have gone haywire," Maureen tuts. "When Mr. Simeon gets back we'll have proper dining times, with everybody present."

Serge shrugs. He eats some bread and honey, then wanders up to Sophie's room to see if she's still sleeping. She's not there. He heads back down the stairs and out across the maze towards the Mosaic Garden. The day's calm; spring flowers are lolling open in the late-afternoon sunlight; others, budding, secrete their own sticky juice, attracting bees. As Serge approaches Sophie's lab the smell of flowers gives over to another, sourer smell that reminds him at first of marzipan. The door's open; when he steps inside, the smell becomes much stronger—stronger and more sharp, like apple brandy. Sophie's sitting in a chair holding a glass in her hand, but the glass is lolling at an almost horizontal angle. Sophie's hand is stiff; its middle finger points in the direction of the chart. Her eyes are open: it seems that she's trying to show him something among the sprawling web—some new word, or figure, or associative line. It's only as Serge turns his eyes up to it that he registers, like an after-impression, the flecks of brine that cover Sophie's lips like bubbles blown by a departed insect.

iii

The funeral arrangements take some time. A quick burial was never on the cards: there are the autopsy and coroner's report to be completed, as in any case of death by poisoning. Serge's father busies himself with arrangements over the next week: distributing invitations, developing and printing programmes, discussing the contents of the buffet with Maureen and Frieda, consulting weather forecasts in the newspapers each day . . .

It's to be held outdoors, same as the Pageants—but in the Crypt Park, not on the Mulberry Lawn. The vicar of St. Alfege's is to say a few words, the Day School pupils are to perform a recitation and Sophie's to be buried in the Crypt, or rather under it; there's no more room at ground level. Carrefax has devised an elaborate construction whereby Sophie's coffin will be lowered into the ground beside the Crypt, slid along rails into an enclave burrowed out beneath the edifice itself, then slightly raised so as to slot into its designated space between the bodies of two ancestors, with the communicating tunnel to be filled in once the manoeuvre's completed. The excavations are installed two days before the funeral itself: supporting pillars with winch-levers on them for the lowering; a second, horizontally operating winch for the sliding, and a pump-lever contraption for the final hoist. By the time the workmen have finished, piles of dug-up earth line the edges of the trench, and the sound of hammering and tapping that's filled the estate's air falls silent, leaving only birdsong in its place.

Dr. Learmont, general practitioner of long standing for the districts of West Masedown and New Eliry, comes in person to tell Serge's father that the coroner has reached a verdict of accidental death. Carrefax concurs:

"The cyanide was right next to her lemonade glass. Easy to confuse the two. And then she'd been up all night, working on the compounds. Best female student Imperial has had since they admitted them, according to her tutors . . ."

Learmont looks at Serge; Serge looks at Learmont. The doctor's kind face and brown leather case seem to multiply for him, vaguer and more mythical with each iteration, down a telescoping corridor of memories: of strep throat, measles, chickenpox and other, nameless illnesses that always, whatever their distinctive unattractive qualities, returned him to a pleasant and familiar zone of honey-and-lemon tea, boiled sweets and picture-books—a zone where Maureen plumped his pillow every hour, Sophie brought the Berliner down from the attic and played him records, Mr. Clair waived all table-learning or essay-writing deadlines and, whatever time it actually was, it always seemed to be the calm, drawn-out stretch of mid-afternoon. Repeating the gesture with which he used to reach towards him then, Learmont extends his arm now and taps Serge on the chin.

"You keeping fit?" he asks.

Serge nods.

"Be needing all you able-bodied young men soon," the doctor says.

"Apropos of—what? Imperial, yes: I wanted to ask you . . ." Carrefax says to Learmont. Learmont raises his eyebrows; Carrefax continues: "As you'll doubtless be aware, it's not unknown for death to be misdiagnosed, which makes for a certain . . ."

"You think it might not have been accidental?" Learmont asks.

"Not—what? No, no: that's not what I meant. I was referring to the rare—yet still, I believe, well-documented—instances in which a death is recorded, only for the so-called deceased to awake several days later and recover their full capacities."

"I'm sorry to say that in this case we can entertain no hopes, not even the faintest, of—"

"Bells were used, in times less technologically advanced than ours, with cords running from within the coffin to miniature towers mounted on the tombstone, should the incumbent come around and wish to signal the fact to those in a position to liberate them—a vertical position, as it were . . ."

"But your daughter's been . . . I mean, after the autopsy, there's simply no way that—"

"Yes: splendid! So I was thinking that perhaps we could avail ourselves of more contemporary hardware. I've arranged for a tapper-key, donated from Serge's arsenal of such equipment, to be placed beside her in the coffin, and will attach a small transmitting aerial to the Crypt's roof, should she—"

"Which one of my keys?" Serge asks. "You never consulted me!"

"That way, she won't need to rely on the circumstance, far from guaranteed, of someone happening to pass by the Crypt at precisely the moment she comes to and rings. The signal emitted will be weak, but strong enough to cover the estate, should, for example, Serge be experimenting with his wireless set, as I believe his wont is these days . . ."

Serge's mother spends her time in the spinning houses, working on a shroud. Bodner plies her with tea: Serge sees him moving between his garden and the Weaving Room or Store Room virtually each time he looks in that direction from the attic window. He's spending lots of time up in the attic these days. It's the spot with which he most associates hours spent alone with Sophie. The cylinders and discs are still there. When he plays them now, her voice attaches itself, leech-like, to the ones recorded on them—tacitly, as though laid down in the wax and shellac underneath these voices, on a lower stratum: it flashes invisibly within their crackles, slithers through the hisses of their silence. He looks out over the flat, motionless landscape as he listens. The sheep never seem to move: they just stand still, bubbly flecks on Arcady Field's face. The curving stream also seems completely still, arrested in a deathly rictus grin. Only the trees in the Crypt Park seem to have any movement in them: they contract and expand slowly, breathing out the sound of the Day School children practising their recitation:

Soon as the evening shades prevail
The moon takes up the wondrous tale,
And nightly to the listening earth
Repeats the story of her birth . . .

The looping, repeating lines mutate and distort so much that, even when the words come out correctly, they seem like a mispronounced version of something else, other sentences that are trying to worm their way up to the surface, make themselves heard. Kneeling on the window-sill three floors above them, Serge strains his ear to pick these buried phrases up, but gets just inarticulate murmurs. The estate's layout, too, seems to be withholding something—some figure or associative line inscribed beneath its flattened geometry, camouflaged by lawns and walls and gardens . . .

The day of the funeral is warm and sunny. The mourners' tread as they descend the gravel path is muffled, cautious. They gather, all in black, outside the Crypt Park's gates, beneath the obelisk-topped columns, and make quietened small-talk with each other, glancing nervously around as they try to spot their host, hostess or Serge. After a while, Carrefax strides out of the house and greets them boisterously.

"Wonderful that you could come! There'll be refreshments afterwards. For now, we should proceed into the park. What? Splendid! Yes, no seating, I'm afraid. Where's Miss Hubbard?"

As though taking her cue, Miss Hubbard emerges from the school-rooms with seven or eight pupils in tow. She steers the children through the Crypt Park's gates behind Carrefax and the other mourners. Serge meanders in behind them. By the Crypt, the vicar's waiting. So are Maureen, Frieda and their girls. Frieda and the girls are crying; Maureen's got a stoic, grim expression on her face. The vicar has a consoling beam on his. He flashes it around, as though trying to attach it to the face of each arriving person. Beside him, mounted on a small wooden podium, is the coffin. It's made of dark wood, with brass handles; from a small hole in its lid probably imperceptible to anyone but Serge and his father, a small wire spills and dangles down the side. On each side of the trench Carrefax has designed, a workman's standing between piles of earth, holding a spade: they look like soldiers standing to attention as they line a dignitary's route. The mechanical set-up has become even more complicated than it was last time Serge saw it: now, a new rail is supported in the air above the rail-lined furrow, cutting across it perpendicularly—a curtain rail, with black drapes pegged to it on hooks. A little metal switch-box is set into one of this rail's supporting columns. Carrefax steps over to it and clicks the switch on, then off: the box gives a little moan, the rail's pegs jerk and the drapes, one hanging on each side of the trench, hems bunched up on the ground, twitch briefly, then lie still again.

"Splendid!" says Carrefax. "All set to go. We'll start with—"

He's interrupted by a general rustling as all heads turn away from him towards the Crypt Park's gates. His wife is making a late entry between these, with a train of women. She's holding something in front of her, cradling it in upturned hands. The train is moving in formation, like a set of rugby forwards: advancing in rows, arms locked together. Their faces are neutral and impassive, like statues' faces. With long dresses covering their feet, they seem to glide above the lawn, as though mounted on their own rails made of air, invisible in the long grass. The other mourners watch their slow approach in silence; Carrefax, the vicar, Miss Hubbard and the Day School pupils watch them too. They glide towards the main group slowly but ineluctably, as though bearing down on them. Then, just as it seems they're all going to collide with the posts beside the trench, they stop, as one body, a few yards from the coffin—all of them apart from Mrs. Carrefax, who proceeds onwards to the coffin and, placing on its lid the shroud that she's been carrying in her arms, unfolds it until it covers the whole thing. It shows, in red and green silk on a white silk background, an insect feeding on a flower.

Carrefax nods to the vicar, who coughs, then starts to speak:

"Friends," he beams, "we come here not in despair but in gratitude: for the gift of these past seventeen years . . ."

A sob breaks loose from the main crowd of mourners. The vicar's beam grows more pronounced and aggressive as he continues:

". . . in gratitude also that the soul of Sophie Annabel Carrefax has been reclaimed—redeemed, as one redeems a ticket or an object given out on loan—and done so, I'm quite certain, with great joy, by he who crafted it in the first place. When we consider—"

"Him," says Carrefax.

"I'm sorry?" asks the vicar.

"By *him* who crafted," Carrefax corrects him.

"Him who crafted it, indeed," the vicar says. He foists his beam about again before continuing: "When we consider that we all are here on loan, then we might come to see that those the earlier gathered back are perhaps those most valued. Think of the cherished objects you yourselves might once have lent . . ."

Serge stops listening after a few sentences. He can still hear the vicar's words, of course, but they're just sounds. His pick-up's set beneath them, lower. He looks down, and sees among the grass a beetle pushing an earth-clump several times its size. The beetle's trying to move this forwards, but the clump rolls back onto the beetle every time the latter shoves the former up the little incline in its path. Is it a Balkan beetle, Serge wonders? A bloody-nosed one? He looks at the flower and insect embossed on the coffin's drape. The drape's thin, and it fits the coffin loosely; sunlight, after passing through its fabric, bounces back up off the coffin's copper handles to travel back up through it from the inside, making its white silk luminescent and its insect and flower dark, like silhouettes; they seem almost to move across the fabric's surface, as though animated. The sunlight's also spilling across the large earth-piles by the trench, blurring their edges; it looks as though tiny clumps have broken loose and are slightly levitating. The steel rails in the trench glint blue and silver. They seem to hum, like railway lines hum when a train's approaching in the distance, just before you hear the train itself . . .

The sensation of humming, real or imagined, grows: Serge can sense vibrations spreading round the lawn. He feels them moving from the ground into his feet and up his legs, then onwards to his groin. They animate his own flesh, start it levitating. He can't help it. He crosses his hands in front of his crotch and looks about him: everyone else is looking at the vicar, or the coffin—not at him. The vicar's still beaming aggressively, talking of heaven. Looking around him, trousers bulging, Serge is filled with a sudden and certain awareness that there is no such place: there's the coffin and the Crypt, the lawn, these conker trees above them, this fresh-smelling earth. One of the workmen's scratching his nose. A fly's buzzing around the vicar's head. The vicar tries to ignore it, but it brushes his face, tickling his lips and making him half-blow, half-spit his next few words out. If the fly hatched on Arcady Field, it will have come from sheep-dung. Serge pictures minute dung-flecks being deposited on this man's mouth, the even tinier bacteria inside them turning inwards from his lips, swimming against his phlegm through crashing rocks of teeth, past lashing tongue and gurgling epiglottis down towards his stomach . . .

The vicar's words tail off. Serge's father marshals the Day School pupils into place and they perform their recitation:

The spacious firmament on high,
With all the blue ethereal sky,
And spangled heavens, a shining frame
Their great original proclaim . . .

Their pronunciation's more distorted than it usually is in Pageants: they've had less time to rehearse, and are more nervous. "Spacious" and "spangled" are drawn out forever; "proclaim" becomes "co-caime." The sky is blue and shining though: this much is true. Serge raises his head from the ground towards it. Birds are far away, which means high pressure: he should get good reception tonight. Another sob comes from one of Frieda's girls; another mourner sniffles. The Day School pupils, voices dull, monotonous and out of synch, intone the second verse, describing evening shades, the moon and all the planets, which

Confirm the tidings as they roll,
And spread the truth from pole to pole . . .

Serge, mind still wandering, recalls a photo in the latest *Wireless World* showing the earth's southernmost Marconi station, in the Chilean archipelago—four giant tethered pylons with row upon row of wires running between their peaks, cutting the air into grid squares which hovered above a tiny operator's cabin. The operators had to spend up to six months at a time there, waiting for their relief. What truth might they be spreading to the pole? Telegrams, news, weather reports, cricket scores, the day's closing prices . . . ? A female mourner's gazing at him, tearful, pitiful eyes trying to tell him that she understands his grief. He looks away. She can't: he doesn't feel any. He knows he's meant to—but it's not there, and that's that. What he feels is discomfort: at his priapic condition and, beyond that, at a sense he has of things being unresolved or, more precisely, undivulged. The charts, the lines, the letter-clusters and the fragments Sophie was pronouncing as she wandered round the Mosaic Garden—and, beyond these, or perhaps *behind* them, the vague, hovering bodies and muffled signals he's been half-seeing and -hearing at the dial's far end, among those crashing and erupting discharges of meteoric events, galactic emanations: these, he's more and more convinced, *mean* something and are issuing from *some*where, from a place he hasn't managed to track down before the one person from whom he might have learnt the what, where, and why of it all elected to go incommunicado . . .

The pupils pause, then launch stumblingly into the final verse:

What though in solemn silence all
Move round the dark terrestrial ball;
What though no real voice or sound
Amid the radiant orbs be found?
In reason's ear they all rejoice . . .

The voices run out to their furrows' end, and trail off into silence. There's a pause. Serge hears a motor car go by on the far side of Telegraph Hill, then looks again at the beetle, still carrying on its battle with the earth clump. His father issues an instruction to the two workmen, who transfer the draped coffin from its podium onto the platform suspended above the trench, then winch it down onto the rails. One of them steps over to the other winch-handle and starts cranking it; the coffin begins to slide towards the Crypt. Carrefax nips over to the column supporting the curtain-rail and flicks the switch on. As the coffin slides beneath the perpendicular bar above the trench, the drapes jerk into action, their long hems slipping from the higher ground to fall into the trench and, to the sound of an electric whirring, draw closed across the coffin as it passes through their axis. That's what's meant to happen, at least: in fact, one of the hems catches on the coffin and gets pulled backwards, sending the electric motor first into whining overdrive and then into suspension.

"Blast the thing!" says Carrefax. He switches the motor off, tugs at the curtain to unsnag the hem, then flicks the switch again. The coffin slides right through the curtain now, which falls back into place behind it.

"She's gone!" sobs Frieda.

Her girls whimper agreement. Serge, still hard, can't stop himself from smiling: the coffin's not two feet from where it was before. If they moved round to the side they'd see it, dumb and wooden and unaltered. It strikes him that this whole event's more amateurish than the Pageants—more contrived, more sloppy. The curtain's just a curtain, and a badly designed one at that. His hands still covering his crotch, he runs his eyes beyond it, to the Crypt's wall. Is that meant to be the edge, the portal to beyond, the vicar's heaven? And its far wall, then: would "beyond" stop there? He runs his eye on further, to the grass behind the Crypt, moist and stringy and no different from the grass they're standing on back here—then onwards, to the dung-filled, sloping field beyond the water, the telegraph line on the hill. He pictures the cars beyond that, then the boats, the towers, the stations, archipelagos . . .

The workmen have moved along the trench's edge to operate the pump-lever contraption. As they hoist the coffin up into its slot inside the Crypt, Serge feels a heaviness enter his stomach, as though something foreign were being lodged there. It's a pronounced, visceral sensation—strong enough to make him release one hand from his crotch and rub his midriff, in the manner of a pregnant woman. He closes his eyes in discomfort, and sees dark globes orbiting in seas of light. When he opens them again, the workmen have finished pumping and are standing back, rubbing their own hands. Several mourners are sobbing. Mr. Clair is weeping quietly. Not Serge: for him, this shoddy, whining spectacle has nothing to do with death, nothing to do with Sophie either. Both death and she are elsewhere: like a signal, dispersed.

6

---

i

K loděbrady is a twenty-three-hour journey from Portsmouth; from Versoie, twenty-eight. Serge and Clair board first a train, then a boat, then another, grand train laid on by the International Sleeping Car Company and, finally, when this pulls up somewhere near Dresden, a series of smaller trains that carry them across borders of countries, time zones, principalities and semi-autonomous regions Serge has never even heard of. If the names sliding across the compartment's window beside telegraph poles, red-roofed farmhouses and haystacks that seem to float ten feet above the ground seem vaguely familiar to him, this probably owes more to the fairy tales Maureen would tell him as a child than to anything he's learnt from Clair of geography or history. He's passed through zones of boredom and exhaustion too, emerged from them and started waking up now for the journey's last leg. His senses, though out of kilter, are alert; the lethargy that's hung above him like a pall for months seems to have lifted—not completely, but a little: lifted and lightened.

The train's come to a stop. It's not a station: they're just waiting for a signal to change, or a point to switch, or an instruction to be shouted from the track-side in a foreign language. Serge stands up, pulls the top half of the window down, leans out and looks around. It's the end of summer: bushes and trees beside the lines are overgrown and faded; dandelions and weeds stand a foot tall between the sleepers. A stone post has been painted black and yellow, in straight stripes. A small electric box clings to one of the rails, short legs clamped around it like the femurs of a tick while a longer, more tentacular protuberance drops from its underbelly to send currents through the earth. The countryside is flat. A mile or two away, a smokestack seems to rise straight from it. Nearer by, an earthworks plant groans as its stilted runways convey ballast before dropping it onto a growing mound. Other, fully grown mounds of the stuff stretch for hundreds of yards beside the railway line, strangely black against the blue sky and golden foliage.

"It's the cysteine," Clair says, noticing Serge looking at the mounds.

"Sistine? Like the chapel?"

"No, what makes it black: the chemical. Cysteine and sulphur, chloride, sodium, what have you. That's what's going to cure you."

He tosses Serge a brochure from among the papers lying beside him on the bench-seat. The train's almost empty; with the compartment to themselves, they've spread out. Serge lets the brochure land on his own bench-seat, then sits down again and picks it up. The front cover bears a drawing of an elegant lady strolling with a parasol along a boulevard lined with Greco-Roman buildings, a glass in her hand. Beneath this image's border and slightly in front of it due to the perspective adopted by the brochure's illustrator, a large red heart's held aloft by a jet of water while a cherub, balancing above the heart on one foot, breaks across the border into the main picture to strew roses across the lady's path. It's that depth thing again: the technique Serge could never master in his drawing lessons. It's not *right:* the cherub, occupying the same plane as the master image, couldn't simultaneously be several feet in front of it, and therefore couldn't strew the flowers from outside its frame—unless he's reaching up from beneath a screen onto which the picture of the strolling lady's being projected and, holding the flowers in front of the path, performing some clever optical trick. Above the lady's parasol, shot through with black sunrays, are the words "Klodĕbrady Baths."

Serge flips through the brochure, past photographs of gentlemen and ladies very like the lady in the drawing strolling past domed mausoleums or posing in front of fountains, also with glasses in their hands. The accompanying text gives the town's history, which seems to consist of a series of invasions, wars and squabbles over succession. One such squabble, dwelt on at some length by the brochure's author, sees the heirs of a King Mstislav accusing the pretender to his throne, one Vladimir, of poisoning their father, only for it to turn out that he'd died of "corruption of the blood due to bad humour"—a cue for Vladimir, cleared of foul play, to decapitate his libellers. This Mstislav, or perhaps another, is mentioned a few paragraphs later, only now the humour has become a *tumour:* he (or his namesake) it was, the brochure says, who, "seeking for his way in the labyrinth of events and social problems" prior to his blood's corruption, established Klodĕbrady as a centre for "radical social oppinions"—laying the ground for the progressive reign of the man who, emerging eighty or so years later, would eventually become the town's saint, Prince Jiři. Under Jiři, Serge starts reading out loud to Clair, society and culture flourished in the mid–fifteenth century, and the town "undoubtably attained the zenith of its import."

"As your father would point out, it should be indubitably," Clair says.

Their train's pulled off again. A goods train passes them, heading in the other direction, its carriages laden with the same type of black ballast they were watching pile up in the earthworks.

"This is interesting," Serge continues, flipping past more Mstislavs and Vladimirs into the nineteenth century. "The whole town burned down in 1805. When it was rebuilt, the Bavarian king and his Spanish wife brought in the water-diviner Baron Karl von Arnow, who discovered the spring in the grounds of their own castle."

"How convenient," snorts Clair. "A subterranean water-source that big would have been found under a peasant's hut if Baron von Aristo had divined there."

"No," says Serge. "This engineer, Maxbrenner, had to lay pipes beneath the whole town, leading out from under the castle, in order to create the spa. He plumbed in pumps, and heaters, and all sorts of things. So now, it says here, 'all visitors may divertise themselves imbibing of the restorative balm.' Oh, look: here's a list of what it's got in it."

His eye runs down a table in which cysteine breaks down into sulphur, which in turn subdivides into various chlorides, carbonates and sulphates: chloride of sodium, chloride of lithium, of potassium; chloride, sulphate and carbonate of magnesium; carbonate of lime; then, intriguingly, "free and easily liberated" types of carbonic acid. The heaviness inside Serge's stomach that's a constant presence for him these days makes itself felt as he reads the table. He flips the page and finds a photograph of Klodĕbrady's Grand Hotel, its terraces alive with water-swilling people, flags of all the states of Europe fluttering above them and, above these, the heart-and-cherub logo once again.

The logo's waiting for them at the station, painted on the wood beside the town's name, its heart blackened by grime. Porters load their bags onto a trolley and push this rattling up the main drag. There are the domed mausoleums, set among a park; there, too, the strollers, just like in the brochure, only not so many. There are nurses, chattering in groups of three or pushing wheelchaired cripples past kiosks selling trinkets and chemists' shops above whose doors hang model scales with snakes coiled round them.

The Grand Hotel's terraces are half-empty. Chairs are leaned up against tables. Only three flags are out today: they hang limp above two old men nodding on a bench behind newspapers. The porters hand Serge and Clair over to their counterparts in the hotel, who take them to their rooms. In his Serge finds, beside the bed, a season ticket to the baths, two bottles of sparkling but slightly murky-looking water and a book of writing paper with the heart-and-cherub logo on it—only now the heart itself is sprouting flowers, dishevelled ones that look like the dandelions and weeds along the train tracks, while four cherubs hovering beneath it struggle to hold it up. There's also a menu of the therapies on offer, with a list of prices: inhalation, twenty-nine crowns; gas injection, twenty crowns and fifty; underwater massage, twenty-two; and so on. How much is a crown? Serge thinks of those covetous Mstislavs and Vladimirs again, of their corrupted blood and rolling heads.

Dinner's at seven. The long dining room has a bar at one end behind which a white-coated waiter stands, hands on the counter, bottles rising up from staggered shelves like organ pipes behind him. On one wall, beneath curled-vine cornicing, a fresco shows, in Greco-Roman style, ladies and gentlemen in togas sipping water while divertising themselves in games of discus- and javelin-throwing over which a togaed judge presides. The room's just under half-full. Serge and Clair are seated by a waiter at a small round table and served quail and boiled potatoes with a bottle of red wine.

"Drink it slowly," Clair says. "It's supposed to be good for digestion."

Serge shrugs. The other diners glance their way occasionally while speaking a mish-mash of languages. Serge can pick out French, German and Spanish; Clair identifies Hungarian, Serbian and Russian on top of these. English is spoken as well, but, exchanged as a currency of convenience between people to whom it's not native, sounds foreign too. After dinner, while they're taking coffee in a lounge whose walls are lined with local wildlife specimens—otters, eels, pikes, water-rats and toads—stuffed behind slightly darkened glass, a German man comes up and, introducing himself to them as Herr Landmesser, asks them what they're "in for."

"It's the boy," says Clair. "*Das Kind.* Stomach complaints. Me, I'm as right as rain."

"If you can say that, you are a lucky man," Herr Landmesser answers with a deep, sardonic laugh. "Or happily ignorant. Which doctor will you see?"

"Dr. Filip," answers Serge. "My first appointment is tomorrow morning."

"My doctor also, Filip. Gout, for me." Herr Landmesser points down at his foot. "For Filip, it is all the same: all moral."

Serge begins to ask him what he means, but is cut off by the arrival in their group of a tallish, middle-aged lady.

"So young!" she says in a grainy voice as she looks at Serge. "I have a niece so young as you. You should meet her, when you would be in Rotterdam one day. Me, I have heart problems. How long will you stay here?"

"Three weeks, I think." Serge looks at Clair to confirm this, but Clair seems too offended, or worried, by Herr Landmesser's jibe to take part in the conversation.

"You missed—it was five days ago," the Dutch woman continues, "the spectacle. Dressed as the sun, the people of the town and doctors, nurses: sun, and clouds, and weather. Very funny. You and my niece would much have liked it, both. More people were here then. *Pani!*"

She calls this last word after a waiter who's just passed by with a coffee pot. He doesn't hear her, so she sets out after him. Herr Landmesser, too, moves away from them towards some bookshelves. Clair and Serge sit for a little longer in depleted silence, then retire upstairs. Serge drifts off to the sound of running water not far from the hotel, a stream his mind makes flow again internally, recasting it as dark, with creatures moving slowly through it.

ii

He wakes up early, some time before Clair, takes a light breakfast, then wanders along the paths that join the small domed buildings to each other in the park. An orchestra is playing beside one, in a bandstand. As he approaches it he realises that the seated musicians are arranged in a heart shape; also that the mausoleums are in fact not mausoleums:

they're pavilions housing fountains. People stroll from one to the next, holding their glasses out beneath the jets until they're full, then slowly sipping as they move on. A group of kaftaned Jews with beards and side-curls chat in Polish and Yiddish as they drink; two Russians talk to one another loudly, gargling and spitting between sentences. A French couple discuss the music:

"Mais c'est Debussy, n'est-ce pas?"

"Non, non: c'est Brahms . . ."

Serge doesn't have a glass. He cups his hands and holds them out into the fountain. The water's not particularly cold and, bizarrely, doesn't feel particularly *wet* either. It's got a kind of sooty feel to it. He draws his hands up to his face and looks at it: it's cloudy, slightly dark, with bubbles in it. He takes a sip: it's cloudy-tasting too, and a little bitter. A nurse wanders up and says something he doesn't understand. He raises his shoulders and looks blankly back at her; she makes a drinking-from-glass gesture with her hand, and points towards a kiosk selling glasses of the same slightly opaque quality as the wildlife cases in the hotel's lounge. Beside it, a signpost's arrows bear four names, each painted in large capitals: MIR, MAXBRENNER, ZAMACEK, LETNA. None of them say GRAND HOTEL, but Serge manages to find his way back there by following the same drag he walked up with the porters yesterday, past the trinket-selling kiosks and the chemists' with their scales and snakes.

He finds Clair waiting agitated for him on the terrace.

"Your appointment's in five minutes. Hurry up!"

"I'm ready," Serge shrugs back.

They head in the opposite direction from the fountains, past a statue of a crowned horseman and a large building up and down whose steps columns of nurses move, until they arrive at a smaller building. Here, beside the front door, is a plaque with the name FILIP and a string of letters on it. Inside, a receptionist directs them to a waiting room. Several other patients are sitting in this, most of them holding jars half-full of some sort of dark, silky material: they're the same size as the ones Bodner stores the honey in at Versoie, with the same bronze screw-on lids. After a few minutes Serge's name is called.

"Do you want me to come in with you?" Clair asks.

"No," answers Serge.

Dr. Filip is a small man with unkempt white hair and a stringy beard and whiskers. From behind thin, steel-rimmed spectacles, his eyes fix

Serge with a disapproving look. Around him, tables, trays and treadmills are arrayed like the musical instruments of some outlandish orchestra. There are tubes and pumps and cylinders, and scales attached to handles that in turn trail wires towards black sub-boxes. Strangest of all is a large machine that takes up a whole bench. Its cogs and filaments conjoin parts that look like they belong to printing presses, breweries or miniature railways. In its central segment, a dome the same shape as the fountain-pavilions rises up, a spiral staircase carrying a copper cable from its apex down its side and on towards a fuse to which it's soldered.

"Carrefax, with *C*, not *K*," says Dr. Filip. "Sit down."

Instinctively, Serge looks around the room for his father before realising that "Carrefax" means him and complying with Dr. Filip's order.

"Notes from English doctor indicate chronic intestinal problems," Dr. Filip continues. His voice is sharp, and seems to issue from the tiniest of apertures nestled among the whiskers. "Please to describe them."

Serge sticks his hands beneath his thighs and shuffles in his chair. "It's like a big ball in my stomach," he says. "A big ball of dirt."

"Why you say 'dirt'?" asks Dr. Filip.

"Well, because it's dark. It seems that way."

"You having constipation?"

Serge nods, reddening.

"And lethargy?"

"Yes," Serge says. "Very much."

"Headache?"

"Also."

"Please to lie on table." Dr. Filip rises brusquely as he indicates a kind of folding slab that's held up by a complex frame of interlocking metal legs. It looks a little like an ironing board divided into segments that, hinge-mounted, rise and fall abruptly. "First remove shoes and shirt."

Serge slides his shirt and shoes off and climbs up onto the table. Dr. Filip pushes Serge's shoulders down into its flannel-covered surface with cold hands which then move down to Serge's stomach, which they tap, as though sounding a box or wall. Serge begins to speak but Dr. Filip cuts him off:

"Shh . . ."

He holds his hand over Serge's midriff and, tapping it a few more times—gently, as though nudging a dial—lowers his head and listens.

"Not good," he says after a while. "A blockage. Stagnant. You are having autointoxication. Skin is dark, eyes too. You seeing well, or not?"

"Not," Serge says. "I mean no. It's kind of . . ."

"How is?" Dr. Filip asks, impatient.

"Furry."

"What is meant?"

"Furry, like fur. The hair of animals. Small hairs. It's like . . ."

His voice trails off. It's hard to describe. Fur's not quite right. It's more like tiny filaments. The closest thing he could liken it to is one of his mother's silks—the really fine, dark ones—held right up to his eyeballs and stretched out in front of them, making the world gauzed: dark-gauzed, covered in fleck-film. It's been like this for months. When it started, he'd try to blink a hole in it, or wipe it away, peel the veil back; but that only ingrained it further, lodging it beneath the surface of the eyes themselves. He tried washing them, but this just made the filament-mesh run and stain, gauzing everything he saw before he'd even looked at it.

Dr. Filip says: "Please to provide a sample."

"Sample of what?" Serge asks.

"Stool," Dr. Filip answers. His cold hands pull Serge's shoulders upright and turn them towards a low chair with a hole in its seat and a kidney-shaped tray beneath it.

"I can't," Serge says.

"Not to be embarrassed," Dr. Filip sneers disdainfully.

"It's not that," Serge explains, reddening again. "I mean I can't. It doesn't want to . . ."

"You speak of what *it* wants?" Dr. Filip's stringy eyebrows climb up towards his hairline, and his glasses ride up with them. "So: I am arranging enema for you this afternoon. Also," he continues, turning to his desk and picking up a pen, "I am giving you diet from which not to digress. Lactose: soured milk and cereal. And fruit. No meat. You give this to hotel kitchen; they will administer." He hands Serge two cards. "And you will follow hydrotherapy course. Here is schedule." He slides from a drawer a sheet of paper and, reaching behind him, pulls from a shelf a honey jar, then passes both these to Serge. "Please to go now. Return tomorrow afternoon at four. Also drink constantly the water: from the fountains, with your eating, at all times. Every opportunity, you drink."

Serge walks back to the hotel holding the jar, wondering what he's meant to do with it. He tries to hand it in with his menu card, but the maître d' returns it to him, instructing him to take it to his next appointment, which turns out to be in the building that he saw the nurses entering and leaving. The nurse Serge sees, in a room sharp from disinfectant, makes him lower his trousers and pants and bend across another segmented table whose lower end is ramped down to the ground; then she inserts a rubber tube in him and turns a tap on. As the warmish water enters and then leaves him, carrying no more than a small fragment of whatever's in him out with it, the fabric of the veil that's darkening his vision seems to expand and open slightly, making the objects in the room stand out more sharply: the taps and tubes, the tiled gutter running by the walls, the door's handle and the nurse's shoulders as she bends towards the gutter to retrieve the sample.

"You have bottle?" she asks.

"Bottle?" Serge says. "No. Should I?"

"Doctor has give you one, I think . . ."

The honey jar. "I didn't realise that was meant for . . ."

"I use another," she says. "Show me card."

He shows it to her. She copies his name and number onto a small piece of paper and hands the card back to him. "Next time, bring."

"Next time?"

She looks back at him without replying. Her look's not unkind, just knowing and indulgent, like Maureen's back at Versoie.

The sharpness brought on by the enema stays with him for a while: the air around the park as he walks back through it seems brighter, clearer and less flecked. The feeling lasts for an hour or so; then the gauze contracts and thickens again, veiling the world back up. As he heads to his bedroom after a dinner of soured milk and what looks like horse-food, he passes the stuffed otters, eels and pikes, and realises that he should have compared his vision, when describing it to Dr. Filip, to the glass of their cases: it has the same clouded quality, the same fine-filamented graininess as everything he sees. The glass of the bottled water in his room as well: when he picks one of the bottles up, it's like holding a miniature and concentrated version of the world—his world at least. The bottle's got the heart-and-cherub logo on its label and, beneath that, a patent number. Serge pops its top and pours the water out: it, too, is cloudy, darkened, sooty. As he lies in bed, its bitter taste lingers in his mouth despite two vigorous brushings . . .

The hydrotherapy begins the next morning. After a fruit and yoghurt breakfast and a wander round the Mir fountain with a glass purchased from the kiosk by the signpost, he visits the complex in which hydrotherapy is offered. It's the Maxbrenner building, built, like the Letna one in which he got his enema yesterday, around the spring whose name it bears. Serge presents his card at the front desk, and is ushered on towards the building's innards. A musty smell fills its corridors; the air itself is moist and sulphurous. Opening the door of the room he's been directed to, he's attacked by vapour which invades his nostrils and half-scalds his lips. Inside, against a wall, are rows of cabinets, large escritoires with hinged covers, like the one that Widsun did his correspondence at when he was visiting Versoie. Some of these are open; others, closed, contain men, locked inside them with only their heads protruding from the top like unsprung jack-in-boxes. Other men's heads jut out horizontally from blankets wrapped tightly round their bodies as they lie on benches, steaming. They look like insects, like pupating larvae lifted from boiling water. Tubes loll and snake around the room, running from cabinet to cabinet and bench to bench, forming a vapour-gushing mesh in which the human chrysalises all sit, lie or swoon.

A nurse takes Serge's card and leads him first to a changing booth, then, towel-loined, to a cabinet inside which she seats him, clamping its door shut around his neck. Steam swirls around his enclosed limbs and torso, making them wet and dry at the same time, immersing him without immersing him *in* anything. Drops form on his forehead and run down his face. It's sweat and sulphur mixed together: licking it from his lips since he can't use his constrained hands to wipe it off, Serge tastes the bitter sootiness again. He spends what seems like hours inside the cabinet. To pass the time, he thinks of the ink set next to Widsun's headed government paper: how he'd dip the signature-seal in the ink and stamp the man's name out across his forearm while Sophie sat at the desk learning all those cipher sequences. When he's finally released he sees that the sweat that's poured from him is dirty, a blue-black, as though he were full of ink.

He's sent through to an adjoining room to be massaged. The nurse who performs this is only two or three years older than him, short and dark-haired. Her hands make circular passes around his navel, the ball of the hand pressing down into his abdomen before descending in spiralling ovals towards his pelvis; then they move up and down his sides, slapping and sawing. Her body, as she bends above him, seems a funny shape. Her skin is ruddy; her arms and chest give off the same musty, sulphurous smell that pervades the corridors, as though her flesh had imbibed it and turned each of her pores into mini-fountains. When she finishes the massage and straightens up, Serge realises that the unusual shape of her body wasn't just due to her position as she bent, stroking and kneading, over him: her back is slightly crooked.

"Finish now. Same again tomorrow," she says. Her voice is low and earthy. She has a glazed look, not quite in the present, as though she were staring through him, or around him, at something that was there before he came and will be there after he leaves.

Serge is meant to have a class with Clair after lunch, but he's too exhausted. He sleeps till almost four, then makes his way over to Dr. Filip's. In the waiting room he picks up the *Lazensky Soutek,* which, as far as he can make out, is a kind of local *Bathing Times.* It's amateurish, badly printed onto thick, rough paper. On its front page is a grainy image showing some kind of spectacle taking place, with girls on a stage holding up cut-out suns. That's what Serge assumes the objects are: they're sun-shaped but, due to the saturation in the printed photograph, much darker than the girls who hold them. Is that what the Dutch woman was talking about? Do they do Pageants here, just like at Versoie? There's a text beneath the image, but Serge doesn't understand it. He looks up from the paper. The other patients are resting their sample-filled jars across their knees, or on the seat beside them. His is waiting for him in Dr. Filip's office: the doctor's holding it up, turning it around and inspecting it when he walks in.

"Not good; very much not good," Dr. Filip says disapprovingly. "Please to look."

He hands the jar to Serge. On its outside is a label bearing the hand-writing of the nurse who hydro-mined him for its contents. The matter inside is solid, liquorice-black, with an undulating surface in whose folds and creases small reserves of dark red moisture have collected.

"Blood," says Dr. Filip, pointing. "You have cachectic condition: encumbrances in bowel causing autointoxication. Ptomaines, toxins, pathogens all enter bloodstream. Look how dark it is."

"You mean the blood?" Serge asks. "Or . . ."

"Both," snaps Dr. Filip. "And if not treated, more. You have a poison factory in you that secretes to arteries, liver, kidneys and beyond. To brain too, when we don't prevent."

"What's causing it?" Serge asks.

"Morbid matter!" Dr. Filip's thin voice pipes from his small mouth. "Bad stuff. If I am speaking several hundred years ago I call it *chole,* bile—black bile: *mela chole.* Now, I can call it epigastritis, alimentary toxemia, intestinal putrefaction, or six or seven other names—but these do not explain what causes it. It needs a host to nurture it, and you are willing. Yesterday you spoke to me of what *it* wants, which means you serve its needs, make them your own. This we must change."

"How?" Serge asks.

Dr. Filip's whiskers rustle as his lips curl in a wry smile. "I cannot tell you this," he says. "You must discover. I can prescribe treatment and diet, monitor symptoms. The rest is for you." He slips a sheet of paper from his drawer and starts to write. "Take this to chemist," he tells Serge. "The pills, one time each day—not more: too many all at once will kill you. And drink the water, always, all day long. If abdomen distends a little, not to worry. Like your own Lord poet Tennyson has said of faith: 'Let it grow.' " His eyes glow slightly, like thin filaments, registering satisfaction at the quip he's just made. Then their grey-metallic colour returns as he tells Serge: "Please to go now."

iii

Serge settles into a routine. Each morning he wanders through the park and sips from the Mir fountain to the sound of the orchestra's music, then heads on to Letna for a water-and-paraffin-oil enema, then to his hydrotherapy and massage session with the musty-smelling, crook-backed nurse. The lightening effect produced by the enema stays with him through the massage and on until just after lunch, when the veil thickens again and he sleeps for an hour. In the afternoons he has his lessons (Clair's intent on teaching him German these days, deeming him old enough to start reading Marx) and takes walks around the town. He dines with Clair each evening, then spends an hour or so reading or playing games in the parlour: dominoes or bridge if in a group of four or five, or, if alone with Clair, chess. At first Clair always wins, but after a week Serge finds in the hotel's library a book about the game and, learning the numbers and letters used to denote pieces and positions, starts applying the manoeuvres, familiar to him from nights of transcription, that the

Marconi operators would tap across the sea to one another; now he wins each time. Whenever in his room, he drinks the bottles that are left for him every morning, with the heart-and-cherub logo and the patent number on their labels; each night he falls asleep with sulphur and soot on his tongue.

Serge gets to know the other patients staying in the hotel. They're always kind to him: as the youngest one, he's treated like a type of mascot. Besides Herr Landmesser and the Dutch woman, Tuithof, there's a Frenchman, Monsieur Bulteau, who takes pleasure in explaining how each person's diet acts on their metabolism, trotting out the names of chemicals, compounds and gastric juices; a Russian, Pan Suchyx, who reads sheet music in a deep armchair each evening, humming the odd snatch out to himself as though pondering a proposition or a line of argument; an Austrian banker named Kleinholz who keeps whipping from his waistcoat pocket a notebook full of columns of what Serge assumes are ledgers or accounts, and annotating these with a pen he keeps attached to it; and a score of vague Hungarians, Swedes, Serbs and Italians who nod and smile at Serge each time they pass him beside the stuffed animals or on the staircase. Nationality seems less of a defining label here than type of illness: the K4-to-X move of most long-serving inmates when they meet a fresh one is to enquire not where the new arrival's from but rather what he or she's got wrong with them, and patients subsequently tend to gravitate towards those with the same complaint. There are the arthritics and their outriders, people with sciatica and neuritis, who of an evening gather round a puzzle table, their stiff fingers prodding and poking the pieces into position; then there's the skin-disease gang, the eczematics and psoriasistics, who generally loiter in the hotel's interior courtyard (an area the other patients unkindly refer to as "the Leper Colony"); then the ones with urinary-tract infection, arterial spasm, hypertension, renal calculus, functional and organic diseases of the heart or chronic diseases of the liver—in short, what Serge and Clair call "the picklers," people who've come here to douse their organs in the water in the hope of cure. They're usually Dr. Filip's patients. You can spot his patients all around Kloděbrady by the sample jars they carry about with them like passports. Serge wonders, as he waits outside the doctor's office, where the samples all end up. Do they get filed in some huge archive? Or stored in a cellar, laid down in comb-shaped cubby-holes like a thick-set honey made from bees fed only on black flowers? There must be so much of it, enough matter to rival the mounds of cysteine rising from Kloděbrady's outskirts and the countryside around it and constantly being loaded onto trains, carted away who knows where . . .

M. Bulteau has a theory about the cysteine, which he expounds one morning in the drawing room:

"For gunpowder, *n'est-ce pas?* Explosion: *pow!*" His hands fly apart in an explosive gesture. "The Prussians take it to their *arsenales,* prepare for war."

"Ganz lächerlich!" a German lady mutters as she sips her coffee. Kleinholz, notebook out, starts annotating figures with more rigour. Herr Landmesser declares:

"The earth belongs to Prussia from long time ago, so she may use it as she wishes."

"How does it belong to Prussia?" Clair asks.

"The whole region is Germanic, from way back," Herr Landmesser explains. "This Jiři in the statue, patron saint, is just new, Christian name for old Germanic god."

"What god would that be?" a Hungarian demands to know.

"Jirud. He was a prince expulsed from kingdom after he became diseased, and wandered as a swineherd. When he saw his pigs rolling in earth here, and their diseases ended, he did same and was himself cured. Then founded new kingdom here, and conquered back old one too. He was father of Volsung, who is father of Sigmund, father of Siegfried."

"But," says Serge, "no one knew about the healing powers of Kloděbrady until Baron von Arnow found the water under the castle and Maxbrenner plumbed it through the town."

"You have eaten modern version of story like a good boy taking medicine," Herr Landmesser informs him with a patronising glance.

"This is Prussian arrogance *typique!*" M. Bulteau almost shouts, his hands still gunpowdering apart. "They think all Europe's theirs, and make these stupid *mythes* to justify their avarice for land and power."

"*Mossieu!*" The German lady slams her coffee down, red-faced. "You are not polite."

"She's right: you should apologise," Herr Landmesser tells M. Bulteau.

"I shall not!" M. Bulteau answers.

The argument rumbles on throughout the day, with the German delegation demanding in increasingly aggressive terms an apology from the lone Frenchman, while Hungarians, Serbs and Italians first take sides then splinter into smaller groups who've found subsidiary grievances with one another. Only Pan Suchyx remains neutral, although not unaffected, humming first one melody and then another, contrary-sounding one to himself, as though weighing and counter-weighing the claims of each. People argue in Dr. Filip's waiting room; their raised voices draw the doctor out to sternly tell all parties to desist, his white coat at this point, for Serge, resembling the toga of the Greco-Roman judge in the hotel's dining-room fresco.

"Same problem in their heads as in your body," he tuts as he prods Serge's abdomen back in his office, ear lowered as it tunes into his intestines again. "Blood of Europe poisoned and cachectic; ptomaines and pathogens in system. Now the black bile is everywhere: the *mela chole*. All have clouded vision, just like you."

Discussions, hostile or otherwise, become less common as the hotel's population dwindles in late August. Each day the porters' suitcase-laden trolleys clank and trundle down the main drag from the hotel to the station, not the other way. The orchestra by the Mir fountain reduces its appearances to two a week, and even then is made up of fewer musicians than before, its heart shape retained but shrunk, the music now competing with the sound of workmen's hammers banging at stone and plaster as they renovate the mausoleums. Sections of the fountain complex are switched off, drained and repaired. Serge spends whole mornings following the piping's layout, fascinated by the bare mechanics of it all: the joins and junctions where the network splits, the small electric pumps beside the pipes, the insulated wires threaded through these. The habit catches: he starts looking at the ground all day whatever part of town he's in, inspecting the cracks that run through it like skeins, its dark and viscous colouration, or the discarded stubs of bath season tickets and medicine labels ground into it and broken down until they seem as old and organic as earth itself.

iv

At the beginning of September, an arrival creates a small eddy in the flow of leavers from the town. She turns up in the Grand Hotel's lobby with a large round hatbox, a mink stole, a folded parasol of the same light blue as the hatbox, a black handbag and a flotilla of smaller bags and boxes. As porters duck and tack around her, she stands static as a lighthouse in a busy harbour, leaving her older chaperone to issue instructions and distribute tips.

Serge is heading out of the hotel towards the Mir, and half-stops when he sees her. She's about his age—perhaps a year or two older, like the crook-backed nurse. She looks at him quizzically when his passage through the lobby falters, which makes him look back quizzically at her, as though he knew her, or perhaps were supposed to perform some task for her that's slipped his mind—which makes her stare back too, bemused. She seems to understand the situation sooner than he does—to understand there *is* no situation—and releases his gaze with a confident, if mannered, kind of smile.

He sees her next that afternoon, in the town's museum. The museum's in the castle; Serge didn't even know of its existence until Mevr. Tuithof gushed about it over dinner last night. When he buys a half-crown ticket at its entrance, the old lady in the ticket-booth comes round to his side of the window and leads him towards an ancient sub-Berliner in the main gallery.

"Deutsch? Französisch?" she asks, smiling up at him.

"English," he replies.

"Ah!" She seems a little shocked, and scurries back to her booth, returning with a record that she lowers to the turntable with shaky hands. Stooping slightly, she leads the pickup's arm across, then down. She turns to Serge now, and makes to say something—but, lacking the English words to do so, merely points to her ear: *listen.* Serge listens. A deep, male, English voice comes crackling through the speaking horn:

"Of all the towns in Central Europe," it informs him, "few have had a history so steeped in violence as Kloděbrady." As though to illustrate its point, a scream—perhaps a child's, perhaps a woman's—interrupts the monologue. "Here it was," the deep, male voice continues after the scream fades out, "that the child-prince of Kutna Hora was beheaded at the order of the *Hauptmann* of Olbec; here it was that Vincenzo and Rosnata, the sons of Mstislav, were killed by Vladimir after their own father's demise."

Serge nods at the old lady knowingly:

"The tumour-humour thing," he says.

She smiles back at him anxiously, then beats a slow retreat towards her booth. The deep, male voice continues telling him of wars and purges, plagues and fires. He looks around the gallery: its vitrines, made from the same murky glass as the pike-and-otter cases in the hotel, hold illuminated manuscripts depicting scenes of battle and execution. Larger images of similar events hang on the walls. A tapestry of roughly the same size as the one above the staircase at Versoie shows some kind of torture taking place: an unhappy-looking character's being carried by two soldiers up a ladder leading to the rim of a huge vat from which steam rises, while a courtier-type points to the vat malevolently. Serge wanders over and inspects the scene more closely. The courtier has the same sharp, narrow features as Dr. Filip. Maybe Dr. Filip's just the latest incarnation of a character as old as this town itself, Serge thinks to himself—a figure who reappears in era after era, like Dr. Learmont's face repeating through the sickbed afternoons of his childhood, but on a larger scale, one to be measured not in the memories of a single life but over centuries. The borders of the tapestry are embellished with insects. Serge turns away from it and feels his veiled vision darkening further, and feels too the dark matter in his stomach tightening, solidifying. The deep voice on the gramophone is talking about the region's landscape:

". . . already crossed by an extremely important long-distance trading route linking the centre of the country to the Kodsko region and Silesia inking the centre of the country to the Kodsko region and Silesia inking the centre of the country to the Kod . . ."

The record's stuck. Serge turns and makes to walk back to the gramophone so he can release the needle, but sees that he's been beaten to it: a woman, not the ticket-lady, is lifting the arm up and sliding it above the record's surface before lowering it back again, allowing the monologue to advance:

". . . for the transportation of the mineral-rich earth of the surrounding countryside, which remains a valuable resource to this day. At the beginning of the thirteenth century . . ."

The woman turns around now, and he sees it's the new arrival. She's changed since this morning, and now wears an emerald-green knotted cloche hat and a sea-blue shawl.

"My stumbling porter," she says. "What's your name?"

He tells her.

"Serge like 'sedge,' or 'urge'?" she asks.

"Just like I said it," he replies. "What are you called?"

"Lucia," she answers. "It's Italian."

"You don't sound Italian," he tells her.

"It's my mother," says Lucia. "She's from Genoa. My father's English. 'Serge' sounds French."

"It is. My mother also: her family."

"You have brothers and sisters?"

"No," he says. "I had a sister, but not anymore. What are you here for?"

"Here? To see the museum," she says.

"No, I mean here in Kloděbrady."

"Oh, anaemia," she tells him, rolling her eyes up like a naughty schoolgirl. "My blood's too light or something. How about you?"

"The opposite: too dark."

Lucia giggles. "How perfect. Shall we visit the gallery?"

They walk through the large hall beneath tapestries and past illuminations, while the gramophone's account of wars against the Turks, Hungarians and Czechs, of infanticide, betrayal and sedition, echoes at them from the room's high walls. The words soften and run together as they step into the cellar, in which rotting boat-fragments, the charcoaled skeletons of old canoes, are laid out among sepulchres whose stone reliefs level accounts between aggressors and their victims by giving the faces of both the same worn-down, characterless quality. When they come up to the main gallery again, the voice is telling them how Mstislav tried to buck the murderous local trend by developing and implementing pacifist strategies.

"He was the one with radical oppinions," says Serge. "I read about this earlier. He lay the groundwork for Prince Jiři to ... Listen ..."

"... for the reign of Prince Jiři," the deep voice says as though completing, or rephrasing, Serge's sentence, "who submitted to the royal courts of Europe, under the title of *The General Peaceful Organisations,* a blueprint for universal peace."

"Well, well," Lucia says, nodding at him wide-eyed and amused. "Impressive."

Serge holds up his finger like the ticket-lady did a while ago; they listen as the voice continues:

"Although not immediately adopted, Jiri's vision is now blossoming among all nations, and amicable trade has replaced warfare as a means of competition."

"Has it?" Lucia asks, more to the voice than to Serge. "That's nice."

The record's ended now; the gramophone's speaking horn hisses. For a moment, Serge is back in the attic at Versoie, looking out over the rainy garden, shunting ghosts around its grid-squares. The ticket-lady's shuffling over to retrieve the disc, smiling at them exaggeratedly as they pass her on their way to the exit. As she's returning the pickup to its cradle, she must clumsily allow her shaky hand to drop the needle back onto the disc's surface: the child's or woman's scream erupts once more, following Serge and Lucia out into the courtyard.

The heart-logo's embedded in the castle's masonry; it hovers above them as they head beneath an arch, only this time it's held up not by cherubs but on strands which protrude from its underside like fleshy tentacles, giving it an octopus- or jellyfish-like look. They pass out of the courtyard towards the town's river, where, beside a boathouse, rowers are lowering their not-yet-charcoaled canoes from a jetty while swimmers in trunks and bathing caps splash friends in paddle boats. A bridge crosses this; Serge and Lucia walk to its middle, then pause and, leaning on the rail, look down over a large double-decker pleasure boat that's waiting for a lock to open. On the boat's stern is painted its name, *Jiři*.

"How did your sister die?" Lucia asks. They haven't spoken for a while: just walked and watched the river. Looking at the swirls emerging from beneath the boat's hull, Serge replies:

"She drowned."

The lock door opens; bubbles rise up from the churning water; the pleasure boat moves on; so do Lucia and Serge. After a few more yards the bridge turns into a weir. Sluice-gates beneath it channel and filter the water; above it, at intervals, gate-houses rise like watchtowers. Beyond these, a generating station runs from the weir to the solid ground on the river's far side. Through its mesh windows, Serge can see turbines grinding and whirring, their wheels and belts resembling the strange machine in Dr. Filip's office. The building's electric moan hangs in the air and merges with another hum that comes from somewhere else—from higher, growing in volume and aggression like the buzz of a malignant insect. Serge looks up and sees an aeroplane flying low above the river. Lucia grabs his shoulder as it passes over them.

"Look!" she shouts, all excited. "Look at that!"

"It's taking people on an aerial tour of the town and countryside," Serge says. "They do it two or so times each week, when the weather's good."

"Have you flown on it?" she asks.

"No." Clair suggested it one day but he declined, for the simple reason that he didn't believe that all his weight could possibly get airborne. He knew it could, of course, knew that the laws of physics would allow the machine to bear him on its wings and propeller up into the sky—but *psychologically* . . . In his mind the morbid matter Dr. Filip spoke of has taken on proportions far, far larger than his stomach could ever accommodate, and expanded to become a landscape, a whole territory: the land itself, and then the murky, gauzy air above it, the dark waters flowing beneath this . . . How could all *that* be elevated? His abdomen's swollen since he arrived here. Dr. Filip said that this was good—that it was the pure, air-filled water that was swelling it, that purity, like faith, would grow. But something else is growing inside Serge. He feels its heaviness. He *sees* its heaviness everywhere: in the scales hanging above the doors of chemists' shops, the snakes that curl around them, weighing them down, in the cysteine-rich ballast being crane-hoisted onto groaning trains, or in the hearts that jets and cherubs strain to hold up against dragging weeds and tentacles. He's taken to colouring the hearts black in idle moments in his room: on the stationery beside his bed or on the labels of the mineral-water bottles . . .

He sees Lucia often. They take walks together on most afternoons. Both Clair and Lucia's chaperone, the fifty-odd-year-old Miss Larkham, seem to think their company is good for one another. Lucia likes his, certainly: each time she laughs she fixes his eyes with hers, aquamarine and pale, holding them for longer each time. After a few days she starts punching him lightly on the arm whenever she makes a light-hearted comment, or grabbing his shoulder like she did when the aeroplane flew overhead and leaving her hand there, letting him support her as though she were about to lose her balance even though the patch of ground they're on is straight and flat. He senses that she'd let him return the gesture if he felt like it, and hold her as closely or tightly as he liked, kiss her, do whatever he pleased . . .

But he's not sure that he wants to. For all Lucia's levity and brightness, he prefers the company of his crook-backed masseuse. Her name's Tania, he found out the third or fourth time she massaged him. He likes the way her hands circle around his stomach, the aggression of the palm's ball pressing down into his flesh and muscles, the spiralling descent that follows, then the way she slaps and saws his sides. He likes her ruddy skin and musty, sulphurous odour; as she bends above him he inhales it deeply, as though breathing in, through her, the sulphurous fumes gushing straight from the springs. Walks with Lucia are enjoyable and pass the time, but sessions with Tania fill him with anticipation, so much so that he finds himself growing impatient for the next morning's one each afternoon, losing the signal of whatever Lucia's talking to him about as his mind tunes forwards to the mustiness, the pressing and descent . . .

He and Tania talk little. Once he asks her how she came to be a masseuse and she tells him that she contracted polio as a child, and came to Kloděbrady because her family wanted her to benefit from the healing powers of the local earth. They weren't wealthy enough to keep her here as a patient, so she became a chambermaid's assistant; then, when she was thirteen, started training at the Letna. Despite working in hydrotherapy, she's adamant that it's the earth and not the water here that's special.

"You're like Jirud, then," Serge tells her as she pounds him.

"Who he?" she asks.

"He came here with pigs, and the earth cured them—or at any rate that's what Herr Landmesser says. Is he one of yours?"

"I do not know either Jirud or Landmesser," Tania tells him. "But the earth here is good. Without it, I would have much pain. You turn over now."

As he turns, her distended shoulder looms above him. He likes her crippled body, the illness inside it. Like her smell, it seems to convey something else—something gurgling upwards from below, running through her as though she were a conduit, a set of pipes. Her glazed look too: the way her eyes seem almost oblivious to what's in front of them, fixing instead on something other than the immediate field of vision, deeper and more perennial . . .

Does his health improve? Not really. Its progress certainly isn't to the satisfaction of the old judge and torturer. He sees Dr. Filip once a week and, lying on his back while the detector-whiskers twitch and bristle and the tapper-arm hovers above his abdomen, is lectured on his failings as a patient.

"So: appears your body is responding to the treatment only so it then can re-intoxify," the doctor's sharp voice scolds.

"What's re-intoxifying it?" Serge asks.

"*What?* There is no *what*. It re-intoxifies itself."

"*With* what then?" Serge tries.

"Not *with* either. Your illness is not a thing; it is a process. A rhythm.

Toxins are secreted around body, organs become accustomed and, perverted by custom, addicted. So when toxins are gone, organs ask for more. More ptomaines, please! More pathogens! And body makes more. The rhythm is repeating, on and on. It will repeat until you—I mean your will, your mind—tell it to stop."

"How do I tell it that?" Serge asks.

Dr. Filip stops tapping; his thin eyes lock on Serge's from behind their steel-rimmed spectacles. "Tell me," he says; "you like it here?"

Serge shrugs. "It's fine."

"You like the rhythm of your days? The enemas, the hydrotherapy, the walks . . ."

"It's rather pleasant," Serge tells him.

The thin eyes glint metallically. "See? You find it pleasant—and I think you find the rhythm of your illness pleasant too. It pleases you to feast on the *mela chole*, on the morbid matter, and to feast on it repeatedly, again, again, again, like it was lovely meat—lovely, black, rotten meat. And so the rotten meat pollutes your soul."

"But if I like it here," Serge counters, "and follow what's prescribed, doesn't that mean I'm accepting of the treatment rather than resistant to it?"

Dr. Filip turns from him and fiddles with his instruments. His small, tight back seems tense with thinking. After a while he answers:

"Things mutate. That is the way of nature—of good nature: things pass through on their way to somewhere else, and both they and the things they pass through are thereby transformed. You following me?"

"I suppose so," Serge says hesitantly.

"You, though," the doctor continues, "have got blockage. Jam, block, stuck. Instead of transformation, only repetition. Need to free what's blocking, break whole rhythm of intoxication—then good transformation can resume and things will pass through you and make you open up. You still are only adolescent: still have much transformation to perform. Blockage must be broken, then body and soul both will open up, like flowers."

Still lying on the segmented table, Serge sees in his mind's eye cocooned men, trapped in escritoires or trussed up in sweat-filled blankets, pulsing in figures of eight as they mutate into resin-oozing, black silk-larvae that will never become moths. From the recesses of his stomach, as though from a box, he hears again a child's or woman's scream.

"Out now," says Dr. Filip. "Go and start transforming."

In mid-September there's a religious festival. Clair thinks it's the Exaltation of the Cross; Miss Larkham thinks it's the Nativity of the Theotokos; Serge doesn't care what it is; Lucia finds it all very amusing. She and Serge shadow the procession as it emerges from the doors of the town's church and makes its way towards the castle, after which it heads down to first the Letna, then the Maxbrenner buildings, pausing to perform a ceremony on the steps of each. It then moves past the rows of chemists' shops, the statue of Prince Jiři and the kiosks lining the main drag, each one of which it blesses too; then, finally, across the lawns of the fountain park, where it takes in all the mausoleums before ending up beside the Mir. At its head a priest, holding aloft a cross, intones liturgical script, while sub-priests and altar boys murmur assent. The orchestra, heart shape abandoned, follow behind, intermittently striking up tunes that sound rather funereal, breaking these off, then striking them up again, reprising the same passages. The townspeople who move along its route with Lucia and Serge join in at regular intervals, reciting short phrases in their own, non-liturgical language.

"What do you think they're saying?" asks Lucia, holding Serge's arm.

" 'O holy water, please keep bringing us rich foreigners so that we may take their money,' " Serge answers.

Lucia flings her head back in a peal of laughter and throws both her arms around his neck. A couple of townspeople turn round and cast them disapproving glances. A hush spreads through the crowd as the priest dips his cross into the Mir; then all heads bow as he holds it submerged beneath the water. He keeps it there for a long time. Watching him, Serge remembers what Herr Landmesser said about the old, Germanic origins of the town's myths. As ancient and obscure words waft over the devoted, cowered crowd, it strikes him that Herr Landmesser was probably right—and strikes him too that all the water that's gushed through the Mir since its inception would never purify him, wash his dark bile away, because the water's dark as well. It's bubbled up from earth so black that no blessing could ever lighten it, been filtered through the charcoaled wrecks of boats and tumour-ridden bones of murdered ancestors, through stool-archives and other sedimented layers of morbid matter. Serge turns his veiled gaze away from the priest—and as he does, sees Tania looking back at him with old, glazed eyes.

V

By late September only Serge and Clair, Lucia and Miss Larkham and a gaggle of full-time patients who've resigned themselves to the knowledge that they'll never leave the place alive remain in the Grand Hotel. The poles outside stand flagless; the terrace, cleared of tables, collects leaves. Inside, the dining room is being redecorated: a large sheet hangs over the Greco-Roman judge and athletes of the fresco; the white-coated waiter manning the bar beneath it doubles to serve the four or five tables at which guests still sit. Beside the Mir the orchestra no longer plays; the floor of its bandstand, like a horizontal version of the fresco, is covered in sheets as workmen repaint the trellised ironwork of its rails and columns. Wandering out to the fountain every morning, Serge feels like an interloper, someone who's found his way, like the rose-strewing cherub in the drawing on the brochure, into a picture to which he doesn't rightly belong. The townspeople, who earlier were so attentive to the visitors, accommodating to the point that their lives, their daily movements and activities, revolved around them, now seem to orbit their own, obscure suns, ones that Serge can't quite discern. The concierge and maître d', as often as not out of uniform, chat to one another across the reception desk even when guests are waiting; men with ladders assume right-of-way in corridors and streets alike, leaving visitors to skirt and squeeze around them: this is *their* town now . . .

The general relaxation of formalities makes itself felt in Serge's sessions with Tania. There's nothing tangible that's changed: she still wears the same coat and presses, slaps and saws in the same places—but her hands move over him more casually now. Each session seems like a weekend one, as though they'd both just popped in to an empty office before slipping off on an excursion. One morning, Serge asks her what she's doing later; when she answers "I do nothing" he suggests they take a boat-ride on the *Jiří* together.

"Pleasure boat finished now," she answers. "Not tourists enough."

"Well then, we'll hire a paddle boat," Serge answers. "Want to come?"

Without pausing her rubbing she replies: "What time?"

"Six o'clock," Serge says. "Make that five. It's getting dark earlier and earlier these days."

The boathouse by the lock turns out to be closed. He wonders what to do with Tania while he waits for her in front of it. He waits until five-thirty, then five forty-five, then six. At quarter-past he spots Lucia wandering alone beneath the castle. She hasn't seen him yet; he nips across the bridge until he's out of sight but still able to watch for Tania's arrival. He sits there for another hour or so, looking at bubble-clusters moving from the weir's sluice-gates to the water's edge. *Free and easily liberated,* the brochure said; *too many all at once will kill you,* Dr. Filip warned. Behind him the generating station's turbines clank and moan. Beyond it, just before the path gives over to fields, there's a small substation: an urn-like building from which wires emerge and lead to poles, then wind round rubber spindles fixed to horizontal arms on these and split out into smaller wires, like organzine combining, only backwards, each separated strand then disappearing inside a metal casket that's half-buried in the ground. Between the substation and the main one, vines emerge from the same ground—three rows of them, attached by strings to nursery posts that they've outgrown. Serge walks up to the knitted fence around the substation and, resting his fingers in its weave, looks at the vines more closely. They have fruit on them: dark-red grapes bursting with ripeness. He lets his eye run onwards, to the fields. Beyond these there's a wood, already darkening in the dusk. Perhaps he could take Tania there, he thinks, if she turns up . . .

She doesn't. The next day, as she massages him, he asks her why.

"Boathouse closed," she says. "Other nurse tell me."

"Well, we could have gone for a walk," Serge says.

"Where?" she asks.

"In the woods, for example. They look nice. Why don't we do that this evening?"

"Six o'clock again?" she asks. "Turn over now."

"Five," he says as her shoulder looms above him. "On the far side of the weir, by the power station."

"Power?" she asks, sawing his back.

"Yes. You know: electricity." He makes a moaning noise and wheels his arms around beside his waist.

"I understand," she says, pushing them down again. "I come."

She stands him up again. As he waits by the substation he watches soldiers practising manoeuvres in the fields. They run a few feet forwards and lie down, pointing their dummy-rifles at the wood, then jump up and run a few feet further before throwing themselves at the earth again, advancing in stops and starts towards some imaginary enemy within the trees. Serge thinks of what M. Bulteau said about the Prussian arsenals, of what he called their *avarice* for land and power. Widsun thought the same. *Advance thy empire,* Venus said to little round Giles. The deep, male voice on the record said that Jiři's peace-blueprint was flowering among all nations. He remembers the way Lucia smiled at that, then, longing for Tania's musty smell, turns back towards the weir to look for her, and sees that a door in the generating station is opening. A man walks out and says something to him.

"I'm sorry . . ." Serge shrugs.

"Deutsch?"

"No: English."

"Oh! You English!" The man's face lights up. He's fifty-ish, well-built, with thick grey hair and bronzed, sinewy arms that look like the vines in the patch he's just stepped out into. "English good people!"

"Thank you," Serge says to him. "Are these vines yours?"

"Vine? Kystenvine, special of region. You like vine?"

"They look nice," Serge answers.

"I get for you," the man says, then turns and heads back to the generating station. He emerges a few moments later with a bottle.

"Here: *Geschenk* for good English!" he says, pushing it through the mesh with his strong, wood-dark arm. "Electro-vine. You take!"

The bottle's made from the same murky glass as everything else around here. Its contents are so dark that at first Serge thinks the man has handed him some bottled local earth; but when he takes it through the fence he realises there's liquid in it. As he turns it in his hands the liquid runs inside, its silky, deep-red filaments stirring and catching the light until they seem to glow.

"It's wine?" he asks the man. "From these vines?"

"*Da—ja*—how say? *Yes!* Kystenvine: we make here, only few bottles, for us. Electro-vine for good electro-men!"

He lets out a deep, hearty laugh, then disappears into the generating station once more. Serge thinks of taking the wine to the field's edge and drinking it as he watches the soldiers train, but realises that he doesn't have a corkscrew. Returning to the hotel, he slips the bottle beneath his shirt so Clair won't see it.

In his room, a letter's waiting for him. It's from his father.

Dear Son,

he reads,

I trust the water's to your liking. As you'll doubtless be aware (or perhaps not, bathed as you are in splendid isolation), the Pontic seas of politics are flowing with compulsive course to the Propontic and the Hellesport. Should a retiring ebb not be felt soon, I fear we'll have to curtail your stay among the Nix and bring you home, lest *Vernichtung* lay down a barrier preventing your return. Await instructions.

On another note: I have been experimenting greatly of late with Crookes Tubes, in the manner of Lenard, and feel—with great excitement and not a little trepidation—that I am close to submitting a patent for approval by the great and austere offices of our—his—majesty's government. Without going into too great detail, and not unaware that in times such as these the intimacy of one's communications cannot be assured—a fact which does not make me any less loath to engage in the dark, cryptographic art to which your godfather some time ago sold himself *corps et biens* as the saying goes—What? Yes, what I have in mind involves not only the projection by means electronic of images across a screen—a task which, after all, the kinematograph performs more than adequately—but their transmission across long distances, by wires or, indeed, wirelessly, just as sound is wirelessly dispatched at present. There is no reason this could not be done: indeed, successes have already been claimed by others in the passing of static images via radio—you of all people will be privy to that fact—but my ambition is much higher: to transmit *moving* pictures over distance, such that life in all its full, vibrant immediacy may be relayed without any delay. Yes, you read that right: what I'm inventing is no less than a remote, instant kinematoscope!

Why do I tell you this? you ask. Because I intend, *filius meus*, or rather *fili mi* (I hope, dear boy, that Clair is not letting your Latin rust, nor any other branch of the great tree of learning up whose trunk you are climbing, like the squirrel in the Norwegian—no, the Finnish—is it *Kalevalla*, or *Kavelavela* or—anyway)—I intend, once my patent is granted, to *incorporate:* that is, to set up commercially. What do you think of *Carrefax Cathode* for a name? More to the point, what would you think of becoming, if not immediately a partner, then at least, and, if required, by legal proxy till you turn eighteen, a signatory to the incorporated body? I have been pondering the question of an identificatory visual motif, or *logo* if you will, and feel that a photograph of your late sister would complement, nay complete, the family nature of our undertaking. The love of technology shared by the three of us has always been a font of pleasure—of the greatest pleasure—for me; and I see no reason why your sister's death should interrupt this interfamilial communion, far less call a halt to it. When Bell's brother, with whom the great man had spent so many hours working towards the telephone's invention, passed away, this merely spurred Bell on to create a machine sensitive enough to enter into discourse with him should the existence of an afterlife turn out to be not merely a metaphysical presupposition but a physical fact too. No contact was made—but did the brother not still play a part in the invention? Should his contribution be forgotten? So it is with Sophie, I believe. When future generations watch images, borne by fiery electric particles, dancing on their walls, relayed thither from distant lands, should it not . . .

Serge sets the letter down. He had a fluoroscopy session one day, quite early in his stay in Kloděbrady, when Dr. Filip wanted to ascertain the extent of the encumbrance in his bowels. In a windowless room buried deep in the entrails of the Maxbrenner building, he stood between a lead-lined X-ray box and an empty wooden frame that Dr. Filip shifted slightly up and down on its supporting post until it was positioned just in front of Serge's midriff. The doctor then slid a screen into the frame's groove and, stepping away from Serge, switched the room's lights off and the contraption on. There was a whirring, then a flash, a smell of calcium tungstate; and then a glowing pool collected in the air just on the far side of the screen, as though Serge's stomach were seeping light.

"Please not to move," the doctor's voice instructed him from the darkness as Serge tried to crane his head forwards to see the light-source. "I can show you with mirror."

A scraping came from beneath the voice, then the sound of something being lifted from the floor—then there it was, reflected back at him: the inside of his belly, etched in blocks and lines of black against the fluoroscope screen's sickly calcium-white, suspended in a void that detached it from anything and everything. Organs, tubes and bones quivered and oscillated against each other awkwardly, like animals—reptiles, molluscs, nether-dwelling creatures—who, crammed together in a space too small for them, bristle with aggression towards one another yet understand, through some vermicular, primordial instinct, that the survival of each depends on that of its unwanted neighbours. Both Serge and Dr. Filip watched the scene in silence for quite some time. Serge's stomach, and not the vacuum in which it was held, was the living, moving part of this new film that was being projected and viewed in the instant of its creation—and yet, rendered negative and ghostly by the rays, it seemed to Serge more dead than all the meat inside it. Lying back now on the bed trying to picture his father's putative invention, he sees skinless bodies moving through empty space: hundreds of them, stretching, bending and gesturing, like the dancing skeletons of folklore and travelling carnival displays. "Carrefax Cathode": whatever vibrant immediacy this might possess, all Serge can see is death—death broadcast out of Poldhu, Malin, Cleethorpes, flung across the seas, pulsed out on the hour from Paris, relayed from mast to mast and station to station, from Abyssinia to Suez to Crookhaven and on to homes in Europe and across the world. Can death be patented? He reaches for the mineral-water bottle by his bed and, holding it up to his face, rotates it so the seven-digit number on its label ticker-tapes past his eyes . . .

"Why didn't you turn up this time?" he asks as Tania presses her balled palms into his abdomen the next morning.

"I have thing to do," she answers.

"I met a man who gave me wine," he tells her.

"Cystenwine?" she asks him.

"That's what he called it, more or less."

"Is very good."

"We could drink it together," he says, "if you come this evening."

"Okay," she says, "I come."

To his surprise, she does. They meet on the weir and stroll over to the far bank, past the generating station. Serge can see figures moving around inside, but can't tell if his vine-limbed benefactor is among them. He and Tania pass the substation and head into the fields. The soldiers are all gone; the whole landscape seems empty—even the train pulled up beside the earth-mounds a quarter of a mile or so away has been abandoned, its driver probably drinking with the shovellers and soldiers, the bandstand-painters and dining-hall decorators in one of the town's inns. Serge has the Kystenwein on him; he also has a corkscrew borrowed from the hotel's kitchen. He looks at Tania, wondering if he should break the bottle out right now. She doesn't seem impatient for it. Her eyes, dimmer than usual in the dusk, stare vaguely ahead, towards the woods. A path leads into these; they follow it. After a while the woods end temporarily and a strip, too narrow for a field, runs between them and the next block of woods.

"Against fire," Tania tells him—the first words she's spoken since they started walking.

"What's one disaster more or less, in this town?" Serge murmurs.

She doesn't respond. To their right, in the fire-break's middle, there's an indentation: a kind of mini-quarry where the ground's been hollowed out. Its black-soiled surfaces curve in a way suggestive of soft chairs.

"Why don't we sit there?" Serge asks.

Tania shrugs. They enter the indentation and sit down, leaning back against its edges. Serge pulls the corkscrew from his pocket and opens the bottle.

"I didn't bring any glasses, I'm afraid," he tells her.

Tania takes the bottle from his hands and drinks from it, throwing her head back. The liquid casts a deep-red glow across her neck. She hands it back to him. He brings it to his lips—and tastes on its rim the warm, bitter residue of Tania's spit. The wine itself he doesn't taste till further back, down in his throat: it's bitter too, in a rich, dirty way.

"It's different from the one I had on my first evening here," he says. "My tutor said that it was good for my digestion, but Dr. Filip's only letting me drink—"

"Why you come alone with teacher?" Tania interrupts him. "Why not parents too?"

"They have things to do, like you."

"Take care of brothers and sisters?"

"No," Serge replies. "I don't have those. I had a sister, but no more."

"She died?" asks Tania. Serge nods. "How?"

Serge ponders the question for a while, then answers:

"She fell from a height and hit the ground."

Tania reaches for the bottle and drinks again. When she's done, he drinks too. The wine's making him warm; he feels the silky hotness moving outwards from his stomach, to his arms, his legs, his head. Tania takes the bottle again and drinks once more, this time taking long, deep gulps. He does the same. Some of the wine's escaped from the side of Tania's mouth; it runs down her chin and dribbles onto her blouse. Serge reaches out his hand and spreads the wet film from her chin around her cheek. She doesn't stop him, or react in any way. Her eyes, glazed as always, stare through him at the black earth. He brings his mouth up to her face and licks the wine from it. Her neck, beside his ear, emits a low, guttural sound, of the same character and pitch as low-frequency radio waves. He can smell the musty odour rising from her body—from its corners, enclaves, holes. He tugs at her blouse and, meeting no resistance, pulls it off completely, then does the same to her skirt and underclothes.

"Turn around," he says. "I want to see your back."

She turns. There it is, right under his face: the crook, rising beneath her shoulder like a ridge with valleys running down its side, flesh-rills held up by bones under the skin. He touches it, then runs his fingers up and down the rills. Still kneeling behind her, he pulls his own clothes off and, holding his penis in his right hand, feeds it under and inside her from behind while clasping her back's crook in his left hand. The guttural sounds in her neck increase in volume; the musty smell grows stronger, sharper. Serge shuts his eyes and, for some reason, sees the ruddy, marble eyes of the stuffed Spitalfield, the corrugated surface of his hairy skin. He opens them again and, looking straight down, sees the earth rising between Tania's fingers where her hands push into it. He runs his own hand down her back, so hard the nails puncture its surface, and moves inside her violently, like he's seen animals and insects do it. Her thighs push back at him, pulling him further in. He closes his eyes again and feels a burning growing in his stomach.

"*Poisonberry,*" he says, barely audibly.

The word hovers in a small gas-cloud of breath over Tania's skin before spreading outwards, dissipating. The burning's spreading outwards too, just like the wine; it's spreading beyond his body, moving out to fill the hollow, and beyond that too, across the fire-break to the woods on either side. A scream, or the echo of a scream, erupts from neither him nor Tania but, it seems, the night itself; and with it comes a tearing sound, as though a fabric were being ripped. Serge opens his eyes now, and finds that the gauzy crêpe that's furred his vision for so long is gone—completely gone, like a burst bubble or disintegrated membrane. The surfaces of ground and woods and clouds are gone too, fallen away like screens, encumbrances that blocked his vision, leaving the hollow—not of the indentation but of space itself: an endless space in which he can now see with piercing clarity. What he sees is darkness, but he sees it.

TWO

Chute

7

i

Circumferenced by first brass and then mahogany, the steel minute hand of the large wall clock jumps forwards, its point lodging in the gap between the *X* and the first *I* of *XII*. The invigilator announces:

"You may now begin."

Like so many extensions of spring, fusee and escapement, thirty-eight left forearms and two rights reach across desktops and turn back the covering page of the School of Military Aeronautics' General Knowledge Paper. Serge, seated four desks from the front of the row nearest the window, reads:

1. What causes an eclipse of (a) the sun (b) the moon? What will be the state of the moon in the latter case?

He smiles and, without hesitation, picks his pencil up and writes:

Eclipses occur when two celestial bodies arrange themselves in linear formation with a star, such that one crosses the plane between

He pauses, turns his pencil on its head and erases the last seven words, then resumes:

such that the body closest to the star casts a shadow over the one furthest. This is also known as *syzygy.*

He writes each letter of "syzygy" separately, relishing its vowel-less repetition.

Thus,

he continues scribbling,

in a solar eclipse the moon casts a shadow on the earth; in a lunar eclipse, vice versa. This shadow can be divided into *umbra* (area of total occultation), *penumbra* (partial) and *antumbra* (in which the shadow nestles in the sun like a dark pupil in a bright eye).

He sits back, sets his pencil down and looks out of the window. Turreted stone walls and wrought-iron weathercocks shape the Oxford skyline. Below them, out of view, a bicycle squeaks and tinkles over cobblestones. Serge turns back to his paper and re-reads the question's second part. He closes his eyes, thinks for a while, then, leaving a space beneath his previous paragraph, writes:

Dark.

The next question requires him to draw arcs and tangents, and compute their lengths and angles. He slides open a pencil case, removes a compass and a ruler and does this. The third reads:

3. What precautions are taken on railways to prevent the train from leaving the rails when rounding a curve? Do any extra precautions have to be taken in this respect in the case of a single-track railway which carries traffic in both directions?

Once more Serge raises his left forearm, and holds it three inches above the desktop, the hand flat, palm down, fingers pressed together and extended. The wrist swivels to the right to form a curve, and from his elbow to his fingernails he runs an imaginary train, inclining the track inwards as the speeding engine rattles past the bump of his sleeve's hem. Dismantling train and track to hold his paper down, he writes:

The track should be banked, such that the inside of the curve is lower than the outside.

And if the direction were reversed? The forearm's up again, and a second train run from nails to elbow. The banking should remain the same, it seems to him. "No further precautions need be taken": he composes the words in his head but doesn't write them yet because he's still looking at his forearm. The new train's hurtling up it, tilting as it runs into the wrist-curve—but the first train's still there too, racing down to meet it. He moves his head back, hoping that the extra surface view created by this action will reveal a switch, branch-line or siding into which one of the trains could be diverted—or, if not, at least a signal further back to warn each of the other's presence. Yet even as these things take shape in his imagination he realises that not only will they fail to prevent the collision, but it was they *themselves,* in their amalgam, who caused it in the first place: the catastrophe was hatched within the network, from among its nodes and relays, in its miles and miles of track, splitting and expanding as they run on beyond the scope of any one controlling vision; it was hatched *by* the network, at some distant point no longer capable of being pinned down but nonetheless decisive, so much so that ever since this point was passed—hours, days or even years ago—the collision's been inevitable, just a matter of time. The exam hall and its rows of desks fade for a while, and Serge finds himself carried on the buffer of his mind into a storm of steel rods, axels, crankshafts and combustion chambers, all impacting: pistons plunging through sheet metal, ripping seats from gangways, gangways from their chassis; valves screaming ecstatically and flying loose; pure-molten brake shoes splashing streaks of light; track lifted and contorted beyond recognition, as though space itself were crumpling under the weight and force of the demands being made of it, the sheer insistence of machinery breaking its bonds as it comes into its own . . .

Two days after sitting the examination, Serge takes a real train down to London. He travels through winter fog made luminescent by a sun that won't reveal itself. When he emerges from St. Pancras the fog's lifted but the air's still hazy; taxicabs leave knee-high smoke-clouds that drift slowly over pavements as he makes his way by foot through Bloomsbury towards St. James's. A thin mist sits above the park; the roofs of White-hall Court, black pyramids that join with domes and cupolas as they mount upwards, fuzz and blur in this like spires and bell-towers of some legendary castle. The War Office building is bathed in pale sunlight, but its deep-sunk windows cut dark shadow-sockets in the alabaster façade. Serge tells the soldier at the main door that he has an appointment.

"Who with?"

"Lieutenant General Widsun."

The soldier looks him over for a second time, as though taken aback. He asks Serge's name, then steps into a cabin and picks up a telephone, watching him through the glass while mouthing inaudible words. After half a minute he emerges and, pointing into a courtyard, says:

"This way, sir: up the staircase to room 615A."

The building's corridors have marble floors; Serge's feet click as he moves across them. In one, twenty or so men his age fill forms out as they wait on benches; one of them shuffles over to make space for Serge—but he, shunning this gesture, clicks his way onwards, turns a corner, heads up a smaller staircase and enters a new corridor in which plush armchairs overhung by large plants offer themselves up to older men in clean-creased uniforms. The door of 615A leads to an inner waiting area; a secretary seats Serge here, beneath a portrait of a sly-looking Tudor or Elizabethan man holding a quill above a sheet of paper covered in black ciphers, slips through a second door, then slips back out again and tells him to go through.

Widsun's office is large; his desk alone could have a model battlefield laid out on it. Behind it, framed by the grid-squares of a double-sash window, Widsun's face beams at him from atop stiff folds of khaki.

"Serge, my boy!"

"Hello, sir."

"Sir, nothing! Sit yourself down."

Serge sits across the desk from him.

"My Kinetoscope enthusiast!" Widsun guffaws. "My feathered witness! Twice the size, at least! And handsome as a prince: the world's fresh ornament, and only herald to the gaudy spring!"

Serge looks down at the desktop, towards a blotting pad and ink set. Instinctively, his hand reaches for the stamp, before pausing and retreating.

"You hungry?" Widsun asks.

"I suppose so," Serge says.

On the way out, Widsun hands his secretary a sheet of paper and instructs her to CC it to three of his colleagues. While he slips on his jacket, Serge watches her line up three sheets of white paper with two black ones, alternating tones; the click and hammer of the keys against the five-deep stack starts up as they pass through the outer door and follows them along the corridor.

They lunch at the Criterion in Piccadilly. Widsun orders beef Chateaubriand for the two of them, and a bottle of Châteauneuf-du-Pape.

"Your health's fine now, I take it?" he enquires.

"Oh yes," answers Serge. "They tested us for everything at SOMA: measles, polio, consumption . . ."

"SOMA: so you'll be one of Boom Trenchard's bird-men. Have they filled your head with sky and wind, then?"

"Well, we haven't actually flown yet. It was mainly theory. We did mapwork, and learnt how to use compasses, correctors, stuff like that. And we learnt principles of gunnery: line, elevation, aiming points and mean points, all those things."

"*Ligne de foi*: that's all I remember. What you aim down, isn't it? 'Faith Line': has a nice ring to it."

"They didn't mention that," Serge tells him. "We were led more down the artillery side of things. They'd give us distances and ranges, and we'd have to calculate the angle of sight from the horizontal; then we'd have to set this off against the error of the day, and work out the trajectory and angle of descent and—"

"Error of the day?" asks Widsun.

"Oh, you know: atmospherics, wind speed . . ."

A pianist starts playing. The room is filling up. Waiters glide up and down the rows of tables as though slotted into grooves laid in the floor. Widsun holds Serge with his gaze and tells him, in a voice full of affection:

"I never had you down as a mathematician."

"Oh, I don't think of it as mathematics," Serge replies. "I just see space: surfaces and lines . . . and the odd blind spot . . ."

A waiter turns up with their wine. Widsun inspects the label and nods approval; the man sets about opening the bottle. Widsun turns to Serge again and asks:

"What about wireless? I was informed some time ago that you were quite the little radio bug . . ."

"I was," Serge smiles. "But at the school it was different. They'd put eight or ten Morse buzzers in a room, and you'd have to learn the tone of each, and transcribe from first one and then another. It's to train your ear. And we were told the principles of signalling from the air, like don't send on a turn, or right over the ground station; or not to make the dots too short or dashes too long; or how you don't need to send the number after the squadron letter—that kind of thing."

The cork's pop rises above the piano music and room's murmur. A mouthful of wine is poured into Widsun's glass. He holds it up towards the large, arched windows.

"How are your eyes?" he asks Serge while he's doing this. "Still sharp as ever?"

"Oh," says Serge, "they gave us wool balls full of different-coloured strands to pick out and unravel."

"How's your mother?" Widsun enquires, rolling the wine around the glass to check its legs.

"She's busy," Serge replies. "There's lots of demand for silk these days."

Widsun's swilling the liquid round his mouth now, looking intrigued. Eventually the look goes; he swallows and nods at the waiter, who pours two glasses out and glides away again.

"Lots of demand for silk," says Widsun. "Yes, indeed there is. Well, here's to the demand for silk, and your good health."

They clink glasses. Serge sits back again, but Widsun's upper body stays above the table, leaning forward; it makes it look as though the arches and gilded ceiling of the room were being held up by his shoulders. Cigarette smoke curls round these as he murmurs:

"Error of the day . . ."

ii

Serge is sent to Hythe. He's lodged with five other cadets in the dormitory of a requisitioned school. From Romney Marsh, where they do four-mile runs along the Royal Military Canal, the rumble of the guns in Ypres can be picked up. He thought it was distant thunder the first time he heard it, but the sky was blue and cloudless.

"Fifteen-inch howitzers, I'd say," their instructor smiles at them as they scour the heavens. "Carries nicely, dissent it? Now pick thet pace ap!"

The instructor's name's Lieutenant Langeveldt; he's from Port Elizabeth, South Africa. One of his eyes, the right one, points slightly to the side, as though trained down a line of sight that, although different to that of his vision's central axis, nonetheless complements it, like a corrector. On Serge's third day in the school he takes the cadets to the airfield and introduces them to the machines.

"A Maurice Farman Shorthorn," he announces as mechanics wheel out from a hangar a large boxed kite made from odds and ends of wood bound together by bailing wire. Its two wings are held up, one above the other, by a flimsy set of vertical struts; in the space between them, a rectangular box five or six feet long seems to float unsupported as it protrudes forwards from the frame. Two makeshift chairs are lodged within the box which, like the wings, has canvas patches sewn around it; the rest of the fuselage is naked.

"Also known as a Rumpitee," Lieutenant Langeveldt continues. "A monosoupape pusher, twin-seater. This part is the nacelle: that's where you sit. This part behind it is the engine, with propeller mounted on it; here's where the explosive mixture enters, through the skirt."

"Is this one finished?" Serge asks.

"Finished as it'll ever be, Carrefix. You can be first ap with me."

He's thrown a leather jacket, a soft helmet and some goggles. Tentatively, he grabs a vertical strut, climbs onto the lower wing and hoists himself up into the back seat.

"Not there," snaps Langeveldt. "Thet's my seat!"

"Why's it called a Rumpitee?" Serge asks as he clambers over to the front.

"You'll soon find out," says Langeveldt. "You others, stend beck."

The mechanic plants himself behind the nacelle and yanks at the propeller. Nothing happens. He pulls it down again, this time with both hands, and the engine catches. Black smoke fills the space between the wings. Serge coughs and turns to face the front. The engine noise increases, and the grass beneath the wheels starts rolling backwards as though a giant winch were pulling it away from under them. The faces of the other cadets are shaking—not just up and down with the bumping of the wheels over the grass's surface, but also with the faster and more regular vibration of the engine, which shouts from behind Serge, in a mechanical voice amplified by the plane's frame:

Rumpiteerumpiteerumpiteerumpiteerumpitee . . .

The shaking faces swing away, as do the hangars and the woods behind them, the whole disc of ground revolving till the field's main expanse lies in front of him. The *rumpitee*s heighten their speed and tone, growing hysterical; the grass races away beneath him, so fast that its bumps disappear. The *rumpitee*s smooth out too, merging together in a constant high-pitched whine—and then he's up, his face slicing the air in two, a slit right down the middle of its fabric as it rushes past him. He looks down: as the landscape falls away, it flattens, voids itself of depth. Hills lose their height; roads lose their camber, bounce, the texture of their paving, and turn into marks across a map. The greens and browns of field and wood seem artificial and provisional, as though they'd just now fallen from the sky. Now the land's surface starts to tip, its horizontal line rotating round the Farman's nose as though the vegetation, soil and brick that formed it were all one big front propeller. Buildings, ditches, hedgerows turn and re-align themselves like parts of a machine, then shift and re-align themselves again as the line rotates back the other way, cogs and arms swivelling around an axis at whose centre Serge's own head sits. He feels a tapping on his back, and turns round: Langeveldt, strangely outlandish now that his offset eyes have disappeared beneath goggles, is pointing to the right. Serge looks that way, and sees the town: the parallel rows of its terraces, the plan view of a St. Leonard robbed of elevation, steeple pushed down and compacted like a collapsed telescope. Beyond the town, the canal forms a dark line across the marsh; beyond that, the rim of shore is marked in white by waves that have become entirely static, as though no independent movement were permitted of the landscape anymore: all displacement and acceleration, all shifts and realignments *must* proceed from the machine . . .

The coast peels away now and the land tilts towards him, swinging from a hinge running perpendicular to him and his box, along the same line as the Farman's wheel axle. It lifts up to meet him: a flat earth-plane rising to join a wooden rectangle held in a wiry frame set in a huge white-and-blue circle of sky. As it does, depth starts returning. Detail too: he can pick out the airfield, the hangars, the cluster of cadets. Then these things are right on him as they land with a bump and *rumpitee* across the grass back to the group, who wave and cheer.

"Your face is black!" they shout at him as he steps out of the nacelle and slides down off the lower wing.

"Tar in the explosive mixture," Langeveldt says as he peels his helmet off. "How did you like it?"

"I liked it a lot," Serge replies. "It was just right."

"Just right?"

"Yes, sir: just how things should be."

They fly on most days for the next month. Only when the clouds are too low or the air is plagued by thunderstorms do they stay earthbound. They're shown how to ascend in gyres, stall, dive, pull out of spins, stand the machine on its tail and hang on the propeller, perform sideslips and Immelmann turns. The fallen landscape prints itself on Serge's mind by dint of his repeated passage over it: its flattened progression of greens, browns and yellows, patches of light and shade; the layout of the town and of the marsh beyond it; the ribbon of the Hythe-to-Folkestone road; the thread of the Light Railway joining Dymchurch and St. Mary's Bay, then running on across the Romney sands; the dots of the Gypsy encampment outside Dungeness. He likes to move these things around from his nacelle, take them apart and reassemble them like pieces of a jigsaw. When he loops, they disappear completely, the whole horizon sinking from the bottom of his gaze and everything becoming sky, then, after a pause in which time itself seems to be held in abeyance, the rim reappearing at his vision's upper edge and sliding down his eyes like a decorated screen being lowered just in front of them . . .

For the first two weeks they fly with dual controls. Langeveldt and his assistants will guide the Farmans up, then, at a moment chosen at their whimsy, tap the cadets on the back and hold their hands up in the air— their passenger's cue to unclip the paddles by his seat and ply the side-wires till the rudder starts responding. Sometimes the instructor stalls or goes into a spin just prior to handing over, leaving the cadet to coax the chaotic world back into shape. By the end of April they're going up unsupervised, in pairs. In early May Langeveldt starts poking holes in the machines' canvas hides and knocking the odd strut out with a mallet before sending them up.

"Brought a machine down safely with the whole tail shot off once myself!" he tells them. "If you can't do without a strut or two then you're not made for the high life."

Serge has been paired off with a Londoner named Stedman. Stedman does most of the flying: Serge himself, it's been decided at some juncture higher up—a meeting in a room thick with cigar smoke, or an encrypted communication sent down wires from Oxford via London via who-knows-where—has all the makings of a good observer. He's given extra lessons in cartography, and taught Zone Call and Clock Code systems. When he and Stedman go up in the air they're given a list of spots to drop flares on, or photograph, or, if the spot's a military barracks, land at and persuade the CO to sign their logbook. After a few days of this, a camera-gun is mounted on the nose of his nacelle, and he and Stedman have to careen around the Kent coast photo-strafing castles, churches, train stations and gasworks. The results are developed as soon as they land, and posted in the School of Aerial Gunnery's briefing room for Langeveldt to grade in front of them.

"Pepperdine, three hits. Biswick, two. Spurrier, three. Carrefix, five—on top of which you've taken out the Dover pier, which wasn't on the list. What did you do thet for?"

"It looked nice," Serge replies. "I wanted to photograph it."

"It looked nice?"

"Yes, sir. I liked its shape."

By mid-May they're firing live rounds out of Lewis guns. The guns have Aldis sights, harmonised for deflection. Serge likes the way the reticules grid space up when he looks through them, but finds he can perform their main task on his own. The trick's to point the gun not where the target is right now, but to discern its line of movement as it travels through your vision and to run that on into the space in front of it, shooting there instead. Serge develops a knack of splitting his gaze in two, locking the line with one eye while the other slides ahead, setting up camp in the spot at which a successful hit "happens" and thus bringing this event to pass. He experiences a strange sense of intermission each time he does this, as though he'd somehow inflated or hollowed out a stretch of time, found room to move around inside it. It occurs to him that perhaps doing this is what made Langeveldt's eyes go off-kilter, and wonders if his own eyes look like the lieutenant's when he shoots . . .

They do most of their target practice over water, peppering rafts moored just off the shoreline. Serge gets into the habit of firing in certain rhythms, ones that carry with them first words, then whole phrases, spoken in the boom and sent up his arm into his body by the recoil. His favourite consists of a first, short burst of six shots followed by a longer one of eight; each time he fires it out he hears a line that's stuck in his head from the Versoie Pageant, from the year when Widsun visited:

> of purpose that your thought
> Might also to the seas be known . . .

The words fly from his gun into the sea, hammering and splintering its surface, etching themselves out across the rafts' wood: *of-PUR, pose-*

THAT, your-THOUGHT . . . Later, they fire over land, swooping low to take out rabbits, foxes, badgers, hares and hedgehogs, then touching down to bag their sometimes still-quivering score. They gun down the odd farm animal as well, although it's against regulations and draws complaints from irate farmers.

"Another accidental lamb-strike?" Langeveldt tuts as Serge and Stedman unload their bloodied tribute at his feet. "Thet's the third this week. Take it over to the kitchen."

The guns jam all the time. On days when there's no flying to be had they're made to take them apart and assemble them again—six, seven, eight times, all day long. The other cadets try to force the trigger sears and firing pins together, swearing when they won't fit, but not Serge: he finds the process pleasing, an extension of the logic he's developed from the Farman's front seat. In the click and swivel of machinery being slotted together, moved around and realigned, its clockwork choreography, he relives, in miniature, the mechanical command of landscape and its boundaries that flight affords him, the mastery of hedgerows, fields and lanes, their shapes and volumes . . .

Sometimes, when he's out free-flying, and especially when Stedman loops the loop, Serge experiences an exhilarating loosening of his stomach. As they level out one afternoon above some little village, he turns round and points down towards the ground.

"You want to land?" shouts Stedman. "What's here?"

"I've got to shit," Serge shouts back.

They bounce across the village cricket pitch. Serge slides down off the wing, lowers his trousers and relieves himself above the wicket, just short of a length on middle and off.

"What village is this anyway?" he asks as he strolls back towards Stedman, who's stretching his legs beside the machine as he consults a map.

"Tenterden, I think," Stedman answers. "Population six hundred and twenty-nine."

"Six hundred and thirty now," Serge tells him. "Let's go."

The next day they spot what looks like a small battle taking place on a square field below them, and descend to take a closer look. The combatants turn out to be girls playing lacrosse. The game stops as they pass above it, pink and white faces staring up at them through netted sticks. Stedman climbs two thousand feet and pulls the Farman up into a loop that levels out low, just above the playing field, sending sticks and faces scattering. He turns the plane around and lands more or less exactly on the centre circle.

"You could have killed one of my girls!" the whistle-necklaced mistress shouts at them as they pull off their helmets and goggles.

"Terribly sorry, madam," Stedman smiles back. "Thing is, a part seems to have come loose and fallen off the engine just as we passed by."

"Will you be able to fix it?" she asks him, softening.

"Depends. Some of these things just won't fly without the requisite bits and bobs."

"I think I saw it fall behind those bushes," Serge says, shuffling off towards them.

When he strolls back a few minutes later, the girls are gathered round the machine, being treated to a lecture on aerodynamics.

"What does he do?" the tallest one asks Stedman as Serge sidles up to him.

"I observe," says Serge, "and navigate. I make everything fit together."

"No luck finding the whatsit?" Stedman asks.

Serge sadly shakes his head.

"I've worked out what it is," Stedman announces. "A bolt's come out in the skirt. It's simple to fix, but will take a while. Be dark before we're finished: we won't be able to take off again until tomorrow. Perhaps we could use your phone to contact our headquarters, tell them not to worry . . ."

"But of course," the mistress tells him, all smiles now. "We'll put you up for the night."

"Where will they sleep, miss?" a round-faced girl asks, fingering her net.

"They can sleep in the Bursar's lodging; he's away."

"Oh, we couldn't leave our machine unattended," Stedman tells her in a solemn voice. "We'll sleep right out here with it. It's not cold . . ."

"Well, at least let us bring you sandwiches and a flask."

"Too kind, madam," Stedman answers. "I'll come in and fetch them myself."

It's the tall one and the round-faced one who sneak out to see them after dark: two distinctive silhouettes making their way across the field. Stedman and the round-faced one do it on the grass beneath the lower wing; Serge helps the tall one into the nacelle, where, wrapping her arms around the Lewis gun (whose safety catch, fortunately, is on), she bends forward and lets him wriggle off her pants from behind. They leave at dawn. Over the following two weeks, three more planes lose parts above the same spot.

In all his time at Hythe, Serge sees two accidents. The first one happens right in front of him: he and Stedman are waiting to take off when Quinnell and Kirk, who've gone up just ahead of them, stall, go into a spin and hurtle back down to the airfield, landing in the right place but the wrong direction, nose-first. Kirk is killed; Quinnell's spine is broken and he's carted off to hospital in Dover. Their machine stays in the field for several days; the cadets gather round it every morning after breakfast to stare in contemplation at the strange and useless geometry of its upended beams, the decorative wind vanes of its rudders.

"It looks like the Eiffel Tower," says Serge. "The Eiffel Tower if one of its legs snapped off and it started tilting."

"Or an oil well," Payton counters; "a slant one: those bits that they build above the ground to mount the pumps in."

The other accident he doesn't see take place—only its aftermath. Beswick forgets to strap himself into his seat and falls out when his pilot loops the loop. He plunges three thousand feet and lands in a nearby field. A Beswick-shaped mark stays in the grass for weeks: head, torso, legs and outstretched arms.

"The acid from his body," Stedman says as he and Serge stand above the patch one afternoon. "Stops new grass growing."

"It's a good likeness," Serge says.

"All his memories, and everything he ever thought about or did, reduced to battery chemicals."

"Why not?" asks Serge. "It's what we are."

iii

He's passed out in June, and assigned to the 104th Squadron as an observer. He leaves from just down the road, in Folkestone, travelling on a hospital ship alongside several thousand troops, all armed.

"Isn't that cheating?" Serge asks the loading sergeant when he sees the green strip and red cross painted on the hull.

"It's what's available," the sergeant replies. "Came here for disinfection, needs to go to France. If you'd prefer to swim . . ."

They all embark, then for some reason disembark again, spend the night in a dirty hotel, then re-embark and set sail the next day. Serge wonders what disease the ship had on it before it was disinfected; he pictures it floating above the decks, licking its way around the stays and pulleys of the lifeboats' gantries in a yellow cloud, like cholera. Arriving in Boulogne, he finds the whole dock area turned into one giant hospital ward, with sick men lying in rows on stretchers, waiting for evacuation. The landscape around the town looks sick too: trees droop languidly; fields that should be full of wheat at this time of year stand bare. Following the instructions he was handed before leaving Hythe, he joins a transport barge at a small inland jetty, and is carried slowly to Saint-Omer along melancholic waterways, past tin-roofed sheds on edges of ramshackle villages. Rusty cans and floating refuse strew the boat's route like sarcastic flowers. Further down, the river opens out more, splitting into channels in which water-weeds stream indolently in long swathes below the surface. Sedge and bulrushes blur its edges; from within their dense thatch Serge can hear the calls of wild ducks, coots and herons sounding and responding cryptically across the water, as though issuing and forwarding their own sets of instructions. Over this noise, like a low mist, hangs the sound of guns, more substantial than it was in Hythe: the front may still be distant, but the rumble's *here* now, graticuled, almost tangible . . .

The same melancholic lethargy prevails in Saint-Omer. All around town, men are sleeping: on benches and grass verges, outside cafés, on the requisitioned Pétanque court. Serge can't tell if the omnipresent rumbling here is guns or snoring. He picks his way past eighteen or twenty legs sprawled out across the steps of the building he's been ordered to report to, and finds a bored NCO sitting behind a table smoking cigarettes, one straight after the other.

"One hundred and fourth?" the NCO says when he reads the piece of paper Serge hands him. "They're fully manned at the moment. You'll have to wait."

"What for?" Serge asks.

"Someone to die." The NCO stubs out his cigarette and lights another before adding: "It shouldn't take long."

"What do I do while I wait?" Serge asks him.

"Sleep, have an omelette in the bistro, pick your nose—what do I care?"

Serge has an omelette in the bistro. He gets talking to some other RFC men awaiting deployment. They laugh when he tells them that he trained on Shorthorns.

"That's like learning to drive horse-carts before being sent out in a motor-car race!"

"What did you learn in?" Serge asks.

"Well, we started out on *Long*horns, then moved on to Avros."

"An Avro is a pile of shit," another man says. "Its ailerons are useless, it stalls on right turns and it's got no elevator. Three of the cadets I trained with died on them while I was there."

"We lost three too," Serge says. "Only one was just crippled."

"We lost five!" the first man asserts triumphantly, thrusting his spread fingers out across the table top. "And two more have died just in the time that I've been here."

"How?" Serge asks.

"This flight sergeant went out swimming and drowned in a deep pool. And then another man got crushed unloading coal."

"There was another one too," a third man chips in. "Got shot through the heart when someone else's gun went off."

"That was his own gun," a fourth man says.

"No, that was another man who died the week before," the third man corrects him.

Serge, chewing on his omelette, wonders if it's really necessary to fight the Germans after all: they could all just lounge around, each on their own side, dying in random accidents until nobody's left and the war's over by default . . . He does a brief tour of the town after his meal, then settles down beside a pond in the main square and, gazing at a lotus flower lying on its surface, drifts off like everybody else.

He spends the next few days like this: reporting to the smoking NCO each morning, eating in the bistro, wandering, dozing. Eventually, on the fourth or fifth day, the NCO informs him that a squadron slot's become available for him. He's taken in a Crossley lorry alongside ten others. They sit in the back, on cushions that do little to absorb the shock and rattle of steel-studded tires on cobbled roads. The air smells of castor oil; Serge can't tell if it's the lorry or the landscape. The landscape is vast and empty; skylarks cut across it, making for no spot or destination that he can discern. At one point they pass a group of Hindu soldiers bathing in a stream. Three of them are splashing around, calling to each other in their language; two more stand facing outwards, backs to the road, their lower halves submerged while their cupped hands scoop water up and hold it aloft in a kind of votive gesture before pouring it across their foreheads. Every so often the lorry stops, the driver calls a name out and a man slips off to become swallowed by the terrain as the Crossley trundles on. Serge finds himself among the last three left in the back; then the last two; then the last one. The driver cuts the ignition and steps down to the ground to take a leak. With the engine's noise gone, Serge can hear the front's rumble loud and clear; it makes the truck's metal bars vibrate against the wood. The driver, as he heads back to his cabin, turns to him and says:

"May as well join me up front."

The road ahead is split. As Serge climbs inside, the driver's looking down first one fork, then another. He has a map in front of him, but he's not consulting it: instead, he's sitting still and listening, ears perked, as though homing in on some signal lodged in the guns' static. He seems to find what he was listening out for, sparks the ignition up again, heads down the left fork and trundles on.

Eventually they turn off at a farm and bump along the ruts of a small, winding track. The track leads between two colonnades of poplars, passes a potato field, then runs down to an L-shaped airfield flanked by woods.

"The runway's got cows grazing on it!" Serge says.

"You want it to look like an aerodrome?" the driver asks. "Besides, they keep the grass down."

At the woods' edge, Serge can see a large Bessoneau hangar with about ten machines drawn up inside it. They look much solider than Shorthorns; their fuselage is brown and has concentric circles painted on the side. From this angle, it looks as though their propellers have been placed at the wrong end. Some eighty yards away, beside a small copse, more planes are parked inside a makeshift hangar topped with canvas. Nissen huts are planted thirty feet from this, near a farmhouse with red gables. The driver draws up by the farmhouse's front porch and lets Serge out.

The 104th Squadron's commander's name is Walpond-Skinner. He must be in his mid-forties. He seems pressured, and avoids eye contact.

"How many flying hours have you got?" is his first question when Serge steps into his office.

"I'm not sure, sir. Maybe twenty."

"Jesus Christ! Like feeding children up to Baal. I see they're still only giving you half-wings."

Serge runs his fingers over the badge on his lapel: a single wing with a round O beside it.

"That'll change soon," Walpond-Skinner says, his gaze travelling on past Serge to flit across the wall and doorway. "You people are just as important. In the early days it was the observer who was in command of the machine; pilot was just a chauffeur."

"Early days?" Serge asks.

Commander Walpond-Skinner's eyes alight on Serge's for the first time as he answers, with a bemused look:

"Of the war. At least now they're giving you full officer status. As they should. I see you boys as grand interpreters. High priests." He leafs through a dossier, then says: "From Lydium, Masedown."

"Near there, sir," Serge answers.

"Train on Salisbury Plain?"

"No: Hythe."

"That's strange. Says here you have a good eye. And a protector among the Whitehall gods. Let's hope you haven't skimped on hecatombs of late."

Serge doesn't answer. Walpond-Skinner taps a bell lying on his desktop. He flips open a black ledger, takes a rubber and erases something from it, then continues:

"We have three flights here; six machines in each. You'll be in C-Flight. Any questions?"

"I don't think so," Serge says.

A batman arrives and is instructed to escort Serge to "the Floaters." As he leaves, Walpond-Skinner wipes the rubber residue from the ledger's page, picks up a pen lying beside it, then, realising his mistake, sets it down again in favour of a pencil, with which he writes on the spot he's just cleared, murmuring:

"Carrefax, C-eee."

The batman leads Serge across the field. Outside the Nissen huts he sees a group of men in pilots' jackets standing as though on parade—although they're scruffily dressed and their formation isn't one he's ever learnt: it seems to consist of four men planting themselves in a kind of square, all facing inwards, then each rotating forty-five degrees (two in a clockwise direction, two anti-) to face down the square's side, towards the man positioned at an adjacent corner, whereupon the two sets of two men start to circle one another in slow *pasodobles,* before looping round and rejoining the square with each man at a different corner so that, while the positions shift, the overall formation stays the same.

"If he turns left," one of the men is saying, "you turn right. If he turns right, you turn left. If he then turns left after that, you turn left too; and if he turns right, you turn left as well."

The men act these moves out, pacing and turning, as he speaks.

"You mean right," another of them says, halting in his tracks. The whole formation grinds to a halt too. The first man continues:

"No, I mean left. Then you come back at him from below the tail."

The belt of internal movement shuffles into action once again. Serge follows the batman on towards the woods at the field's edge. Taking a little path through these, they come to a row of houseboats moored on a canalised section of river.

"This is your one, sir," the batman tells him as he ducks through a low doorframe. Inside, there's a small stove, a bookshelf and four beds. Three of the beds are in a state of disarray, with sheets pulled back and clothes flung across them; the fourth is neatly made, and has a package bound with string lying on its surface.

". . . should have been sent to his family already," the batman mutters. "I'll take it. Why don't you settle in, then I can show you round the airfield."

Serge unpacks, then steps onto the deck. On the canal's far side another row of slender poplars sways lightly above reeds that bend over the water. The poplars' leaves are dancing, but Serge can't hear the rustle: the guns' noise is loud here—loud and precise, its tangled thunder now unravelled into distinct volleys and retorts. A scow passes by, carrying scrap or machine parts covered by tarpaulin. Its captain looks at Serge, then at his load, then dead in front.

He's taken to the Bessoneau hangar first. Machine parts lie around this too: propellers, wheels and engine cylinders, sorted into groups or mounted on laths and workbenches over which mechanics bend and solder as though studying and dissecting specimens. Towering above these are the aeroplanes he saw from the lorry: large, brown solid things with no nacelle, just a scooped-out hollow in the fuselage between the wings with two seats in it.

"RE8s," the mechanic informs him, tapping an exhaust pipe running above a set of gill-like silver slits. "Hispano-Suiza engine, air-cooled."

"Why's the engine at the front?" Serge asks.

"The RE8's a tractor, not a pusher."

"Doesn't the propeller block the observer's view?"

"Observer sits in the back, facing backwards."

"*Back*wards?" Serge asks. "How can I see where we're going?"

"You can see where you've come from," the mechanic smiles back. "Don't worry: you'll come to like it. It's a great, sturdy machine. Both the pilot and the observer can get killed and it'll fly on for a hundred miles and land itself quite safely back on our side of the lines—if it's facing that way, of course; bit of a disaster if it's not . . ."

They stroll on to the Nissen huts, and Serge is introduced to the other pilots and observers.

"This is Gibbs, then Watson, Dickinson, Baldwick, Clegg . . ."

The men are dressed in non-uniform shirts unbuttoned halfway down the front. Their hair is grown out in long locks. They greet him casually.

"Which flight you in, then?" Clegg asks.

"C-Flight."

"Aha: you're hosting us tonight. Better break out the good stuff."

The good stuff turns out to be local dessert wine with a glowing yellow hue and bittersweet taste. As they hold their glasses up, the men sing:

We meet neath the sounding rafters;
    The walls all around us are bare (are bare);
They echo the peals of laughter;
    It seems that the dead are there (dead are there).

Serge doesn't know the words, but kind of murmurs as he half-mouths to them, rising with the others for the second verse:

So stand by your glasses steady,
    The world is a web of lies (of lies).
Then here's to the dead already,
    And hurrah for the next man who dies (man who dies)!

After the meal, they crank up a gramophone and play music-hall songs. Serge slips out and makes his way in the dark through long grass, then across the shorter grass beside the woods, back to his houseboat. He sits on its deck and watches another barge slide through the oily water, laden once more with objects whose shapes beneath the covering suggest broken and twisted metal, or perhaps animals, the bumps and folds of their limbs and torsos. In the waves left by its passage when it's gone, Serge sees a water rat swimming towards the far bank. The black surface of the water around the rat's head is laced with garish streaks of colour: orange-yellow, greenish white, reflections of the gunfire flickering across the sky. The sound of each volley arrives late, often after its own flash has faded from both sky and river; new waves of flashes catch up with the residual noise, overtake and lap it.

"Intermission," Serge says, to no one, or perhaps the rat.

For a moment, the flickering stops and the whole countryside falls silent. A calcium flare descends noiselessly not far away, silhouetting the poplars and rimming their leaves with frozen light, as though with hoarfrost. Behind it other, smaller lights glow on and off, like fireflies. Then their pops arrive, then louder stutters, then high, booming eruptions: sounds and lights meshing together as the air comes back to life, like a magnificent engine warming up.

8

i

Zero hour today is 7 a.m. Serge is up two hours before it, woken by the plash of a tug's wake against his houseboat's hull. He performs his ablutions, makes his way over to the mess and eats two slices of dry toast washed down with gunfire tea. Fifteen or so other pilots and observers shuffle into seats around him, bleary-eyed, coughing and farting themselves towards full consciousness. Cigarettes are smoked throughout the meal, stabbed into mouths still full with food, balanced on the sides of plates, stubbed out in hollow eggshells. Walpond-Skinner marches in at six to hand out copy orders.

"Five machines on Art Obs today; three SE5s escorting them. Four batteries to each machine: two to be ranged in the first hour, two in the second, all four kept on target during the third. Individual calls on all your sheets."

Serge glances down at his. His batteries are E through H, his own call 3. The print on his paper is mauve and imprecise: third in a CC'd triplicate, the furthest from the ribbon and keys' touch. Beneath the copy order sheet, on whiter and less grainy paper that's been folded and compressed, is a large map. Serge opens it across the table top and sees, among grid squares bent out of line by cup and toast-rack, his objectives marked with arrows, their coordinates written beside them in red ink: two hostile batteries, an ammunition dump, a crossroads. The dump and crossroads are new for him; the batteries he's been targeting for over a week now, on and off.

"Memo from Central Wireless Station: ground operators still reporting too much jambing," Walpond-Skinner reads. "Keep to the wavelengths and notes that you've been allotted. And make sure you're always half a mile—at *minimum*—from the next machine. Any questions?"

His eyes skirt the floor; the men's eyes do the same.

"Then up, Bellerophons, and at 'em!" Walpond-Skinner snaps.

Chairs slide back, cups are swilled from and abandoned, burps sounded like last calls above remains of plates; then the men trudge outside. The sun's not up yet; dew still hangs about the long grass; the odd strand of spider-web filament floats just above this: it's not cold. The mildness of the summer morning makes the behaviour of the men as they slip into thick leather jackets, gloves and fur-lined boots seem quite incongruous. The pilots and observers of the SE5s are pulling muskrat gauntlets over the silk inners on their hands and feet and rubbing whale oil on their cheeks and foreheads: they'll be flying much higher. In the field beside them, mechanics pace round the machines, patting their tails and engines as though leading greyhounds or racehorses to their starting boxes. Serge's RE8 is near the pack's rear; Gibbs is already inside it. Serge climbs into its back seat, wedges the biscuit-box and brandy-flask that he's been carrying under his right arm in between the spark set and its six-volt battery, gives the Lewis gun a swivel, then eases himself into a dew-damped seat as the mechanics throw propellers into motion all around the field, cutting arrowhead-shaped streaks into the grass where it's blown down in diagonal lines behind the wings.

They take off to the west, then turn across the wood, skimming the treetops. The poplars opposite the houseboats bend as they pass over them. Gibbs puts one wing down; for a while the machine seems to drag, as though still connected psychologically if not physically to the ground. Serge feels gravity tautening around him, like elastic. Then the wing rises, the elastic snaps and he's flung, back first, into the sky. It feels like falling, not ascending—but falling upwards, as if sucked towards some vortex so high that it's above height itself. The land accelerates away, its surface area expanding even as it shrinks. Gibbs levels the plane; the countryside slants till it's horizontal and starts running from beneath the fuselage like a ticker-tape strip issuing from a telegraph machine, the flickering band of the Lys racing away beside a thicker belt of forest, villages and hamlets popping up to punctuate the strip like news reports or stock-price fluctuations before Nieppe's large brown stain pushes these out to the margins. A heat bump throws them as Gibbs angles up again; the landscape shakes beneath them and becomes illegible, just for a moment, before settling back into its horizontal run, its centre perfectly aligned with the plane's tail. The bumps continue till they clear a haze that's been invisible up to now: it always is when they're inside it. As it sinks from him like a pneumatic platform being lowered, Serge can make its upper surface out, clear-cut and definite, a second horizon hovering like a muslin cover just above the first . . .

They pass a kite balloon. It, too, seems to strain upwards, pulling at the winch-line tethering it to its truck. Serge waves to the man in its basket; one of the man's hands flies up in response; the other clasps the basket's rail, as though to hold him back. The front can't be far now. Gibbs turns the machine round and Serge, now facing east, looks down onto a vapour blanket that's darker and more murky. Through it, further off, he can see gun flashes twinkling all around the countryside in little points of blue flame. Flares glow down in the trenches. A mile or two behind the German ones, the white plume of a train forms a clear, silky thread. He runs his eye along its tracks, the telephone lines beside these, the cables of a bridge, a pipeline leading from this across open ground before it burrows down to carry out of sight the metal and electric musculature of the land. A new flash appears on the horizon and grows brighter, dazzling him and warming his face: sunrise. Serge takes his watch out: twenty-two minutes to seven, time to test the sigs . . .

Reaching down between his legs, he turns the aerial crank. He pauses after a few revolutions, looks over the side and sees the copper aerial trailing in the slipstream like a fishing reel, a lead weight at its end. He takes his spark set out and starts transmitting B signals to Battery E. They pass the kite balloon again, heading the other way, then fly over a pockmarked village, a road down which a transport column's moving, then some woods until they find, nestled among these, the battery. The Popham strip's already laid out for him on the ground: three white cloth lines, one upright like a backbone, the other two angled into this like a lesser-than sign to form a K. Serge turns round, taps Gibbs on the shoulder and gives him the thumbs-up; they turn and fly out east again.

The sun, although at Serge's back now, bounces off the top wing's underside to light up his little cabin. Once more the kite balloon, its occupant now busy talking on his phone line; then a mandala of small roads and pathways, at least half of them unusable, criss-crossing and looping over open ground; then rows of empty trenches—last month's, or last year's, the year before's; more open ground; more tracks. It's only when the tracers start to rise towards him that Serge realises he's passed onto the German side. It's always like that: on his first few outings he'd anticipate the moment when he'd move across the deadly threshold, bracing himself for it, as though there were a real line strung across the air like a finishing ribbon for the machine to thrust its chest against and breach. But that moment never came—or rather, turned out always to have come already, the threshold to have lain unmarked, been glided over quite unnoticed. Even looking down, it's hard to see which are the front positions: trench after trench slides into view, parallel lines conjoined in places by small runnels as communication trenches link up with evacuation trenches, third-line and supply trenches . . . At times the network opens into a wide mesh; at others it closes up, compact. The tracers rising from it lend structure to the air, mesh it as well. Puff balls of smoke appear as if by magic all round the machine.

"Archie pretty light today," Gibbs leans back and shouts into his ear, quite nonchalantly.

A German kite balloon emerges from beneath their tail. Serge thinks about strafing it, but sees that it's being hurriedly winched down out of his range. It rises again as he draws away from it—strangely elongated, like a floating intestine. He unfolds his map and, holding it across his knees, runs his finger to the square in which the first hostile battery position's marked out: should be about here . . . He taps Gibbs's shoulder again and signals for him to fly in a square holding pattern. As Gibbs turns, then turns again, patrolling their small area's boundaries, Serge can see the machines to his left and right describing the same patterns half a mile away. He looks down and, moving his eyes first in diagonals from corner to corner of his quadrant, then in smaller, darting cat's cradles between landmarks, picks up the battery, secreted within a copse but nonetheless betrayed by the anachronistically autumnal patch of scorched and thinned-out leaves made by its discharges. He picks his spark set up again and taps in *C3E*, then *A*, then *MX12*, the target's map coordinates. Then he signals to Gibbs to fly back to their side.

Travelling in this direction, the tracer fire appears only after it's already passed the plane, cutting long, slanted corridors into the air above him. It tilts up vertical, then starts angling forward, managing, through some optical and geometric sleight of hand, to reverse its direction without altering its flow until it's rising at him from the ground. The intestinal kite balloon's down again, then up; the magic puffs materialise beside them; the front line slides by unperceived once more, revealing in its wake a mesh of interlocking trenches which the same old English kite balloon announces as their own. The pockmarked village, road and woods run past below them one more time, then they're back above Battery E. One of the Popham strip's white lesser-than lines has been removed, the other straightened and lowered to the backbone cloth's base, joining it at a right angle to form an *L*. Serge points Gibbs back towards the lines again, sending down A signals from his spark set as they go.

They're back above their target with three minutes to spare. The other machines are in position too: two to the north of him, one to the south, each marking out its assigned grid square, while a fifth machine moves up and down in long, straight lines behind them. It reminds Serge of a ritual he once saw illustrated in *Boy's Comic Journal:* a ceremonial Red Indian dance to call down rain. The men in feathers marked their patterns out across the ground and the gods, summoned into action by these, sent down water. As the second-hand needle moves across the final quarter-segment of his watch's face, Serge feels an almost sacred tingling, as though he himself had become godlike, elevated by machinery and signal code to a higher post within the overall structure of things, a vantage point from which the vectors and control lines linking earth and heaven, the hermetic language of the invocations, its very lettering and script, have become visible, tangible even, all concentrated at a spot just underneath the index finger of his right hand which is tapping out, right now, the sequence *C3E MX12 G . . .*

Almost immediately, a white rip appears amidst the wood's green cover on the English side. A small jet of smoke spills up into the air from this like cushion stuffing; out of it, a shell rises. It arcs above the trench-meshes and track-marked open ground, then dips and falls into the copse beneath Serge, blossoming there in vibrant red and yellow flame. A second follows it, then a third. The same is happening in the two-mile strip between Battery I and its target, and Battery M and its one, right on down the line: whole swathes of space becoming animated by the plumed trajectories of plans and orders metamorphosed into steel and cordite, speed and noise. Everything seems connected: disparate locations twitch and burst into activity like limbs reacting to impulses sent from elsewhere in the body, booms and jibs obeying levers at the far end of a complex set of ropes and cogs and relays. The salvos pause; Serge plots the points of impact on his clock-code chart, then sends adjustments back to Battery E, which fires new salvos that land slightly to the north of the first ones. Each one's fall draws from the wood a new yellow-and-red flame-flower, with an outer white smoke-leaf that lingers after the bloom has faded. Serge sends one more correction; the shells shift fifteen or so yards to the east, and start arriving in regular fifteen-second bursts, their percussions overlapping with those falling in the neighbouring zones in sequences that speed up and slow down, like church bells' chimes. A larger, darker bloom erupts from the copse beneath him: it seems to have more volume to it, more mass, billowing out and upwards like a dense, black chrysanthemum . . .

"I think we got it," Serge turns round and shouts to Gibbs.

Gibbs points to his ear and shakes his head. Easier to communicate with the ground than with the man in the machine beside you. Serge sends an *OK* down to Battery E, then signals to Gibbs to move on to Battery F. They fly back across the lines and find this in the ruins of a village, Popham strips K'd up in response to their B sigs. They fly back again; Serge ranges the guns, plots the shells' points of impact on his clock-code chart; then they move on to Battery G and do the same. Each time they shuttle to and fro, they pass through residues of tracer, Archie smoke and their own exhaust fumes hanging in the air. The shapes made when trails intersect, lines cutting across other lines at odd angles or bisecting puff-balls' circles to form strange figures, remind Serge of the phonetic characters his father would draw across the schoolroom's whiteboard, the way the sequences would run and overlap. The lower section of this board's become so crowded that it's half-occluded: the morning's light vapour blanket's thickened to an opaque shawl. They have to fly lower to see where shells are landing, or even to get their own bearings. At one point a howitzer shell appears right beside them, travelling in the same direction—one of their own, surfacing above the smoke-bank like a porpoise swimming alongside a ship, slowly rotating in the air to show its underbelly as it hovers at its peak before beginning its descent. It's so close that its wind-stream gently lifts and lowers the machine, making it bob. Serge knows that planes get hit by their own shells, but this one seems so placid, so companionable—and besides, if they're travelling at the same speed then both it and they are just still bodies in space, harmless blocks of matter. In the instant before their paths diverge, it seems to Serge that the shell and the plane are interchangeable—and that the shell and *he* are interchangeable, just like the radians and secants on his clock-code chart, the smoke-and-vapour-marked points and trajectories around him, the angles of his holding pattern's quadrant and the Popham strips' abrupt cloth lines. Within the reaches of this space become pure geometry, the shell's a pencil drawing a perfect arc across a sheet of graph paper; he's the clamp that holds the pencil to the compass, moving as one with the lead; he *is* the lead, smearing across the paper's surface to become geometry himself . . .

On their way back to base, they strafe the German trenches. While Gibbs holds his line above them, Serge points his Lewis gun down and nudges it from side to side until its point seems to slot into their groove. A sixth sense tells him when he's found it: he just *feels* it go in, somehow; when it does, it starts to play, the same track every time: *of-PUR, pose-THAT, your-THOUGHT* . . . Enemy gunfire crackles back at them like angry static. They reach the limit of their area, pull out and turn towards their own lines. The air over no-man's-land is thick with cordite smoke: it has the rich, livery smell of homecoming. The kite balloon's on the ground being deflated, the Popham strips rolled back up. The woods beside the airfield rustle as they skim them; the row of poplars bends the other way. Gibbs puts the wing down; the ground locks them in its drag; and then they're taxiing across the field towards the Bessoneaus. Serge jumps out before the machine's come to a complete standstill, while mechanics are still harnessing it with chocks and halters. With his brandy-flask and biscuit-box beneath his arm, he strolls towards the Nissen huts.

"Narrative, Carrefax." The recording officer, seated behind a table with a stack of papers at the hangar's exit, stops him.

"What?" asks Serge, taking his glove off and wiping his hand across his face.

"Flight narrative for Corps HQ. I have to remind you every time."

"Oh," says Serge. "Well . . ." His hand has gathered a thick wedge of tar. He looks at it, then up at the recording officer. "We went up; we saw stuff; it was good."

ii

Once, returning from the lines in fading light, zigzagging to dodge blue-black storm clouds, Serge and Gibbs find themselves landing on an aerodrome that's not their own. They're pretty sure it's not a German one:

the way the rain-curtains that sweep the ground are lit up, gold and precise with miniature rainbows in them, lets them know they've being flying west—but you can never be sure. The machines lying across the field are neither RE8s nor SE5s, and have storks painted on their fuselage. When Serge and Gibbs descend from theirs, mechanics greet them in a foreign language.

"Perdu la route . . ." one of them shouts.

"Oh, fuck!" snarls Gibbs. "Distract them while I climb back in and get my pistol. We can take off again before those others by the huts get over here."

"They're French," Serge tells him.

"Français," the mechanic nods—before, as though to prove it, launching into a rendition of "La Marseillaise." Four pilots saunter over and serve them glasses of eau-de-vie, then stroll away across the field towards two sleek black cars against which elegantly dressed ladies lean smoking cigarettes through long ivory holders.

"Bloody Cigognes," snaps Clegg when Serge recounts the episode back in the mess. "Nothing but playboys: race-car drivers, fly-half of the national rugby team, the Compte de Trou-de-Cul. Balloon-busters: all they ever dare attack. Show them an EA and they'll cack their French *pantalons* faster than the *jardin de mon oncle*. But soon as they get down from each day's chicken run they've got Parisian hostesses whisking them off to see *Manon* and *Salammbô* while we sit here listening to scratched-up Felix Powell. There's no justice in this war."

The Felix Powell is pretty scratched, it's true. So are the Marie Lloyd, the Vesta Tilley and the Ella Shields. As they play them in the evenings, some of the officers dance together, drawing lots to see who'll do the woman's steps; others, meanwhile, reminisce about the war's "golden era":

"Pity we don't use parasols and Moranes anymore," Watson sighs nostalgically. "Do you remember drop bags?"

"Those things were great fun," Dickinson says. "You'd scrawl your message in them, then just hurl them overboard above the reporting station, watch them drop. Radio killed all that."

"There was this pilot here when I first came," Baldwick tells them. "Said he used to wave at EA pilots when he passed them. You had no beef with one another. He said the first time one of them took a pop at him, he couldn't believe it: seemed so low . . ."

"What happened to him?" Watson asks.

"What do you think?" answers Baldwick. "Last year, or maybe late in 'fifteen. He was a flamer: *carbonisé*."

"*Carbo-nee-zay*," Dickinson and Watson repeat in unison, as though the word held some kind of mantric power, like an "Amen."

"He was a real old-timer," Baldwick tells them; "twenty-four or so."

Baldwick is twenty, one year older than Serge; Watson, twenty-one. They could have been flying with the 104th before he was born, as far as he's concerned. Each month is like a generation here. This makes the twenty-four-year-old who used to wave at passing Germans like a distant ancestor, belonging more to an order of stone reliefs, illuminated manuscripts and tapestries whose stories don't quite lend themselves to comprehension than to any present in which Serge might also have a place. Mess talk is full of predecessors such as him: the dead get more attention than the living. Each week, one or two more airmen join their Olympiad; as new ones replace them, Serge and the others move up the ancestral chain, one generation with every arrival. Before they take off for Artillery Observation or Contact Patrol work, pilots and observers pool their wages in a small iron commode that's been chosen for this purpose for a reason—a precise one, yet one whose particulars have become so subject to conjecture and apocrypha that they've grown obscure; if one of the men doesn't come back, his portion buys the rest an outing to the Encas Estaminet in Vitriers.

The Encas's décor is low-key. The walls of its two rooms are panelled with fly-brown mirrors; the zinc bar-top looks like it's been reclaimed from a shot-down aeroplane or crashed Crossley truck, and hammered repeatedly in an attempt to flatten it that's had the opposite effect: it's all but impossible to keep a glass upright on its surface. The table tops are marble slabs that must have lost their lustre many years ago, worn down by greasy hands and dirty elbows, stained with wine. The whole place smells of spilt wine. Two waiters with hair so greasy that Gibbs once drunkenly accuses them of pilfering from the squadron's engine-oil supplies move like slow spiders though a web of grey cigarette smoke that lingers as insistently as vapour trails and Archie-puffs above the battlefield.

"Hey, *garsson*!" Clegg says as one of them sets two bottles down in front of him. "Send two more to those homosexuals from the Eighty-ninth in the next room. *Comprennay*? Two *bootay*; *'omosexuelle, katrer-vangt-nerf*..."

Serge explains in French to the waiter what Clegg means, and takes the bottles through himself. They often see the 89th men here; their aero-drome's only four miles away. There's one man named Carlisle whom Serge gets talking to each time they meet. Carlisle's neither a pilot nor an observer, but an artist. He was studying at the Slade before the war, and got assigned to camouflage work, devising a whole system based on Goethe's theory of colours and applying it to machines, painting blue, violet and yellow stripes across their wings and fuselage—before discovering that these only camouflaged the planes when seen against the ground, an asset deemed of such limited value that it was scrapped after only two machines had been thus decorated. Rather than recall him, the war office has kept him out here as an official War Artist, on secondment to the 89th. He hasn't taken to his new post well.

"It doesn't work," he moans as Serge pours him a glass. "It's just not possible once you're in flight."

"What's not?" Serge asks.

"Art! Tell me, Counterfax: what's the first rule of landscape painting?"

"Carrefax." Serge thinks back to his afternoon sessions with Clair, but draws a blank. "Don't know."

"Horizon!" Carlisle slaps the table. "Got to have a damn horizon if you're going to paint a landscape! And what's the first thing to disappear when some madman at your back is loopy-looping?"

"Horizon?" Serge ventures.

"Carvers, you're a man of intellect. But you don't understand the half of it, my friend! It's not just the horizon that goes. Oh no. Look at this." He moves three half-full wineglasses together. "Here are some clouds. And here," he continues, dipping his finger in a wine-puddle and smearing it around the table top, "are the French fields with all their pretty patterned colours. When you look at them from here—" he pulls Serge's head across to where his own was—"they run together. Which is cloud? Which land? Can you tell what part of the liquid's in the glass and what's on the table top?"

"Does it matter?" Serge asks.

"Course it bloody matters!" Carlisle shouts back. "How you going to paint something if you can't even see what it is?" His voice goes hushed and urgent as he grasps a bottle and, moving it slowly above the three glasses, says: "A thundercloud passes over; a patch of woodland goes dark—or was it dark already? Who knows? And then, to make it worse, you suddenly come across a block of writing set bang in the middle of a clearing."

"Popham strips," Serge tells him. "It's because the batteries can't send back wireless signals: only rec—"

"I can't paint words!" Carlisle's voice rises half an octave. "Painting's painting, writing writing. Never the twain. It's all wrong, aesthetically speaking: all the depth and texture of a summer countryside steam-rollered into a flat page."

"That's what I like about it," Serge says.

"I try not to look down," Carlisle carries on, ignoring him as he drinks one of the clouds. "But looking up is just as bad! There's no per-spective in the sky, my friend. Some dot in front of you could be an EA swooping down to kill you, or a fly that's landed on your nose, or for all I know the moon of Jupiter. You don't have any measure to position yourself with . . ."

"Yes you do," Serge tells him. "You're connected to everything around you: all the streaks and puffs . . ."

"Ah, right: but how do you show those? The aircraft shell burst lasts a second—at its peak, I mean, the explosion itself, the bit I should be painting, seeing as I'm a War Artist and all that. A cloud is there forever—or at least for longer. What's the honest thing to do, then? Give the shell the same substance as the cloud? How am I meant to paint time? How am I meant to paint anything?"

"Why not just paint it as you see it?" Serge asks.

"Can't even do that," Carlisle wails. "The stuff won't stay still to be painted! Ground won't stay still, air won't stay still, nothing bloody stays still. Even the paint jumps from its bottles, gets all over me."

"Maybe that's the art," Serge says. "I mean the action, all the mess . . ."

"Now, Carefors, you're just talking rubbish," Carlisle admonishes him in a disappointed tone. He drains another glass, then mutters bit-terly: "It all comes from that show."

"What show?" Serge asks.

"The bloody *show*!" Carlisle hisses. "Fry and his buddies. All this . . . *this*—" he gestures at the ceiling, or rather the sky, then at the cloud-glasses and field-puddle on the table top—"is just an extension of *that*." He jabs a finger towards London. "Soon as the cork popped at the Grafton and the poison genie seeped out, this war was a foregone con-clusion. Just a matter of time."

Cécile slips into the room through a side-door and walks towards the exit. Serge catches her eye and she waits.

"Headquarters are complaining that my images aren't photographic enough," Carlisle's grumbling. "I tell them: 'Well, take photographs.' Jesus! Meanwhile, the officers in the mess want me to paint their caricatures. I studied under Tudor-Hart and I'm being asked to churn out caricatures!"

Serge rises from his seat and moves over to Cécile.

"You weren't here in over a week," she says.

"I was flying," he tells her. "Can I see you?"

"Come to my place," she says, slipping a key into his hand. "Wait for ten minutes, then follow."

She leaves. Serge returns to the first room to drink with the 104th, then slips away and walks through a maze of unlit streets, past open windows through which he sees meagre suppers being laid out on cracked and termite-eaten tables. Cécile's lock is well-oiled; her staircase is dark. He feels his way up it towards her room, which a paraffin lamp illuminates in dim, flickering patches; as Serge brushes past it, the room's shadows elongate and wobble over the bare walls and floor. There's not much there: most of the space is taken by a double bedstead whose black, shiny frame's surmounted by brass knobs. A coverlet of coarse crotchet-work has been peeled and folded back on the side nearest the door. The one small window's covered by a blind. In front of it a table stands; a mug on this has coffee dregs in; beside the mug, two empty eggshells sit in blue cups, flanked by wooden spoons.

"My breakfast from yesterday," Cécile says.

"You eat two eggs every day?" he asks.

"No," she replies, undressing. "Just one."

They don't talk much—not beforehand, at any rate. Serge turns Cécile away from him, towards the blind, and kneels behind her on the bed, running his hand up and down her back. Her sounds are feline: quiet wails that lose themselves among the shadows on the wall. Afterwards, she lies on her back beneath him and he scours her stomach.

"You've had something blasted away here," he says, prodding a spot beside her belly button.

"It was a mole," she tells him. "I burnt it off."

"You can see that," Serge says. "The scorch marks are still there."

He looks across the floor beside the bed, and sees a book. He reaches down and picks it up: selected poetry of Friedrich Hölderlin, in German.

"A friend left it for me last year," she explains. "An officer."

"A German officer?"

She shrugs. "They were here first."

After she falls asleep, he reads it for a while, then sets it down and drifts off watching gnats hovering beneath the ceiling just beyond the bed's foot. The gnats travel in straight lines towards each other, then separate, each gliding to the spot another occupied seconds ago, before repeating the procedure, again and again . . .

There are insects forming patterns outside Battery M as well—only these ones aren't moving. Corps HQ issues a directive that observers should pay a visit to at least one of the batteries with which they work, in order to foment a better understanding between air- and ground-based ends of Artillery Ops. Packed off to M by Walpond-Skinner, Serge finds a cratered moonscape. Rising from its surface like the mast of an interplanetary Marconi station is a fifty-foot pylon held by four guide-ropes. Its copper-gauze earth mat sits across a sheet of hessian on which thousands of dead moths, bees, butterflies and dragonflies lie, their bodies forming contours, swirls and eddies against its surface.

"Poison gas," the operator explains when he notices Serge looking at them. "The hessian keeps it out—enough to stop it killing us, but not enough to stop us all getting catarrhs."

"Where's the receiver?" Serge asks.

"Down here," the man answers, holding up the sheet for Serge to duck beneath it through the entrance to a kind of burrow.

"You're listening to my sigs *beneath* the ground?"

"You wouldn't have an audience for long if we stayed over it," the man tells him. "The German kite-balloons pick our flashes up once we start firing, range their batteries on us. Here's what we've got."

Leaning against one of the burrow's earth-walls, sitting on a wooden table, is a small Mark 4 receiver.

"Pelican crystals?" Serge asks.

"Two," the operator says. "And two dials: aerial condenser and signal. We have to keep the first one turning constantly; then once we've caught your clicks, we crank the condenser up to max. Makes our ears bleed."

Serge looks at the man's ears. He's not exaggerating: his drums are caked with dried blood, and red streaks run down both sides of his neck.

"Sorry," Serge murmurs.

"Not your fault. Wouldn't hear them otherwise."

"Oh, look," says Serge, "the gas hasn't killed all the insects."

The wall behind the receiver has lice on it. So does the receiver, and the table, chair and floor.

"Curse of the trenches," shrugs the operator. "Still, I wouldn't swap with you people for all the world. Need to feel ground beneath my feet. Over my head as well, these days. I get all anxious if I'm in the open for too long—even way back from the lines, on leave or what have you: like something's going to come and land on me . . ."

The man's words give over to coughs. Serge runs his eye around the burrow. There are passages leading off from the main chamber, presumably to other chambers which in turn have passages connecting them. This chamber has a bed in it; beneath the bed, two tins of pork-meat and a tattered copy of A. E. Housman.

"You too?" asks Serge.

"Calms me down," the operator tells him. "When the ordnance is falling, or taking off from here, or both. I think of Shropshire hedge-rows . . ."

This is what the 104th men say as well. They've got at least two copies there—one in the mess, one on his houseboat. He saw a soldier reading Housman on the boat over from Folkestone too. Half the front must be thinking of Shropshire hedgerows. Serge doesn't get it, and one day finds himself arguing the case out with the other officers, holding his ground against first one, then two, then three opponents.

"It's deep," Watson insists indignantly. "He looks at the cherry tree and has a vision of time passing." Straightening his back and dropping his voice to a solemn register, he starts reciting:

Now, of my threescore years and ten,
Twenty will not come again,
And take from seventy springs a score,
That only leaves me fifty more . . .

"Seventy minus twenty equals fifty," Serge replies. "That's deep."

"You have no sense of poetry, Carrefax," Baldwick joins in. "These things can take you away from all the rage around you, keep you safe . . ."

"Why would I want to be taken away?" asks Serge. "Where danger is, there rescue grows."

"What?"

"Hölderlin." He tosses Cécile's copy onto Baldwick's lap.

"This is a German book!" Baldwick gasps, recoiling.

"He was a German poet," Serge replies.

"You could be . . ." stutters Baldwick, "I mean, it's virtually . . ."

"It's virtually treason," Dickinson helps him out.

"You should read it," Serge informs them. "Learn some phrases: help you if you get shot down behind enemy lines and they don't understand what Shropshire hedgerows are . . ."

None of them take his offer up; the book lies around the mess unopened for one week, then gets returned to Cécile. Serge takes some of its lines into the air with him, though: they start jostling for space with the ones from the Pageant. He still hears the latter every time he shoots his gun; but when Gibbs turns, or dives, or pulls up suddenly and catapults him backwards to the sky, he hears the opening words of "Patmos":

> Nah ist
> Und schwer zu fassen der Gott . . .

He feels the *schwer* inside his stomach, tightening like gravity; the *Nah* is a kind of measuring, a spacing-out of space in such a way that distant objects and locations loom up close and nearby ones expand, their edges hurtling away beyond all visible horizons to convey and deliver the contents of these to him. The *Gott*'s not a divine, Christian Creator, but a point within the planes and altitudes the machine's cutting through— and one of several: the god, not God. And *fassen . . . fassen* is like locking onto something: a signal, frequency or groove. The word speaks itself inside his ear each time he taps his spark set or amends his clock-code chart. When arcing shells respond and hit their target, another phrase of Hölderlin's hums in the struts and wires, its syntax rattling and breaking with the pressure from the rising blasts: the line from "Die Titanen" about *der Allerschütterer,* the One Who Shakes All Things, reaching down into the deep to make it come to life:

> Es komme der Himmlische
> Zu Todten herab und gewaltig dämmerts
> Im ungebundenen Abgrund
> Im allesmerkenden auf.

He thinks of the sky he's held in as an *Abgrund:* an abyss, a without-ground—yet one that's all-remarking, *allesmerkenden,* scored over by a thousand tracks and traces like the fallen earth below him. Which makes him *der Himmlische,* the Heavenly One, calling down light, causing it to burst forth and rise upwards, to the partings of the Father's hair, so that . . . *wenn aber . . . und es gehet . . .* Here the sentences fade in and out, like wireless stations, before climaxing in a stanza that Serge once spends a whole night sitting on his houseboat's deck translating:

> und der Vogel des Himmels ihm
> Es anzeigt. Wunderbar
> Im Zorne kommet er drauf.

> and the bird of Heaven
> Makes it known to him. Upon which,
> Wonderful in anger, he comes. .

These lines, and others, echo for him on another occasion too: his visit to the sounding range near Battery F. This visit's not directive-prompted. Quite the opposite: it takes place by accident and, Serge suspects, against the orders of Headquarters, who have always maintained an air of secrecy about what goes on in the woods just north of Vitriers. He's being driven in a Crossley truck to Nieppe one afternoon, to buy spare aerial copper from a local metalworker (ordering it up from England would take months) when the driver announces, on the way back, a short detour to drop off some piano wire in Sector Four.

"They're playing pianos amidst all this racket?" Serge asks him, incredulous.

The driver smiles. They leave the road and slalom between tree trunks, pulling up eventually beside a small cluster of huts. As the driver carries the looped coils to one of these, Serge wanders off among the trees, unzips his trouser-fly and starts to urinate onto the ground—only to be chastised by a voice that issues from the foliage around him like some spirit of the woods:

"Don't piss against the wire!"

"What wire?" he asks. "Who said that?"

The wood-spirit emerges: a short man with slender fingers.

"Just under the earth's surface," he says, before adding, no less obscurely: "You'll cause interference from the mikes. Who are you?"

"Observer from 104th Squadron," Serge tells him. "I stopped by to drop off the wire."

"The wires are already in place," the slender-fingered man says, pointing at the ground. "Six of them, running from the microphones to here."

"Microphones in the woods?"

"Yup: six mikes, one for each wire. They're in cut-out barrels arranged in a semi-circle quarter of a mile away."

"Attached to piano wire?" asks Serge.

"You brought new piano wire? Why didn't you say so? Where is it?"

"Being carried into those huts," Serge tells him.

The man hurries back towards the huts. Serge follows him. Inside the main one, he finds a huge square harp whose six strings are extended out beyond their wooden frame by finer wires that run through the hut's air before breaching its boundary as well, cutting through little mouse-holes in the east-facing wall. In front of the harp, like an interrogation lamp, a powerful bulb shines straight onto it; behind it, lined up with each string, a row of prisms capture and deflect the light at right angles, through yet another hole cut in the hut's wall, into an unlit room adjoining this one. There's a noise coming from the adjoining room: sounds like a small propeller on a stalled plane turning from the wind's pressure alone.

"What is this place?" Serge asks.

"You're an observer, right?" the slender-fingered man says.

Serge nods.

"Well, you know how, when you're doing Battery Location flights, you send down K.K. calls each time you see an enemy gun flash?"

"Oh yes," Serge answers. "I've always wondered why we have to do that . . ."

"Wonder no more," the man says with an elfin smile. "The receiving operator presses a relay button each time he gets one of those; this starts the camera in the next room rolling; and the camera captures the sound of the battery whose flash you've just *K.K.*'d to us. You with me?"

"No," Serge answers. "How can it do that?"

"Each gun-boom, when it's picked up by a mike, sends a current down the wires you just pissed on," the man continues, "and the current makes the piano wire inside this room heat up and give a little kick, which gets diffracted through the prisms into the next room, and straight into the camera."

"So you're *filming* sound?" Serge asks.

"You could say that, I suppose," the man concurs.

"What's the point of that?"

"Here, follow me."

He leads Serge from this hut towards another. Pausing at the door of this, he knocks; then, when a voice inside shouts "Enter," opens it no more than a slit's width and ushers Serge inside. The interior's suffused with red light. At a trough propped up against the far wall, a man with rolled-up sleeves is dunking yards of film into developing liquid, then feeding it on from there into a fixing tank. As the film's end emerges from this tank in turn, he holds it up, inspects it and tears off sections, clipping these with clothes pegs to a short stretch of washing line, from where they drip onto the discarded strips on the room's floor below them.

"Yuk," Serge whispers beneath his breath.

"What?" the slender-fingered man asks.

"Nothing," he replies.

"Look here," Serge's guide says, unclipping a strip of the developed film and pointing at dark lines that run, lengthways and continuous, along its surface. The lines—six of them—are for the most part flat; occasionally, though, they erupt suddenly, and rise and fall in jagged waves, like some strange Persian script, for half an inch, before settling down and running flat again. On the film's bottom edge, beside the punch-holes, a time-code is marked, one inch or so for every second. The jagged eruptions appear at different points along each line: staggered, each wave the same shape as the one on the line below it, but occurring a quarter of an inch (or three-tenths of a second) later.

"So," Serge's elfin guide continues, "these kicks are made by the sound hitting each mike; and they get laid out on the film at intervals that correspond to each mike's distance from the sound. You see them?"

"Yes," Serge answers. "But I still don't—"

"These ones ready to take through?" the guide asks the developer.

The other man nods; with his piano-player's fingers, the guide unclips the other drip-dried strips, then leads Serge out to yet another hut. This one's wall has a large-scale map taped to it; stuck in the map in a neat semi-circle are six pins. Two men are going through a pile of torn-off, line-streaked film-strips, measuring the gaps between the kicks with lengths of string; then, moving the string over to the map slowly, careful to preserve the intervals, they transfer the latter onto its surface by fixing one end of the string to the pin and holding a pencil to the other, swinging it from side to side to mark a broad arc on the map.

"Each pin's a microphone," the slender-fingered man explains. "Where the arcs intersect, the gun site must be."

"So the strings are time, or space?" Serge asks.

"You could say either," the man answers with a smile. "The film-strip knows no difference. The mathematical answer to your question, though, is that the strings represent the asymptote of the hyperbola on which the gun lies."

"But there are several guns," Serge says.

"And several types of kick on the film," the man replies. "You can tell from their shape and thickness which are primary and which secondary, tertiary and so on. You just keep plotting all the intersections and eventually the whole thing maps itself out. It changes every few days, of course: soon as you people take one battery out, another one pops up for us to pinpoint . . ."

The Crossley's engine comes to life outside. Walking back to it, Serge is acutely conscious of his feet percussing on the ground, and starts to tiptoe lest he cause more interference to the wires, even though the truck's noise is much louder. On the way home, once they've left the woods and joined the road, he starts to drift off. To his mind, held in a web of strings and arcs above a darkness lit up by diffracted flashes, it seems that the groaning of the guns now comes as much from below as above. He sees it travelling through earth on worm-like cords, then seeping out like methane. As it rises past him, its vibrations make the truck's metal bars pronounce, over and over again, the word *Allerschütterer;* then it rises further, up towards a high spot where a keen ear inclines above a battlefield that's turned into a giant sounding-board. Just before he loses consciousness entirely, Serge sees Dr. Filip's thin, filament-eyes glow above metal-grey whiskers—and hears, at a pitch barely audible and issuing from a spot that no amount of intersecting arcs could pinpoint, a little not-quite-German, not-quite-English voice describing twangling instruments humming about his ears.

iii

On days when they're assigned to Artillery Patrol, Serge and Gibbs fly further over on the German side than the machines on Art Obs duties, sending zone-call rather than clock-code signals back. The sequences are longer, running into double-figured strings of numbers, letters, dots and spaces: *BY.NF.B30 C 8690; BY.COL.FAN NW B30C8690 . . .* His fingers ache by the end of every mission. When he's not tapping sigs out, he's photographing the ground with a camera attached to the plane's lower wing. They have to fly in pre-set patterns and maintain a stable altitude to keep their photographs in sequence and to scale. They liaise with the photographic unit regularly; it's in a former slaughterhouse two miles behind the airfield.

"I'd say this emplacement's a dummy one," Lieutenant Pietersen opines as he passes the monocular to Serge. "The tracks leading to the copse are so clear you could see them from ten thousand feet up. They may as well have drawn an arrow on the ground . . ."

"I see flashes from there a lot," Serge tells him, "but they never seem quite right. Haven't got that forward kick . . ."

"Stage effects," Pietersen tuts. "Smoke and mirrors."

He pins the photo to a board—askew, and covering the bottom corner of another photo which is slanted to the other side. Eight or nine more photos cling together to produce a mosaic of landscape across which lines—straight, curved and dotted—cut and swirl like markings on butterflies' wings.

"Now, this part's changed since yesterday," Pietersen says, replacing one tile of the mosaic with a new one that contains a dark, concentric set of ripples moving outwards from a spot covered by trees. "But I'm not sure we've knocked the big gun out. When you fly over it tomorrow, try to ascertain whether the scorch marks fall along the main diameter of all these circles, or if they're off-centre."

"I'll snap the area, but I don't know if I'll be able to tell that with my naked eye, through all the smoke," Serge replies.

"Try rubbing cocaine in it," Pietersen tells him.

"Cocaine?" Serge asks. "Isn't that for teeth?"

"Yes, but it works wonders on your vision: sharpens it no end. Go pick some up from the Field Hospital in Mirabel."

Serge does so. He's given a small make-up tin of white powder, a little of which he daubs onto his retina just prior to take-off the next day. It takes effect as they're clearing their own kite balloon, which starts beaming up at him taut and alert, a big white eyeball. The lines of tracer-fire stand out more starkly a few seconds later, their velocity and inclination bold, insistent. The mesh of trenches, the coloured flames of guns and flares, distant roads and railway lines, the markings on the ground: all these things come at him more cleanly, more pronounced—but then so do Archie puffs, vapour trails and cordite smoke-clouds, not to mention the real clouds above him and the sky's deep blue.

"Did it work?" Pietersen asks him next time he visits the slaughter-house.

"I'm not sure," he answers.

"You can get a stronger effect by snorting it," Pietersen tells him.

"What, like snuff?"

"Knock a little out across a table top or mirror," Pietersen says. "Lay it in a line, and snort it through a rolled-up banknote. I'm afraid the scorch-marks are off-centre."

"Sorry?"

Pietersen's finger taps the mosaic on the board. This shows the same territory as it did yesterday, but most of the landmarks on this have mutated: changed their shape, grown blast-wrinkles, become scarred by craters or even, in some cases, simply disappeared. Sliding his mind's gaze between the old images and these updated ones, Serge has a flickering apprehension that the landscape's somehow moving, as though animated.

"Like a cat's leg," he says.

"What is? Which bit?"

"The whole thing."

Pietersen steps back and tilts his head at the elongated spit of land formed by the collated images. After a while he nods and murmurs:

"I suppose it does have that shape, a little."

The next day, Serge taps a small mound of cocaine onto his shaving mirror, pushes it into a line, rolls up a twenty-franc note and breathes the powder up towards his cranium. It stings behind his eyes, then numbs the upper part of his face. As Gibbs takes off, Serge feels a lump of phlegm grow in his throat. He swallows; it tastes bitter, chemical. The tracer-lines this time are vibrant and electric: it's as though the air were laced with wires. Higher up, the vapour trails of SE5s form straight white lines against the blue, as though the sky's surface were a mirror too. Scorch-marks and crater contours on the ground look powdery; it seems that if he swooped above them low enough, then he could breathe them up as well, snort the whole landscape into his head. The three hours pass in minutes. As they dip low to strafe the trenches on the way back, he feels the blood rush to his groin. He whips his belt off, leaps bolt upright and has barely got his trousers down before the seed shoots from him, arcs over the machine's tail and falls in a fine thread towards the slit earth down below.

"From all the Cs!" he shouts. "The bird of Heaven!"

From this day onwards, he develops a keen interest in the contents of the medicine box in the RE8's cabin, tucked between the aerial's copper reel and the second set of controls. He experiments with benzoic acid, amyl nitrate, ether and bromide before discovering diacetylmorphine. Held in injectable phials, the liquid floods him with euphoria each time he pushes it into his flesh: a murky, earthy warmth that spreads out from his abdomen in waves. Then everything slows down and seems to float: the tracers rise towards him languidly, like bubbles in a glass; Archie puff-clouds hang about his head like party bunting. He likes it when the bullets come close—really close, so that they're almost grazing the machine's side: when this happens he feels like he's a matador being passed by the bull's horn, the two previously antagonistic objects brought together in an arrangement of force and balance so perfectly proportioned that it's been removed from time, gathered up by a pantheon of immortals to adorn their walls. The sky takes on a timeless aspect too: the intersecting lines of ordnance residue and exhaust fumes form a grid in which all past manoeuvres have become recorded and in which, by extension, history itself seems to hang suspended. Flashes tincture the lines green, lace them with yellow, spatter them with incandescent reds. The colours look synthetic, as though they'd been daubed and splashed on from bottles, like Carlisle's oils, aquarelles and acrylics; it seems to Serge that if he had a jar of turpentine or camphor and a sponge then he could wipe the whole sky clear . . .

In states such as this, he finds his attention captivated by the German kite balloons. He'll gaze at them for endless stretches, measuring his position not from the grid squares on his map but from these strange, distended objects as they rotate to his view. Unlike the English ones, they're coloured the dark, putrid tone of rotting flesh. They may have the shape of intestines, but their rising, falling and eventual deflation makes him think of lungs—diseased ones, like the catarrh-ridden lungs of the burrow dwellers whose flashes they pinpoint. When he sees one being inflated on the ground, it calls to his mind the image of ticks swelling as they gorge themselves on blood. He fires on airborne ones that come into his range not out of hatred or a sense of duty, but to see what happens when the bullets touch their surface, in the way a child might poke an insect. When flame-tendrils push outwards from inside the balloons and climb up their surface before bursting into bloom, he watches the men in their baskets throw their parachutes over the side and jump. Often they get stuck halfway down, tangled in the ropes and netting. Seeing them wriggling as the flame crawls down the twine towards them, he thinks of flies caught in spiders' webs; when they roast, they look like dead flies, round and blackened.

He starts picturing the batteries he's targeting as insects too, ticks that have burrowed into the ground's skin and embedded themselves there: his task's unpicking them. Pinned to the slaughterhouse's wall, the photographs take on the air of dermatological slides.

"I don't think that one'll be troubling our boys much more," Pietersen declares triumphantly, tapping a deeply pockmarked patch on his mosaic. "The whole sector's dead now."

"Dead?" asks Serge.

"Yes," Pietersen replies. "You've killed it."

"I don't see it that way," Serge murmurs back.

"You think there's still an emplacement there?"

"That's not what I mean . . . It's just that . . ."

He can't explain it. What he means is that he doesn't think of what he's doing as a deadening. Quite the opposite: it's a quickening, a bringing to life. He feels this viscerally, not just intellectually, every time his tapping finger draws shells up into their arcs, or sends instructions buzzing through the woods to kick-start piano wires for whirring cameras, or causes the ground's scars and wrinkles to shift and contort from one photo to another: it's an awakening, a setting into motion. In these moments Serge is like the Eiffel Tower, a pylon animating the whole world, calling the zero hour of a new age of metal and explosive, geometry and connectedness—and calling it over and over again, so that its birth can be played out in votive repetition through these elaborate and ecstatic acts of sacrifice . . .

And in the background of these iterations, like a relic of an old order, the sun: intoxicated, spewing gas and sulphur, black with cordite smoke and tar. As the summer months draw on, it seems to sicken. Rising beneath him on early-morning flights, its light's infected by the ghostly pallor of the salient's mists, driven a nauseous hue by green and yellow flashes. It darkens, not lightens, as each day progresses and the puff-balls, vapour clouds and tracer-lines build up. Its transit through the air seems laboured, as though the whirring mechanism that dragged it along its tracks were damaged and worn out. As afternoons run into evenings, it becomes so saturated with the toxins all around it that it can no longer hold itself up and, grown heavy and feeble, sinks. Serge watches it die time and time again, watches its derelict disc slip into silvery, metallic marshland, where it drowns and dissolves. When this happens, a chemical transformation spreads across land and sky, turning both acidic. In these moments, he feels better than he's ever felt before—as though his rising were commensurate with the sun's sinking. As space runs out backwards like a strip of film from his tail, the world seems to anoint him, through its very presence, as the gate, bulb, aperture and general projection point that's brought it about: a new, tar-coated orb around which all things turn.

9

---

i

By September, more than two-thirds of the pilots and observers who made up the 104th when Serge arrived have been killed. The ones who remain undergo a similar set of transformations to the landscapes in Pietersen's photographs. Their faces turn to leather—thick, nickwax-smeared leather each of whose pores stands out like a pothole in a rock surface—and grow deep furrows. Eyelids twitch; lips tremble and convulse in nervous spasms. Arriving back from flights, they stumble from their machines with the effects of acceleration and deceleration, of ungradated transit through modes of gravity alternately positive and negative, sculpted in the open mouths, sucked-in cheeks and swollen tongues that they present to the airfield's personnel for the next few hours. *Clown Bodners,* Serge tells himself. Sometimes they laugh uncontrollably, as though a passing shell had whispered to them the funniest joke imaginable, although often it's hard to tell if they're laughing or crying. The engines' pulses have bored through their flesh and bones and set up small vibrating motors in their very core: their hands struggle to hold teacups still, light cigarettes, unbutton jackets . . .

"It's the flying circuses," Clegg croaks shakily to the mess orderly in front of Serge one afternoon. "The Jastas. They move up and down the front in huge formations. When they get all around you there's not that much you can do. They come at you from everywhere . . ."

"I'm rigging my plane up against them," Stanley, a recent arrival, tells them.

"How?" ask Serge and Clegg in unison.

"Pike principle," answers Stanley, enigmatically.

"You mean the fish?" Serge says.

"No, pikestaffs," Stanley tuts. "You'll see."

The following day he wheels out of the Bessoneau an SE5 to which no fewer than seven Lewis guns have been attached. They poke out of the machine in every conceivable direction; there's even one hanging below the tail.

"To guard against the bites of sharks," Stanley explains as he taps this last one.

"How will you operate them all?" Serge asks.

"I'll dart from one gun to another, depending on where they're coming at me from. I'll learn to play the whole contraption like an instrument—an organ, say: you can't be at all the stops and pedals at the same time, but you can still make it do its thing when you know how . . ."

Walpond-Skinner nixes Stanley's pikery:

"If the RFC had wanted three-hundred-and-sixty-degree bullet dispensers, they'd have built them. Your task is to fly. Two guns for each machine—that's it!"

Stanley is killed a week later. Serge inherits his copy of Shakespeare's Sonnets, and finds, in the very first one, Widsun's line about being the world's fresh ornament, herald to the spring and so on. The phrase that his mind snags on, though, comes from a later sonnet, number 65: the line about love shining bright in black ink. He keeps on hearing it: as he reads copy orders, wipes tar from his face, or watches the dark water flowing by the Floaters. Clegg and Watson, meanwhile, scoop fish from the river and, placing them in a glass tank in the mess, study their formations.

"He was right, you know," says Watson. "You do need an anti-shark gun. That spot beneath the tail's unguarded and unsighted."

"Look at this one," Clegg says, pointing to an upward-angled perch that's nibbling a toast crumb on the water's surface. "It's hanging on the propeller."

"These two orange ones have taken up a good position," Watson comments. "No one below them, lots of clear air to rise through . . ."

The fish-tank modelling affects the way Serge sees things in the sky: now heavy clouds above him look like the huddled bellies of a school of whales; the tall, waving poplars become fronds of seaweed; the ashen ruins of bombed villages, clusters of coral. *To the seas.* On days when rain, uninterrupted, washes away the line dividing river-water from the air above it, the men move around the mess like fish inside a tank, with liquid sluicing through their gills.

"Says here two measures whiskey, one Champagne," Gibbs announces as he pours the contents of three bottles into a metal bucket.

"Ella's stopped singing," Clegg complains, face sunken in guppy-like despondency.

"Then give the gramophone a drink," Gibbs tells him.

"The Bellerophone!" the others shout out drunkenly. They commandeer the bucket, drag it over to the music corner, crank the machine up again and start dribbling the cocktail down the speaking horn's throat. As it trickles out across the disc at the horn's other end, the music goes faint and warbly, as though it were being performed underwater. The men fall about laughing. When Ella drowns completely, they burst into song themselves:

Take the cylinder out of my kidneys,
The connecting rod out of my brain, my brain,
From the small of my back take the camshaft
And assemble the engine again.

In the lulls between songs, the conversation reverts, like a pickup's arm returning to its cradle, to discussions of the dead.

"I saw it all," some pilot says of some other one who could as well be here describing yet another. "The fuel tank caught fire at the front of the machine, and so he put the tail down, to keep the flames from the cockpit. But they'd spread already. Then he tried to swat them out. When that didn't work, he climbed out of his seat and started walking back along the fuselage. By the end he was crouching on the tail. Then he jumped."

"Did they find his body?"

"In some old woman's laundry yard."

"That Trenchard is a lunatic," snarls Gibbs. "The kite balloon-men, who've got winches tied to them like apron-strings, are issued parachutes. But we, who fly ten times as high without any cord to haul us back, get nothing."

"He thinks they'd slow the machines down," Serge tells him, "also, that they'd encourage us to jump instead of land each time we had a problem. Then there's the silk shortage . . ."

"What silk shortage?" Gibbs sputters through his drink. "The Germans have parachutes made from British silk! We've got enough to sell it to them, but not enough for our own side?"

Serge says nothing, but in his mind sees tall piles of fresh crêpe, Jacquard and moiré being stitched into large jellyfish-shapes by women who, at least in the scenario his mind's concocting for him right now, cavort with lions and sheep beneath a hybrid Sino-German flag, while generals smile and whisper in the background. His mother's somewhere in this picture, consorting with a buyer who, his face obscured by a thin silk sheet, talks loudly in an accent as strange as her own, pronouncing words Serge can't make out.

"I dream of going down in flames each night," Clegg mumbles. "It's always the same: the bed's on fire. It starts at its foot, and moves up. I try to tip the whole thing back, then stall and side-slip down, but it never works."

"You could put it out by wetting yourself," Serge tells him.

The men all burst into laughter again, but this time it's hollow. They're all terrified of becoming *carboneezay*, flamers. Candles are now banned on board the houseboat lest, by setting fire to its wooden beams, they allow the "orange death" that stalks them in the sky to catch up with them even on the ground; paraffin lamps have been replaced by electric bulbs inside the mess; even sparking up cigarettes causes the men to shudder as they flip the lighter's lid shut with a kind of angry vehemence. Of all the pilots and observers, Serge alone remains unhaunted by the prospect of a fiery airborne end. He's not unaware of it: just unbothered. The idea that his flesh could melt and fuse with the machine parts pleases him. When they sing their song about taking cylinders out of kidneys, he imagines the whole process playing itself out backwards: brain and connecting rod merging to form one, ultra-intelligent organ, his back quivering in pleasure as pumps and pistons plunge into it, heart and liver being spliced with valve and filter to create a whole new, streamlined mechanism. Sometimes he dreams he's growing wings and, waking up, prods at his breastbone, trying to discern an outward swelling in it; each rib feels like a strut. He shakes after flights just like the others, but he doesn't mind: the vibrations make him feel alive. He buzzes with kinetic potency as he carries them to Vitriers, to Cécile, where they make the brass knobs above her bedstead shake and bore their way on into her flesh too . . .

Cécile's place is unheated. By October, evenings there are cold. He brings her a dead observer's jacket to keep warm in.

"If he was killed, how come his jacket came back?" she asks, slipping it over her bare skin.

"Oh, he came back too," Serge answers. "Just not alive. Look, you can see the bullet holes."

Her eyes peer down her nose while her hand presses the leather to her stomach.

"On the left side," he helps her out.

"Ah yes," she purrs, poking her finger through a hole. "Direct dans la poitrine."

She keeps it on while they make love again. Serge, kneeling behind her with his face pressed into collar fur, imagines the bullet piercing the jacket's leather and travelling onwards through both the observer and Cécile, then, broken down into a million particles, lodging in him not only harmlessly but also beneficially, as though he were both its and the other two's final destination, the natural conclusion of a process whose trajectory conjoined them all. Afterwards, he picks one of her stockings from the floor and, holding it up to his face, stretches its fabric.

"What are you doing?" she asks.

"If you could spare this, it would really keep me warm up in the air."

"Your legs will be too big for it," she says.

"It's not for my legs," he says. "I'd wear it on my head, beneath the helmet."

Cécile shrugs. A clunking sound comes from the street outside. People are moving stuff around all the time these days: chests of drawers, tables, bathtubs, cookers, sinks. The German ordnance has been falling closer and closer to the town, destroying outlying villages and pitching their inhabitants up on the doorsteps of relatives who themselves are beginning, as stray shells start breaching civic limits, to gather together family heirlooms or at least saleable objects, tie them to carts and trundle down potholed roads towards imagined safety. Those who've stayed lug buckets and cylinders from house to pump and shop to house: the water and gas pipes feeding half the populace have been destroyed. Drains and sewers have been snapped and dragged up from beneath the ground to spew their mess across the cobblestones. Even a graveyard on the edge of town has been blown up; the stench of unearthed corpses carries through air whose coldness crystallises and preserves it. Serge can see the graveyard from Cécile's window. Beyond it, two dead horses lie with swollen stomachs in a field. Beyond them, past the rubble of the farmhouse that once marked the field's boundary, blackened and splintered tree-stumps litter a winter landscape that he couldn't imagine ever having been another way.

One afternoon in January, Walpond-Skinner gathers the men together in the red-gabled house's main room and informs them that a major push is being prepared. Serge, Gibbs and several other pilots and observers are taken off flying duties above the front and sent ten miles back to practise Contact Patrol work. This turns out to consist of flying low over advancing infantry who have mirrors attached to their backs, sounding a klaxon from the cockpit to solicit from the ground flares which, in turn, indicate positions and accomplishments. Bengal lights mean a wood has been captured, Aldis ones a trench, and Hucks a battery—or is it Aldis for battery and Hucks for woods? And is a copse a wood? How many trees . . . ? Serge suspects, even as they learn the signals and run through the klaxon sequences, that the system's flawed. The mock-battles that they act out over unmined, undefended fields usually manage to degenerate into confusion. In the week he spends there, three machines crash: two of them into each other, pilots glare-blinded by mirrors . . .

Serge finds it hard to sleep. It's not the gentle rocking of the houseboat that he misses so much as the front's sounds all around him: they've become his nightly lullaby. He can still hear the howitzers from here, of course, but they're too distant—and besides, their sound is drowned out by the noise of Crossleys carrying troops eastward: convoy after convoy of them, trundling past the window of his cabin in an unbroken supply chain. Infantry march by round the clock as well, the rhythm of their step setting off in Serge's head the lead-up lines from Sonnet 65:

Or what strong hand can hold his swift foot back,
Or who his spoil of beauty can forbid?

Returning to the 104th at the week's end, he whoops for joy as the poplars, Bessoneaus and grazing cows appear beneath his wing, then runs along the path that leads through the wood (or copse) to the river and, throwing himself on the bed, flips Stanley's book open so that he can read 65's riposte line, already firmly scrawled across his memory, with his own eyes:

O none, unless this miracle have might,
That in black ink my love may still shine bright.

"So when's the big day, then?" he asks Walpond-Skinner.

"Firstly, Carrefax, it's 'big day, sir'—or, strictly speaking, 'big day, sir, then.' "

"Sir, then," Serge corrects himself. "Then when—?"

"And secondly, that's privileged information. I would tell you that it's mine to know and yours to wonder about—if I knew myself, that is, which I'm afraid I don't. The moles have to finish their work first."

"Moles, sir?"

"The tunnellers. They're digging all the way through no man's land, so they can lay explosives underneath the trenches, gun emplacements and what have you. Got to proceed slowly: make sure it doesn't cave in, make sure they keep quiet, listen out for Germans counter-tunnelling beneath them, all that sort of thing . . ."

Serge becomes fascinated with these tunnellers, these moles. He pictures their noses twitching as they alternately dig and strap on stethoscopes that, pressing to the ground, they listen through for sounds of netherer moles undermining their undermining. If they did hear them doing this, he tells himself, then they could dig an even lower tunnel, undermine the under-undermining: on and on forever, or at least for as long as the volume and mass of the globe allowed it—until earth gave over to a molten core, or, bypassing this, they emerged in Australia to find there was no war there and, unable to return in time for action, sat around aimlessly blinking in the daylight . . .

In anticipation of the push, there's almost constant bombardment of the German side. It's barrage bombardment: the shells advance in lines, like the teeth of a giant comb moving up warp fibres, ten or so yards each time. For Serge, sleeping in his houseboat once again, the booms of the guns' discharge to the west, spread out along a line of well over a mile yet sounding almost simultaneously, and the consequent, equally elongated blasts of their detonation to the east, a little further away with each round, become the sounds of waves rolling past him, moving towards a shoreline that's retreating; no sooner does the longest-travelling one peter out on distant shingle than a new, close-range set swells up and starts bursting energetically. After five days and nights of this, though, he wakes up to silence. Not only have the shells stopped: so, too, have most of the small-gauge gunfire, Archie pops and flares. Nothing at all seems to be happening. All of the squadron's flights are in the hangars. Scouring the unusually bright winter sky, he fails to pick out a single aeroplane against its blue. It looks desolate and sad, as though aware that it's being spurned by beautiful machinery and at a loss to understand why.

The push begins the next day. Almost all the 104th's planes are involved in it in one way or another. The RE8s are to fly in holding patterns until the tunnellers' mines are detonated at half past eleven on the dot—their cue to swoop down low and monitor the progress of the infantry battalion to which each of them has been assigned, tracking the soldiers through no-man's-land towards the target destination. They're to report the battalion's advance to stations set up a mile or so behind the front for this very occasion, which in turn will relay the troops' positions back to HQ—where, Serge presumes, they must have a warlike version of the Realtor's Game laid out across a table, with helmets instead of top hats, trucks instead of cars and rabid, snarling dogs being shunted over flattened icons representing trenches, hills and machine-gun nests. Serge and Gibbs have been assigned the 10th Battalion; their target destination is a spinney.

"Spinney, now, is it?" Gibbs snorts. "They should've given us a course on forestry before sending us out here."

"What are you taking a shaving set with you for, Sassen?" Walpond-Skinner asks a pilot in the front row.

"Case I get shot down and taken prisoner, sir. Want to keep up appearances."

"Why not just send your silk pyjamas over, and arrange for your mail to be forwarded? Go and put it back in your quarters! The only thing you'll need with you if you get shot down and end up in one piece is a Verey gun, to torch the machine with."

"I've got to pop over to the Floaters too," Serge mumbles to Gibbs. "Our medicine box is low."

Gibbs shrugs. He's tried the cocaine-in-the-eyeballs trick, but doesn't get the point of snorting it, and even less so of injecting stuff into one's arm. Serge, for his part, can't imagine flying without diacetylmorphine. He's been making regular trips into Mirabel for months now, appointing himself, as far as the quartermaster there's concerned, the squadron's pharmaceutical liaison officer. Back on the boat, he stabs a phial into his wrist, then, catching sight of Cécile's stocking, two round peep-holes snipped out of its fabric, picks that up and slips it over his head, brushing his face briefly with a honey-like genital scent. He pockets two more phials on his way out, then pauses for a last look at the river and the poplars, still and impassive against all the excitement. He can hear the engines catching on the field, the first planes moving through the long grass. The diacetylmorphine takes hold as he glides back up the path and over to his RE8, turning the machines' manoeuvres as they taxi, pause and pirouette, escorting one another into position, into ballroom-dance steps, the roar of their engines into symphonies whose every chord is laden with insinuation . . .

Flying towards the lines, Serge has the same sensation as he had in massage sessions with Tania towards the end of his Klodĕbrady sojourn. The whole front has a weekend feel. No round, white balloons are up; no blue and red lights flicker in the trenches. There's no cordite smoke, no vapour blanket, nothing. It looks like the entire war effort has been stood down—or, rather, put into a casual mode in which formalities have been relaxed and, consequently, anything is possible. As he nears the English lines, he notices a change in the texture and colouration of the ground behind them. Its surface, previously pale and washed-out, has become darkened by spiky dots. They're everywhere, crowded together like ants. In the relatively quiet air, Gibbs has no problem making himself heard as he shouts back to Serge:

"Men!"

They spill out of the trenches, flecking the circles and mandalas of the ruined roads and pathways. In some places Serge can make out subdivisions in their mass, semi-discrete clusters; in others the clusters are so large that they've run together and eclipsed the ground entirely. Unlike ants, though, they're not moving: packed together with their bayoneted rifles pointing upwards, they're sitting still as encrustations on a rock or hull, waiting for the signal to move. Serge reaches down between his legs and lowers his copper aerial. Testing the sigs, he leads Gibbs to above their interim receiving station, marked by a semi-circle of white cloth beside which, in place of Popham strips, a black-and-white Venetian blind opens and closes, winking Morse OKs at him. Then they turn back towards the lines and climb. Their route is slightly different to the normal one; the shift adds to the sense of strangeness brought about by the guns' silence. The men in the German trenches seem to have noticed the changes too, to sense that something new is coming their way: they're too nervous to send more than a token spattering of tracer fire towards him. The German kite balloons have picked up on the break with protocol as well: all down the line they're up as high as they can go. The one emerging from beneath his tail doesn't bother to winch itself out of range, so intent is it on fixing its gaze on the dots massing on the far side—and Serge, caught in the same spell of anticipation, doesn't bother to strafe it.

They find their position just back from the German lines at three-and-a-half thousand feet. Serge looks up and sees the squadron's SE5s patrolling in formation high above them. He looks at his watch: twenty-eight minutes past eleven. He looks down: the whole battlefield is static, calm; only the planes move, serenely etching out their patterns. As Gibbs turns, then turns again, Serge runs his eye along the earth below, wondering in which part of it the moles have secreted their explosive droppings. For a while, he feels the presence, composited from blocks of air and tricks of the light, of that faceless diviner Baron Karl von Arnow: he's hovering beside him, holding a dowser's stick; and the wind buffeting the struts and wires is pronouncing his name—insistently, repeating it over and over: *Are-NOW, Are-NOW, Are-NOW* . . .

Then, as though summoned upwards by this incantation, the earth rises towards him. At first it looks like a set of welts bubbling up across its surface; the welts grow into large domes with smooth, convex roofs; the roofs, still rising upwards and expanding, start to crack, then break open completely; and through their ruptured crusts shoot long, straight jets of earth: huge, rushing geysers that look as though they're being propelled upwards by nothing but their own force and volume, the dull brown matter defying both height and gravity through sheer self-will. As the closest geyser funnels up past the machine, its dizzy clods glitter in the air. Serge looks out horizontally, first north, then south: the whole German line is punctuated by these earth jets. They look like columns holding up the sky; it seems that if they crumbled it would fall. Their apex is much higher than his plane; for the first time, he has the impression that he's flying not above the earth's surface but below it—or, rather, within some kind of enclave contained inside it. A few seconds later, particles start raining down on the machine: small clumps and flecks, beating against the wings and sprinkling his cabin. The jets evaporate, and Serge looks down again to see two enormous holes in the ground beneath him. They gape like hollow eyes, the sockets of some giant who's been lying beneath the landscape buried—perhaps for centuries, or perhaps even longer—and is only now, part by part, being disinterred.

"Shall I go down?" Gibbs shouts.

Serge doesn't answer, hypnotised by the evacuated eyes.

"Shall I go down?" Gibbs shouts again.

Slowly, Serge moves his gaze to the east. The spiky dot-men on the ground have started moving. They're swarming forwards, trickling through no-man's-land's rills and gullies. Every so often parts of their mass are thrown into the air by landmine explosions that, compared to the enormous ones that have just preceded them, seem no more substantial than the bursting of small spots. Shells have started falling too, machine guns chattering. Serge can pick out the starting-flare of 10th Battalion; he signals to Gibbs to fly towards it. As they make their first pass, the mirrors on the men's backs flash; by the time they've turned around and made their second, there's so much smoke around that none of the sky's luminescence makes its way down to the mirrors and back up to Serge; by the third he can't even see the men. He sounds his klaxon, but its noise is lost amidst gunfire. He can hear another machine's klaxon sounding too, and presses his own again, to let it know he's nearby; other planes apply their horns as well, like ships in fog. Serge taps Gibbs on the back and shouts:

"Up again."

Gibbs points to his ear and shakes his head: too loud to hear each other now. Serge jerks his finger upwards. As they climb out of the smoke, he tries to send a signal to his ground station, but finds he can't: the hurled-up earth has gritted up the spark set, jamming its parts. When he bangs it on the cockpit's side in an attempt to shake the earth out, the whole tapper-key comes loose; trying to reattach it, he severs a wire. Gibbs is holding a position at three thousand feet, awaiting instructions, but Serge has none to issue. His spark set's demise is giving him a strange, almost electric sensation: it feels as though he were flying naked, as though a layer of insulating hardware and a softer, inner one of message-lace had suddenly been stripped away and he himself were the thing riding the air's frequency, pulsing right up against it. Despite his diacetyl-morphine-induced languor, he begins to feel a buzzing in his groin again. More blood runs to it as Gibbs plunges back towards the smoke. Tilted back and facing upwards, hardening, Serge can see why Gibbs is diving: a whole Jasta has descended on the SE5s. The colourful German planes and the more sombre English ones turn around each other in confused whirlpools, their vapour trails forming a vortex that's drifting to the side with the wind. They look like bees swirling around a honey jar. One of the English machines is on fire. Two of the German ones have broken loose and are now hurtling downwards.

"Albatroses," Gibbs shouts back to him, his voice amplified and made audible by fear.

As they sink through the smoke-cloud, Serge sounds his klaxon again, then looks down. The battlefield's now strewn with fragments: of machine parts, mirrors, men. Legs, wedged in by earth, stand upright in athletic postures, crooked at the knee as though to sprint or straightened into sprightly leaps but, lacking bodies to direct and complement their action, remain still; detached arms semaphore quite randomly across the ground; torsos, cut off at the waist, mimic the statues of antiquity. Gibbs flies above them for a while, then pulls the plane up and takes them back for a peep above the smoke. No sooner have they cleared it than Serge hears a rhythmic tapping: it's as though a mechanic were standing beside the machine rapping on the fuselage to get their attention. The taps make the canvas on the plane's back section tauten and jump; little holes appear in a straight line along it. They look like a row of popper-buttons springing open, starting at the tail and advancing towards his cabin, which they then move across as well, pocking its floor. A mass of shadow runs behind them, bringing with it a loud sound he doesn't recognise. As the sound climaxes and falls off, Serge looks up and sees, coming from where the sun should be, a wave of brightly-coloured metal hurtling downwards. It sinks beneath them; he swivels his head to follow it, and watches the mass resolve itself into the shape of an Albatros. It's turning below them, getting ready to come back; then it's climbing behind them, just out of range, amassing altitude so it can dive again. Colours radiate from its underbelly—the central part of which, the lower wing, has words painted across it. He can't make the words out, but he can see some of their letters: there's a *K*, an *m*, a *c* . . .

"Shoot at them when they come back!" Gibbs shouts, pointing to the Lewis gun.

Serge turns away and gazes at the Albatros as it turns gracefully above them. He looks at the gun: should he shoot? The German aeroplane is beautiful, elegant and agile; and it's selected them, of all the men and machines in the battlefield, to bear down on with its colour and its words—as though, like an annunciating angel, it had a message to convey, one just for them, for him. It's hovering five hundred feet above him, shedding speed, nose angling downwards; then it starts diving, its front spitting out streaks of yellow and orange, like a splashing paintbrush. More buttons pop along the fuselage; struts leap out from between the wings. It passes above the RE8 this time; as it does, the phrase painted on its lower wing streaks by again: the *m* is actually two *n*'s; the *c*'s part of the sequence *sch,* like in *schwer.* Serge sees a *t,* then loses sight of the plane; Gibbs, meanwhile, turns, then turns again, trying to shake it off their tail.

"Shoot!" he screams back at Serge.

Serge isn't going to shoot. He feels tranquil, passive. He wants the Albatros to come and pluck him from his nest and carry him away in a long, whispered rush of consonants. He still can't see it—but a set of bumps rising from the undercarriage lets him know it's coming back at them from the shark angle, the blind spot. The bumps are followed by a jolting at his back. He turns around to see Gibbs's shoulders first straighten suddenly, straining against the belt, then slacken and slump forwards. One of the plane's wings snaps; the machine lists to the side as the landscape below it starts elevating. As the smoke cloud rises up to meet them, the Albatros looms once more into Serge's vision. It hovers above them, the one bright object in the darkened sky, the phrase written across its lower wing now finally legible. Painted in black, Gothic script on a red background, it reads:

Kennscht mi noch?

The phrase stays with him as the sky falls away. It seems to flicker all around the machine, seeding the air with a significance whose essence eludes him. "Do you still recognise me?" the painted words have asked him. Tilting his head back as he waits for earth to gather him, he wonders who the "me" is, or what time, what tense, what moment might be indicated by the "still." The RE8 flattens out a little. A last dark, elongated kite balloon flashes by, burning. The plane hits something, but it's not the ground: it feels more like a buffer, a soft boundary beyond which the air has a heavier, slower texture. He can feel this texture all around him too—see it as well: it's silken, swirling about his shoulders and enveloping the whole machine, thin fibres at its rear expanding and contracting in the slipstream like a jellyfish's tentacles, shooing the world away. Within its canopy, the humming of the plane's struts and wires is amplified and softened; light is filtered, made to glow. Then the light dims, the sound fades out and there's nothing.

iii

When he wakes up, there's brown fabric covering his vision. It's right up against his eyes: a diagonal grid that stays still as he glances left and right. Inhaling, he breathes in again the rich and honeyed smell of cunt. Touching his hand to his face, he feels the thread of Cécile's stocking. The peep-holes have slipped down towards his mouth; he gouges a finger into one of them and tears the whole thing off. His view's still blocked by fabric, though: the white, silky stuff that wrapped the machine as it fell forms a sac around it. Serge runs his eye down past the tail, to where the sac's thinner fibres are—and sees, at their end, lying on the ground fifteen feet away, a human figure in a harness.

"It's a parachute," he says to Gibbs. "We hit a parachute on the way down."

His voice is strangely muffled: he can hear himself—but only silently, inside his head. Gibbs doesn't seem to hear him either: he doesn't answer—or if he does then his voice isn't loud enough for Serge to pick it up. Serge turns round. Gibbs is dead: stuff from his chest is spattered about the cockpit. Serge unclips his own harness, levers himself from his seat and drops to the silk-coated ground. Pushing his hands against a roof and walls of silk, he makes his way along the soft, white tube towards the opening by the strings and, emerging through this, prods the man tied to them. He's dead too, head split open from its impact against the earth. He must have jumped from the burning kite balloon, only for his parachute to be run into by their machine and carried along horizontally—or, rather, on a diagonal descent—dragging him with it.

Serge looks around him. The landscape is nondescript, brown and broken, like all the front's terrain. Twenty or so yards away, a section of it jumps into the air as a shell lands on it. The explosion is silent: it's as though he were watching one of Widsun's films. Even the rushing air and the earth clods it brings smacking against his face carry no sound in their

174

wake. He traps one of the clods against his skin, holds it out and inspects it. Viewed from this close, the earth takes on a similar resolution to the one it has in those photographs he shoots for Pietersen, pockmarked and lined with patterns. He lets it drop, from sympathy: it's been churned up enough. Watching it fall past his groin, he realises he's still got an erection. He looks about him, embarrassed, before remembering that there's no one else around. He could be anywhere. The fact that they hit a German kite balloon's occupant, or ex-occupant, on the way down suggests they were heading east, in which case . . . Should he torch the machine? As he wonders this, the pressure grows inside his ears—and with it comes, at last, a sound. It's a quiet one, resonating at a low frequency and emerging from inside the parachute: an electric buzzing spilling out of the inflated pod. He heads back through its opening towards the broken wings and bent propeller blades that, like a set of irregular tent-poles, hold the structure up. The buzzing's coming from the cockpit—from the back half of it, his half . . .

Pulling himself up again and peering in, he sees that it's his spark set making it. The six-volt battery has fallen from its spot and half-smashed on the cabin's floor; the wires issuing from it are sparking intermittently; and the unregulated flow of electricity into the tapper key is making the latter twitch, as though the current—and with it, the entire signalling regime—had been reversed and the set were now receiving rather than transmitting. Serge reaches past it for the medicine box, then realises that the two phials he picked up from the houseboat are still in his pocket. He takes one out, rolls back his sleeve and injects its contents into his forearm, then leans over Gibbs and grabs hold of his Verey gun.

"Silk pyjamas."

Did he say that or just hear it in his muffled head? He looks at the buzzing radio set again. The sparks are spreading further down the wires now, spreading too across the cockpit's floor, where engine oil is flickering alight. Serge drops the Verey gun, yanks what remains of the transmitter loose, lowers himself to the ground once more and walks slowly down the tube again, then past the dead parachutist and across the churned-up landscape. He turns back after a while and, cradling the spark set in his arms, watches the parachute and machine burning. The silk turns black, then orange, then falls away to reveal the wooden skeleton beneath it blackening as well. Small collapses and eruptions take place within the flames' mass, but they make no noise: the only sound's the low-resonating buzzing which, despite the spark set being both smashed and disconnected, is still echoing inside his head. He stares at the flames for what could be seconds, minutes or hours, then turns again and walks away.

After a while he finds himself strolling beneath mutilated willows at the edge of what must once have been a picturesque country pond. The water, frosted over in parts, has a rust-brown texture laced with silver threads of mercury. Pieces of shell-casing, ripped and jagged, protrude from its surface. At its sides yellow, erect reeds tremble and shudder. Serge can't tell if it's wind or buffeting from ordnance fall making them move. He can't hear any rustling—but he does start hearing a high-pitched note, breaking through the buzzing in his head: it seems to come from somewhere else, somewhere exterior. Is it connected with the reeds, their oscillation? He can't tell. The ground around the pond is coated with military refuse and metallic dust, as though fragments of the sky had flaked off and fallen to earth. Birds are moving among these: jack-daws, crows and ravens, picking through the pieces with gestures as mechanical and irregular as the broken parts themselves. Smoke drifts around their beaks. As Serge comes near they all take off and fly in a long, funerary procession towards nearby woodland, their shadows strafing the ground.

He follows them. What draws him towards the woods isn't a reasoned need to find cover or hide, but rather the high-pitched note piercing his ears: it seems to carry from among the trees—to emanate from within their dense mass with a kind of intent, like an electric summons. The sound grows louder as he threads his way between the trunks, as though held in and concentrated by the canopies and branches, bounced back up by moss to linger at head height. Listening to it more carefully, he discovers that it's actually composed of several notes and pitches, weaving into and out of one another like the strands of interference you get when you nudge through the dial. When he stands still and tunes his ear to them more finely, the notes amalgamate into two trunk-tones: the high-pitched one he first picked up and, nestling within its sonic shadow, a deeper one that has the pitch of trumpets. Together, the two tones form a melancholy wail, like the long-drawn-out scream of a fall that never hits the surface towards which it's falling.

An animal darts past his feet and vanishes as soon as it appears. Was it a fox? A dog? It had something in its mouth. Serge, still cradling the broken spark set, presses on into the woods. More animals disperse as he comes near. They're all holding things between their teeth, grey morsels laced with scarlet; even the black birds perching in the trees pinch titbits in the beaks down which they peer at him disdainfully. He's come to a spot where all the trees are crippled: trunks riven, branches snapped, both scorched and covered in large patches of tar. Tar coats the ground in intermittent patches too, countering its winter hardness with soft, insulating accretions. The accretions grow more frequent as he treads towards a small clearing secreted among the trees: the tar-coat covers the floor of this almost completely. Men are sitting on the tar as though on a padded blanket, backs propped against the trees' bases, packs and weapons at their feet. There must be ten or fifteen of them, wearing German uniforms. They're all dead. They slump against the trunks like over-ripened fruit that's lost its shape, begun to rot. Their faces all wear grimaces, as though frozen in a grotesque laughter bordering on the insane. Serge looks at their mouths: some of the jaws are dislocated and hang loose; two of them have been ripped open by shrapnel wounds extending from the chest, or neck, or cheek; one has been blown off entirely, leaving a hole through which broken shards of jawbone poke.

The sound's loud here. The men's deformed mouths seem to be either transmitting it or, if not, then at least shaping it, their twisted surfaces and turned-out membranes forming receptacles in which its frequencies and timbres are unravelled, recombined, then sent back out into the air both transformed and augmented, relayed onwards. Their eyes, despite being empty of perception or reaction, seem electrified, shot through with a current that, being too strong for them, has shattered them and left them with a burnt-out, hungry look. Their clothes have streaks of red on them. The tar's black is streaked with red as well, just like the Albatros's fuselage. It's a bright red: a kind of scarlet, rippling across the tree trunks like an ensign fluttering in wind. It gives the tiny, overhung clearing a cosy glow that complements the sweet smell of tar and corruption lingering about its air. The sound vibrates about the air too, infusing the whole scene with what feels like a kind of heat: it seems as though, despite the cold, the earth were sweating, yielding up these phantoms, passing their bones and flesh on through its strata, up past layers of frosted mulch and tar, delivering them back to life, albeit in a dead form. They almost seem to move. One of them *is* moving: dragging himself upright against his tree trunk, then, placing one foot in front of the other, lurching forwards along a line that leads past Serge towards the clearing's far side.

". . . Engnis," the man tells him, not unkindly.

Serge smiles back apologetically. It was somewhere like "End this"—or perhaps, conversely, "Endless" . . . A new soldier appears and the others turn to him and talk. This one is more smartly dressed, an officer. He steps over to Serge and takes the spark set from him; as he does, the high-pitched noise stops suddenly and Serge can clearly hear the man say:

"*Zu Gefängnis.* Prison. You are prisoner."

iv

He's sent away from the frontier: eastwards, to the interior. Having ascertained that he's an officer, his captors group him with his peers and transport them initially in first-class carriages, then second-class, then third, downgrading their conveyance every hundred miles or so. Eventually they find themselves in cattle trucks. A German corporal and three privates stand guard above them, jerking and swaying in front of neat fields, canals, factories and towns that follow one another with a progression whose logic seems both perfect and impenetrable. Occasionally, they pause at stations; while they're handed bread and coffee, women stare at them malevolently from the platforms; as the train pulls off again, sliding past houses whose doors wear wreaths and crosses and whose windows, covered by black blinds, transmit in Venetian Morse the same message each time, Serge understands why. On every road, in every town and village, columns of soldiers pass by marching in the opposite direction, the neat stamp-and-click of their swift footfall drawing briefly into line with the rhythm of the steam and pistons' chug and hissing before disengaging, fading and dying away . . .

He gets passed through a series of processing stations and transit camps. At each one they ask his name and rank. His answer to the former question never fails to elicit a humorous comment:

"*Chafer?* You are *Insekt,* beetle?"

"Carrefax," Serge answers, stretching the *x* out into a long, steam-like release of breath.

"*Käfers?* Then you are more than one: many *Insekts!*"

After running through the fourth or fifth variation on this exchange, he finds himself inducted into an *Offizierslage* in Hammelburg. Ham-

179

melburg is a barracks town: the prison's just a section of the town that's been wired off from the surrounding streets. The dormitories in which the prisoners sleep eight or ten to a room line a cobbled square that's hemmed in by sharp-angled red- and brown-slate roofs rising above the yellow and red houses, tradesmen's premises and municipal buildings that jostle and collide with one another with Germanic closeness and compression. The guards who police the penned-in sector of the town are old, shoddily dressed, confused. Several of them limp; one of them's missing an eye. On the far side of the wire, in the same square, new recruits are drill-marched up and down all day long. Often, when the prisoners are lined up in the open during roll call, the recruits cast anxious glances their way, as though trying to catch a glimpse of what awaits them. Serge tries to smile back each time one of their eyes meets his, as though to reassure them that it's not that bad—until it strikes him that what's putting the fear into their faces might not be the enemy but rather their own veterans: the thought that they'll end up like *that* . . .

Roll-call is taken round the clock: in the square, in the dormitories, routinely first thing every morning, without warning in the middle of the night. When they're not standing to attention, prisoners mooch around, play bridge, attend (or deliver) lectures on a variety of subjects ranging from history and medicine to religion, or study French, German or Latin. Serge inscribes himself in Moreton's course on Problems in Philosophy.

"The history of our thinking on free will hinges around the question of determinism: are events pre-scripted, as it were—by God, our cells or an invisible engine driving history's course? And even if they are, are we still free to *choose* to do what we were destined to do anyway—standing face-to-face with its implications, in full awareness of its consequences? Hume thought so, and allowed this liberty to, as he put it, 'everyone who is not a prisoner and in chains.' "

"Our current situation kind of pisses over that one, doesn't it?" Serge asks.

"Not necessarily," Moreton answers, pushing his glasses up his nose's bridge, "not necessarily. To find our way round that we'd have to look to our captors' philosophical tradition. Rudolf Steiner has recently argued, after Schopenhauer, that we're free when we're able to bridge the gap between our sensory impressions of the outer world, on the one hand, and, on the other, our own thoughts."

"So if I think of barbed wire fences, then I'm free?"

The nose wrinkles as the glasses slide down them again. "Well, I suppose, if you put it that way: yes."

The men in the *Offizierslage* are definitely free to queue—for food, mail, laundry, medical supplies or almost anything else. Queues form around the camp at the slightest provocation. One day, bored, Serge persuades two pilots to line up with him in front of the door to a coal cellar just for the hell of it: within five minutes twenty other men have fallen into line behind them without even asking what it is they're queuing for. The food queues break down into two types: those for the camp food with which all prisoners are provided, and those for the food sent in Red Cross parcels to individuals and distributed among recipients' compatriots. The French eat the best: their tables are adorned with marinated mackerel, cold chicken, foie gras, peas and ham, all sent in tins. The Russians eat the worst: sustained by nothing but dried fish, they spend their time and energy building a chapel with ad-hoc interior decorations. Serge visits it one day to find they've fashioned icons out of wood splinters and strips of cloth, using dirt, resin, wax and blood to paint emaciated saints with sorrowful faces: eyes turned ever upwards, importuning the skies for delivery, or at least for an explanation of their circumstances. The English are somewhere in between: they get sent tins of tongue, pork shoulder, broad beans, brawn, the odd plum pudding. All of them eat better than the guards, though, who are restricted to the very slop they serve out to the prisoners: turnip stew, broth with horse-meat in it, liquid cheese and nine-tenths of a loaf of black bread every week. They're visibly hungry. They make the prisoners kick back a little of their Red Cross supplies, but know better than to demand too high a cut: the parcels would stop coming if they did . . .

It's not just the guards who are hungry: townspeople habitually gather beneath a third-floor dormitory window overlooking Hammelburg's "free" sector to beg food from the prisoners, who toss hunks of their regulation black bread to them. Sometimes they'll throw in a chunk of meat, wrapping it in paper after removing it from its tin. The tins themselves they never throw: these are precious.

"Why?" asks Serge as a lieutenant holds his wrist back when he makes to chuck one from the window on his first day in the camp.

"Tunnelling," the lieutenant nods back at him.

"You do that here too?"

"All the time, young fellow, all the time: what keeps us sane."

He's not overstating the amount of time spent tunnelling—although whether it keeps them sane or not is another question. On Serge's very first evening, and all subsequent ones, as soon as roll-call has been taken and the lights turned out, the men, moving with balletic deftness, cover the window with a blanket, light several candles, remove a bed from the room's corner, lift up two of the floorboards beneath it and, tying a long cord around the designated tunneller's feet, send him head-first into the hole armed with two empty tins to dig with. As the roll-call's fall and cadence is repeated in the dorms along the corridor one after the other, fainter and fainter every time, they watch the cord worming its way into the ground—two cords: a second, smaller string held in the burrower's hand is attached, Ting-a-Ling-style, to a third tin that's perched on a shelf back in the room. If the tunnel collapses or the tunneller begins to faint, he pulls on this, the tin falls and his comrades yank him back, feet first. That's the idea, at least. Yet more tins, bases all removed, have been laced together to form a loose tube: this is shoved down the hole as far as it will go, to provide air in the manner of a snorkel. It amuses Serge to see the vegetables on the tins' labels heading into the ground, in a long column, one after the other—as though, having shed the grit and lowness of their origins, become refined to the point of weightless, bulkless images, they'd now come full circle and were sinking back down to rejoin their dirty, material roots. The sound of hacking, scraping and panting spills from the tube's opening into the room's air; some tunnellers sing quietly to themselves, or strike up strange, subterranean monologues whose sense, if they had any in the first place, is distorted beyond any comprehension by the hollowed-out reaches along which they travel.

"Where does this tunnel go?" Serge asks one night as a man they all, despite his shortness, call "Lofty" toils away beneath them.

"Go?" the dormitory captain, a colonel named Craddock, counters.

"Where will it come out?"

"That's proscribed knowledge. Escapee Committee take care of all that. They dispense info on a firm need-to-know basis."

"Shouldn't it be 'Escaper Committee'?" Serge asks. "I mean, strictly speaking, the prison is the escapee, the thing escaped from. We're escapers—and in fact not even that, not having yet escaped. More like escaper-aspirants. Who are 'they,' anyway?"

"That's proscribed knowledge too."

"You mean you've never met them?"

"I'll have passed them in the square, chatted with them, played cards and so on. Perhaps we even share this dormitory with one or more of them. But their identity qua Escapee Committee members is at all times and in every circumstance withheld."

"Then how do you know which direction to dig in?"

"It's communicated to us via intermediaries, on a need-to-know basis, as I intimated. The committee have it all worked out: I've heard they've got a chart of all the gas-pipes, sewers and what have you, and are using those as guidelines—following them, crossing them, whatever. There's a logic to it all . . ."

The man listening at the door hisses and signals to them to restore the room to its original state. No sooner has the corner bed been slid back, candles snuffed out and men reinserted beneath sheets than a guard shuffles into the dorm and moves up and down the rows, counting heads. As he passes the bunk on whose top half Lofty should be lying, the man in the lower half pulls a string to make the dummy that's been placed above him roll over in its sleep.

"Did you see the way his hand flopped?" Craddock asks as soon as they're all up and at it again. "Wasn't realistic enough. We should stitch it to his face: that's how people sleep."

"Or have another string to control the whole arm," another man says.

A third, spurred by talk of strings, retrieves the alarm-tin from its hiding spot beneath the bed and returns it to its shelf.

"You okay down there, Lofty?" Craddock stage-whispers down the tube. He lowers his ear to it, then decides: "We'd better haul him up."

Lofty throws up across the floor when he emerges. Someone else goes down to bring up his loose earth, which they add to the mass stuffed in draws and cupboards, behind wall-panels, beneath other loose floorboards. As the weeks and months go by, it occurs to Serge that, far from removing earth between them and the outside world, they're adding it around them: digging themselves *in*, not out. Men throw up often when they emerge from the hole; several of them, over time, become too scared to tunnel. Not Serge: he likes being down there, for one reason more than any other: it's the only place in camp where he can masturbate. There's nowhere else you get the requisite solitude. He wonders if the others do that too: wonders if that's what lies behind the panting, or if the murmurs unravelling along the breathing tube are fragments of dialogues held in the dark with soft, imaginary mistresses . . .

He never gets brought face-to-face in full awareness with an Escapee

("Escape," he realises as spring runs into summer, would have avoided the inaccuracies of that term) Committee member, and by autumn has started harbouring doubts about their existence. Their logic, if there is one, is skewed: tunnels frequently run headlong into impassable sunken metal joists, or into one another, or surface in other dormitories, or even, on more than one occasion, cause small sections of the cobbled square to collapse while prisoners and guards are standing on it. One tunnel still in progress in November, not originating in his room, is rumoured among the inmates of several dormitories to have breached the camp's wire fence, although nobody will say which dorm it leads out of, where and when it will eventually surface or who will exit the camp through it— facts that lead Serge to suspect that it, too, might be no more than a collective daydream. He never finds out whether or not he's right: in February, by which time not a single prisoner has managed to escape, he's transferred to another camp.

This new one's several hundred miles away, in Berchtesgaden. He's moved around by rail again, one train after the other. The landscape changes: lowlands criss-crossed by canals give over to ravines along which brooks sparkle and fall. Sheep and cows become lopsided, grazing on sharp inclines; the shuffle and click of soldier columns is replaced by solitary figures weaving their way down hillside paths towards small stations, heading back from leave. The train starts groaning as it strains against the gradient; its puffs grow shorter and more frequent, as though it were running out of breath, which it could well be: the air does seem thinner. More refined too: Serge misses the smell of smoke, of oil and tar . . .

The *Offizierslage* in Berchtesgaden turns out to be just beyond it, separated by a stretch of rocky scrubland from the village above which it perches: used to be a monastery, one of the guards tells him. The guards here are more on-the-ball than their Trier counterparts. The officers are sharper too, but not unfriendly. The *Feldwebel* runs a bridge club composed mainly of his prisoners, jovially telling them they'd better not escape as it would break the fours up. He even lets them leave the camp—but only on parole. The parole system's so absurd and contradictory it could have been devised by one of Moreton's philosophers: prisoners are handed their freedom on condition they won't use it, and must pledge to this condition with their word—whence the convention's name. They trade this word against a pass that's issued to them at the front gate as they leave; on returning an hour or so later, they hand the pass back, and their word becomes their own again. For Serge, the whole practice belongs to the same order as the sleeping dummy: it's as though, each time he takes the word-card out, he duplicates himself and leaves a double behind as a marker. Or perhaps the other way round: *he's* the double, his sensations and encounters as he wanders round the village and the fields no more than dummy ones, hallucinations given the air of veracity by contractual and linguistic strings. He even dreams once that he's strolling around an airfield nestled in the monastery's shadow (in reality there is none), climbing into a machine, taxiing across the grass— all perfectly legitimately, sanctioned by parole—then, as he takes off, trying to explain to some vague, airborne invigilator that the word, *the* word, has altered, and now lies back in the camp with his stuffed simulacrum, leaving him at liberty to fly back to the front. The invigilator, still faceless, asks what the new word (password? keyword? call sign? it's not clear) is, posing the question by quietly whispering: *"Kennscht mi noch?"*

One day, during the second spring of his captivity, American prisoners arrive in the camp. They receive much better parcels than the others: salami from New York, ground beef from Chicago, endless medical supplies. Serge sets about befriending their dispensing medical officer, and trades several jars of honey and crab-apple jelly sent to him from Versoie against phials of diacetylmorphine.

"You like your sister, huh?" the dispensing officer, a Barney from Queens, New York, joshes him the third time he negotiates a trade-off.

"Sorry?" The question takes Serge aback.

"It's what the *Negroes* call it up in Harlem."

"Call what?"

"This," Barney answers, pointing at the phials. "Sister, dope, Big H: heroin. You don't call it that here? I mean in *Eng*land?"

"No," Serge answers him after a pause. "I don't think we do."

The arrangement becomes a regular one: every week Serge hands over to Barney the fruit of Versoie's trees and beehives, Barney hands over the goods, and sister roils and courses through his veins. Out on parole, he'll sit among the scrub, his mind at once both perfectly replete and empty. Airfields, tennis courts and cityscapes merge into and out of one another across contours of rock and hill. Gorse curls around his forearms; lichen stains his clothes: the landscape seems to penetrate his skin and grow inside him, replacing viscera and brain with heather, lavender and fern, as though he really were no more than a stuffed dummy . . .

The tennis courts, or at least one of them, have some basis in reality: there's one down in the village. Officers less lethargic than him play games on it regularly, while others look on, mingling with villagers whose resentment of the enemy's been pushed to one side by their need for food. This suits the prisoners just fine: they trade some of their tins (useless for tunnelling in this rocky terrain) against civilian clothes, which they then smuggle back into the camp and mix and match in covert fashion shows conducted with a view to finding what the French officers call *"un look"* that will enable them to sneak past the gate word-lessly and uncontracted. Serge, happy to spend whole afternoons watching the ball arcing back and forth across the gridded net and bouncing among painted lines, gets charged one day with slipping some of these clothes on under his own, but, too lazy to take his shirt off, pulls them on over it instead, an oversight that results in him getting caught out at the gate and sent, sisterless, to solitary for two weeks.

The first few days are dreadful, full of fits and fever. By the fifth these have subsided, leaving him wakeful and alert. He notices that two veins on his forearm have collapsed, like shallow tunnels. By the second week he feels quite good: resilient, self-sufficient—and besides, there are advantages to being alone. He spends the last three days of his confinement masturbating. There's a smell that seeps from the cell's walls, floor and ceiling when he does this, and only when he does: it's musty, earthy, old but somehow fresh at the same time. Although he always starts out trying to picture Cécile—her back, the blind, the brass knobs of her bedstead, wobbling shadows on her wall and broken eggshells—these images soon give way to new ones of tunnels viewed from the interior, of fruit and vegetables being returned to earth, of tins with strings attached . . .

By the time autumn's come round again, the *Lage*'s guards have become lax. They start going around without their uniforms, in civvies. They don't bother checking prisoners' parole cards, instructing them instead to collect them from and slot them back into a set of pigeonholes outside their cabin. "Punching the parole clock," the Americans call it. As the men sally out around the village, its inhabitants come up to them and, speaking in whispers even when there's no one there to overhear them, say:

"Kaiser kaput . . ."

The officers start wearing civvies too. They appear in camp less and less frequently, then withdraw from it completely, leaving a dwindling number of guards behind. In late October it's decided by someone or other, and communicated down to all the men, that the escape plan will be put into action. Two prisoners, dressed as local tradesmen, collars turned up to cover their faces, walk out of the gate. Not only does their exit go unchallenged, but their absence isn't even noticed in the following days. Two more men leave, disguised as cooks; then three more, hauling rubbish bins; then four, got up as nothing in particular. Then there's an exodus: men leave at will, realising that the remaining guards simply don't care enough to stop them.

Serge travels through the countryside with one other prisoner, a pilot from the 55th Squadron named Hodge. They stick to small paths and open fields, sleeping in ditches, pilfering from farmsteads clinging to the edge of hills: eggs, chickens, even dried maize. On the roads below them, they sometimes see troops marching away from the front. One day, they're sitting on a wooded slope watching a battalion of infantry cross a river, waiting until they've disappeared so that they can cross it in the other direction, when a British aeroplane, an SE5, appears overhead and starts strafing the soldiers. They all run for cover: some of them duck beneath the bridge's columns where these join the land; others throw their packs and rifles to the ground and plunge into the water; the majority of them, however, crawl up the very slope on which Serge and Hodge are sitting.

"English Offiz-ee-er!" Hodge says, a tad unwisely given what's just happened on the bridge, to the soldiers who surround them with bemused looks. No longer having guns to point at them, the soldiers just stand facing them, motionless. The sound of the SE5's engine dwindles as it goes in search of other prey. A sergeant, one arm streaked with blood, shows up.

"Wer sind die?" he barks at his men.

The men repeat what Hodge has told them. The sergeant steps right up to Hodge and, with the arm that's not hurt, pulls Hodge's coat back. He lifts his jersey up, then tugs the shirt loose from his trousers.

"Das ist keine Englische Uniform!" he growls.

"What's he saying?" Hodge asks Serge.

"You're not in uniform," Serge translates for him.

The injured sergeant looks at Serge, then yanks at his clothes too. He's civvy-clad as well, *cap-à-pied*.

"Deshalb sind sie Spione!" shouts the sergeant.

"What's he saying now?" Hodge asks.

"He says we're spies," Serge tells him. "Technically, he's right."

"So what does that mean?"

"I imagine we'll be shot."

He's spot on. The next morning, after being held in the same woods (the battalion camps there while it licks its wounds), Hodge and he are marched towards an area where the trees clear and the hillside flattens off.

"A pleasant location," Serge comments. They didn't pass it on the way through the woods yesterday, despite coming from the direction in which it lies.

Hodge doesn't answer. He's gone white. The sergeant who captured them presides over the ceremony. Still holding his bad arm in his good one, he orders his soldiers into line and, standing to the side of them, barks commands. As these mix with the click and shuffle of the rifles' pins being pulled back, Serge experiences a familiar buzzing in his groin. He looks up. The trees' trunks seem to incline slightly inwards as they rise. The sun's out: blocked by the trunks in places, it casts shadows on the ground. Among the mesh of twigs and moss an insect's moving, traversing the huge geometric patchwork of triangles and semi-circles formed by the alternating light and shade. At one point it pauses briefly, as though remembering something, and then trundles on. Finding its path barred a moment later at an obtuse angle by a twig that, to it, must seem as monumental as a fallen oak, the *Käfer* mounts this, then slips off again, then mounts once more. Watching it rise several times its own height, Serge gets a sense of elevation too: without leaving his body, he can look down on the whole scene. The arrangement of the soldiers, their position in relation to the clearing's edge, the shapes formed by their planted feet, the angle of the guns against their shoulders: somehow it all makes sense. Seeing it this way, as though from above, appreciating all its lines and vectors, its vertical and horizontal axes, and at the same time from the only place from which he can see it, the spot to which he's rooted, affords him, hand in hand with the feeling of rising, the vertiginous and pleasant sense of falling. It's not just him; everything seems to be falling back into this moment, even the sky: a breeze is touching down now, making the trees rustle. From among the sound's static there forms, like a clear signal, a familiar phrase:

Serge murmurs the words himself this time, letting them echo from him as though he were some kind of sounding box, hollow and resonant. As he does this, their meaning becomes clear; he knows exactly what he's saying. The question of who "me" is, or what time the "still" refers to, is no longer irksome: the dispersed, exterior *mi* previously held captive by the air, carried within its grain and texture, has joined with the interior one, their union then expanding to become a general condition, until "me" is every name in history; all times have fused into a *now*. It all makes sense. He's been skirting this conjunction, edging his way towards it along a set of detours that have curved and meandered like the relays of a complex chart, for years—for his whole life, perhaps—and now the conjunction, its consummation, tired of waiting, has found its way to him: it's hurtling back towards him on the line along which the bullets will come any second now. As he waits for the sergeant to give the command to shoot, Serge feels ecstatic.

The soldiers await the order too, with a perfect immobility, as though time had stopped, or run into itself so fully that it's breached and flooded its own borders, overflowed. They could have shot already; Serge could be already dead, his consciousness held back within some kind of intermission that's been opened up by the intricate physics of it all, or held suspended while time loops: it's just a matter of waiting for its rim to reappear and slide back down his vision; then he'll be gathered up by the overlap, disappear into its soft accretion. It's not until he notices some motion behind the soldiers that he realises there's a reason for the pause: a man, some other kind of sergeant, captain or subaltern, has appeared and called the first sergeant over to him. They're talking together. They talk for a while—and while they do, time seems to fall back into its old shape, the accretion to withdraw. It's not a pleasant feeling. Now the sergeant's talking to the firing squad: he mutters something to them and they drop their guns.

"Was passiert?" Serge asks, indignant.

It's the subaltern who answers him, in English:

"Finished. It's over . . ." He starts to walk away.

"What do you mean it's over?" Serge calls after him. "It hasn't even started yet!"

"War over," the subaltern shouts back across his shoulder.

Hodge drops to his knees and starts to cry. The soldiers begin walking away too, withdrawing. Superimposed across the clearing, as though projected there, Serge sees the image of a boat pulling off from a jetty at a point where several canals intersect: as the boat draws away, it takes the intersection with it, leaving him behind. For the first time in the whole course of the war, he feels scared.

"Hey!" he calls after the soldiers. "You can't do that. Wait!"

THREE

Crash

and interactions he might undergo—has dwindled so low that they could be itemised on a single sheet of paper. The exchanges he has in shops or in the post office, the movements and gestures these involve, seem so limited, so mapped out in advance, as to be predetermined—as though they'd already happened and were simply being re-enacted by two or more people who'd agreed to maintain the farcical pretence that this was something new and exciting. He's taken to walking out on the charade halfway through: stepping into, for example, the cheese shop, responding to the usual questions about how his parents or the Day School pupils are, agreeing how nice it is to be back after serving his country so bravely, admitting that the weather isn't quite doing what might be expected of it at this time of year, and so on—then, just as the shopkeeper shifts his stance above the rows of Lancashires and Stiltons and asks him what he'll have, turning round and pushing the door open, leaving its *ting!* hanging in the air behind him with the ruptured conversation. He once did this on three premises in a row—neighbouring ones: newsagent, baker, fishmonger—not out of maliciousness but simply to identify and breach the boundary of each situation, one after the other, to let it form a box around him which he could then step out of . . .

The same restless impulse sees him whipping up and down between Versoie and London. He enrols at the Architectural Association, then gets it into his head that he should study engineering instead; visiting Imperial College to sign up for this, he changes his mind and decides to follow in his sister's footsteps and join the natural science department; but, realising after a week that he has no aptitude for this discipline, he cools on the idea of being at Imperial at all and re-enrols at the AA. The restlessness, he comes to realise, is in truth an attempt to achieve its opposite: stasis. It's as though if he moves about enough, the world will fall into place around him. He experiences this most viscerally when driving across Salisbury Plain. Summoning up with his right foot a roar of snarling teeth and whirring cylinders, feeling beneath his hips the force of however many horses surging forwards, he watches the hedgerows run together till they blur into a tunnel of green speed. As this streaks by and the horizon accelerates towards him, it seems that he himself has become still—and, in these moments, he feels the same sense of satisfaction that he used to in the nacelle of the Rumpitee or the cabin of the RE8: the sense of being a fixed point in a world of motion. Holding this point against the landscape with the wheel, he pushes back into the air that screeches along his cheeks the word *fassen,* although this modulates amidst the noise sometimes to become *fast* or *faster.* The air carries a smell of lime—not the fruit but quicklime: the plain's been used as a giant burial ground for victims of the recent flu pandemic. The calcium oxide penetrates his nostrils and sinks deep into his lungs, making him feel alive and good.

It's not just Masedown's humans who've been struck down by disease: the mulberry trees at Versoie have caught an infection—something called Dieback. It takes the form of a fuzzy white mould, like the mould you get on stale bread, growing around the leaves and branches and extending out from these in wispy strands from tree to tree—as though the vegetation had, as Clair's heroes advocated, taken control of the means of production and, cutting out the parasites both insectoid and human who exploited its resources, started weaving for itself. The effects of this insurrection are quite tangible: most of the silk-making staff have been laid off; the spinning sheds are empty. Only Bodner can be seen from day to day: a small, lone figure trudging around the Mulberry Lawn with a bucket into which he dips a brush, painting the trees with disinfectant.

Serge's father has a theory about the cause of the disease: electric blighting.

"Under times of great stress or excitation," he explains to Serge over a glass of port one afternoon in Sophie's former lab, "the body emits an increased static charge. Police forces in America and France—" his finger points vaguely left to indicate the former place; his thumb jerks back over his shoulder for the latter—"are already making use of this phenomenon, measuring electric levels on the skin to ascertain when a suspect is lying."

"How does that blight our trees?" Serge asks.

"Blight—what?" his father barks. "Ah! Well, these electrical disturbances, once created, outlive the moment of their generation. If they remain behind indefinitely, they're detectable indefinitely, *n'est-ce pas?*"

"By what?"

"By what?" repeats his father. "Why, by detecting devices, of course. You of all people should know that!" He switches on one of the many radio sets lying on the shelves behind him. As it warms up, and familiar tweets and crackles start spilling from it, he turns the dial. The static gives over to music, then to static again, then to a voice reading what seem to be sports results. This is new, hearing voices over the receiver:

started this year, first of the new decade. Nowadays when you trawl the ether you get loads of little stations sending fully formed, audible words out to who-knows-where: songs, personal messages, phrases whose nature and purpose Serge can't work out but has spent hours listening to nonetheless, charmed by the sequences' sounds, the images that they evoke, their modulating repetitions. The string of names and numbers gives over to old-fashioned Morse beeps, then once again to static. His father, still turning the dial clockwise, turns to Serge and asks: "What do you think most of that stuff is?"

"What do you mean?" asks Serge.

"What is it?" his father repeats.

"It's messages," Serge answers.

"From when?" his father shoots back at him.

"From all over."

"I didn't ask from where: I asked from *when*."

"When? From now . . ."

"Aha!" guffaws his father. "That's where you're wrong—or, at least, not entirely right." He leans towards Serge and, his tone changing, tells him: "Wireless waves don't die away after the ether disturbance is produced: they linger, clogging up the air and causing interference. Half the static we've just waded through is formed by residues of old transmissions. They build up, and up, and up, the more we pump them out."

"And that's what's blighting our trees?" Serge asks him, incredulous.

His father downs his port and, reaching behind his work table, pulls out a device in which a needle sits behind glass within a hand-sized box.

"What's that?" asks Serge.

"An ammeter," his father answers. "Come with me."

Serge knocks his glass back hurriedly and follows his father out into the Mosaic Garden, where he holds the device out in front of him and, pointing to its face, announces:

"Low levels of static here. Just standard background discharge."

Serge peers at the needle, resting between zero and five micro-amperes. His father strides on into the Maze Garden and, holding the ammeter in front of him again, declares:

"Increasing. Five to ten."

He's right: the needle's started stirring. He strides on, through the Maze Garden's wall, across the gravel path and on towards the Mulberry Lawn, his upturned palm holding the instrument before his portly stomach all the while. Marching past Bodner, who ignores them as he daubs low-lying branches, he booms out triumphantly:

"Twenty to twenty-five!"

Serge peers around his forearm, and sees that the needle is, indeed, straining round to the dial's right-hand side.

"That's . . . I mean, how do you . . . ?" he stutters.

His father beams a satisfied smile back at him.

"Pretty conclusive, isn't it, my boy?"

"But . . . why here?" Serge asks. "My old mast was in the Mosaic Garden."

"Oh, you're being too literal," his father scolds. "Things move around, accumulate in ways we can't anticipate. Besides," he continues, eyes still on the needle as he takes two paces forwards, "I'm not even claiming that it's radio per se that we're detecting here."

"What else could it be?" Serge demands to know.

"I refer you back to what I said about the body and its discharges," his father tells him. "If the ones emitted by the brain are anything like the wireless waves that wend their way around the earth, they'll leave a trace for a considerable time after their creation."

"But that doesn't work," Serge says. "Transmissions *travel*. They go somewhere else, and then they're not here anymore."

"Ah: you're behind the times, my child." His eyes move from the dial to Serge, bathing him in pity. His left hand starts rising and sinking at an angle, cutting diagonal peaks and troughs in the air. "Imagine a ball bouncing around a dome, and hardly losing any energy in doing so—bouncing around the inside of a sphere and ricocheting off the outer surface of a smaller, solid sphere inset within the larger sphere . . ."

Serge cast his mind back to the tennis court in Berchtesgaden. He tries to roll its asphalt flatness up into a tarry sphere, to coil the outlying landscape into a larger, hollow ring around it, and to bounce a tiny, yellow ball between the two, but finds the mental space through which the smaller orb should move filling up with crackling gorse and heather. His father's explaining:

"Waves move around the globe, bouncing off the ionosphere. The ones that make their way through this—" his left hand, rather than angling down here, continues its upward rise until his arm's extended at full stretch—"go on until they hit some object out in space, and—" now the hand falls—"bounce off that. They all bounce back eventually, or loop round: everything returns." The hand starts looping as he carries on: "Now, if—*if*—the electric charges generated by our organisms move in the same way . . ."

"Then they can be detected later?" Serge completes his sentence in the interrogative.

"Why not?" his father answers. "In principle, it shouldn't be any harder. If a measuring device is present at a scene of great mental stress—and at the right time in the cycle according to which the electrical disturbances created by the event pass by the spot again, then the whole scene might be replayed, albeit in decayed form . . ."

The hand-loops slow down, then stop, and the two men stand in silence for a while, the regular plash and scrape of Bodner's paintbrush punctuating their thought. Then Serge says:

"If your theory is right, there's no reason why one spot should be any better than another."

"Why not?" his father asks.

"Because the ball bounces all around the space between the dome and sphere, hitting one place with as much force as it hits another. An event could replay elsewhere."

"I never said I had the whole thing worked out," his father harrumphs. "This is new research. Cutting edge. I'm corresponding with von Pohl about it on a weekly basis. He, like me, is of the opinion that it is these cycles of return that are responsible for lack of germination in certain ground areas. He's already done extensive research on the subject. I, for my part, have suggested to him that the curious groups of three staccato signals that one commonly picks up amidst the interference on one's receiver are none other than the echo of Marconi's first three 'S' signals, transmitted on—"

"It's true," Serge interrupts. "There's often three beeps in the background. But that doesn't mean—"

"—on the twelfth of December, 1901," his father concludes, adding: "If I'm right, the implications are enormous."

He's started walking away from the mulberry trees as he speaks. Serge follows him across the lawn and through the Crypt Park's gates. As he strides through the long grass, his father's still holding the ammeter out in front of him.

"Imagine," he confides to Serge, lowering his voice as though they were being overheard, "just imagine: if every exciting or painful event in

history has discharged waves of similar detectability into the ether—
why, we could pick up the Battle of Hastings, or observe the distress of
the assassinated Caesar, or the anguish of Saint Anthony during his great
temptation. These things could still be *happening,* right now, around us."

He pauses, and looks down at the ammeter before lowering his voice
right to a whisper as he says:

"We could pick up the words, the very *vowels and syllables,* spoken
on the *cross . . .*"

His voice trails out in a hiss. Serge peers down at the needle once
more: it's veered way over to the right side of the dial, past forty. He
looks up again, letting his gaze sweep the Crypt Park. As it does, he
seems to detect a general static hovering round its grass and trees: a static
through whose reaches, it strikes him for some reason, bounce the cries
of all the men he's killed—ranged guns on, strafed, pinpointed with pho-
tography, failed to protect from shark-bite, snagged from their cush-
ioned downward drift and slammed into the earth. He closes his eyes for
a moment, and sees, behind the static, an operator: a female one, sitting
at some kind of switchboard shaped like an outlandish loom.

This ghostly operator's face is mirrored in those of the Day School
pupils. These have changed since he left for the war—grown older, been
replaced—but seem strangely familiar, even the new ones. It works both
ways: a sense of recognition seems to flicker over the faces when they
meet his, as though their owners were somehow privy to what happened
out in France and Germany, could hear it rebounding round the reaches
of their deafness. Bodner too: in his immense indifference to almost
everything around him there seems to lie a tacit understanding and
acceptance of anything Serge might have undergone, as though he'd
undergone it too. Perhaps this is because Bodner, unlike the shopkeepers,
or Dr. Learmont, or each and every member of the stream of visitors who
pass by Versoie, makes no demand to have Serge's adventures recounted
to or summarised for him. He chews his tongue-stump like he always
used to, shunts wheelbarrows from one garden to another, makes tea for
Serge's mother, all just as before . . .

His mother's aged. She looks depleted, like a silkworm that's secreted
all it can. Her eyes have sunk into their sockets; her cheeks have contracted around her jaw and cheekbones. Despite having no production
line to oversee, she still spends long stretches of time inside her store-
room, itemising the few remaining silks, doodling designs for new ones

to be made once the blight lifts, or sitting at her low table staring into space. Serge joins her there most afternoons: they now take tea together. When the weather's nice they adjourn to one or other of the gardens and sit there in silence, untroubled by the bees and flies that hover around them, land on them, take off and land again quite nonchalantly, confident in the knowledge that they won't be swatted off.

ii

Serge's London flat is in Bloomsbury, on Rugby Street. It's on the second floor, above a dairy shop. Each morning he's awoken by the rattle of glass bottles and the tap of hooves, mingling with men's voices as they rise through his dreams to break their surface like the tentacles of some primordial kraken. He stops off around the corner for his breakfast, in a Turkish café on Lamb's Conduit Street: a syrupy, layered baklava. Sick children, let out of Great Ormond Street Hospital on parole, are wheeled by like the cripples were in Klodĕbrady. Sometimes their parents or nurses stop and buy them pastries, which the children never seem to enjoy much. Their faces have the look of old people's: disillusioned, sad, resigned. *Sins of the fathers,* Serge thinks as he watches them each day. Sucking walnut pieces from the gaps between his teeth, he strolls through Russell Square Gardens, trying to work out the logic governing the fountains' spurting sequences (a task to which he sets his mind obsessively for as long as it takes to wander past them, but instantly forgets as soon as he's left the square), then skirts the stone lion-guarded rear wall of the British Museum and, finally (and always anticlockwise), follows the fence-rails round the closed garden in Bedford Square until their long ellipse deposits him a few yards from the Architectural Association's front door.

Mornings are taken up by lectures. Theodore Lyle, FRIBA., holds forth in the ground-floor seminar room on the influence of ancient Greece on the architecture of the Roman, mediaeval and—to cut a long list short—all subsequent periods:

"The modern tendency," he declaims without notes, turning to face the students from plan drawings of the Parthenon and Hephaesteum into which sketches of peripteral and prostyle columns, metopes and triglyphs are inset, "is to consider these structures as ruins rather than as functioning buildings. The temples, as they present themselves to us today, stand stripped of their original stucco, colour and so on. What we lose is the effect of reflected light flowing over the smooth, coloured wall surfaces, across the bronze grills and balustrades, the gold, ivory and precious stones. I want you, when contemplating the incomplete edifices of the Attic and Hellenic periods, to turn back the clock and think of them as *under* construction, not beyond it . . ."

Fittingly, the refurbishment of the room in which these thoughts are being delivered is not yet complete. Window-sills stand upright in the corner, waiting to be affixed to the wall; cornicing smells of wet plaster, floorboards of fresh varnish: the school's only just moved premises from Tufton Street. The canteen downstairs is still being painted. Students show off their command of building structures as they lunch in it:

"This sausage is like a fluteless column," one says as he prods his toad-in-the-hole.

"Then my poached egg is a gilded saucer dome, rendered in bird's-eye perspective," says another, not to be outdone. "What have you got, Carrefax?"

Serge looks down at his plate: all he's got is a roll and a slab of butter.

"A burial mound, with gravestone on the side," he answers.

He never eats much for lunch. In the afternoons they're meant to do site visits—cathedrals, schools, train-stations and the like, producing sketches—but he usually ducks out of these and slinks off towards the web of streets that lurk within the triangle formed by Shaftesbury Avenue, Charing Cross Road and the north edge of Leicester Square. He first stumbled across the area when he went to Mrs. Fox's Café in Little Newport Street to meet a mechanic who'd offered to fix a minor problem with his father's car (he'd brought up his trunks in it the week before; his father was to drive it back the following week). The man had procured a machine part at a knock-down price, and brought it to the café swathed in a sheet which he unwrapped as though it contained contraband, which it effectively did. Most of Mrs. Fox's clientele seem to be criminals of one sort or another. They sit at tables nursing single coffees for hours on end, communicating with their fellow customers in nods and murmurs. Serge sometimes spends whole afternoons in here, drawing plan sketches of imaginary spaces. He likes the ambience: the sense of being in some kind of nether world whose air is rich with covert signals . . .

One day in Mrs. Fox's, Serge finds himself in the corridor off the main tea-room, in the company of a woman of about his age. The corridor is narrow; Serge squeezes past her, tries the bathroom door, then realises that she, too, is waiting. He smiles at her as though to say as much, and she smiles back—and as she does, her nose wrinkles to execute a type of sniff he recognises all too well. It's an energetic, forceful sniff, one that's at odds with her full, healthy complexion and the absence from her face of any cold-like symptoms. His smile changes into a knowing and complicit one; hers does the same, the eyes above the curling lips illuminated in a way that, although he's never seen another set of eyes lit up like that, is also instantly familiar to him.

"Lots of snow in London at this time of year," she says.

It's autumn—a warm one. Serge answers:

"Snow's fun."

A flushing sound emerges from the bathroom, followed by a thin man in a cap and waistcoat. In unison, Serge and the girl look down and press themselves against opposing walls to make way for him; when the man's gone, she takes Serge by the sleeve and pulls him into the bathroom behind her. There's an outer washroom in here (a *pronaos* area, it occurs to him, would be the technical term for it) and, half-separated from this by a stall, an inner toilet *(cella)*. She takes a vanity case from a pocket in her skirt and, handing it to Serge, says:

"Do the business. I've got to pee."

With that, she disappears into the stall. Carefully, Serge opens up the vanity case, taps a small bunch of the white powder it contains onto the counter beside the sink, and separates it out into two lines. A trickling sound comes from the toilet, strengthening into a steady, leisurely cascade.

"What do you do?" her voice calls out to him above it.

"I study architecture," he calls back as he takes a banknote from his wallet and starts rolling it into a tube. "How about you?"

"Theatre."

"You study it?"

"Study it? Why would I do that?"

"I don't know. It seems you can study anything these days."

"Well, I don't study. *Under*study sometimes . . ."

"Understudy?"

"I'm an actress."

The cascade dwindles to a trickle, then stops. There's a rustling, the sound of fabric being hoisted, then a flushing; then she's out again, inspecting the two lines he's made. He hands her the banknote.

"After you."

She takes it, pushes her hair from her face and bends over the counter to sniff the cocaine. She throws her head back, neck straining towards him, and hands back the note. After he's snorted his line they stare at one another, flushed, in silence for a few seconds.

"Well," she says.

"Well," he repeats. There's another pause, then he tells her: "I've got to pee as well."

"Come join me for a coffee afterwards," she says, heading for the corridor again.

He does. Her name is Audrey. She turns out to be almost exactly his age, born in '98. She's "currently appearing," as she puts it, in a musical comedy called *The Amazonians*.

"It's playing at the Empire," she tells him, "just round the corner from here. I can get you a ticket if you'd like to see it."

Serge accepts the offer. The following evening, he presents himself at the theatre's box office and is handed an envelope on the front of which someone, perhaps Audrey, has misspelt his name so that it reads the way his father speaks it: "Surge." Opening it, he finds an upper-circle ticket, and, after purchasing a programme from a liveried young lady on the staircase, takes his seat. The theatre's pretty full. Most other people seem to have come in twos or threes: there's the occasional conventional man-woman couple, but many more pairs and groups of women unaccompanied by men. They talk to one another loudly, smoking, laughing, exuding an air of masculinity. Serge flips through the programme. On the inside cover there's an advertisement for Good Printing, proclaiming that the Finest House in London for Commercial Typesetting, Lithography and Account Books is the House of Henry Good and Son. Serge wonders if that's their real name, or whether the father and son exist at all. Carrefax Cathode: his father never mentioned that plan again. Maybe Henry lost a child, too, in the war. Serge thinks of ink and ribbons, floating letter-blocks. On the next page the cast are listed: Serge runs his eye down the column, past the principal, then secondary parts, and on into the chorus. Finding Audrey's name there, in the smallest print, makes him feel fond of her, more touched by her invitation than he would have been if she'd been one of the show's stars. The next page carries a "historical note" about the production:

Far from simply being mythical creatures,

it explains,

Amazons are in fact figures of genuine historical record. Dwelling in Scythia, they were revered throughout the ancient world for their fierce, war-like character. Though their by-laws forbade marriage and, indeed, all other forms of congress with men, an annual excursion to the neigh-bouring all-male Gargarean clan furnished them with daughters enough to extend their line. Male children born of such trysts were variously returned to their fathers, put to death or sent out into the world to fend for themselves . . .

His reading's interrupted by the dimming of the theatre's lights. The band start playing; the curtains draw back to reveal a magnificent court in which all tasks—guarding the ruler, fanning the ruler, being the ruler—are carried out by women. The court burst into song, lauding their queen, Penthesilia, warning putative male English suitors that she's not much of a one for Anglophilia, and would-be pretenders to her throne that a single blow from her can killya. Penthesilia introduces her sisters Antiope and Hyppolite, who sing a short, plaintive duet about every man they ever thought was half-alright turning out to be a dope. Penthesilia answers their complaint by summoning onto the stage a cho-rus of female soldiers holding bows and arrows, little-round-Giles-style. Audrey's one of these. Thrusting their weapons aloft, they launch into a rousing anthem:

Oh, of Thracian and Spartan,
Of suits tweed or tartan,
We've all had our fill. (How much more can we kill?)

Frenchmen and Italians
From chariots and stallions
Have fallen before us. (They bore us! they bore us!)

Trojans, though cogent,
Don't impress us. No, gent-
lemen, be you Gentile or Jew,

Whatever your qualities,
Your mores or polities,
We'll get along fine without you.

For a girl today
Doesn't have to say
"I do" as the church bell rings . . .

Who needs a man
When you're an Amazonian?
We're keeping abreast of things!

There are two more verses, each rounded off by the "abreast" refrain. An anachronistic newspaper vendor-girl then enters and announces the outbreak of another war, which the soldiers promptly set off to and win quite easily, bringing back harems of female prisoners whom they quickly convert to their Amazonian ways. Twenty or so minutes into the production, Serge is expecting a male hero to wash up on the Scythian shore and introduce a basic conflict into the prevailing orthodoxy, but no such event takes place: instead, the play runs through a gamut of light-hearted sketches in which aspects of contemporary London life— hailing a taxi, ordering in restaurants, navigating the new telephone-number system—are satirised through a thin Amazonian veil. He loses interest; when Audrey's not on stage, he flips his way further through the programme, his eyes having by now become accustomed to the auditorium's lighting. There's an advertisement for Osram Lamps ("Brilliant, Economical, Lasting, Strong, Sold by All Leading Electricians, Ironmongers and Stores"), and one for War Seals. Initially, he misunderstands this second term and pictures a blubbery, black-metal object, a hybrid between sea-lion and submarine. On the next page there's a notice advertising Aerial Joy Rides above the capital, taking off each day from Croydon Aerodrome. For a moment, Serge is transported back to Kloděbrady: standing with Lucia by the weir as the prehistoric aeroplane buzzes above them; then Kloděbrady's ground-plan—the interlocking lines formed by its avenues, the circles of its mausoleums' roofs, the inner and outer squares made by the castle walls and the meandering path leading from these to the river, past the boathouses and on towards the forest—morphs in his mind into a mesh of trench-grids, paths leading through scorched woods to ruined villages and vacant ground scarred by blast marks. He imagines taking a pleasure flight over a war-zone, looking down on all the killing from above; then, glancing again towards the stage on which another battle has commenced, reasons to himself that perhaps that's just what he was doing in France day after day: watching it all from the upper circle, for his pleasure. Joy Rides: he recalls the way the seed fell from him that time, arcing over the plane's tail . . .

He heads backstage after the show to look for Audrey, and finds her amidst a clutter of horse-heads, silhouette-outlines of vanquished cities, false restaurant interiors and two-dimensional cars.

"I was in a play with a car once," Serge tells her as she pecks him on the cheek.

"You've acted?" she asks.

"Only as a child."

"I bet you were as sweet as sugar," she says. "Wait for me. I'll take you to the Boulogne: the whole gang's going there."

The gang have a dining room to themselves, on the Boulogne's top floor. Serge hears them as soon as he and Audrey enter the restaurant: they're singing the "abreast" song, raucously and a capella. As Audrey presents him to her fellow chorus-girls (the likes of Penthesilia, Hyppolite and Antiope seem to be dining elsewhere), they emit war-like whoops and whistles, then slide over to make room for them. Waiters bring out plates of chicken, lamb and fish, but these are merely nibbled at, passed around and played with as carafe after carafe of wine is knocked back. Pretty soon the table looks like one of *The Amazonians*'s battlefields, post-battle. Audrey's friends drape their arms around each other's shoulders, laugh and caress one another. Cigarette cases and purses change hands; trips to the bathroom are frequent.

"You come here every night after the show?" Serge asks.

"We start here, then move on to the 52," Audrey tells him. "Here, go powder your nose."

She hands him her vanity case; he heads off to the bathroom too. When he comes back the girls are getting ready to leave.

Just hailing a taxi
Is Amazonomachy!

several of them trill outside. They find cabs eventually, and ride the short distance to Gerrard Street. A small crowd is hovering around the door of number 52; they stride belligerently through this, are whisked en masse by the doorman down the club's narrow staircase and ushered towards several of the dance floor's tables, where they set up camp. The room has long, much-dented floorboards. At one end a stage rises roughly the same distance above the floor as Schoolroom One's podium at Versoie. A jazz band is playing on this: four men—one Indian, one West Indian, two white—frenetically vibrating as they clasp their trumpets, saxophones and drum-sticks, as though these were wired straight into electric currents lurking beneath the wood. Behind them, on the wall, a moon winks out at the clientele; around the moon are planets: Saturn with its rings, red Mars, another one that could be any in the solar system or beyond; and, interspersed among the planets, cat-faces, leering like primitive masks. Trellises extend from each side of this scene and run down the club's side-walls, trailing green foliage. Flowers are laid out on the surface of each table, in small glasses.

Champagne is ordered, and consumed. Some of the girls start dancing. They dance with one another: there are men in here, but not that many; at least half the couples on the floor are women. They vibrate like the musicians, their whole upper bodies shaking like the pilots' used to after flights. Balloons float above them, bouncing off their heads and shoulders. Cocaine is sniffed at tables here, quite openly. After serving him up a snuff-sized pinch from the back of her hand, Audrey leans across to Serge and says:

"Let's go to mine."

They leave, and wander down to Piccadilly Circus. While Audrey hunts down a cab, Serge stares up at the giant electric advertising hoardings: hundreds and thousands of lightbulbs—brilliant, lasting, strong, pulsing back to life again and again as they scrawl the names of the *Evening News*, of Venus Pencils, Monaco and Glaxo out against the sky. The G of "Glaxo" has a swoosh beneath it, a huge paraph forming from left to right as though being written out in pen-strokes, like a signature, each bulb a drop of ink, then disappearing and re-forming. All the names fade into the black and reappear, signing themselves obsessively against oblivion. Only the tyre beneath the word "Firelli" stays illuminated constantly, its rim-circumference, spoke-radii and hub-centre anchoring the elevated and abstracted spectacle in some kind of earthly geometry. Beneath the hoardings cars stream by with their headlamps on, barges of light flowing in the darkness. One of them's detached itself from the stream and pulled over.

"Marylebone," Audrey tells the driver.

They start kissing in the taxi. They snort more cocaine. Audrey lets Serge slip down her dress's shoulder; while he strokes her upper breast she runs her hand over his hardening crotch. Her flat, like his, is on the second floor. It's strewn with stockings, blouses, camisoles. Clearing some space on a divan while she goes into the small kitchen to fetch two glasses of whiskey, Serge finds a song-sheet marked with pencil annotations; perusing it, he learns that, in the original draft of the "abreast" song, "of suits" was "in suits" and the line "Your mores or polities" was the vastly inferior "Your offers of jollities." Beneath this sheet lies a flyer for a weekly spiritualist meeting taking place in Hoxton Hall. These papers and all other paraphernalia are swept to the floor as Audrey takes her place on the divan beside him, passing him his whiskey. They take one sip each, then continue where they left off in the taxi. She removes his clothes herself, firmly unbuckling his belt and yanking down his trousers. When they're naked he tells her to turn round.

"Why?" she asks.

"I like it that way," he replies.

Afterwards, as they lie on the divan, she makes quiet sniffing noises. Serge thinks it's the cocaine at first, but realises, as the small, short sniffs continue, that it's him she's sniffing at, his chest.

"You smell like my brother," she says.

"Is that good?" Serge asks.

"Yes," she answers. "I always liked Michael's smell."

"You don't anymore?"

"I doubt he smells as good these days," she tells him. "He's been dead for three years."

"The war?" Serge asks.

"Verdun," she replies. "We've had contact since, though."

"How?"

"Through séances." Her finger draws a circle on his chest, as though sketching a group of sitters round a table. "He's not always there—quite rarely actually. But it's always good to go."

"In Hoxton, right?"

"How do you know?"

"I'm psychic."

She snorts derisively; her fingers clench into a fist and thump his chest. His own hand reaches down and, rustling through the below-divan debris, hoists into view the flyer.

"Oh, of course!" she giggles, her hand softening and stroking his chest better again. "I'll take you sometime if you like. It's really good."

Serge thinks of his father's theories about static residues, bouncing electric waves. He's got the ammeter right here in London, in his flat: his father asked him to take readings at various spots around the city, a task he's signally failed to carry out . . .

They try to sleep but can't: the cocaine's made them jittery. Audrey offers to go and get some veronal to help them come down from it, but Serge has a much better idea:

"Do you know where to find heroin?"

"Oh, Becky's into that," she says.

"Becky?"

"The one who chopped off the Sumerian warrior's head. She was sitting across from you in the Boulogne."

"You think she's still up?"

"Only one way to find out."

They take a taxi to Bayswater. Becky is up, but has no heroin. She knows where they can get some, though: a woman named Zinovia or Zamovia in Primrose Hill.

"She runs a kind of salon," Becky tells them.

It's mid-morning by the time they find themselves riding across town in yet another taxi. As they pass through the West End Audrey makes them stop so that she can pick up a pair of ballet shoes from Arthur Frank's.

"You like them?" she asks, slipping the shoes on and straightening her feet against the driver's partition as the cab pulls off again.

"Dr. Arbus buy them for you?" Becky half-sings. Audrey nods.

"Who's Dr. Arbus?" Serge asks.

"Her mentor," says Becky in a mock-stern voice.

"Protector," adds Audrey, equally faux-solemnly.

"Instructor," Becky elaborates, nodding slowly.

The two girls start laughing. Serge laughs too, although he doesn't get the joke, and looks out of the window. Streets are growing leafier, houses bigger and smarter. They chug uphill for a while, then stop beside a house whose entrance is held up by light-blue columns (Ionic, Serge deduces as they wait between them for admission). A servant opens the door; Becky enters into an exchange with him whose phrases don't make sense to either Serge or Audrey but result, like combination lock-dials rotating to their designated slots, one after the other, in a second door being opened and the three of them being led up a finely carpeted staircase into a living room with sensual curtains and hangings, low-shaded purple lights and an uncanny atmosphere of lassitude. People—some in dinner jackets, some in suits, and some in what look like elegant pyjamas—are strewn around this room like clothes at Audrey's: draped across divans, curled up on rugs, slumped in lush armchairs.

"This is like the Mogul's opium dream in *Sunshine of the World,*" whispers Audrey. "You know, Niziam-Ul-Gulah, or whatever he's called, in the first act."

"Niziam's the Vizier," Becky whispers back. "The Mogul's called something else."

"Isn't that the lord who's chasing Mabel?" Audrey says, nudging Becky. "You know, the political man. Lying on the sofa, with that girl you always see in the lounge of the Denmark Street Hotel."

"I think maybe it—" Becky begins, before catching her breath and gasping: "Oh, look! It's the chap who's in that film we saw last week!"

She clasps both Serge and Audrey with excitement. Audrey squints piercingly towards the man in question, but is unable to confirm or deny Becky's claim, as her view's blocked by the approach of an ageing lady who floats towards them with an indolent, cat-like gait.

"My angel," the lady, whom Serge presumes to be their hostess, this Zarovia or Ferrovia, purrs as she gathers Becky's hand between her own, smiling at her with a languid and matronly look. "So glad to see you."

Her voice is husky, foreign: maybe Greek or Russian. Becky introduces Serge and Audrey to her; she takes their hands too. Her hands are limp and clammy; she reeks of perfume. Her eyes move from one of them to the other with a dull and heavy motion as she asks:

"What will my angels have? Pipe or syringe?"

The two girls turn to Serge, who answers:

"Syringe, definitely."

Their hostess leads them to an enclave in which poufs lie in a circle round a Persian rug, sits them down, then floats away, returning shortly afterwards with three loaded syringes. Serge injects himself, then watches Zoroastria inject first Becky and then Audrey. By the time she's got to Audrey he's already under the drug's spell; watching an air bubble rise through the liquid in the barrel as the *madame* taps it with her clammy finger, he feels himself rising too, shedding gravity like clothes, like curtains, hangings, tapestries . . .

Serge, Audrey and Becky visit the salon several times over the next few weeks. After a while Becky teaches them the password sequence so that they can go without her: it consists of the visitor enquiring whether there'll be a piano recital today, and the servant (since Madame Z's seems to be open round the clock, these keep rotating) asking whether they've come to hear the Chopin or the Liszt, to which the visitor must answer "Liszt." There is a piano in the main room, as it happens; from time to time, one of the guests will play it for a while, but their recitals never get completed, any more than the intermittent conversations rippling about the place, which fade away almost as soon as they get going. Serge learns other passwords too: there's one that works at Wooldridge and Co. chemist's shop in Lisle Street, and another in a taxidermist's store in Holborn; at a confectioner's in Bond Street, by announcing himself favourable to liquorice, then purchasing either a flask of perfume or a box of sweetmeats, Serge is able to procure much more than he ostensibly requests; at an antique dealer's out in Kensington, the code works the other way, one or other (sometimes both) of two Oriental objets d'art, calligraphic watercolours bearing (originally, at least, quite accidentally, Serge imagines) the likenesses of the Western letters C and H, appearing in the window to indicate the availability of various stock. He starts seeing all of London's surfaces and happenings as potentially encrypted: street signage, chalk-marks scrawled on walls, phrases on newspaper vendors' stalls and sandwich boards, snatches of conversations heard in passing, the arrangements of flowers on window-sills or clothes on washing lines. He also comes to realise just how many of his fellow citizens are subject to the same vices as him. He picks up the tell-tale signals all over town: the sniffs, the slightly jaundiced skin, the hands jerky and limp by turns, eyes dull yet somehow restless too. Sometimes a look passes between him and a chance companion on the bus, or in a queue, or someone brushed past in a doorway, a look of mutual recognition of the type that members of a secret sect might give each other: *Ah, you're one of us . . .*

The 52's maître d', Billie Lee, has that look in spades. He's half-Chinese, and has a liquid, silken voice that lingers like Madame Z's clammy hands do when she greets her guests. He has a lisp as well, which Serge always associates in his mind with the word "Liszt" in the salon's entry-dialogue. His gait also strikes Serge as cat-like, although Serge knows he's probably only thinking this because of all the cat-masks leering at him from the stage. The more drugs he takes, the more associatively his mind seems to work: the circulation of dancers over the long floorboards, interlocking bodies moving on collision courses towards other conjoined bodies, pausing to let them pass then advancing again, suggests for him the way that London's cabs and busses pulse and flow, negotiating space; then aeroplanes circling and passing one another; gnats above a bed; orbiting planets. The bold, confident women sitting around tables, painted in stylised geometries of black, white and scarlet, the stark angles of their bare spines, stockinged legs and forearms that extend and retract triangular cocktail glasses or long, straight cigarette holders, summon up the image of new, shining engines, the sleek machinery of luxurious, expensive cars, their brazen pistons, rods and cylinders. Men—both in the 52 and Madame Z's salon, and for that matter in most other places—seem diminished by comparison: retracted, meek, effeminate.

"Dear *Szerge*," Lee susurrates at him one night, "you're minus*z* your lovely Audrey this evening."

"She's meeting her guardian," Serge tells him.

"Ah! The doctor." A soft chuckle emanates from Lee's mouth. "A fine man. Devoted to her."

Serge shrugs. He still hasn't worked out the nature of Audrey's relationship with this Dr. Arbus. Lee half-gasps as he remembers something.

"*Szerge!*" he says. "You must bring all your Folies-Bergèrs*z* to the party that I'm organising down in Limehous*ze* next week. It's a *z*secret party. Exclusive, but huge. It'll be a blas*zt* . . ."

"Consider them brought," Serge answers.

Audrey arrives soon afterwards, flush to the gills with money. She buys them both Champagne and smothers his cheek and neck in apologetic kisses. He turns from her wordlessly and watches the jazz band play. They look like machine parts too, extensions of their instruments, the stoppers, valves and tubes. Their bodies twitch and quiver with electric agitation. So do the bodies of the dancers. One girl, gyrating with another, lets a shriek out: it's a shriek of joy that manages to carry on its underside a note of anxiety, a distress signal. The music carries signals too: Serge's eyes glaze over as he tunes into them. There are several, gathering within the noise only to lose their shape again and slip away. Dispersed, they rise up silently towards the winking moon and bounce off this to Mars and Saturn before travelling along the cat-masks' whiskers and being granted structure and form once more by the trellis and the plants, which they cause to slightly tremble. When Serge closes his eyes, the signals become images: words and shapes being written out in light against a black void, then erased, then written out again, worlds being made and unmade . . .

At the beginning of November, Serge is summoned by the AA's provost, Walter Burnet, ARSA. On his office walls hang photographs of previous years' hockey teams (Burnet has been the school's hockey coach for the last twenty years).

"Not one for sports, Carrefax?" he asks, following Serge's gaze.

"Not so much, sir, no."

"Good for the health, both physical and mental. Teaches team spirit. An architect's only as good as the team he works with, and vice versa. We try to instil that principle right from the get-go here: collective site visits and the like. Can't have our players slacking off . . ."

"I've been doing some independent research," Serge says. "I find it easier to sketch when I'm alone."

"You've got the drawings to show for it?"

"Yes, sir," Serge replies. He saw this coming, and has gathered all the sketches idly dawdled in Mrs. Fox's Café into a large dossier which he now hands the certified disciplinarian.

"What are these of?" Burnet asks.

"Well, they're hybrids really. Plans for . . ."

"For what?"

Serge's mind runs through the taxonomy of edifice-types, grabbing at terms. Laying hold of the one that seems most current, he tells Burnet:

"Memorials."

"Ah!" Burnet says. "A worthy line of investigation. Do I take it you'll be entering the competition to design the school's own war memorial?"

"I hadn't really thought of it, sir," Serge shrugs.

"You should, Carrefax; you should. It's a blind submission: there's no reason why the likes of you can't win." He flips through a few more sketches, then asks: "Why are these all in plan view?"

"It's my preferred projection."

"So I see. As you're no doubt aware, though, the syllabus for the first year requires you to become proficient in not only plan but also section, elevation and perspective. Which brings me to—"

"I haven't quite begun to—" Serge begins, but Burnet cuts him off:

"Which brings me to the question of your course attendance record. I'm afraid Mr. Lynch has complained to me that he's only seen you once in his drawing class all term."

"I find perspective hard, sir," Serge says.

"All the more reason to attend—that, and the fact that your continued membership of this institution demands it."

Serge has nothing to say. Burnet returns the sketches to the dossier and hands this back to him. He looks at Serge in silence for a while; then his tone softens as he says:

"I know it's difficult to readjust."

"It just seems odd to draw things out into relief when they're—"

"No, Carrefax, I don't mean the perspective thing. I mean to life in Civvie Street. You've lived through war and all its horror, and—"

"But I liked the war," Serge tells him.

Now it's Burnet who's stumped for words. His eyebrows wrinkle in concern as his eyes move from left to right over Serge's features, as though trying to draw their flat inscrutability out into some kind of relief. Serge looks back at him, frankly, letting his face be scrutinised. There's no reason to resist it: Burnet and his like will never disinter what's buried there, will never elevate or train it; Serge hasn't made himself available for his team, never will. Besides, he doesn't buy the line, much peddled by the newspapers, that tens of thousands of men his age are wandering around with "shell shock." He sees symptoms around London all the time: the deadened, unfocused eyes and slow, automatic gait characteristic of the NYDNs he'd see at the field hospital in Mirabel, or of the pilots and observers for whom Walpond-Skinner had to write AAF-3436 forms—but these are general. Billie Lee displays them, and he spent the war years overseeing his family's business interests in Shanghai. Madame Z displays them, and she's been running salons for as long as anyone can remember. Commuters trudging to work each morning display them as well, as do the pleasure-seekers shuffling around the West End. They can't *all* have been at the front. The children outside Great Ormond Street display them. The dope fiends, especially, display them; the cocaine-sniffers too, when they're not temporarily fired up with charges that will run down in minutes, leaving them more empty than before. It's like a city of the living dead, only a few of whose denizens could proffer the excuse of having had shells constantly rattling their flesh and shaking their nerves. No, the shock's source was there already: deeper, older, more embedded . . .

Serge decides to go and visit Mr. Clair, who's working for the Fabian Society. He visits him at home, a flat in Islington.

"It's not much," Clair tells him. "I've only had it for a year or so."

Clair looks older: thinner, more worn—and, beyond this, as though the anger at society's condition that peppered his speech when he was Serge and Sophie's tutor at Versoie were no longer coming from some abstract, intellectual font of righteous youthful rebelliousness but had been rubbed into him from outside, almost physically ingrained, leaving him bitter.

"Where were you before that?" Serge asks.

"Farming in Yorkshire. I was made to: conscientious objector. Forced to till the earth for refusing to participate in the conquest of it."

" 'Advance thy empire,' " Serge says, smiling.

If Clair understands the reference he ignores it.

"Some of us were even put in prison. But we've brought changes about. In future no one will have to—"

"Where's the one with the jetty in it?" Serge asks. He's been looking at the paintings on the walls while Clair's been speaking.

"Sorry?" Clair asks.

"When you lived with us, you had a painting of a boat pulling off from a jetty. There were two canals meeting each other, and the boat was pulling off. You told us that you'd painted it yourself."

"I did lots of paintings in the old days," Clair says.

"You know when you gave me and Sophie art lessons?" Serge asks.

"Yes," Clair answers. "She always did plants, or insects. You did maps."

"Exactly," Serge says. "You were trying to teach us depth."

"I didn't do a very good job there," Clair murmurs sadly.

"Can you remember what you told us? About how to do it, I mean . . ."

Clair ponders Serge's question for a while, then says:

"I probably gave you basic principles of one-point or two-point perspective: picture plane, rectilinear scene, horizon line . . ."

"You've got to have one of those if you're going to paint, right?" Serge asks.

"To tell you the truth," says Clair, "painting's not really my bag these days. My interests have moved on to the artisanal side of things. I like the work of craftsmen, the aesthetic of the labourer. It seems less disingenuous, more honest . . ."

He stares out of the window, his face earnest but joyless. Looking at it, Serge sees reflected there a vision of the future—the collective future, or a version of it, at least: a fairer, saner, soberer one that leaves him cold.

Billie Lee's party is the next day. Serge, Audrey, Becky and the other Amazons ride in a long procession of taxis along the Embankment, past Tower Bridge and into the East End. They pass a market that's still going at this late hour: Jews, Poles, Russians, Turks and others bustle around in the smoky glare of naphtha flames exchanging nondescript bundles of fresh produce, fabric or electrical equipment, haggling with each other in a dozen languages.

"We could be in Smyrna," Serge says, which prompts the girls in the cab to sing, in unison:

That Smyrna-Myrina
Enchants all who've seen her . . .

Both people and lights grow sparser as the cortege moves down Cable Street. Dark, empty roads run off this towards Shadwell and Stepney. After Limehouse Canal the street lamps give out entirely; only moonlight reflecting off the muddy creek illuminates their passage through the night. The lead taxi pauses, then turns down the narrowest of alleyways and draws to a halt beside a warehouse from whose small side-door a pool of yellow light is spilling. Other cabs are pulled up outside. Serge and the Amazons disembark and make their way through the door. Much to their consternation, they're relieved of one pound each, then led along a dusty corridor and up a rickety staircase towards a large internal doorway from beyond which the familiar sounds of jazz are streaming. Passing through this, they emerge into a vast industrial space, a storage room or assembly hall, that's been transformed into a setting as fantastic as an emperor's opium-dream or some exotic film. The room's pillars, coiled about with red-grape-heavy vines, tower above the room like columns of a bacchanalian temple. Crane-hooks around the walls are similarly vine-decked, as are gantries hanging from the ceiling. On a platform raised much higher than the 52's stage, between fixed machine-parts, an expanded jazz band is playing double-time, as though possessed by the deity that's being invoked by the outlandish décor. Above them, like the god himself, Billie Lee stands looking down from a raised walkway, resplendent in a blue overcoat with a luxurious fur collar.

"For once, we're underdressed," Audrey shouts at the other girls.

It's true: most of the women here are wearing chiffon dresses trimmed with lace and crêpe-de-chine tea gowns; the men, like some of those he saw in Madame Z's salon, seem got up for a pyjama party too. Waiters wearing laurel wreaths are gliding around with trays of Champagne. Serge, Audrey and the Amazons down a few glasses; then the girls skip off to join the crowd of dancers on the floor beneath the stage.

"Dr. Arbus is here," he hears one of them say to Audrey as they slink away.

Serge looks around, wondering which reveller he might be. The dancers are mostly women. He can make out Amazonian segments interspersed among the limbs and faces: bare shoulders turning and vibrating, hands pulling vanity cases from purses (they're so adept at sniffing cocaine that they don't need to stop moving in order to do it). Serge has his own medicine, procured from the objet d'art–displaying antique dealer this afternoon, an *H* day. He retires into what seems to be a small electricity cabin and doses himself up. When he emerges, all the dancers are moving like the actors in a film that he and Audrey saw played at the wrong speed by a novice projectionist a week or so ago: slowly, their frenetic twists and shudders broken down to gestures that ooze into one another at a pace so languorous it's almost static. Skirts draw together and apart like clouds merging and separating over the course of a whole afternoon; eye contact between partners takes as long to establish as trunk-call connections, and is taken leave of lingeringly, sadly; wisps of smoke turn solid as they extend from cigarettes to coil like lace round limbs and clothing. Viewed like this, the scene looks more melancholic than celebratory or jubilant. Even two women who are kissing each other passionately seem caught up in the grip of a slow desperation: their mouths suck at one another, as though struggling to draw oxygen out of the lungs beyond them; one of their hands is grappling at the other's breast as though clutching at a fixed object to prevent a fall. As the breast breaks free of its clothing, the hand slips and its owner emits a shriek that takes an age to reach him and stays with him for even longer, drowning out the music: a slow, drawn-out version of a shriek he's heard before . . .

Serge finds himself, much later, standing on a fire escape that overlooks the Thames. Audrey is nowhere to be seen. There's someone with him, though: another male reveller who's expounding to Serge his theory that jazz and morphine compliment each other: something to do with frequency and synchronising, how the waves of the brain need to be brought into step with those of the music, Africa and America, ancient and modern, something, something . . .

"Words on the cross . . ." Serge tries to murmur, but discovers that his own words won't emerge from him. In any case, his interlocutor seems to have vanished, if he was ever there at all. A dull metallic pressure on his knee causes Serge to realise that he's lying, not standing, on the fire escape. He looks down at the river. The tide's out; the exposed mud is deep and black. "Maybe it'll be like this, when it comes," he finds himself saying to nobody, not knowing what he means.

iii

In mid-November, Audrey repeats her offer to take Serge to one of her Hoxton Hall spiritualist meetings. Serge accepts. They set out from his flat, and take a bus along Clerkenwell Road and Old Street.

"What's that?" she asks, feeling an object in his jacket pocket prod her as they press together: it's rush hour and the bus is crowded.

"Leveller," he says. "A surveying instrument. I was meant to drop it off at home."

He shifts his position so it doesn't prod her anymore. As he does the object digs into his ribs in reproach for the lie: it's not a leveller but an ammeter, his father's one, smuggled along to take a surreptitious reading, gauge the "spirit level" as it were . . .

"Last week we had the relatives of two people in the room pop up," Audrey tells him as they walk up Hoxton Street together.

"What, jump out of a box and stroll around?" Serge asks.

"No, of course not," she scoffs at him. "They get channelled through the medium: their voices. Through her, and the control too. You'll see."

There are people milling around outside the hall, watched over by two sentinel lamps that protrude from the building's white façade. As Serge and Audrey make their half-shilling contributions at a table in the vestibule, they're each handed a couple of leaflets. They pass into the main room, a homely little place with rather shabby chairs scattered around, all facing a small stage fringed with plush red curtains. In the middle of the stage a table sits. It's a round table with a single, thick stem-leg holding its top up: a dining table, of the type you generally get in middle-class homes. A single chair is drawn up at the table, facing the audience from behind it. Several yards to the table and chair's left, at what Audrey would call "stage right," a second chair sits facing the same way. Between the two chairs, mounted on an easel, is a blackboard. To the table's right (stage left), a second, smaller desk has a chair placed in front of it, facing back inwards towards the big round table. This chair alone is occupied, by a thin, mousey woman who sits, pencil poised, above a notepad resting on the surface of the desk.

"Is that the medium?" Serge asks.

"No," Audrey tells him. "She's a secretary or something like that. She takes notes throughout the session, for a scientific organisation who research this kind of thing."

They head towards two seats near the hall's rear, drape their coats over the back of these and sit down. Other people drift in slowly. Some of them are clearly ingénues like Serge: on entering the room, they pause and stare around, wondering what they're meant to do, before falteringly making their way to vacant seats. Others are habitués: they stride in confidently, looking left and right to see which of the other regulars are here. Serge glances at the topmost leaflet of the little handout sheaf he's holding. It contains a short biography of Miss Ann Flannery Dobai, their hostess medium. Born of humble immigrant stock in Baltimore, this account informs him, she and her five siblings spent their childhood following their father, a railway worker, from city to city. It was in Kenosha, Wisconsin, that her gift was discovered, quite by chance, in 1884:

On meeting with a group of music hall performers, the adolescent Ann entered a trance and listed, quite accurately, the names of each of their maternal grandfathers. Shortly thereafter, she began performing apports and materialisations throughout the American Midwest. As news of her psychic powers crossed the Atlantic, she was invited to the capitals of Europe, and granted private audiences to the Austrian Emperor, the Italian King, and numerous heads of state. Finding herself persecuted by malicious sceptics on her homecoming, she resolved to once more offer her gift to the more open-minded peoples of the Old World . . .

The two sheets beneath this one have hymns printed on them.
"What are these for?" Serge asks Audrey.

"To vibrate the air," she says. She nods hello to a gentleman in a fedora seated a few yards in front of them. "He's always here," she tells Serge.

A door at the room's far end opens and a man strides through it and onto the stage, pausing beside the stage-right chair. A hush descends on the audience as he addresses them.

"Ladies and gentlemen—and, above all, *friends*," he announces, "Miss Dobai will commence her sitting in a moment." His accent is English, not American. Sweeping the hall with his gaze, he continues: "I see a number of familiar faces among us—but for those of you here for the first time, I shall briefly outline the extraordinary procedure we are about to undergo together. Miss Dobai will initially, with your help, attempt to make contact with a control and to channel the ensuing communication by means of her vocal cords. Once contact has been established, you are welcome to put questions to the control: it is to you, after all, that he or she may wish to speak."

He pauses, and lets his gaze alight on individual people, impressing this possibility upon them, then adds:

"This procedure is, as you might appreciate, quite strenuous, demanding huge reserves on physical and mental energy on Miss Dobai's part."

" 'Procedure,' " Serge mumbles to Audrey. "Makes it sound like an operation."

"Don't be flippant," she hisses back at him. The man on the stage continues:

"Once her vocal cords have been exhausted, Miss Dobai will request of the control that its communication be continued by means of the table-tilting method."

"What's that?" Serge asks Audrey.

"You'll see," she says.

"Miss Dobai," the master of ceremonies tells them, "will join us presently, but she has let it be known that she'd like us to sing the first of the two hymns that you were handed on your way in, 'Abide with Me.' "

There's a general rustling of paper, and the audience launch into the hymn. The tightness of the singing falls off as the side-door opens once more and a woman glides through it, passes the master of ceremonies and assumes her seat behind the table. Miss Dobai is middle-aged; her blouse, red like the curtains on each side of her, is décolleté; her cheeks are rouged; her hair is got up in a bun. Serge stops singing and pictures train-yards, circus wagons and European palaces, flickering in the air around her. When the hymn ends, she clasps her hands together; the master of ceremonies makes the same gesture, holding his conjoined hands out towards the audience in instructive illustration; people around the room start shyly turning to their left and right, linking hands with their neighbours.

"It's to form a circuit," Audrey whispers to Serge.

Miss Dobai gestures to her master of ceremonies, who announces:

"Miss Dobai has let it be known that she'd like you to join in singing the second of the hymns you've all been given, 'Now Thank We All Our God.' "

Easier said than done: the congregation's hands are bound. Breaking the circuit briefly, they balance the hymn-sheets on their knees or the chair next to them, then reconnect their hands and launch into song once more. Halfway through the first verse, the master of ceremonies takes his own seat. Miss Dobai sits impassive at her table, staring vaguely in front of her. She remains impassive through the second verse; during the third, though, a strange metamorphosis overtakes her. It starts with a few light hiccups, which grow heavier, making her chest and shoulders heave until the hiccups have turned into sobs that rattle her whole upper body. Her eyes roll up in their sockets, red-veined balls of fish-white. One by one, the congregation break off singing, captivated by the medium's contortions. In the silence, her rapid, gasping breathing can be clearly heard: the gasps are deep, and growing deeper. As they deepen they slow down and even out, until they sound more like the long, yawning groans of an awakening male slumberer.

"Is someone there?" the mousey secretary asks.

The voice groans once more in annoyed response. Then Miss Dobai's jaws clank into action as the male speaker who's inhabiting them pronounces a word:

"Morris."

"Is that Morris?" asks the secretary. "Can you confirm that for us?"

"Yes," growls the voice, breaking into coughs that shake Miss Dobai's frame again. "Deeds aren't right."

The secretary scribbles in her notepad. "Which deeds, Morris?" she asks. "You weren't clear about that last time."

"Property deeds. Cam, Camber, Camley. I was going to transfer before I . . ."

"I heard '*Cam*-something,' " the secretary says after a pause. "Is it a place?"

"Swindled me out of . . . affidavit . . ." Morris's voice continues, ignoring her question. The words lapse back into groans, which shorten, rising in pitch until they're more like Amazonian war-whoops. These whoops, having attained their plateau, mutate back into words again, contracting Miss Dobai's cheeks as they hurtle from her mouth: "Woo yeh-yeh! Comanche Chief here! Yeh-yeh! Kill land-swindler good and proper. Get his scalp. Woo yeh-yeh!"

"Who's this now?" the secretary calls out.

"Comanche Chief, yeh-yeh!" this new, excited voice informs her. "I scalp white man good and proper. In past; now, no enemies where we are. White and red all friends. Yeh-yeh!"

"Where are you, Chief?" the secretary asks.

"High prairies," the Chief answers. "Not American but other place. Ancestors of all men here: white, red, yellow . . ."

Miss Dobai's cheeks contract still further as a sound of rushing wind runs through her lips. The wind's sound changes, growing lispy, then separates out into crackling stops and starts. These, too, rise in pitch, till it's no longer a man's but a woman's voice that's coming from her. The corners of her mouth curl upwards as the sound's pitch rises higher still and childlike giggles burst into the room.

"Is this Miss Sunshine?" calls the secretary. "Tilda?"

A huge, grotesque smile contorts Miss Dobai's face as a small child's voice emerges:

"Not a little Indian girl. No. I'm not. I got long blond curls and big blue eyes, and Billy Parton says I got a snub nose."

"Can you confirm your name?" the secretary asks.

"Firm . . . soft . . ." the little voice giggles again as it replies. "Miss Scarlet calls me Sunshine. Because my hair. My brothers called me Tilly, like the plough."

"She's often here," Audrey whispers to Serge.

"The mother said," the voice continues, "that she got to wear her bonnet and give answers, or she won't. But if she does, then she'll have sweets."

Miss Dobai claps her hands together rapidly. The secretary scribbles more. The master of ceremonies opens his hands to the audience, inviting their participation. Someone near the front shouts out:

"Is there anyone else with you, Tilly?"

Miss Dobai, eyes still vacant, rotates her head slowly to first one side then another. Two-thirds of the way through its rightwards turn it stops, and Tilly's voice gasps:

"Oh! The temper boy."

"Was that 'temper'?" asks the secretary.

"Temper, tempra, temper-ture," says Tilly. "Mercury rising. He's telling Tilly it's a *P*."

A woman to the hall's left stands up; so do a couple to the right.

"Peter?" asks the solitary woman.

"Tilly hears him say it's *P*, then *A*."

The solitary woman sits down. Not the couple, though: they're clasping one another more and more tightly as Tilly continues:

"*P*, then *A*; then there's another one, then *L* . . ."

"Paul!" the wife says, her voice breaking. Her husband asks, in a more authoritative tone:

"Paul, is that you?"

Miss Dobai's head turns a little more, trying to locate either the man who asked the question or the girl who's answering it, or both. Tilly's voice comes from it once more, saying:

"Died of influ-, influ-, influ-ence. Paul said it's very hot. And wet. But now he's happy again. Hello, Daddy; hello, Mummy. You were always good to me."

The voice has altered halfway though this last speech: it's still a child's, but seems more serious than Tilly's.

"If this is Paul," the husband says, "then tell me: do you remember, in the playroom, the big object? The one with the tail?"

"Oh, toy," Paul's voice answers. "Yes, indeed. A rocking horse."

"Well, that was at the nursery school," the husband says. "But I meant at our house. The object pinned to the wall, with the tail . . ."

"A bird," Paul says. There's a pause, then he adds: "Not a real bird. One made of fabric. With a tail . . . and string . . . long string to fly."

The wife, sobbing, has sunk back to her chair.

"Kite bird," Paul says triumphantly. "Pinned to the wall. You got it for my birthday."

Now the husband starts to cry as well. Audrey looks at Serge as if to say "See?" Returning her gaze, he feels a hot and cold rush moving through his veins. Paul's voice, still issuing from Miss Dobai's mouth, says:

"You're having a painting done. Of me."

"Yes!" chokes the husband through his tears. "Can you see it?"

"Oh yes. I like it. I can see it, and I'm beginning to see *from* it as it goes on. And it makes Matilda smile, just like the photo. How I like the soldiers in a row, like toast and egg!"

The voice is slipping back into giggly mode. The secretary, scribbling furiously, asks:

"Is it Tilly again? Are you seeing a painting or a photo?"

Again Miss Dobai's head slowly rotates, getting its bearings on her interlocutors. The grotesque smile returns to her face as Tilly says:

"Two rows of soldiers. Like in school, when the man came with the velvet and the bird. The front ones are sitting, and the back ones are standing."

Several people have stood up around the hall.

"What regiment are they from?" someone shouts out.

" 'Jiment?" Tilly's voice repeats. "The writing has an *E* in it. And an *I*, and an *L* . . ."

"Is it the Leicester Rifles?" someone else asks.

"Oh, they've left their rifles to the side," Tilly giggles. "One of them has got a stick, though: in the back row, one, two, three from the left. But he's not the one who plays with her. It's the other one, in the front, the raifle boy."

"What did you call him?" asks the secretary.

"He told her that a part was gone, and he was choking for a bit, then getting better. He was frightened, like when it's dark; then he passed over, and was comfortable again."

Two men call out, almost simultaneously:

"What's his name? What's he called?"

Miss Dobai raises her hand from the table's surface and traces in the air an *M*. Beside Serge, Audrey tenses up. Miss Dobai's hand then air-draws *O*. Audrey slackens again, disappointed. The next letter's *R;* then *S*. The hand pauses for a while.

"*Mors:* means 'dies' in French, doesn't it?" someone behind Serge mumbles.

"Is that right?" Audrey whispers in his ear.

Serge, veins still tingling, shakes his head. "Dies" is *meurt. Mors* is "bit." He thinks of the birds in the woods after he was shot down: the grey, fleshy crumbs they all had in their beaks. Miss Dobai's hand twitches back into action and traces an *E*.

"Was he a telegraphist?" someone calls out.

His question goes unanswered as the hand sketches two more letters, an *N* and a *T.*

"Tilly," the secretary says, "I've got *MORSENT*. Do you mean that more men were sent to rescue him, when he was choking?"

Her last few words are drowned out by the gasps of another couple, two of the people who stood up when Miss Dobai first started talking about photos.

"It's us!" they shout. "Morsent's our name. The photograph arrived last week!"

Tilly's voice breaks out of Miss Dobai's mouth again:

"Photo-graph, that's it. He's in the front row, in front of the stick-man: Raifle."

"Oh, Matthew: it's our Ralph!" the woman shrills, hugging her husband. She pronounces it "Rafe." "It's true: there's a man with a walking stick behind him in the photo!" she adds, for the enlightenment of others in the audience. Addressing herself first to Miss Dobai, then, shifting her aim slightly, to the air above her, she continues: "Ralph! Are you okay now?"

"Oh, Raifle's happy as a boy can be," Tilly responds. "He has a house, all built of bricks, and there are trees and flowers, and the ground is solid, not all mud. He's met a girl."

"A girl?" the mother asks. "What girl?"

"Ralph wasn't very polite to her when he first came over," Tilly says, giggling. "He didn't expect a grown-up sister here. He asked me: am I a little brother, or is she my little sister? She calls me her big brother, but she's like little sister. What's that, Yafe? You can't have two. Now Tilly doesn't understand."

"Can you ask him—"the father now assumes the role of questioner— "if he's still missing any parts?"

Miss Dobai's head bobs around a little, as though looking Ralph up and down. "Has he got legs and a head?" Tilly asks, answering almost immediately: "Oh yessie-yes! And ears, and eyelashes and eyebrows, all just like before; mouth and tongue too. It all got rear, rear, sembled."

"And his house?" the father pursues his line of enquiry. "If it's built of bricks, then what are the bricks built of?"

"Emma," Tilly begins. "Emma . . ."

"Is there someone else with you?" the secretary interjects.

"Emma-nations," Tilly finishes the word with difficulty. "Raifle says things rise up, atoms rising, and consol, consolidate when they get up here. We collect them, and make them solid again. There's always something rising from your plane; when it comes through the aether, other qualities gather round each atom, and our people manor-factor solid things from it."

A man to the hall's left stands up now:

"I have a question," he says. "If you need the atoms of living things to reconstitute them, why do those things not disappear from our world?"

"Oh, your world sheds bulk," Tilly responds. "You're losing weight right now, so that I and the others may borrow it in order to become present to you."

People in the audience look down at their bodies. Serge raises his back, to see if it feels lighter. Oddly enough, it does. Tilly continues:

"And think of all the things that die, and decay: they're not lost. They may form dust or manure for a while, but that gives off an essence or a gas, which ascends in the form of what you call a 'smell.' All dead things have a smell. That's what we use to produce duplicates of the forms they had before they were a smell. So decayed flowers make new flowers; rotting wool makes tweeds; dung makes food . . ."

Throughout this little lecture Tilly's register and tone have both become elevated, like so many atoms, gathering scientific gravitas. She catches herself now and, giggling once more, says:

"Yes, all right, Yafe: Tilly will go back now. Table-talkie can take over. She'll have sweets, because she did, and she said she could if she did."

The static hissing rushes through Miss Dobai's lips again; then the lids slide down over her rolled-up eyeballs, and she slumps back in her chair and stays there, seemingly unconscious. The audience remain completely still, waiting to see what will happen next. It's the master of ceremonies who makes the first move. Rising from his own chair, he addresses them:

"My friends, these channellings have quite exhausted Miss Dobai. Nonetheless, her comatose state indicates that she is still receiving. With your help, we shall, as the control suggested, move on to the table-tilting method."

He strides across the stage towards the large round table, behind which Miss Dobai sits collapsed and, laying his hand upon its surface, continues:

"First, to dispel any suspicions that the table is mechanically controlled, I would request that a member of the audience, a gentleman rather than lady, step onto the stage and help me lift it."

There's a pause; then a man near the front rises from his chair, mounts the stage and, grabbing the table top's rim while the master of ceremonies clasps the thick stem-leg, helps him raise the whole thing from the floor. The two of them then walk the table round the stage.

"As you can see," the master of ceremonies says to the audience, his voice a little strained by the exertion, "no strings or wires or any other mechanism connect this object to a point from which lever or switch might influence its movement."

He motions to his volunteer to set the table down again, in its original spot. When they've done this, but before the volunteer has left the stage, he tells him: "Stay here, sir, if you will—just here, beside the black-board." He positions him accordingly, between the table and his own spot at stage right, in front of the easel-mounted board, before continuing: "And if a second volunteer would be so kind as to make him- or her-self available . . ."

Two people rise from chairs: one male, one female.

"We will use the lady," the master of ceremonies says. "Your task, madam," he continues as he leads her by the hand onto the stage and places her beside the secretary, "will be to call out, slowly and clearly, all the letters of the alphabet, in the correct sequence. Should the table respond at any point during your recitation, you shall pause; the gentle-man shall mark down the letter you've just called out; then you shall re-commence pronouncing all the letters, beginning once more with *A*. Have I made the procedure clear to both of you?"

Both gentleman and lady nod. The master of ceremonies moves back to his spot at stage right, casts a glance across the now quite populated stage—the blackboard-staffing gentleman with chalk in hand, the sopo-rific medium behind her table, the mousey secretary at her desk and the nervous lady standing beside her—and, satisfied, instructs the lady to begin. Blushing, she calls out:

"A, B, C, D, E, F, G . . ."

Serge shifts his gaze back and forth between the table and Miss Dobai. Both seem perfectly inanimate. The nervous lady moves on through the alphabet's middle stretch:

"L, M, N, O, P, Q . . ."

Still nothing's happening. When she pronounces *Y*, though, the table top dips—unmistakeably, a clear forward tilt towards the audience, who gasp in amazement.

"Mark it down," the master of ceremonies instructs the man at the blackboard. He does so, drawing a *Y* in its upper left corner. The table top tilts back until it's even again.

"How can it do that?" Serge asks. The tingling in his blood is growing stronger. It's not a sensation he's experienced before; nor is it pleasant: it's a bad type of tingling, as though he'd been injected with a mixture that was somehow not quite *right*.

"Shh!" Audrey whispers back. "Just watch."

The nervous lady composes herself and starts again:

"A, B, C, D, E . . ."

This time it tilts at *O*. Then *U*. After five minutes the blackboard is displaying the sequence *YOURLOVEBRIDETYPEKILL*. Then, as the alphabet loops round two more times, the table stays quite still.

"We have 'YOUR LOVE BRIDE TYPE KILL,' " the secretary says, speaking directly to the table. "Is that message correct?"

The master of ceremonies nods at the nervous woman, who recommences calling out the letters. Again, the table tilts at *Y*, then *O*, then *U*, and spells out the same sequence as before—until it gets to the *E* of 'BRIDE': this it replaces with a *G*; then the *E* comes, followed by *S*, the tilts continuing until the blackboard bears the more intelligible phrase *YOURLOVEBRIDGESTHEGAP*.

" 'YOUR LOVE BRIDGES THE GAP' is what we've got now," calls the secretary. "Is that what you meant? Perhaps you could give one tilt for yes, or two for no."

The table tilts once. The secretary asks:

"With whom are we conversing now? Is it still Tilly?"

Two tilts provide a negative response. On the master of ceremony's cue, the nervous lady embarks on another set of alphabetic recitations, which coax from the table the word *SCIENTIST*.

"What type of scientist are you?" the man who asked the question about atoms calls out.

ALL, answers the table. *CHEMISTSPHYSICISTS*.

The blackboard's pretty full now. Casting an inquisitive glance at the secretary, who nods at him that she's got it all down, the transcriber picks the duster up and wipes it clean. As the letters of the alphabet are paraded by aloud again and again, a new sequence is written out on it:

FINEAETHERIALMATTERVIBRATES.

The top half of the board is wiped again as the message continues:
WEHAVEINSTRUMENTSPICKUPVIBRATIONS . . .

The tilting and transcribing take a long time, but all the people in the hall are rapt by it. The very voice in which the alphabet's letters are called out seems electrified by the possibility that it will, at any point, prompt a new tilt.

. . . *SYNTHESISENEWMASS,* the table continues.

"Who makes these instruments?" the atom-man calls back.

INVENTORS, the table answers. *ENGINEERSSS.*

The alphabet runs round three more times, each time stopping at *S.* In the gap between each nervously enunciated letter, Serge can hear his heart beating. He can feel it too: it's fast, making his chest throb against his shirt. As it does, he grows aware once more of the object hidden in his inner jacket pocket: the ammeter. He looks around the hall: everyone else, Audrey included, has their eyes glued to the table and the blackboard. Slipping his hand beneath the lapel and pushing the jacket's breast out, he eases the instrument up until its face is visible to him. The needle's at zero. He's about to let the thing fall back into the pocket once more when it leaps right up to twenty and hangs there, suspended, for three or four seconds before dropping, just as suddenly, back to zero.

"A, B, C . . ." the nervous lady's voice intones. As it pauses on *N,* the needle again leaps to twenty. Serge looks up, and realises that the table's tilted forwards. As it straightens, he looks back down and sees the needle drop, again, to zero.

"A, B, C . . ." the letters start again. Once more, the needle leaps as they are stopped, at *T,* by a new table-tilt; once more it falls back as the table's upper surface straightens and the lady's voice restarts. Serge looks around the hall again, scrutinising each member of the audience intensely. While their heads are all pointed the same way, one of their bodies' postures stands out. It's the man in the fedora a few yards in front of him: his shoulders are tensed in a different way from all the others. His elbow's different too: it's twitching just before each table-tilt, each needle-jump. Running his eye along the forearm, to the point where the hand disappears into its own jacket, Serge sees why: the fingers are manipulating something secreted within this just like the ammeter's secreted in his own.

"Wireless control!" he says, almost inaudibly.

"What?" Audrey asks him.

"Nothing," he whispers back. He knows immediately how they're doing it: he read about it in *The Broadcaster* a month ago. A small transmitter sends a signal to an even smaller receiver that, in turn, activates a mechanism in the object to be acted on: the technique has been used in music halls to play pianos without pianists, or make model airships fly around above the stalls and dock unaided in their moorings on the stage. The article's author speculated that it could be developed to make guns fire remotely, or have sirens sound, or even to command an entire warship, bypassing the need for sailors. The table's still tilting, spelling out the sequence *DECAYEDSUNLIGHTRECONSTITUTED . . .*

"Is the sunlight bright, or dark?" the atom-man is asking.

LOVERAYSNOCOLOUR, the table's answering. *AND WHEN . . .*

Serge's pulse is still racing, but now it's with fury. He wonders if he should jump up and denounce the sham. How many people in the room are in on it? The secretary? The transcriber? Atom-man? He looks at Ralph's parents, then Paul's: they're hanging on the table's every tilt, the blackboard's every slowly transcribed word. So is Audrey; so is everyone apart from him. The isolation makes his heart beat even faster, so fast that he starts to worry that he'll have a heart attack and die: he spends the next ten minutes, while the letters flow, halt and restart, trying to calm himself down. He talks to himself internally, telling himself that "pass over" would be the correct spiritualist terminology for "die," which sends a nervous laugh up from his chest into his throat which he then has to stifle. By the time he's coaxed both mind and body back to a safe state, the table's stopped tilting and the session is being wrapped up by the master of ceremonies, who, after thanking all "collaborators" in the séance, helps Miss Dobai from her chair and supports her as she falteringly walks across the stage and disappears through the side-door from which she first entered.

Outside, Audrey is buoyant:

"Did you feel the weight come off you?" she asks, skipping back down Hoxton Street.

"I did, in fact," Serge answers, honestly.

"I felt mine going straight to Michael," she says. "I could tell he wasn't far away when Tilly was talking with Ralph."

"Can I come with you again next week?" Serge asks.

"Of course you can!" she answers. She kisses him on both cheeks, then buries her face in his neck and sniffs it lovingly.

He spends the week making a remote controller. It's not difficult: he mounts a small ignition coil on a baseboard, adds an accumulator, two antennae, a switch and a telegraph key. He estimates the amount of power that Fedora's controller has, and gives himself more. As a result, the mechanism's too big to fit in his jacket pocket: after a little experimentation, he manages to bind it to the inside lining in such a way that the fingers of his right hand can manipulate the key without him needing to see it. The next Thursday, he and Audrey ride the bus along Clerkenwell Road again. He stands two feet from her, sideways-turned and slightly stiff.

About half of the audience from last week have returned; the rest are new. Paul's parents are here; Ralph's aren't, though.

"You'd think they'd come back, after what happened last time," Serge says.

"I thought I'd want to after Michael spoke to me," Audrey tells him. "But you don't need to communicate with them all the time, any more than when they were alive. Just knowing someone's fine is enough—that, and the odd 'hello' now and then . . ."

The atom-man is here too; so's the secretary, poised above her notebook. So, of course, is Fedora. He nods to Audrey like he did last week, including Serge within the gesture this time. Serge sends a big smile back at him, trying not to look too hard at the bulge on his chest but finding his eyes wandering towards it all the same, hoping he's guessed the level right: accumulator *can't* be more than four volts, surely . . .

The master of ceremonies gives the same spiel as last week. The same hymns are sung. The same sequence of hiccups, sobs and heaving rattles Miss Dobai's frame, then modulates into the deep and plaintive tones of Morris, who grumbles about codicils and proxy signatures. The Comanche Chief's on holiday today: his place is taken by a South Pacific fisherman who drowned diving for abalone and now drifts through balmy waters in a place where all seas meet. Tilly's on fine form, though, giggling as she mediates between another infantryman and his parents, then a submariner and his brother (there's a nautical theme to the evening). This second spirit accurately describes the contents of a box of his effects received by the brother just a week ago, even naming the sorting office whose stamp the package bore. Serge realises, as the brother gasps his confirmation of the objects and the name, that the network of Miss Dobai's collaborators extends far beyond this hall: she must have postmen working for her, nurses, undertakers, clerks in the Bureau of

Records, domestic servants, painters and photographers or their assistants, people scouring newspapers like Sophie and Widsun used to, tabulating death notices, auction listings, engagement and marriage announcements and who knows what else. His hand keeps slipping beneath his jacket, feeling the circuit-board lurking beneath it, his own secret network—then withdrawing, lest it attract attention: it's not time, not yet . . .

When Miss Dobai slumps back in her chair, exhausted by her vocal mediation, her master of ceremonies busies himself setting up the table-tilting phase of the séance. A different gentleman comes forward to help him demonstrate the table's lack of external attachments and to staff the blackboard, and a different lady volunteers to call the letters out. They're not part of the sham after all, Serge reasons: why should they be? As long as Fedora does his job, only Miss Dobai and her master of ceremonies need be in on it. Serge wonders if it's Miss Dobai who calls the shots, or this other man. Perhaps there is no Miss Dobai, Baltimore immigrant, frequenter of trains and boats and courts: perhaps the woman on the stage in front of them's a Londoner, from no further afield than Hackney or Mile End, picked up in some bar where washed-up cabaret performers drink and trained to do the voices, all the sobs and hiccups. Maybe neither she nor he's behind it all, but someone else entirely, a "control" not even in the room but sitting back at home counting the proceeds of this remote manipulation of human automata. Serge slips his hand back underneath his jacket as the lady starts calling the letters out. He lets the first few sequences be dictated by Fedora: WEHEARWHENTHEYCRY is scrawled across the blackboard after a while.

"How do you hear?" the secretary asks, addressing herself to the table as before.

Fedora's halfway through spelling out RESONANCE, or maybe RESONATIONS, when Serge intervenes. He flips the switch on in his pocket and, tapping the key to join the circuit, cuts in after the A, just as the lady calls out H. It works: the table tilts; the blackboard-staffing gentleman writes down an H. In front of Serge, Fedora's shoulders lock up. He looks around, confused. Serge makes the table tilt again at I, then S. He manages one more letter, a T; then, as he waits for U to come round, Fedora, elbow twitching, cuts in again and tilts on E. Serge takes the next round with an R.

"I've got 'RESONAHISTER,' " the secretary reads. "It's not a word."

On a cue from the master of ceremonies, the lady volunteer goes back to *A*. Fedora's taken his hand out of his jacket now, and is trying to attract the master of ceremonies' attention, but to no avail. Serge has a clear run at the next eleven letters, and dictates the sequence *DOBAI-ISFRAU*.

"That's German for 'Mrs.,' " someone near him murmurs.

D, he adds.

Now Fedora has got the master of ceremonies' attention: the latter stares at him wide-eyed and apoplectic, urging him to get his act together. He, though, is in no state to do this: Serge can see, even from behind, that he's panicking. His head's turning from side to side; his hand is nowhere near his jacket.

"I've got 'DOBAI IS FRAUD,' " the secretary says, taken aback. "Who's saying this? Where are you?"

UPMISSDOBAISCUNT, Serge dictates. So intent is the master of ceremonies on communicating with Fedora that he doesn't pay attention to the letters being called out. By the time he glances at the board again, the last message has been supplemented by the sequence "*AUDREYITSMESERGE.*"

"I think we should curtail this session," announces the master of ceremonies. "Miss Dobai is clearly . . ."

But he's lost control of the procedure. Defiantly, the lady volunteer raises her voice above him and continues calling out the letters. As Audrey stares at him open-mouthed, Serge moves in for the kill:

TABLECONTROLLEDBYMANINFEDORA.

The room falls silent as the letter-calling stops. All eyes shift to Fedora, who, as though it made a difference, slides from his head the item in question before making swiftly for the door. Two sturdier men than him detain him there; in what passes for an ensuing struggle, his remote controller falls from his jacket to the floor.

"Two-volt," Serge comments. "I could have gone lower."

On the stage, Miss Dobai snaps out of her lethargy, rises and strides towards the side-door through which the master of ceremonies has already exited. Two more men try to cut her off but they're too late: they throw their weight at the door, then, realising it opens into the room, pull it towards them and rush through it after the duo. Others have stormed the stage: they push past the secretary, who sits at her desk dazed, pencil still in hand, and throw themselves upon the table, tearing at it vehemently, as though the piece of furniture had wilfully deceived them. Next to Serge, a woman's screaming. It could be Paul's mother, but it's hard to tell: the whole place is in uproar, women shrieking and men shouting, running around, grabbing hold of other men whom they suspect of being in on the act. Fistfights are breaking out. Steering between them, Serge wanders to the front of the hall; as the stage empties, its occupants rushing after some poor, innocent detainee who's managed to pull himself loose and make a dash for the main exit, he climbs the steps and walks up to the table. It's been snapped in two, its upper surface ripped clean from the stem—or, rather, not quite cleanly: both parts have splintered where they've been separated. Nestling among the splinters on the base are the cogs of a small, automatic hinge; beside the hinge, glued to the inside of the hollow leg, a receiver with decoherer and coherer, relay, circuit battery and two antennae more or less identical to the ones lightly scratching Serge's side. Serge bends down and inspects the shattered contraption from close up. The table's real enough, at least. Its wood is old, and beginning to rot. A small insect, some kind of wood louse, is crawling out of it, crossing the wires of the receiver's circuit-board as it heads up towards the opening that's miraculously appeared, like a new heaven, in the space above it. The insect's body is dark and wet, like oil or ink. Serge watches it ooze upwards for a while, then turns and walks away.

Scuffles continue outside the hall. People are running up and down Hoxton Street, chasing or being chased or, in some cases, both. Locals who weren't at the meeting in the first place have been caught up in the mêlée. Audrey is standing in the middle of the road, looking as catatonic as Miss Dobai did before her sudden exit. Serge takes her by the arm and leads her down to Old Street, where he hails a taxi.

She doesn't speak during the ride. When they get back to Rugby Street, she stares straight ahead as he leads her up the staircase to his flat. Once inside, she throws herself onto his bed and starts to sob. He sits down beside her and places his hand on her back, but she shrugs it away. The sobs continue for a while, then ease off; her face stays turned away from him, though, buried in a pillow as she quietly weeps. Serge sits beside her for a long time, watching her back rise and fall. It seems bulkier, as though the weight lent by her body to the world of spirits, loaned out through the twin agencies of love and conviction, had been returned unclaimed. Her hair, too, looks heavier, greased by sadness. Her shirt and dress are crumpled. All of her is downward-sagging, solid, heavy. If mass and gravity have been added to her, something's been stripped away as well: despite her layers of clothes, she somehow looks more naked than she does even when undressed, as though a belief in which she's clothed herself till now, a faith in her connectedness to a larger current, to a whole light and vibrant field of radiant transformation through which Michael might have resonated his way back to her, had been peeled off, returning her, denuded, to the world—this world, the only world, in which a table is just a table, paintings and photographs just images made of matter, kites on walls of playrooms unremembered and the dead dead.

Eventually, she falls asleep. Serge leaves the flat and walks the streets, still angry. He's angry at Miss Dobai and her gang, at people for being credulous, at himself for his cruelty to Audrey. He gravitates, naturally, to the Triangle, spends some time in Mrs. Fox's, then stops off at Wooldridge's, then at the taxidermist's. Needing a place to ingest his by-now-considerable haul, and not wanting to return home or retreat to some dingy toilet, he heads for the Holborn basement where his father's car is garaged (he's had the loan of it again for the last two weeks). Retrieving the key from an attendant whose uniform, it strikes him in passing, is very similar to that of the Empire ushers, he sits in the front seat and, in the dark and columned vault, injects and sniffs and sniffs and injects, more and more, to try to make the anger go away. It doesn't: it bears down on him from all sides. He decides he's got to make things move.

He starts the car up, leaves the garage and drives southwest, past Chelsea, Wandsworth, Wimbledon. Soon he's not in London anymore. He doesn't know where he is, or where he's going, and he doesn't care: what matters is to get things moving—get them moving so that he can get them still again, re-find the stasis in the motion. Green, blue and black run by; sometimes an angry shout weaves its way into the air's tapestry, a klaxon whose tone dips and falls off as it passes. The colours run closer and closer to him; the tapestry becomes a screen, a fixed frame through which sky and landscape race, nearer and nearer all the time: soon it's as though he were no longer merely watching the projected image but pressing right up against the surface of the screen itself. *Into* it even: somehow the space around him has become material. It's not just wind whipping his face: the colours, having merged to brown, are on him, scraping right against his skin and pressing down into his mouth. There's some kind of inversion going on too: the screen's surface has rotated and is now above him. From it comes the sound of crashing metal. The noise travels down to meet him, as though from a more elevated world: it sounds like a big iron lid being closed on him. Then it goes quiet. He's in some kind of nether region now: a mole, being stuffed like drawers and cupboards with an old, familiar substance.

"Earth again," he murmurs, tasting it inside his mouth. Flakes of it jump out from between his lips as he begins to laugh. His laughter ricochets off the car's floor, which, overturned and bent now, arches and folds about him like a metal tent or hangar. It's a pleasant noise; reminds him of liturgical chants and whispers echoing around St. Alfege's interior. Pinpricks of light pepper the structure's roof.

"My own crypt," he announces to whoever might be listening. There are people around: he can hear voices, muffled beyond the metal. They can hear him too: they're saying so, saying he must be hurt, that the car should be lifted from above him.

"It won't come off," he tries to call back to them. "It's my carapace."

The words, instead of travelling cleanly and intelligibly to the bystanders, reverberate and distort inside his bunker. Outside it, there's general arguing. A voice suggests a way to lift the chassis off him; another proposes a different way; more join in. There's more arguing, then heaving, then creaking. The misshapen dome is prised away from him; as it comes loose, it affords him a glimpse of the crowd that has gathered round the ditch in which he's lying; then, as a parting gesture, its edge catches his clothes and flips him from his back onto his front. A new argument starts up, about whether or not to turn him over again.

"Don't," Serge tries to tell them. "I'm conversing with an old friend."

But his mouth's too earth-filled for the words to come out. The turners win the argument; flipped onto his back once more, he lies incapacitated, staring at the sky.

"Doctor," someone's saying; then he's somewhere else. It could be his flat, or Audrey's, or Versoie, or the prison back at Hammelburg or Berchtesgaden. There are several doctors round him; then there's just one, Learmont, and it turns out to be Versoie where he finds himself after all.

"You back with us?" Learmont says.

"Did I leave?" Serge asks.

"The way you've been mistreating yourself," Learmont responds, "you're lucky not to be in ten separate specimen jars. I've never seen . . ." Then his words trail off, and it's dark and earthy again.

When Serge wakes up properly, Maureen is sitting at his bedside, watching over him. They're chatting. It's like that: they're already chatting; he seems to have woken up in the middle of a conversation that's been going on for quite some time. She's telling him who's doing what: marrying, leaving the area, being born or dying. The conversation lasts, has lasted, and continues to last for a long stretch, perhaps several weeks, during which time he becomes strong enough to leave his bed and walk around a little. Sometimes Maureen's replaced at his bedside by his father, who's telling him about his latest research, patents pending, business schemes. And sometimes it's his mother, who's sitting in silence, smiling. It doesn't really make much difference. Serge consumes it all quite passively, as though watching a film—one in which he's partly a minor character whose role requires little of him in the way of action, but mainly a viewer, located just beyond the frame. He likes this film, likes his immersion in it, its drawn-out timelessness that has no borders, no beginning and no end . . .

It doesn't last forever, though: eventually he's yanked back into time by the arrival, with his father, of a surprise visitor. Serge senses his presence in the room before he sees or hears him: it's a familiar, regal presence, one that brings with it, or at least implies, lurking somewhere behind it, all the protocols and codes of an official world, a world of influence and power.

"Serge, my boy!" Widsun beams from an odd angle: tall and vertical.

"My own Dr. Arbus," Serge replies. "How are the Whitehall Gods?"

"Recruiting," Widsun says. "I'm working in Communications now, with special responsibilities for North Africa. Thought you might appreciate a short stint on our team in Egypt."

"Egypt?" Serge asks. "What have they got there?"

FOUR

Call

II

_____

i

There's broken masonry along the Rue des Soeurs: window recesses and door frames with chunks missing where bars and hinges have been ripped out, façades chipped and crumbled under battery.

"Last year's riots," Petrou tells Serge.

"That too?" Serge asks as they wander past a row of damaged balusters outside the Bourse.

"No, that's the '19 revolt. Bourse took a hammering, so to speak."

"And this?" Serge asks a little later as they come across a pile of giant slabs toppled over one another in a vacant lot on the Rue Stamboul.

" 'Eighty-two bombardment—although these," Petrou continues, pointing at the oldest-looking ones, "were probably torn down from some other edifice when the Persians sacked the place in the seventh century; and from another one before that too, when Octavian routed Antony. That's the thing about Alexandria: these periods just kind of merge together . . ."

Petrou works in the Ministry of Communications. He's charged with co-ordinating names. There seem to be three different names for every street and square in town: English, French and Arabic—beside which a controversy is raging over whether Arabic names should be translated into French or English on official street maps and, beyond this, which of three English systems, each backed by a rival government department, should be used. Petrou speaks about seven languages himself. He's British, legally speaking, although, apart from a childhood stint in Liverpool, he's never lived in Britain. His family hail from Greece, via Byzantium, or maybe Trieste, Odessa or the Levant, though he's never lived in any of those places either. But he seems to have soaked up the idioms and affects of the cities, countries, islands and homelands-in-exile or -abeyance that lurk in his history, and to exude them to the satisfaction of the Bosnian florists, the White Russian dressmakers, the Syrian weavers, Armenian saddlers, Prussian carpenters, Cypriot haberdashers and Italian gunmakers whose premises he visits, Serge traipsing in behind him, on a daily basis, census-taking, plotting the linguistic layout of the city block-by-block.

"I'm doing *epsilon* through *theta* today," he tells Serge as they down a Turkish coffee and a glass of arak pressed on "dear Morgane" (the tradesmen all call him by a variant of his first name: Morgané, Morjan, Morganovitch) and his "new friend" by a kindly proprietor.

"Yesterday was *alpha–delta,*" Serge replies. "Sounds like we're walking through the alphabet."

"Blocks here have always been labelled like that," Petrou says, adding after a short pause: "This place and lettering go way back together. It was here that the fourth-century Copts devised their alphabet by transcribing spoken Egyptian into Greek figures, then adding hieroglyphs. This city's where it all began: cultures and languages slamming into one another, making new ones. Where co-ordination started too: Rosetta's just a short train-ride away. Just think: a single slab that fits all tongues together; second Babel in three feet of stone. The Rue Rosette's my favourite in all of Alexandria, by virtue of its name alone. Infuriatingly, they're changing that as well . . ."

Serge works in the Ministry of Communications too. As he rode from Versoie to London in Widsun's car, his godfather explained to him what he'd be doing: compiling a report, or reports, that, in ways not yet entirely clear to him, assessed, abetted or advanced, or at least paved the way for the advancement of, the (still largely prospective) Empire Wireless Chain.

"The whole project was mooted years ago," Widsun told him in the backseat of the chauffeured Ford. "The Egyptian station's licence was issued in '14. Why it's still not up and running is beyond me."

Serge, staring through glass at racing countryside, was distracted—neither by memories of his crash nor by pharmaceutical cravings (these have been bizarrely absent ever since his re-awakening; the odd faded track-mark on his arm is the only residue of past drug dependency) but rather by his recollection of the fact that, as the vehicle pulled away from the house and up the sloping path, gravel crunching beneath its wheels, he'd looked back to see that, of the people gathered there to wave him off, it was Bodner alone whose face had displayed signs of sadness.

"Norman's committee proposed eight stations," Widsun went on, voice blending with the motor's drone, "each two thousand miles apart, relaying from here to every corner of the Empire. The Milner-Eccles report seemed to confirm that this was feasible. But the Dominions are being irksome, and the Cabinet now seem to want to set up a new committee and commission new reports, while simultaneously pushing ahead with the Egyptian station that's been sitting around half-built for seven years. You'll be working for Macauley, in Cairo: he'll be having you prepare a sub-report that he'll doubtless amalgamate into his own report to the Telegraphy Committee, who, in turn, will report up to the Imperial Communications Committee, who in turn . . ."

His voice trailed off, and they sat in silence for a while. Then Widsun, shifting his position, stretched his arm out horizontally across the leather bench-seat behind Serge and added, in a confidential tone:

"And if it's okay with you, I'd like an appendix."

"An appendix?" Serge asked.

"An appendix," Widsun repeated. "Addendum, apocrypha, postscript, prolegomena—what you will. A section just for me. Think of it as the lost chapter."

"What should it contain?"

"If I knew that I'd write it myself," Widsun chuckled. "You'll be there; I'll leave it to you to decide what things should come to my attention." He looked out of the window himself, as though scanning the blur of vegetation for a pattern, then continued: "These are 'interesting times,' as the old Chinese curse would have it. There's . . . *stuff* happening in Egypt that I'd like to keep abreast of."

"Like an Amazonian," Serge muttered.

"What's that?"

"It's a . . . nothing. Carry on."

"Send it to me separately. Think of it as our direct line: one that bypasses chains, committees and the like." He brought his head right down to Serge's and half-whispered: "You'll be my little spy."

Serge, digesting this rather cryptic commission, felt a sour taste gathering inside his mouth—a taste that returned each time he subsequently pondered Widsun's request: bitter, and massing from further inside, like some peptic reflux.

After disembarking in Alexandria and reporting to the Ministry's office on the Rue de France, expecting to be handed tickets for that evening's Cairo train, he was informed that he'd be staying here for a while, "surveying damages."

"Damages to what?" he asked.

"His Majesty's communication network," Major Ferguson, head of the Alexandria section, told him. "After we deported Zaghlul, the Egyptians chose to vent their anger not just on our businesses and residencies, but also on telegraph wires, phone lines and the like. Even the poles sometimes: hacked them down with a real vengeance, like a tribe of Red Indians wreaking sacrilege against enemies' totem posts. Which they were, in a way."

"How so?" asked Serge.

"Way I see it," Ferguson said, picking up a salt biscuit from a bowl on his desk, "a phone box is sacred. No matter how shoddy, or in what obscure and run-down district of which backwater it's in, it's still connected to a substation somewhere, which is connected to a central exchange, which itself forms one of many tributaries of a larger river that flows straight to the heart of London. Step into a box in Labban or Karmouz, and you're joined in holy trinity with every lane in Surrey, every gabled house in Gloucestershire." He slipped the biscuit into his mouth like a communion wafer, then continued: "You've been attached to us—semi-attached, until Cairo has need of you—to assess the impact of these acts of telecommunicative blasphemy. You're our attaché for detachment—our *détaché*." Brushing crumbs from his shirt, he smiled, pleased at his witticism.

"Why not just get some engineers to do it?" Serge asked.

"Engineers are engineers," replied Ferguson. "They understand wires and insulators, nothing else. What we want from you is a different angle on it all, a wider perspective."

"Perspective was never my—" Serge began, but Ferguson cut him off.

"You'll be taken around town by . . . Ishak Effendi Benoiel!" he called to his secretary.

"Yes, Effendi?" the man asked, appearing, notepad in hand, in the doorway.

"Go and dig out Petrou for us, would you?"

Petrou shuffled into the office several minutes later. He looked shy, and stood slightly sideways-on to Ferguson and Serge.

"Petrou, Carrefax; Carrefax, Petrou," Ferguson intoned perfunctorily, reaching for another biscuit. "Name co-ordinator and *détaché:* you'll make a great pair."

So it is that, after sitting in on tedious morning meetings at which land purchase, hemp and fibre cultivation, steam-cotton-press importing and coin-mintage or marsh-drainage tendering are discussed in English, Arabic and pidgin French with bureaucrats from two more ministries housed in the same building as theirs and one more housed two Attic blocks away, Serge and Petrou set out on their daily jaunt round Alexandria. The city's long esplanades sweep them from shop to shop, the awnings, balconies and palm trees shading their heads and marking their progress with a rhythm of half-repetition that seems almost regular. Motor cars and horse carts slide around them, cutting into and out of one another's paths like intersecting eras. Native men in European dress embellished by red flowerpot fezzes hurry past them carrying briefcases of legal documents, newspaper copy or insurance claims; others in long robes roll barrels down the road with sticks; groups of schoolchildren in multi-coloured dreamcoats process along pavements hand-in-hand like paper-figure chains. The robes remind Serge of pyjamas, lending the city a sleepy look, as though it had just now been roused, or half-roused, from its slumber. Hawkers' chants float through the air towards them as they pass the French Gardens each day; howls and cries spill out at them from the Cotton Exchange; flag staffs bristle in their honour as they move down the Rue Chérif Pacha. Trams carry them, past churches Maronite, Presbyterian and Anglican, banks Roman and Egyptian, mosques with a hundred different types of minarets, from General Post Office to Canopic Way, past the Gate of the Sun, through Turkish Town, across Mahmoudied Canal from one shore to the other and then back again.

"We'll take the Ragheb Pasha tram to Anfoushi—that's the Red Crescent one; then a Moharram Bey tram on to Karmouz—that's the Red Circle one; and then the Circular tram onwards to Shatby—that's the Green Triangle one," Petrou informs Serge one Monday afternoon.

"Circles, triangles, crescents: how very geometric," Serge replies as they board the double-decker drawing up beside them.

"That started here as well," Petrou says as it pulls off again.

"What did?"

"Geometry. Euclid was Alexandrian: worked under Ptolemy Soter, the first one. Eratosthenes as well: he calculated the diameter of earth from the sun's shadow as it fell across the city's streets at noon. And Sostratus, their contemporary, conceived Pharos, the great lighthouse, as an expression of shape and form and boundaries: dividing sea from land and light from dark, cutting the night up into cones and blocks and wedges . . ."

They're jolted slightly as their tram glides through a junction where the tracks from two lines intersect. The rails form cords and sectors on the ground, arcs, ratios and reciprocals. Another tram slides along a curve, joining the intersection from another angle; as it does, its trolley-poles swing out above its roof until they're almost perpendicular to both it and the overhead wires; then they align themselves again, like arms of gramophones.

"Alexandria was on the Nile as well as the sea," Petrou's telling him. "But the Canopic mouth silted up sometime in the twelfth century, defeating the main purpose for which Alexander built the city in the first place."

"How?" asks Serge, holding the hand-rail.

"He wanted it to be the great hub of the world, connecting everywhere to everywhere else. More than that: it would be Greece's grand self-realisation, its ascent, beyond itself, into a universal condition. Über-Greece: a kind of simulation better than the real thing ever was. His version would assimilate all other cultures, all their gods and figureheads and what have you else, and conjoin these beneath the canopy of a transcendent, modern Hellenism in which reason, science and knowledge would all flourish. Alexander was a co-ordinator too."

"So why didn't it work?" Serge asks.

"He died," shrugs Petrou, "without ever seeing it finished. His fellow Macedonians, the Ptolemies, took over, and started marrying their sisters in the old Egyptian manner. Then the Mouseion and its famous library burned down. Octavian saw the place as no more than a grainhouse, for storage and shipment back to Rome. The later Roman emperors just passed through on their way to visit the antiquities of Upper Egypt, and neither the Arabs nor the Turks saw much of value here. Nowadays we Europeans treat it as a trading colony on the shore of an alien continent. Oh: there's the Ptolemaic dyke. We get off here. If you look closely, you can see the route it took . . ."

Petrou knows everything about the city. He seems to have absorbed it almost chemically: blotted it up, the subsequent reaction dictating his elemental constitution. It strikes Serge that if you cut a graft off him, a cross-section, and mounted it on a slide-tray beneath a microscope, then what you'd see would be a cellular combination of every Greek-speaking Jewish draper whose yarmulke's made from Alexandrian cotton, each partially French-descended native clerk proudly twiddling his Second Empire moustache as he describes the tract he's writing in his leisure hours about the horticultural benefits of Napoleon's Egyptian reign, the Austro-Hungarian confectioners whose Viennese profiteroles bear the distinctive taste of local sugar, the Maltese photographers, Levantine booksellers and Portuguese tobacconists they visit every afternoon—a combination, too, of the cells of the Persians, Romans and ersatz-Greeks who people his daily talk: all of them, right back to the sister-wedding Ptolemies.

One day, their habitual round of morning meetings cancelled due to strikes by native civil servants, they begin their peregrinations early, stopping in on an Albanian shoe-maker whose shop, it turns out, has been vandalised the night before.

"A running battle, Morganou," he half-wails as he crouches on his floor, sweeping up broken glass. "Up and down the street, hour after hour."

"Who was fighting?" Petrou asks.

"Young people: Arabs, Greeks, Italians. Maltese as well, you can be certain." Standing up, he brushes his head against one of the strips of fly-paper hanging from the ceiling, then tears a double-page from the *Egyptian Gazette* lying on his counter. As he lowers himself again to sweep the glass fragments into the paper, Serge runs his eye over the pages now exposed. Their columns, like the flypaper, form long, narrow bands. One lists the ships at quay in Port Said: *Lepanto* in 71; *Nickios*, 28; *Aurora*, 77. Their export manifests descend the adjacent column: ten tons caustic soda, half a million cigarette papers, five tons *haricots*. On the far side, the sports: Sett's taking on Naylor in a ten-round bout at CISC and Othello's favourite over City of Cork and Archduke Ferdinand in the Heliopolis Oasis Stakes at odds of 3–2. Between these long strips, in a thicker column, the Revue Commerciale, in French, compares Nile Gages with last year's. *Coton* is down, *Sel et Soda Egyptien*'s down, the Agricultural Bank's down 1/16, trading at £4 3/16. Along the central crease run ads, all for insurance: Sun Insurance, Anagnostopolou Insurance, Caledonian Insurance (agent: Levant Company, 8c Passage Chérif) . . .

"They sell protection against riots now," the cobbler moans, his own eye following Serge's as he straightens. "I should have bought this last week."

"You'd do well to buy it this week," Petrou tells him. "I fear more trouble's to come."

"I'll buy, I'll buy—but the price doubles now, I tell you, Morganou. And next week, double again! And if," he adds, his eyes rolling heavenwards in deterrent supplication, "independence should come, an emperor's ransom will not guarantee my shop!"

Later that same day, they visit the Cleopatra Stationery Store, and Serge buys a ribbon for the Corona typewriter he's borrowed from the Ministry to write his damage report, his *détaché* dispatch. He buys a small black notebook, and some carbon paper too: official documents, he reasons (although no one's told him this), should be in triplicate.

"She was an Alexandrian as well," Petrou says as they catch a Circular tram outside.

"Who?"

"Cleopatra. Came to the throne at seventeen. Her brother, Ptolemy Thirteen, also her husband, was just ten—and there were two more siblings, eight and five. The whole court was a nursery."

"Didn't she wrap herself up in a tapestry or something?" Serge asks.

"In a carpet, yes. For Caesar. Her real love was Antony, though: that's the one that got immortalised. She poisoned herself after his death, with an asp." Turning to face him, he pokes his pronged hand against Serge's chest and starts reciting:

Dost thou not see my baby at my breast,
That sucks the nurse asleep?

The hand stays there for a while; then Petrou turns slightly sideways again, so that he's partly facing Serge and partly the elegant Ramleh beachfront that's slipping by.

"Dryden has it bite her arm," he carries on after a while. "That's the way Plutarch said it happened. Statues of her and Antony as Isis and Osiris were discovered here . . ."

Serge, watching beach-huts and parasols that seem to move against a sea dotted with small sailing boats that seem not to, pictures a dual-pointed needle sinking into flesh. The tram's slowing down; Petrou's signalling to him to get off.

"Telegraph wires are cut just . . . where is it?" he mumbles as they stand at the trackside, turning left and right. "Ah! Here. See?"

"Yes, I do," says Serge. The wire has been cut in two like a piece of string—and then cut further, with the detached stretch itself snipped into several shorter pieces on the ground. The tram-wires that run beside it are untouched. Petrou steps back and turns half-away again, deferring: telecommunication's Serge's brief, not his. Serge stares at the dead copper snakes for a few seconds, as though they could tell him anything, then follows Petrou's gaze towards the beach. It's late afternoon; beyond the yacht club, on past the casino, the wet sand's turned the colour of oxidised mercury. The scene itself has a *détaché* air: it seems to bear the same relation to reality around it as a photograph—perhaps of somewhere else. The ladies promenading in white hats and dresses, the cravated men hauling their dinghies a few feet up the beach before heading towards the clubhouse, the pale children patting sandcastles: these seem to have been transposed here straight from Torquay, Cannes or Saint-Tropez—as though, in fading light, Europe, like Alexander's Greece, were simulating itself, trying with a dogged persistence to block out the growing knowledge that it can't take root here, that it won't work.

"We should head back to town," says Petrou. "When's the next . . . ?" He runs his finger down the tram timetable. "Would you look at this?" he clucks exasperatedly. "The French and English parts list different times!"

On the way back they pass the Royal Tombs.

"That's the Soma," Petrou says. "Where Alexander's body's meant to lie."

"Meant to?"

"It's almost certain that it never made it here. The Ptolemies liked to believe it did, and had themselves buried on this spot. The prophet Daniel too: his mosque's above the founder's vault. And there's a little Isis temple here as well, just where the Rue Rosette and the Rue Nebi Daniel meet: a whole funerary complex—at the heart of which, unfortunately, there seems to lie a void."

His eyes have been fixed on Serge's chest while he's been speaking, on the spot that he asped earlier. They remain there while the tram pulls up at a stop Serge recognises as his own, and move with it while Serge steps down onto the pavement, saying good night.

He spends his evenings at home, trying to write his report. The

Corona's set up at a writing desk beside the window; on the wall above it, Serge has pinned a map of Alexandria and its surrounding region. He's not sure what to write: the Ministry already know which wires have been torn down, which installations damaged; his brief's the "different angle," the "wider perspective." He glances at the map from time to time, hoping for inspiration, glazing his eyes and moving his head from side to side in an attempt to set its lines, ridges and contours into some kind of motion that in turn might furnish him with what the RFC used to call a "narrative"—but these always seem to sense him coming in advance, and lock themselves in frozen immobility. The Nile's mouth, around Rosetta, forms the shape of a mons veneris. Running his gaze across its inverted triangle back towards the city's more rounded sphere one evening, he passes the dot denoting Ramleh, and recalls the snipped-up snakes. "Wreaking sacrilege," Ferguson said: he was probably right. Closing his eyes, Serge tries to hear what chants, or curses, might have been intoned around the totem posts embodied by the poles, but manages only to pick up game-moves whispered down Ting-a-Ling wires strung up over walls and hedges.

Many attacks on communications,

he starts to type,

seem to be carried out in areas of no military import, and with little practical end. The inconvenience caused to the overall machinery of empire by the interruption of the chain of orders between (for example) a country club and its caterers is negligible. From a symbolic point of view, however . . .

He pauses; it strikes him that he should have used the word "perspective" instead of "point of view." He pulls the paper out—all five sheets of it: the three white ones and the two carbon sheets between them—winds a new stack into the machine, and starts again:

A majority of attacks on communication networks seem to be perpetrated in areas . . .

His knuckle's got a carbon-smudge on it; he wipes this off against his wrist—and, as he does, begins to ponder the issue of Widsun's appendix, his prolegomena. Glancing at Rosetta again as he once more replaces the pages, he types out in block capitals:

PUDENDUM ADDENDUM

Then he leaves, heading for the Iris Cinema. He goes there often: he's seen the film currently showing there, *Love's Madness,* three times. There are bars in his neighbourhood, but he doesn't feel an urge to visit them: he likes the rhythm of typing, watching a film whose every move he knows and can anticipate, returning home, re-reading the pages he wrote earlier, then typing more. Sometimes he just sits and thumbs the carbon paper, letting its smooth, luminescent blackness rub off onto him while he stares through the pane-less window at the other blackness, the one outside. Sounds carry through this: music spilling out of cafés, the clang of metal cups, ships' sirens sounding in the harbour. Beneath this, less audible but equally persistent, a rustling, hissing noise that animates the city at all times. Alexandria's air's electric, harsh with static: lightning discharges flicker above it occasionally, but never bring rain; fireflies glow and fade, like faultily wired bulbs. It seems to Serge at times that in the city's pulses, in its interrupted flows, there lurks some kind of unrequited longing. This is what he hears in the muezzin's chants threading meshed balconies, or in the cries of tradesmen and the wails of beggars filtering through palm trees. More than anything, it's what he hears in Petrou's voice, its exiled, hovering cadences—and what he sees in Petrou's face and body, his perpetual slightly sideways stance: a longing for some kind of world, one either disappeared or yet to come, or perhaps even one that's always been there, although only in some other place, in a dimension Euclid never plotted, which is nonetheless reflecting off him at an asymptotic angle; and reflecting, it increasingly seems, straight towards Serge.

One morning in late February, Serge makes his way to the Ministry through streets thronged with jubilant Egyptians.

"Independence," a sour-face colleague informs him as he enters the half-empty building. "Ferguson wants to see you."

"Independence," Ferguson repeats, equally sourly. "Could have been avoided, if the will had been there. Never trusted Milner, between you and me. He's got one big concession, though, as far as we're concerned."

He looks at Serge conspiratorially, as though the meaning of his statement were explicit. Serge stares back at him blankly.

"Communications!" Ferguson snaps. "Britain reserves the right to maintain both military and civil offices in Egypt 'to protect,' as the wording has it, 'her Imperial Communications.'" His hand dips into the biscuit bowl on his desk and flaps around, finding it empty. "Ishak Effendi —!" he begins to call out, then breaks off. "Opportunist. Can't trust half the people here. They'll probably be back in two weeks' time, promoted to positions of . . ." He shakes his head, then, remembering why he summoned Serge in the first place, announces: "You're being transferred to Cairo. Order came through from Macauley's people just before our operators here abandoned their posts. Seems this independence thing has jolted Cairo, or Whitehall, or whatever ill-informed sub-sub-committee's charged with the issue at the moment, into action: they're finally getting the Empire Wireless Chain's Egyptian station up and running."

"When do I leave?" Serge asks.

"Day after tomorrow. Better go and pack."

"And my report?" Serge asks. "It's finished, more or less."

"What report?"

"Perspective. Sacred phone boxes. I've typed it in tripl—"

"Oh, that. Yes. Drop it off in my secretary's box . . ."

Petrou insists on spending one last afternoon with Serge. He takes him to the museum. The place is virtually empty: Egyptians are too busy celebrating, Europeans cowering indoors, to visit the salvaged jetsam of their city's patchwork past. The two men roam through galleries lined with inscribed tombstones, framed papyri, cabinets of scarabs.

"This is Arsinoe, done as Eurydice," Petrou says as they pause before a statue of a woman holding her distended stomach, as though pregnant. "She was the wife of the second Ptolemy, Philadelphus: his sister, seven years older than him. When she died of indigestion, he was inconsolable."

"Bad ptomaines," murmurs Serge, but Petrou doesn't hear him.

"And this," he continues, laying his hand on Serge's chest once more and drawing him towards the next exhibit, "is Thoth done as Hermes, or Hermes as Thoth, depending on which way you look at it."

"Oh, he's the one with the cap," Serge nods. "Cupid."

"Inventor of writing," Petrou tells him, "god of magic, measurer of time, keeper of divine records. Thoth-Hermes was supposedly the author of the Hermetic books of Roman Egypt. And here's Bast and Sekhet."

"They look like cats," Serge says.

"They are, of sorts: Sekhet has a lioness's head and holds a golden flower, to represent the sun, whose heat she takes into her body and re-emanates. Bast is a standard cat-god. In pharaonic times his statue was everywhere."

"Is that what 'pharaoh' means?" Serge asks. " 'Sun'? Like the *phare* at Pharos?"

"No, it means 'house,' " Petrou answers. " 'Great house.' "

They move on into a room full of small statuettes.

"Funerary art," Petrou comments. "Dead children."

Serge peers at a row of them. One shows a small boy sitting on his mother's shoulders, while the one next to it has the same child, or perhaps one similar to him, riding a toy chariot full of grapes that's drawn by dogs. Another shows seated pupils taking lessons.

"Relics from early Jewish settlers," Petrou tells Serge. "Early Christian too. And Greek, of course: the various religions' figures all blur into one another. This, for example," he continues, leading Serge down the row as though he were a dignitary to whom state officials must be introduced, pausing before a bull-headed figure, "is Serapis, the deity clobbered together for the city by the first Ptolemy, Soter: Dionysus, Osiris, Apis, Zeus, Asculapius and Pluto all rolled into one. It all began here: city of sects and syncretism."

"And incest," Serge adds.

Ignoring his words, Petrou leads him to a large scroll that bears what seems to be a diagram: in black and white, above a set of interlocking rings inset with smaller circles that hold images of birds, compasses or clock-faces, a female figure rises. She, too, is largely composed of circles: round breasts with concentric nipples between which rests a pendant circle with a cross, or aerial, above it; a round womb in which floats a rounded baby; and, above her shoulders, a head formed by the sun, a perfect orb. Words annotate the diagram from every angle: "Lumen Naturae," "Oculus Divinus," "Tinctura Physica," "Water," "Soda," "Terra," "Blood."

"Sophia," Petrou says reverently.

"So fear what?" asks Serge.

"Her name: Sophia. Wisdom of the Gnostics. Syzygy of Christ."

Serge is silent for a while, then says:

"Syzygy: I know about that. That's why those orbs are dark."

He points to two eclipsed suns on the right side of the constellated rings. One of them is blank, like carbon paper; the other has a skull set in it. Above these, to their left, a river, flat as the Canopic Nile-mouth, wends its way up between her legs.

"Philo of Alexandria devised her, to bridge the gap between man and Jehova. She's the Logos, Dweller in the Inmost. Look between her breasts."

He points; Serge follows his finger with his gaze and sees, hovering above the aerial-cross, its frame formed from a square inset with other squares for windows and its roof made of a triangle, a great house.

"Philo was a Jewish Platonist," Petrou continues, "but the Christians picked up the Logos baton and ran with it. For them, Sophia's a sad figure, symbol of our descent. Valentinus—an Alexandrian too—has her undone by love: desiring too ardently to be united with God, she falls into matter, and our universe is formed out of her agony and remorse." Petrou's eyes shift to Serge's chest as he continues: "As an unknown theologian—yet another Alexandrian—wrote of her: 'She is more beautiful than the sun and all the order of stars: being compared to light she is found beyond it . . .' "

It's dusk; the museum's rooms and corridors are murky. The two men stand quite static, Petrou sideways-on to Serge, his gaze fixed on his chest—as though they, too, were sculptures, syncretic overlays of eras and mythologies, gods, mortals and their relics. They remain like this as Petrou continues, in a voice becoming fainter all the time, his recitation:

" 'For after this cometh night . . .' "

His words trail off. Serge turns away from him, towards the window. Through it, in the gloaming, he can see a firefly pulsing photically, in dots and dashes.

ii

The train to Cairo runs through the Wady Natrun soda fields. Serge knows, because he's sat in on at least two meetings about the issue, that the concession to develop these is held by the Egyptian Salt and Soda Company—but it's good to set a proper landscape to an abstract history of bribery, fraud and ineptitude. Between the grey hulk of a factory and the isolated monasteries that wobble in the heat-glare, a giant mineral lake stretches. Despite the heat, the lake seems to be covered with a layer of ice; what's more, the ice has crimson patches on it, as though baby seals had been clubbed there. Trickling streams of claret link the patches to blue and green pools. Above the blushing, multicoloured tracts stand impossibly large birds, perched on lumps of salt that look like towering icebergs.

"The mirage," says the Scotsman sharing Serge's compartment, noticing him staring in bemusement at the scene.

"It's an illusion, then?" Serge asks. "There are no birds?"

"Oh, there are birds all right. But the light's bending and expanding them. Ditto the salt."

"You're seeing it too?"

"We're both seeing what the light's gradient as it hits the warmer air is conveying to our retinas."

"And the crimson?"

"Natron deposits rising to the surface."

This man is an optician, as it turns out. He shows Serge his ad in the *Gazette* (his logo: a hieroglyphic eye-symbol beside a suspiciously anachronistic-looking pair of glasses done in the same style), then retreats behind the same newspaper, emerging from time to time to comment on its contents, none of which are to his liking.

"They're attacking Europeans randomly," he tuts. "Says here a whole train was halted by a mob at Damietta, and white men and women treated to 'the worst indignities.' "

Their train also gets held up, although not by a mob: there's a defect on the Shouba Bridge. It's almost dawn when they arrive in Cairo. Serge makes his way past mini-*phare* lampposts, each casting small cylinders of phosphorous light onto the pavement, to the Ministry. He finds it in a complex so expansive as to dwarf the Alexandria outpost: here are the departments of Unappropriated Revenue, State Properties, Public Works, Justice, Irrigation, Ports and Light, Pensions, Public Instruction, Antiquities, the Army of Occupation, the Suez Canal—and, nestled among these, Communications. All of these seem to be undergoing overhauls: offices lie vacant, their contents packed in boxes on the floor; typewriters, all Coronas, stand stacked up against walls, awaiting relocation or, perhaps, evacuation; people move briskly and anxiously down corridors trying to locate other people who are moving down adjacent ones looking for someone else. Whenever Serge stops one of them to ask directions he's met with an exasperated shrug; it's by sheer chance that he eventually comes across Macauley, standing in the middle of a room supervising the removal of three wall-to-wall shelves' worth of box files.

"I'm Macauley," his new boss, a stout man in his mid-to-late fifties, tells him offhandedly. "If you're from internal accounts then you'll have to wait until I've relocated. Spreadsheets are all packed."

"No, I'm Carrefax," Serge tells him.

"What's that supposed to mean to me?"

"Serge Carrefax. I just arrived from Alexandria. I'm to work on the Empire Wireless Chain. I should—"

"Ah, yes!" says Macauley, turning to face him for the first time. "Widsun's boy. Expected you some time ago."

"I would have been here sooner, but they've had me doing . . . I have it right here."

He opens his case, fishes out the second copy of his *détaché* dispatch and hands it over.

"What am I supposed to do with this?" Macauley asks, tossing it into a box that's being picked up and carried from the room. "First you're three weeks late; now you're one week early."

"Early?" Serge repeats.

"We're shifting operations to the Central Cairo Station. Offices here will be committed to disentanglement: installing native ministers, advising and liaising, other such nonsense . . ."

"And the Wireless Chain?"

"Oh, that'll go ahead—in parallel: through Abu Zabal and another site. That's what you'll be working on—but not yet. Come back in a week. Not here: come to the Central Station. I should be installed by then."

"And what should I do in the meantime?" Serge asks.

"Bed in, attend receptions, buy some trinkets. If you can hunt down Pollard and Wallis they'll take you to the lodgings we've kept ready for you—assuming that these haven't since been taken over by some righteous mob . . ."

The lodgings, near the Ezbekiya Gardens, are intact. From their terrace where he takes his coffee every morning he can see the sun hitting the roofs of Heliopolis, the slopes of Mokatem, the City of the Dead running to Matary. The evenings he spends with Macauley's men Wallis and Pollard, who are a few years older than him. Having first kitted him up with tie and tails in Orosdi-Back's department store, they take him, as their boss anticipated, to receptions: at the Gezira, Turf and Jockey clubs, the Mena House, Shepheard and Continental hotels, or chalet-like private residencies in Maadi, Abdine and Khalifa. One such event, hosted by Conte Mario de Villa-Clary, chairman of the Maltese Colony of Cairo, has an undertone of suspicion laced with resentment: of the civil servants by the Maltese, who feel that the former have never quite accepted them as "proper" British subjects, and of the Maltese by the civil servants, who murmur into their canapés accounts of double-dealing, bet-hedging and convenience-flag seamanship. Another, an annual dinner thrown by the Cairo Horticultural Society, is spoiled by a choice of menu-card background that's deemed unappetising by the majority of those at Serge's table: entitled "De Metamorphosibus Insectorum Surinamensiun," it shows a palisade tree, or *Erythrina fusca*, beset by the moth *Arsenura armida*, depicted in all phases of its life-cycle. Having grown up surrounded by such insectoid mutations, Serge has no problem with the intersecting carapaces and antennae forming a trellis in which the words "asparagus," "saddle" and "parfait" sit; in fact, he quite likes the picture, and slips the card, before the table's cleared, into his jacket pocket to take home with him as a memento.

He spends most of his days trawling the markets—the antiques ones—buying, as Macauley suggested, trinkets. Ankhs and scarabs, signet rings, papyri, necklaces. The scarabs come in many shapes and styles: square, oval, decorated, some with beetle-armour moulding on their backs, others with images (the sun, a bird, a human figure writing something), others still with geometric patterns: circles, spirals, mazes. He buys them for his mother and his father, for Maureen, the schoolrooms. For Bodner he buys jars containing pulverised mummified cat, which, he's informed in broken English by the seller, is a prodigious fertiliser.

"Is that true?" he asks Pollard a few hours later.

"Apparently," Pollard replies. "The tombs they've been unearthing constantly for the last hundred years are so full of these bandaged creatures that they're twenty to the dozen, and quite nutrient-rich to boot. Whether or not you're getting the real thing each time you buy a jar of ground-down ancient cat in a market is another question. Same goes for the scarabs and papyri: half of them are fake."

Wallis, warming to the theme of forgery, tells Serge to double-check his change in shops and cafés: there's a glut of counterfeit 10-piastre pieces and 5–livre égyptienne banknotes going round these days. It's not just currency that's counterfeit: people themselves are often of dubious provenance—especially Europeans. You never know whether the person you meet in a restaurant is a surgeon or minor statesman as he claims, or a card-sharp, pimp or hustler. The *Gazette*'s awash with stories of well-spoken Englishmen who waltz into the Continental, introduce themselves as middle-men for jewellers and take consignment of gold watches and diamond rings to show to clients, never to reappear; or ones who scour the social pages to learn who's pitched up in town and where they're staying, then set out to befriend, seduce and generally swindle them. A well-known bigamist, one article announces, who's wanted for gross deception, extortion and manslaughter, is rumoured to be passing through Cairo incognito: "HE COULD BE ANYONE," the headline shouts excitedly. It's true: anyone and everyone seems to pass through here; it's the gateway to the Middle and Far East. Oil prospectors, irrigation-pump importers, engineers, brokers, general speculators: they're all milling around, waiting for boats or business, trying to buy or sell something or other. One evening, in the Savoy Palace brasserie, Serge runs into his old Hythe training partner, Stedman.

"You survived!" they blurt out simultaneously, equally incredulous.

"Did anybody else?" Serge asks.

"Pepperdine got taken prisoner on his first flight, I heard. Spurrier got wounded and shipped home. The rest are dead, I think."

"And you?"

"Bullet-resistant. Like a reverse magnet: they just veered away from me. Must be some magic powers those lacrosse girls had. I went through five observers—no, six. The best part of the ground crew in my squadron got killed too; but I was in the air each time the bombing raids came. I've been flying ever since: figure it's lucky for me . . ."

"Flying where?"

"Joy rides over London until last year."

"I read about those," Serge says, his head filling with Amazonians and Osram Lamp advertisements. "From Croydon, right?"

"Exactly," Stedman answers. "Now I'm heading for the Levant, to do aerial surveys for the Anglo-Persian Oil Company."

"If they can still afford it, that is," a fellow diner to whom Serge was vaguely introduced some nights ago, and who's been listening to their conversation while he reads the *Gazette* at the bar, chips in. "Their share price is down three-sixteenths."

"Three-sixteenths isn't so bad," counters Pollard, who's wandered over, having failed to secure an invitation to the table of a minister whose wife he's been buying drinks for. "The Agricultural Bank's down a whole pound, and the Banque d'Orient's fallen two since independence. If they can take it, Angie-Percy can drop the odd sixteenth and bounce back."

"Bounce back?" the *Gazette*-reader scoffs. "I'm not sure any of them can 'take it,' as you say. We'll all be lucky to avoid a run."

"I don't think . . ." Pollard begins—but the man, warming to his subject, cuts him off:

"Least of our worries, anyway: says here there's talk of a complete withdrawal."

"I can assure you that that option's not being—" Pollard tries to tell him, but the man continues:

"Even the Copts want us out, apparently. If our fellow Christians won't stand by us, then what hope have we got? And to top it all, we're being assassinated left, right and centre."

"Bit of an exaggeration . . ." Pollard answers soothingly.

The man waves his *Gazette* at him. "Page seven: 'Italian Lawyer Shot in Labban.' Page eight: 'E. Brown, of Ministry of Public Instruction, Shot in Abdine.' Further down the same page: 'F. Bloch, of Egyptian State Railways, Bludgeoned—' bludgeoned!—'in Boulaq.' "

"Got a nice alliterative ring to it," Serge says.

"Meanwhile," the gazetteer continues, "they're not even guaranteeing our pensions."

"Not so," Pollard disagrees. "Pensionable-age officials are being told that they can leave on ad-hoc—"

"Right," the other jumps in again, "but only if we can show that we're working under 'unacceptable conditions.' What's unacceptable? Being shot at's only unacceptable once it's occurred, and by then it's too late."

"What ministry are you in?" Pollard asks him.

"Finance," the man answers resentfully. "I'm having to help ratify this great injustice. And to add insult to injury, I'm being made to divest my own powers to some underqualified and smirking local. 'Disentanglement,' they call it; I call it rubbing ourselves out."

He makes a frotting motion with his hand. Serge, his magnetic thought-poles influenced by Stedman's presence, thinks of Walpond-Skinner's ledger, then of balls of wool, then of Widsun, whose 'appendix' he has yet to write . . .

Besides British officials and their civil servants, labourers from all over Europe and entrepreneurs and hustlers from the earth's four corners, the town's also full of tourists. They seem quite oblivious to the political upheaval taking place around them—yet they have their own brand of disquiet. Serge spends an evening in the company of one: an Abigail he picks up, like some fraudster, at the Continental and, giving her parents, a Chelsea banker and a Lawn Tennis Association social secretary, the slip, takes to one café, then another, then another, the establishments' respectability diminishing as they progress, until they find themselves surrounded by horse-players and their bookies, courtesans on breaks and worse. The conversation buzzing around them is full of High Nile stakes and boxing odds, of anxious speculation about what will happen if capitulations are repealed and foreign miscreants tried in native rather than consular courts before being locked up, unsegregated, in Man-shiyya. Abigail, insensible to these strands that Serge's ear's unpicking, coughs on the Melkonian he offers her and, waving smoke from her eyes, complains:

"The brochure says we're meant to 'discover' the Pyramids. But they've already been discovered. Egyptology's a hundred years old. Did you know that?"

"I suppose—" Serge begins, but she continues:

"I read it in the *Times* before we left: a hundred years exactly since that French chap Champignon deciphered that old tablet."

"Second Babel in three feet—" Serge starts to say, but she interrupts him again:

"I mean, my *grand*father remembers seeing the Egyptian court in Crystal Palace as a child. And I read as well, in the same article—was it the same one? Doesn't matter: that one or another like it—that until recently you could pitch up here with a compass and a map, and your hosts would arrange for you to find—to '*find*'—" her voice goes high and squeaky at this point—"a tomb, which they'd prepare overnight for you, mummy and all, while you slept on Oriental cushions. It's all so . . . *fake*!"

She drags on her cigarette again, then, puffing the smoke out in a rush, continues:

"We got all the guidebooks before we set out. The Cook's one told us we should read Herodotus, so as to come here not as tourists but as 'travellers,' 'individual explorers.' So we got that too. But now it turns out everybody else on our tour is carting round a copy of Herodotus—which they got told to buy by Cook. What's individual about that?"

"Maybe—" Serge ventures; but she's on a roll:

"And we got another book as well, that tells us how to do 'research': we've bought a sextant and chronometer, a siphon and barometer and measuring tape—oh yes: and paper to do pressings of inscriptions on these temples, like they haven't been transcribed a hundred million zillion times before. And then, because it's the latest edition that we've got—of the book, I mean—there's a note telling us it's now acceptable to photograph inscriptions rather than pressing them. Acceptable to whom? Who are we photographing *for*?"

Her voice has gone squeaky and breathless again; Serge, looking at her neck, sees that it's flushed. She pauses for a while and sips her drink. Serge, following the red flush from her neck down to her blouse, recalls his nights spent DX-fishing in Versoie: the sense that, in transcribing all the clicks, notating all the messages, logging the stations and their outputs, he was performing a task so vital that a single wrong entry would have disastrous consequences for whole hierarchies of—of what? Committees, subcommittees? Of *important bodies* who relied on him, who'd process and act on his dispatches, who *needed* them. Beyond that: that the stations at the far end of the dial, the signals on the edge of audibility—from ships, or desert outposts, or more distant ships and outposts ever further still being picked up and forwarded through vast, static reaches—were coming from a place so remote and enchanted as to belong to another dimension entirely, a "there" as far divorced from "here" as angels from the mortals before whom they might briefly appear in flickering electric visions. Now, though, there's no "there": he's here where "there" was and it's not "there" anymore, just "here."

"Do you know," Abigail's asking him, "what happened when we went past Gizah on the steamer? Well, I'll tell you: at exactly half past four the dragoman came below deck and said: 'Ladies and gentlemen . . .' " She slips into a mock-Egyptian accent and repeats: " 'La-dies and gentle-men. If you care to as-cent un-to the main deck now, the marvel of the Pyra-mids will be re-vealed to you.' So we as-cented, and the Pyramids were there, just like in the photographs that I'd already seen in all those bloody books but not looking so nice and aesthetic; and people got their cameras out and started photographing them, although I don't know why, because their photos won't turn out as nice as the ones in the books and brochures either. And they didn't even photograph the things for very long, because there was a buffet laid out on the deck, and they all wanted to get at it before the sandwiches and lemonade ran out; but then of course they realised that they had to show a certain reverence towards the Pyramids, while still not missing out on lunch, so they revered and ate and photographed and drank all at once. And our drago-man said: 'Please don't for-get your tem-ple tick-et, as it's valid for the Sphinx tour too.' "

"And what did you do?" Serge asks.

"What *could* I do?" her voice goes high and squeaky and her neck flushes again. "I looked at the Pyramids, and tried to revere them, and photographed a little. Then I looked at the others looking at the Pyra-mids, and photographed these people too. I tried to eat a little, but I felt sick. It was obscene—like a pornographic film: this dirty entertainment laid on for us all to gape at."

"I had that impression in the war," Serge says.

"You were in the war?" she asks, looking straight at him for the first time. "Doing what?"

"Observing," he says. "Gaping from a plane."

"That sounds quite exciting," she says. "Tell me more."

He takes her back to his place. During sex, her gasps have the same high and squeaky pitch as her voice during conversation, as though arousal, for her, were a heightened form of indignation. Kneeling behind her, he watches the flushes move from her neck down her spine and out along her rib-lines. Afterwards, they lie in silence for a while; then she asks him:

"So, did you kill anyone?"

She leaves the next day—on another steamer, heading down to Luxor and Assuan. He thinks of her two days later, though, when, leaving his flat by foot and turning the corner into Rue de Paris, he hears two gun-shots and, looking down the street to where they came from, sees two black figures running from a growing patch of white that's spreading across the pavement. It's milk: their victim, an English professor at the Law School, had stepped outside his front door to collect it when they shot him—they were lying in wait. The man's already dead by the time

Serge reaches him. His blood, trickling from his head and abdomen, is running into the milk, marbling its pool with deltaed strands, like natron on a lake of soda.

iii

The Central Station has its own building, a much more modern one than that housing the other ministries. Antennae sprout from its roof; soldiers guard the compound that surrounds it: Imperial Communications are indeed, as Ferguson intimated, "protected." Its rooms are full of people and equipment, its corridors of well-directed bustle. Macauley leads Serge past rows of desks at which men sit with headphones on, transcribing letter sequences while other men move up and down the rows gathering the transcriptions and depositing them in front of yet more men who mark them up on blackboards. In a corner two more men are working their way through a pile of newspapers—*Gazette, Wady et Nil, al-Ahram, al-Balagh, al-Jumhur, al-Akbar*—underscoring certain words, then tearing out the pages on which these have been highlighted and passing them to the gatherers, who convey them to the marker-uppers, who, in turn, copy them out to mingle with the letters on the boards.

"They use all kinds of channels," Macauley says to Serge, obscurely.

"Who do?" Serge asks.

"Everyone!" Macauley answers. "We're at the crossroads here, the confluence of all the region's interest groups' transmissions. We're listening to the Wafdists and the Turks; they're listening to Ulamáists and Zionists; the French are listening to us, and we to them—but we share info on the Russians, who we both hate, although not as much as we all hate the Germans, who we listen to as well. Or is it the Spartacans? In any case, we listen to them all. Telegrams, radio messages, acrostics and keywords lurking within print: we try to pick as much of it up as we can. A thankless task, of course; who knows what tiny fraction of it all we actually get?"

"And that's what all these men are doing?" Serge asks.

"All these men and more: my *décryptage* department. Headed up by Egyptologists. Got the right minds: used to cracking New Kingdom texts or something. Rebus logic. It all goes above my head, to tell you the truth. This stuff," he continues, leading Serge through a door into the next room, "I can understand a little better: at least it looks like something vaguely recognisable."

He's pointing to a wall on which a huge map, as big as eight or so of the other room's blackboards, is painted: a map extending from Izmir down to Khartoum and from Tunis to Baghdad. Pins of various colours have been jabbed into this—some small and some with heads as large as ping-pong balls, some all alone and some in clusters. More pins are being added all the time, by men consulting photographs, hand-written notes and smaller maps.

"ImagInt," Macauley says. "Aerial, terrestrial, snapped, painted, scribbled on some scrap of fabric: it's all there. Even livestock movements, locust swarms, what have you. All adds up—or at least, it's supposed to. HumInt too, of course."

"What's humming?" Serge asks.

"HumInt: Human Intelligence. Got agents everywhere: here; Suq Al-Shuyukh, where the sheiks all meet; Nasiriyah, from whence sedition seems to spread down the Euphrates to the Arab tribes; the Shia holy cities, hotbeds of intrigue and points, if memory serves me rightly, of contact with Damascus, which, via them, can exercise remote control of Persia . . . or is it the other way round? Either way, we've got to keep an eye and ear out for what's brewing. We have men doing the Hajj, or wandering around with herdsmen, or hanging out in mosques, bazaars, communal washhouses, village meetings . . ."

"*Folklore?*" Serge asks, pointing to a table labelled with this word, across whose surface lies a mish-mash of handwritten pages crudely illustrated with pictures of lions and eagles.

"Supposed to contain useful information," Macauley responds. "Stories of curses going round, or afrits haunting districts, may be telling us something . . . or not . . ." He sighs. "It's all pretty intangible: whispers and rumours drifting like some kind of vapour across swathes of desert . . ."

"Back in London," Serge says, "I was reading about some chap named Laurice, Lorents, Laudence . . ."

"That fucking twit," Macauley snorts. "Bombards us all the time with useless information. Not just him: every two-bit traveller, 'adventurer,' 'novelist' or general man of leisure who's inherited more money than sense . . . ladies of leisure too: they're just as bad . . . Sending us their 'reports,' briefing their friends on Fleet Street to extol their bravery and cunning to readers who aren't any the wiser, then expecting knighthoods when they get home . . . Fantasists and frauds, the lot of them! The worst part of it is, they're actually quite useful."

"How?" Serge asks.

"With the other parties all spying on us, if we appear to take something seriously, well, they take it seriously too. We call it 'feedback'—no, hang on a second . . . 'bleedback': that's it. Lots of those sequences you saw being written out across the blackboards in the other room get bled back too, mutated but still recognisable, in telegrams, transmissions, new acrostics . . . Make sure they're confused as we are, eh? Plus, who knows? We might actually hit some nerve, activate something . . . maybe . . . Oops! Don't let us get in your way: carry on!"

This last phrase is directed at a man who's arrived bearing more photographs, maps, foolscap pages. As Serge and Macauley move aside, he sets them down on the table next to the folklore one and starts sorting them, stamping each with a different scarab-sized seal as he does so.

"Half the people in the region are spies," Macauley says as they move on. "Engineers, archaeologists, anthropologists: you name it. If they're not spies, they're suspected of being spies, which makes them just as much a part of the whole maddening caboodle as if they had been. To give you an example: we've been keeping a close eye on a consignment of butterflies that's at quay here on its way from Baghdad to the Tiergarten in Berlin. Butterfly eggs, to be precise: they'll hatch when they arrive. The French have been showing a keen interest in the consignment. The Italians too. The Wafdists not—which might be because they already know something we don't. The eggs are being escorted by some acclaimed naturalist, Professor Himmel-This-or-That von Something-Else. Papers in order: all legitimate, perhaps; or perhaps not. We've picked up intimations that the whole operation forms part of a larger German rearmament plan, although how it does this isn't clear; also, that Prof Von's in cahoots with the Bolsheviks; or, in fact, the Turkish CUP. And it has been decided, at some juncture, that, for our part, we should act as though each of these theories held water."

"But what's the truth?" Serge asks.

"The truth?" Macauley repeats. "Who's to say? Scientists—physicists—are telling us that two things can be true at once nowadays. The point is, if we think the butterflies are something other than what they are, or that they serve some purpose other than that which they serve, or if we act as though we think this, then the French will also think they are—do, I mean—or think that they've tricked us into thinking this, and the Italians will follow suit, which means the Germans will . . . I lose track beyond that point . . . It's quite frustrating . . ."

He sighs again, and leads Serge from the room. As they move down a corridor, Macauley continues, wistfully:

"One of my men's working on mirages: trying to prove they're real . . ."

They're in his office now. The box files have been rehoused on new shelves; the desk has one large folder on it, labelled "EmpWirCh." Macauley holds his thumb and finger to his scrunched-up eyes for a few seconds after he sits down, then opens them again and says to Serge:

"So, finally: the pylon at Abu Zabal is to be completed. It'll be switched on in May, they say. About eight years too late—eight years in which the nation that had radio before all others has slipped hopelessly behind. The French alone have high-powered transmitters in Beirut, Bamako and Tananarive; America has five times more foreign stations than we have; even the Germans match us kilowatt for kilowatt world-wide. It's an embarrassment. And all because the Post Office Department and the Committee of Imperial Defence couldn't agree; or if they did they couldn't get the Admiralty on board, or the Treasury, the Board of Trade, the India Office, the Air Ministry or whatever other gaggles of failed politicians had to be in accord in order for the whole thing to progress. Do you know," he asks Serge, "how many committees have been set up to address the Imperial Wireless question in the last eight years?"

Serge shrugs his shoulders.

"Six! The technology's not even the same now as when Marconi first proposed the whole chain idea: arc-transmission's giving over to the valve method; there's talk of a new beam-system that'll enable long-distance communication without intermediary stations; who knows what else? The man himself, meanwhile, seems to have lost his marbles. Last I heard he was heading to Bermuda, to find out if Mars is sending wireless messages to us."

"Marconi?" Serge asks.

Macauley nods.

"But I thought," Serge says, "that he wasn't involved in the whole chain thing anymore."

"Oh, he's not," Macauley reassures him. "The Cabinet felt he'd have a monopoly, which is precisely what they wanted for the Post Office. They forgot, though, to consult with their Australian and South African counterparts, who've thumbed their nose at Whitehall by developing their own high-powered transmitters with him—Marconi, that is. Now Whitehall's worried the Dominions will start distributing counter-productive content through the airwaves—which is why they're setting up, back home, a national Broadcasting Corporation, to pump a mix of propaganda, music and weather reports all around Britain and, eventually, to every corner of the Empire. Which, in turn, is why they've realised that they'd better get the Abu Zabal pylon up and running, and start working on the next one, and the next . . ."

"Strange timing," Serge says.

"What's that?"

"That we start broadcasting central content Empire-wide just as we lose our empire . . ."

"The irony is, as they say, striking," Macauley concurs.

"They should play dirges," Serge suggests.

Macauley breathes out heavily, then tells him, in a voice that's laced with fondness: "I can see your father in you."

"You know my father too?" Serge asks.

Macauley looks back at him bewilderedly. "Well, yes, of course," he says. "After all, he's the one who sent—" He stops, as though catching himself, and looks away, then, shifting in his seat, continues: "The new chain will run in parallel—through Egypt at least."

"Oh yes, you mentioned that," says Serge. "What does that mean?"

"It means," Macauley tells him, "that beside the Abu Zabal pylon, which we'll visit after lunch, Egypt will host another mast. The chains will split beyond here: one running through Nairobi down to Windhoek and the other on to India and Singapore."

"And where will the second Egyptian mast be?"

"Where indeed? That's where you come in. I'm sending you upriver to scout out a possible location."

"When?" Serge asks.

"Few days from now," Macauley tells him. "There's a large party heading up to Sedment. We've been helping them with the Antiquities Service: concessions and the like. French interests prevail there, I'm afraid."

"We're going to a place called Sediment?"

"No: Sedment. Falkiner's the archaeologist: a good man, friend of the Ministry. He's been digging there a while; returning there this week with some equipment too large to transport by train. The Inspector of Monuments is sending a man too. Then there's some Frenchie—chemist, I think. Keep an eye on him."

"And you want me to decide whether the second transmitter should go there?"

" 'Decide' might be too strong a word. 'Advise.' Assess the spot's particulars: whether it's got easy landing, flat ground, raised rather than sunken—that kind of thing . . ."

A bell sounds somewhere down the corridor. Macauley rises from his chair and beams:

"Ah: lunch!"

Their table seems to be the refectory's senior one: its occupants are older, all Macauley's age, and ooze the same air of confused frustration.

"Falkiner got his concession at last, did he?" a moustachioed colonel asks. "Thought the whole thing had passed right out of our hands."

"We had to let Lacau send one of his men along," Macauley explains, buttering his bread.

"Is that the chemist?" Serge asks.

"No: that's Pacorie," Macauley answers.

"That cad?" the colonel snorts, spraying his soup. *"Méfie-toi!"*

"French are being sneaky as hell of late," a red-faced HumInt officer adds, pouring wine for himself and the others. "They're setting up semi-autonomous local states within Syria."

"Why?" asks Serge.

"They're tied in with Amir al-Husayn," the HumInt officer says.

"You think so?" asks Macauley.

"Without doubt," the other answers. "They've been undermining us right from the off by siding with the Arabs."

"We've sided with the Arabs too at times," Macauley reminds him. "Fomenting unrest and all that."

"Yes, but for other reasons than the French," HumInt responds.

"Half the Wafd have spent a good long stretch in Paris," says the colonel, whether by way of agreeing or disagreeing with his colleague Serge can't quite work out. "They were liaising there with Comintern envoys. Bolsheviks are the real villains of this piece."

"Oh, let's not forget Constantinople," cautions HumInt. "They've got their finger on the button as far as Mecca's concerned. They could summon up an armed conspiracy at any moment—one that would spread like wildfire through the entire Muslim world."

"So in stirring up the Arabs, we've been doing the Turk's work for him?" Macauley asks.

"It depends."

"On what?"

"On the role of the Muslim Soviets in Jeddah."

"Exactly!" the colonel sputters excitedly, pushing his bowl away. "It always comes back to the Soviets. Arabia's becoming Bolshevised: the Zionist immigration to Palestine is seeing to that."

"But I thought," Serge chips in meekly, "that the Jews and the Arabs hated one another."

"Maybe they do," says the colonel. "But Moscow's perfectly capable of playing them both."

The main course comes. More wine is poured.

"There's little evidence," the HumInt officer continues after they've all taken a few mouthfuls of lamb chops, "that the Russian residency's actually doing much at present."

"All the more reason to conclude they are," replies the colonel. "Time of study, period of observation and all that. When somebody goes quiet, they're usually cooking something up. Take the Swiss."

"Yes: you've been paying them quite a bit of interest these last few months," Macauley says. "I was wondering why."

"Back door to Germany, and hence outpost of Soviet Marxism. They have their own paper here: read by bankers, watchmakers and the like. Least obvious of all channels, and for that very reason the most dangerous . . ."

"I sometimes think," says HumInt, "that we need to look closer to home: Sinn Féin, the Labour Party . . ."

"Precisely!" snaps the colonel. "And where do those two take their orders from? You want to see what links Sinn Féin, the CUP, Young Persia, Labour, Spartacus and who knows what else: follow the Cyrillic script . . ."

"And Sarikat al Islam?" Macauley asks.

"That's harder to track," the colonel concedes. "India Office back home are uncooperative. We listen in on them too."

"Sarikat al Islam?"

"No: the India Office, for the Foreign Office—who, quite possibly, are having them spy on us . . ."

"Then there's Churchill's old bugbear, the Egyptian Vengeance Society," HumInt adds.

"Does that one exist, or not?" Macauley asks.

"It does now."

"I seem to recall Standard Oil using them to stir up trouble," says the colonel, squinting a little.

"Me too," says HumInt, also staring vaguely in front of him, as though trying to discern some kind of outline. "Them or the Kemalists: that one was never entirely clear to me . . ."

The discussion continues while they ride in a car towards Abu Zabal. As they pass the city limits it winds down, and the four men stare in silence at the desert. The colonel dozes; once, as the road's surface jolts them, he mumbles the word "Comintern" into his moustache, only it sounds more like "coming turn" or, perhaps, "coming term." They pass through groves of date palms, then, just beyond the old Ismailia Canal, a village at whose edge a slaughterhouse stands. Heads and entrails have been thrown over its wall for dogs to pick at; their muzzles, purple with clotted blood caked by the sun, briefly emerge from their carrion nosebags to follow the car's progress before burying themselves in cartilage and membrane again. The station's beyond this. Its four masts, each about two hundred and fifty feet tall, are woven together by a net of wires.

"Like in the Chilean archipelago," Serge says.

"What's that?" Macauley asks.

"It must be powerful," Serge answers.

"You bet it is!" Macauley exclaims proudly. "Got to reach all the way to Leafield in Oxfordshire."

The colonel and HumInt wander off towards a table from which a large urn is doling coffee out to engineers and workers, all European, some of whom wear boiler suits with "British Arc Welding Company of Egypt" printed on the lapels. Further away, scantily clad Egyptian Qufti pass *homrah* slabs down a long chain that runs from the spot where the Mataria railway line ends towards the radio station's compound.

"Before the track came out here," says Macauley, noticing Serge watching them, "we had camels carry it all in: whole caravans of them crossing the sand. Looked like a scene from pharaonic times: building the Pyramids or something . . ."

Serge, looking across his shoulder, sees an arc welder perched halfway up one of the masts' steel frames, soldering a cable into place.

"Look at the terrain," Macauley continues, walking Serge away from the pylons. "Flat, unencumbered, plain. That's the type of landscape our parallel erection needs."

They pause at the compound's edge. Serge stares out at the desert. In the distance, a caravan, or perhaps a line of joined-up, sleepwalking schoolchildren, seems to glide across a shimmering, reflective lake.

"Mirages *are* real," he says to Macauley, suddenly remembering his conversation with the optician on the Alexandria-to-Cairo train. "They're caused by the light's gradient as it . . ."

But Macauley's gone, headed towards the urn. Serge watches his figure shrink beneath the station's geometric mesh, then turns away from this to face once more the utterly ungeometric desert. A squeal carries towards the compound from the slaughterhouse—and makes him think, again, of Abigail, her high-pitched, squeaky voice. He recalls what she told him about feeling sick at Gizah, her impression of watching what she called an "obscene spectacle." Perhaps she wasn't wrong. What if the whole of Egypt were one big, endlessly repeating pornographic film, *Love's Madness* on a loop? The camel-schoolchildren turn into dancing girls with flailing limbs, then flowers or umbrellas opening, or perhaps bodies being torn apart: tricks of the light casting a flickering pageant of agony and remorse across a dense and endless sheet of matter.

12

i

He's to travel upriver on a steel-hulled *dahabia*, departing from quay 29 at Boulaq. He arrives to find the boat already being towed out into the river.

"Not again!" he moans to the docker repositioning the fenders hanging from the berth's edge.

"What's the problem?" the man asks.

"I was meant to be on that," Serge tells him.

The docker stares at him for a few moments, then breaks out in laughter.

"What's so funny?" Serge asks.

"It's not leaving yet," the man says. "They're only sinking it."

"*Only* sinking it?"

"They sink it to get rid of all the rats. Then they refloat it and kit it out with clean stuff; *then* you board it, it's towed out again, they hoist the sails and set off properly. Understand?"

"It's a sailing boat?" Serge asks.

"Has to be for this trip," the docker answers. "Vibrations not good for the instruments."

He jerks his thumb towards a group of men carrying large wooden boxes from a warehouse to the quayside. Overseeing them is a bespectacled European girl; barking orders at both her and the porters is a bearded European man.

"Careful with that box!" the latter calls out in an English accent. "If the theodolite gets damaged, the whole expedition's stuffed. Lawrence & Mayo label upwards."

He looks about the same age as Serge's father.

"Are you Falk—?" Serge begins to ask.

"Label *up*wards!" he shouts. "Who are you?"

"Serge Carrefax. From the Ministry of Communications."

"Ah, yes: Pylon Man. *I know thee, and I know thy name, and I know the name of the god who guardeth thee!*"

He speaks these last few words as though somehow performing them: arms straight by sides, head up, voice measured and incantatory.

"I'm sorry?" Serge asks.

"Look: it's sinking," says the girl, pointing over the men's shoulders.

Serge and Falkiner both turn round. The *dahabia*'s hull, deck and cabins have all disappeared beneath the Nile, leaving only two bare masts to mark its watery burial site. Small eddies whirl around these, giving over to more violent eruptions as air from the boat's interior rises to the surface.

"Rats abandoning: not a good sign," another English voice at Serge's back says, ominously. Turning round again, Serge finds a man in his mid-thirties, in plus-fours and a chequered yellow waistcoat. "You Macauley's scout?" the man asks.

Serge nods, a little apprehensively. "And you?"

"I'm from Antiquities. Alby's the name! Seems we'll be shipmates on this jolly spree."

As Serge and Alby shake hands, an argument breaks out beside the warehouse. This time the voices aren't English: one of them's Egyptian and the other, which belongs to a man wearing a long, black jacket and a matching bow tie, is native to the language in which the argument's being conducted.

"C'est marqué dans le manifeste!" the bow-tied man's trying to convince the clipboard-holding Egyptian, over and over again.

"Pas marqué dans mon manifeste, Effendi," the Egyptian's insisting, tapping his board. "On nous en a donné des nouveaux hier."

"A mon insu!" the Frenchman cries, turning his palms out.

"Désolé: je ne peux pas les embarquer," replies the Egyptian, shaking his head.

"Ce sont mes utils!" the other hisses, gesticulating with his hands in a way that reminds Serge of M. Bulteau's gunpowder-act in Kloděbrady. Running his eye along the quayside, Serge can see the object of the argument—objects, rather: a new set of boxes, smaller ones, have been unloaded from a taxi and stacked up next to Falkiner's surveying instruments.

"Pacorie," Alby mutters to Serge. "Heaven knows what he's got with him."

"No magnets, I hope!" Falkiner barks, walking over to inspect the rival boxes.

"Only *minuscule* ones," whines Pacorie, casting a hurt look back at him.

"Magnets play havoc with my compasses," Falkiner snaps.

"So: I leave behind the magnets, and you tell this *clown* to sign the other *boîtes* for embarkation; is okay?"

Negotiations rumble on for the next hour or so. Serge introduces himself to the girl. She's called Laura and must be about twenty-three or -four, like him. She's been working for Falkiner for six months, she informs him, both in London and here "in the field."

"Field?" asks Serge.

"Desert, delta, bank, whatever," she corrects herself. "Territory."

"You're heading towards some tomb or other, right?" Serge asks her.

"Not just one," she tells him, rubbing her palm against her forehead as she speaks. "Sedment's an enormous burial site. There are thousands of tombs, all stacked on top of one another. Professor Falkiner's one of the men who first excavated there. I studied his work at university."

"So why's he going back again?"

"The layers are—"

She doesn't get to finish: Alby's wandered over and is asking Serge if he's brought picaridine with him.

"No: he came on his own. He's a chemist or something—"

"No, *picaridine*: insect repellent. You'll be needing plenty of it."

"Aren't those mosquito nets?" Serge asks, pointing to a pile of fine-mesh webs folded up on the quayside next to an assortment of mattresses, carpets, blankets, sheets, towels and pillows.

"Nets don't catch everything," Alby tuts in the same ominous tone he used earlier.

"Oh, look: the boat's rising again," Laura says.

The men turn round once more, and see the white hulk break the surface like some wood-and-metal Aphrodite. Muddy water gushes from her every orifice.

"Won't it take a while to dry out?" Serge asks.

"We don't leave until tomorrow," answers Alby.

"I was told today."

"Today's loading. Where's your stuff?"

"I've just got this," Serge says, pointing at the small suitcase by his feet.

"May as well go home, then; get a last night's sleep on solid ground."

Serge does this. Back in his flat, he shuffles aimlessly through a stack of papers and finds, wedged among them, the small, unused pocket notebook he bought back in Alexandria. He slips this into his jacket: it'll be where he sets down his thoughts about the suitability or otherwise of Sedment as a site for the parallel mast. Beneath it lies the sheet of paper with "PUDENDUM ADDENDUM" typed across it. It occurs to him that he should send the third and final copy of his *détaché* dispatch to Widsun: since it seems that no one else is going to read it, it will, indeed, be—as requested—just for him. He digs this out: its print is weak and carbon-smudges cloud the paper's surface, but it's legible. He slips the thing into an envelope that he addresses and is just about to seal when he changes his mind. He slides the report out again and, in its place, inserts the Horticultural Society's illustrated menu-card: the "Metamorphosibus Insectorum," the sick palisade, the hungry and rapacious grubs and moths that scrape and prod at words and world alike with their blunt carapaces and sharp antennae. Then he seals it and leaves it in his post out-basket, to be picked up and sent tomorrow.

The *dahabia,* whose name, Serge learns when he arrives the following morning and sees it painted on the hull, is *Ani,* casts off just before noon. The tug-pilot who tows it from the quay into mid-river wears a look of blank indifference; the *Ani's* crew, too, perform their duties with the same disinterested expression: hoisting the sails, cleating ropes, plying the tiller. They progress at a slight diagonal across the river's surface— not tacking, since the wind's behind them, but not following its course directly either: every so often, as they near first one bank, then another, the boom swings languidly across the foredeck as the helmsman brings the boat about. The wind may be behind them, but the current's not: it runs backwards past the bobbing prow, shunting them constantly to leeward.

"It's counter-*intuitif,*" says Pacorie, noticing Serge watching the flow.

"What is?" Serge asks.

"*Appellation:* Lower Egypt, Upper Egypt."

"You're right," says Alby, who's sitting beside them on the deck. "I always wondered why the northern part's called 'Lower' and the lower 'Upper.' "

"Altitude," Pacorie explains. "The *terrain* rises as the country descends from the sea. The river flows from south to north. One time each year it *débords*, and deposits black silt over the fields. That's why the land is black—but only in a narrow corridor along the Nile."

"A strip," says Serge.

"*Précisement,*" nods Pacorie, approvingly. "Only this strip is cultivated. The silt allows lush *marécages* with fish and birds on either side the river, and soil that is *oxygène*-isated, and so good for food. The villages are just above the line of *débordage*. Then comes hills and desert: no fertile *terrain* there; no habitations either."

"I wouldn't say that," murmurs Alby. "You're forgetting the dwellings of the dead."

Pacorie thrusts his lower lip out and rolls his forearms upwards in acknowledgement. Steamers chug past them, following the river's line directly and at more than twice their speed. Watching them go by, Serge is struck by the strange and slightly dizzying sensation that, in their anachronistic sailing boat, they're somehow drifting leeward in time, too: slipping back—or, more precisely, *sideways*—in it, losing traction on the present.

"Heading for Luxor," Falkiner calls out from midship, pointing at the steamers. "Place is a giant dummy chamber."

"What's a dummy chamber?" Serge asks.

"It's a trick," says Laura, rubbing her forehead again, "used by the pharaohs to fool the plunderers they knew would one day come and disinter their funerary complexes. They'd have a second burial chamber, not the real one, built in a part of the structure that was relatively easy to find, and fill it with a few half-precious things. The thieves, thinking they'd hit the jackpot, would stop digging when they came across it, and the real chamber and its treasures would stay undiscovered."

She looks over at Falkiner expectantly, as though awaiting some sign of approval for her annotation. He neither gives nor withholds this, but continues:

"Draws the tourists to it like so many flies to shit." Raising his fist at the parasoled and safari-hatted passengers who lean across the steamer's railings facing their way, he shouts: "Buzz, flies, buzz!" These people, for their part, wave back excitedly, mistaking his hostility for friendliness.

Falkiner looks like an old sea-dog with his beard. He holds a sextant and a compass, which complete the look. Between bouts of checking the ship's position against these—or, perhaps, since this act is quite redundant in the circumstances, vice versa—he rails intermittently against the Concession system:

"Worse than taxi licences in London! Most archaeologists would sooner die than relinquish theirs—and when they do, they're snapped up by the EES, the Philadelphia Museum or the Institut Français. Your people have a lot to answer for!"

He points an accusatory finger at the prow—a finger that, due to the boat's motion, wavers between designating Pacorie and Alby.

"Whose people?" Pacorie asks. "Mine, or his?"

"Both of yours!" Falkiner barks back. "Department of Antiquities has consistently favoured the French since Lacau's headed it."

"That's not quite true," Alby responds. "Look who's digging right now: Winlock's at El-Kurneh; Fisher's at Asasif; and Carter and Carnarvon—English as you or I, it must be said—are up at Thebes."

"Won't find a single scarab there," scoffs Falkiner. "And even if they did, your man has signed away our rights to anything we turn up!"

"It's not that simple, as you're well aware," says Alby. "The permittee must notify the Chief Inspector of all finds, and the Antiquities Service assume overall jurisdiction of each dig, while still—"

"Overall jurisdiction? They confiscate the whole lot, and hand it over to the Museum in Cairo, who decide what paltry scraps to toss back to the finder's national collections."

"Isn't that fair?" Alby asks.

"Hell, no! The home of Egyptology is London—Berlin too. What's Cairo got to do with any of this?"

"Could it not be argued—" Alby starts; but Falkiner roars back at him:

"Appeasers! Turncoats! Cowards!"

Towards Serge, Falkiner's attitude is softer—not that he bothers to learn his name: he calls him "Pylon Man" each time he addresses him:

"You an engineer then, Pylon Man?"

"Not at all," Serge replies. "I studied architecture."

"AA?" Falkiner asks.

Serge nods, squinting against the light reflecting off the water.

"Old Theo Lyle still there?"

"I went to his lectures every morning—well, most mornings."

"Theo! We studied together at Cambridge. He still banging on about metopes?"

"Metopes and triglyphs—absolutely." Serge tries to recall the other terms that Lyle used in his lectures, but loses these beneath the buzz of half-remembered conversations in Mrs. Fox's Café, titles of West End musicals, narcotic code-words . . . "How did you become an archaeologist, then?" he asks Falkiner after a pause.

"Grew up in Greenwich: used to ride my tricycle across the Prime Meridian, beneath the Royal Observatory. Gave me a sense of measurement and time, I suppose. I'd go around Kent as a teenager, looking for Roman villas, temples, bathhouses, what have you—little knowing there was one two hundred yards from the observatory."

"Oh yes," Serge says. "I was meant to visit that with my class once. Were you involved in excavating it?"

"I was consulted," Falkiner replies. "Didn't like their method, though. More vandalism than curation: coins, vases, tablets and the like were being hauled out as though the place were a house on fire. Wrong way to go about it: you should brush it down inch by inch, notating everything—positions, state of degradation, the lot. Like police detectives going through the scene of a catastrophe."

"It is like a house on fire, then," Serge says.

"Yes—but the fire's already happened. Everyone's dead; the evidence alone is to be salvaged. Same mistake was being made here when I arrived: explorers ripping stuff out of tombs willy-nilly, plundering as fast as they could, rendering artefacts illegible and therefore meaningless. A real disaster!"

"A disaster that the catastrophe was lost, rubbed out?" Serge makes the frotting motion that the man from the Ministry of Finance made in the Savoy Palace.

"Exactly," Falkiner replies. "Pylon Man, you get it. Only here, it's much more complex: there've been generations upon generations of excavation, which you have to disinter and notate too."

"Egyptology's a hundred years old, right?"

"A hundred? Three thousand, more like. These tombs were being dug up from the moment they were made. Romans, Arabs, the pharaohs themselves would delve into and disinter them—and the artefacts they took from them would themselves be re-located and re-used for their own ends. This is part of what we're studying, or should be studying: you have to look at all of this, at all these histories of looking. The mistake most of my contemporaries make is to assume that they're the first—or, even when it's clear they're not, that *their* moment of looking is somehow definitive, standing outside of the long history of which it merely forms another chapter . . ."

He turns away from Serge towards Laura, and the two of them spend the next few hours planning the elaborate trigonometry according to which their Sedment excavations will proceed in light of the new instruments they're bringing with them:

"If we plot it all in three-point," Falkiner says, "reading by verniers to three seconds . . . What's the average error with that?"

"Four-fifths of one second," Laura answers, counting off her fingers.

"Fine. We take the first triangle from *here*—" he marks the map that's laid out on the deck in front of them—"the second *here*—" a second mark—"the third *here,* and so on. We lay down rock-drilled station-posts, and work out the relative value of each station by taking observations from those. If a shift's proved, we treat the observations as two independent sets, not one . . ."

Serge listens to them for a while, thinking of clock codes, zone calls, houses and batteries on fire. Gazing towards the *Ani*'s sails, he lets the rhombi and trinomials of their conversation run across the surfaces of these, their intersecting angles. Beyond the sails, just past the shoreline, irrigated fields form neat-edged planes; beyond these, the desert is, once more, ungeometric. Birds wheel occasionally above it, homing in on prey, or maybe simply signalling to other birds the whereabouts of decaying carcasses. At some point, the boat drifts past oxen yoked to a water-hoisting mechanism, turning its lever in slow, plodding circles.

"Same *méthode* they are using since antiquity," Pacorie says, noticing Serge looking at them. "Greatest *achèvement* of *technologie* in all the history."

"What: ploughs?"

"No: making the water to flow upwards. Once this was realised, the automobile and flight *mécanisé* were no more than a small step away."

"Still took a while, didn't it?" Serge asks.

Pacorie rolls his lip and forearms outwards again, although this time it's less in agreement than in contestation: *Did it really?* Then, turning away from Serge, he sets about unpacking the boxes that he's been allowed to bring on board. Each one seems to contain a larger, more sophisticated version of the old chemistry set that Serge, *The Boy's Playbook of Science* in hand, used to fool around with. Throughout the afternoon he busies himself taking readings from the river, dangling a test tube on a piece of string from the boat's deck, reeling it back in and emptying its contents into beakers into which he then dips various reactive bands. The water's murky, full of the silt with which it's been fertilising fields and smothering transcendent, Hellenistic dreams since time immemorial. While waiting for the bands to give him readings, he watches Serge, as though keeping track of what Serge is looking at. Each time he does this, Serge looks away, usually at Alby, who himself seems to be observing Pacorie and making the odd entry in a notebook: suspicion, like a yoke of oxen, seems to move in a closed circle. Serge, prompted by Alby's scribbling, takes his notebook out as well, but finds he can't think of anything to write in it. The only words that come to him are *Méfie-toi;* he jots them down. After wondering for half an hour or so what Pacorie and Alby are really on this expedition for, or what their respective agencies think the other might be here for, or want the rival agency to think that they themselves are here for, it strikes him that he should be asking that same question of himself: why has he *really* been sent, through endless counterflows of animated sediment, to Sedment? Could he himself be—to his own *insu,* as Pacorie would say—some kind of decoy: a dummy chamber, and a moving one at that, being slowly dragged across the surface of events? If so, by whom, and for whose benefit, or detriment? Dizzy again, he looks back at the two words in his notebook and underlines the second: *Méfie-toi* . . .

Later, as mint tea and biscuits are served, he chats with Laura, who tells him that she studied history at St. Hilda's College, Oxford:

"I did a dissertation on Osiris," she announces. She goes on to outline the well-known myth: the god's dismemberment, his sister Isis's search for his parts, her conception of Horus from the one part of him that she couldn't find and so was forced to remake for herself, and Osiris's subsequent adoption as the deity of death and resurrection by the people of the Nile, who'd depict him in their art with a large phallus, rising to inseminate each day.

"A res-erection," Serge quips. Laura looks back at him through her glasses without laughing. He pictures the girls he'd see emerging from St. Hilda's gates during his stint in Oxford—riding bicycles, chatting with friends or clutching books as they headed to lectures: maybe one of them was her. SOMA: the School of Military Aeronautics' buildings merge in his mind with the funerary complex Petrou pointed out to him from the Circular tram on the way back from Ramleh, the Royal Tombs—and Alexander, a young Macedonian soldier, morphs into an ankh-bearing, hook-bearded god.

"The sun itself entered the body of Osiris," Laura's saying. "He'd swallow and pass it, bringing about the repetition of creation, the timeless present of eternity. The ancient Egyptian cosmology had no apocalypse, no end: time just went round and round . . ."

Her little lecture fades out, and there's silence for a while on deck, broken only by the regular plash of the bow and the creaking of the tiller. The man holding this smokes a black, wooden chibouk; another riverman sits cross-legged at the prow, staring at the water like a mesmerised Narcissus. The crew's completed by two more Egyptians: one of them lounges at a fixed spot on the cabin's roof, reaching up to casually pass the front sail's boom above his head each time they go about; the other lurks inside, preparing food. The landscape slips by indifferently. Like the crew, it looks bored, weary of being stared at. At sunset, it turns a chemical shade of pink, then green, then changes, via white, to the same dark blue tone as the sky. As they drop anchor they're besieged by insects: grasshoppers, cicadas, moths, mosquitoes. They look like flocks of birds, congesting the whole air and covering cabin, deck, sails, crew and expedition members alike in a twitching and vibrating coat.

"Maybe we're the shit," Serge says to Falkiner.

"Get the nets up," Falkiner instructs the helmsman, who seems quite unbothered by the insects—perhaps because his chibouk's smoke is keeping them away from him. The helmsman murmurs something at his crew, who slowly haul mosquito-netting around the deck's rear, from the roof above the cabin's entrance to the helm beside the rudder, wedging two vertical poles between it and the boards so as to form a tent. They then pick some of the larger insects from the netting's outer surface, fry them over a stove and eat them with *dourah* paste. The Europeans, meanwhile, dine on a stew of dates, figs and pigeons. They drink wine too: Serge, Laura, Alby and Pacorie in moderation, Falkiner to excess. He spends a good hour after supper issuing invocations to the night air:

"*Hail, ye gods, whose scent is sweet,*" he chants, arms pressed to his side like they were when he assumed the same declamatory tone on the quayside in Boulaq. "*I am a swallow; I am a swallow. O stretch out unto me thy hand so that I can . . . so that I can . . . so that I may be—may be!—may be able to pass my days in the Pool of Double Fire, and let me advance with my message, for I have come with words to tell . . .*"

"What is that stuff he's saying?" Serge asks Laura.

"It's from the *Egyptian Book of the Dead*," she replies, hand pressed to her forehead as though this action alone allowed her to think. " 'The Book of Stepping Forth by Daylight,' in fact, if I recognise this passage rightly."

"First thing ever written for a dead readership," mutters Alby.

"*Who then is this?*" asks Falkiner. Not waiting for an answer, he continues: "*It is Ra, the creator of the names of his limbs. Who then is this? It is Tem the dweller in his disk. I am yesterday; I know today. Who then is this? It is Osiris; or (as others say), it is his dead body; or (as others say), it is his filth. I gather together the charm from every place where it is, and from every man with whom, with whom it is . . . and though . . .* Hang on . . . Ah! yes: *And though I be in the mighty innermost part of heaven, let me stay*—remain!—*remain upon the earth . . .*"

Serge turns his head towards the river bank, but can't make it out anymore. Water and sky have disappeared too: there's no moon. Only the glow of the helmsman's chibouk lights the scene at all, intermittently revealing, etched across the faces of the crew, looks of bemused indifference to the bearded interloper's drunken incantations.

He wakes just after dawn to a landscape that seems utterly synthetic. The sun, rising behind hills, is tearing the mist into gauzy shreds. The sky's a worn, scratched kind of red, spliced with orange streaks; the desert's laced with purple. The soil beneath the floodline is, as Pacorie pointed out yesterday, black—a painted-on, superficial kind of black, as though some giant inkpot had been knocked over and stained its surface. The Nile water looks synthetic too: grained and oily, like film. It runs past the boat's prow at an obtuse angle; again there's that slight leeward slippage. Again Pacorie observes Serge studying the flow and shunt. As they drift past a village (Falkiner's forbidden any stops, citing reports of plague) from whose tower a muezzin's chant spills, the Frenchman says to him, reprising yesterday's conversation as though no time had passed between it and the present moment:

"It's counter-*intuitif* in more ways than one."

"What?"

" 'Upper,' 'Lower.' 'Upper' should be newer, but it's older. Its formations were made sooner, when the continent was first *construit*."

"Civilisation and culture too," Alby joins in. "This is where it all began."

"I thought it all began in Alexandria," says Serge.

"Alexandria is where it *ended*," Alby corrects him. "The Christianity and reason that took root there were a re-modelling of dead pharaonic fable. Beneath the cross, the ankh; behind monotheism, a plethora of older deities . . ."

The boom of the foresail sweeps slowly through the air above them, guided by the languid crewman's forearm. Pulleys whirr, teeth click. Serge is so used to the boat's rhythms by now that they colour everything around him: he has the impression of being not in nature but in some giant mechanism, like a clock, sextant or theodolite. The stalks and herons that strut and peck their way through marshes look mechanical; the marshes themselves, the fields, settlements and stretches of desert beyond them look mechanical as well, alternating and repeating like a flat panorama that's wound round and round by a dull, clockwork motor. Passages of desert suggest epochs—present, Napoleonic, ancient—which loom into focus like so many photographic slides, one following the other with an automated regularity; sometimes several epochs appear simultaneously, as though two or three slides had been overlaid. Even the movements of humans take on a mechanical aspect: chibouk-stuffing, tiller-plying, boom-guiding, forehead-rubbing, test-tube-lowering and hoisting, spying. Events follow the same sequence as they did yesterday: Alby and Pacorie and Serge conduct their three-way stand-off; tea and biscuits are served; Laura lectures Serge on Osiris, the information streaming out like a strip of punch-card paper issuing from her mouth—constant and regular, as though, by rubbing her forehead, she had set her exegetic apparatus at a certain speed from which it wouldn't deviate until instructed otherwise. This time she describes to him the festivals performed at Abydos:

"People descended with lanterns and statuettes, awaiting his funerary barge. When it arrived they'd shout: 'Osiris has been found!' A priest wearing a jackal mask would lead the cortege to the cemetery, carrying a chest, and people—"

"A chest?" Serge asks.

"A wooden chest containing silt and seeds: his body, which Isis, through her various travails, had recombined. The statuettes—of corn, earth and vegetable paste—were buried in the ground, and the whole ceremony culminated three days later with the building of a pillar in the temple court—"

Serge, listening to her, his thoughts mechanically tinted, pictures the priest's chest as a wireless set, filled with black metal filings. The image forms so clearly in his mind that he interrupts her to announce:

"Isis was a coherer."

"What's that?" she asks.

"The old sets operated through coherence," he explains. "The signal made the particles all jump together and conduct the current, in bursts either short or long. That's how dots and dashes were—"

"What are you talking about?" she asks.

"Radio," he tells her. "It's a gathering-together too."

Falkiner, eavesdropping, grunts in amusement, then calls Laura over to assist him further with his plotting. In the evening, after the insects have descended and the nets have gone up, they eat pigeon and date again. Falkiner gets drunk again. This time he declaims, in Serge's honour, from "The Book of the Pylons":

"Homage to thee, saith Horus, O thou first pylon of the Still-Heart. I have made my way. I know thee, and I know thy name, and I know the name of the god who guardeth thee . . ."

"I recognise this bit," Serge comments.

"Lady of tremblings," Falkiner intones, *"with lofty walls, the sovereign lady, mistress of destruction, who—*wait—*who sets—setteth—setteth in order the words which drive back the whirlwind and the storm . . . Saith the pylon: Pass on, thou art pure . . ."*

"Pylons?" Serge asks Laura. "Is he making this bit up?"

"No," she resumes her role as annotator. "Pylons were gateways—to both temples and the underworld."

"Homage to thee, saith Horus," Falkiner continues, *"O thou second pylon of the Still-Heart. I know thee, and I know thy name, and I know the name of the god who guardeth thee: Lady of heaven, mistress of the world, who terrifieth the earth from the place of thy body . . ."*

"The deceased, who was himself awaiting recombination, had to pass them all," Laura explains, "naming the guardian of each."

And name them Falkiner does. By the sixteenth pylon it's *Terrible One, Lady of the Rainstorm, who planteth ruin in the souls of men, Devourer of dead bodies;* by the twentieth it's *Goddess with face turned backwards, Unknown One, Overthrower of him that draweth nigh to her flame . . .* The twenty-first speaks of her *secret plots and counsels.* Then comes a long list of the names of all the pylons' secondary guards:

"Tchen of At is the name of the one at the door; Hetepmes is the name of the second; Mes-sep is the name of the third; Utch-re is the name of the fourth . . ."

The crew, again, look on indifferently. Eventually the recitation fades out, but Serge hears its loops and repetitions in the chafing of the anchor-chain against the *Ani*'s side, the clicks and beeps of insects, long into the night.

By the third day, the landscape has grown more hilly and less fertile; now the desert extends all the way to the Nile's banks. Its formlessness seems to have overrun not only the feeble effort to contain it within field-boundaries but also any attempt to box it temporally: today, it's no longer epochs that stare back at Serge from it, but time's basic units themselves, its material particles, freed of their hourglass-walls and mul-tiplied to infinity. He still has the impression of being held in a machine, but now it's one whose operator has abandoned it—or, perhaps, died inside it, at its very core—leaving its motions to repeat without a reason for doing so anymore. Actions are reduced to their own remnants: Pacorie's arm flops and reels over the side like a decrepit lever or gear-handle; he, Alby and Serge spy on one another so half-heartedly it's almost comic, their circular choreography of jottings, sideways glances and averted gazes no more than a set of empty and incomplete gestures. After tea Laura, purely out of habit, lectures him, half-heartedly as well, on the more secret ceremonies to Osiris:

"They were held in underground spots," she says slowly, hand resting languidly across her forehead. "We don't know what was said because the contents were never divulged. They could have been tied in with Thoth . . ."

"Why do you say the word in German?" Pacorie asks in a similarly disinterested tone.

"What word?"

"*Tod. Mort.* The death."

"No, Thoth," Laura explains. "The god of secret writing, whose cult centre was Hermopolis."

"Little round Thoth again," Serge murmurs.

"He carried cryptographic hymns and spells." Laura, if she heard his words, ignores them. "Moses, with his stammer and his tablets of the law, grew out of him. He had his own book: with it, it was said, you could enchant the sky and understand the language of the birds, and other animals as well—even the little ones, right down to microbes. But it was lost . . ."

Nobody takes her up on this, and so the conversation ends. When the insects come, Serge watches one caught in the netting and, turning again to Laura, asks:

"What is it with scarabs?"

"How do you mean?"

"Why are there models of them everywhere, all patterned and inscribed and so on?"

"On the underside, for printing," she says, even more slowly: her apparatus, too, seems to be voiding itself. "On the upper side, to represent Khepera, god of both the rising sun and matter—matter that's on the point of passing from inertness into life. His emblem is a beetle."

"*Hail, Khepera, in thy boat,*" Falkiner slurs, already drunk, "*the three-fold company of gods is thy body . . .*"

"Khepera was part of the solar trinity Khepri-Ra-Atum," Laura barely manages to add. "He was a writer too. And a judge. These attributes were important in Egyptian cosmogony; that's why scarabs are common . . ."

"Secret writing," Falkiner announces. "Isis and Horus, the Department of . . . Department of . . . *that shineth . . . doest homage . . . I am . . . I am all that is, was and will be and no mortal has ever lifted my veil . . . and so saith Isis . . .*"

He continues, like a distant and plague-ridden muezzin, to slur out half-remembered snatches of his scripture. When he runs out of phrases to recite, he repeats the single word "Isis," pronouncing it over and over again, more and more slowly each time, before his voice, too, breaks down into grains and runs away.

ii

They arrive at Sedment the next morning. It's an upland of desert, exposed and windy. Qufti, drawn from nearby villages, form a chain from the main site towards a light railway, just like they did at Abu Zabal—only here they don't seem to be carrying stuff in, but taking it away. There are holes everywhere, funnel-shaped pits riddling the ground: some are cordoned off with rope and neatly cleaned-out; others gape in disarray like ruined mine-shafts or natural craters. At the base of some Serge can see hatches, most of which are splintered, giving him a glimpse of lower holes beneath the holes, leading to more splintered hatches which, in turn, lead to lower shafts.

"Most of these top ones are mastabas," Laura says as they walk past one pit after another.

"Mastur*what?*" asks Serge.

"Mastabas: low-lying tombs of the early dynastic period. They had rectangular mud-brick superstructures and hollow substructures of four or five chambers. Below these, there are later tombs."

"*Below* them?"

"Yes: later dynasties buried their dead lower. Then still-later ones built beside, around, through and all over these earlier-later ones, and so on almost endlessly. This place is a giant warren."

"Looks more like a giant dump," Serge says, pointing to the mounds of debris all around them. Shards of broken pottery protrude from these, alongside scraps of paper that he can't, in passing, make out as either old papyri or contemporary news-pages, plus short lengths of what looks like copper. Beetles scurry up and down the surface of these mounds like mountaineers negotiating faces and approaches. He and Laura come to the spot where Falkiner seems to have established his headquarters: a gully or ravine that cuts a gash into the landscape, in which tent-poles support a canvas canopy that extends a more conventionally front-door-like tomb-entrance into a kind of covered porch.

"We've got to get on top of pilfering," are Falkiner's first words to her. "It's become endemic: tools, food, everything. The Qufti say it's Seb-bakhîn and Arabs, but their word's not to be trusted. We must let them know that the cost of anything in their charge that goes missing will be docked from their own salaries."

"Where shall I put my things?" she asks him.

"In the tomb behind me," he says. "Second chamber."

She moves past him; Serge starts walking with her.

"Whoa! Where do you think you're going, Pylon Man?" Falkiner barks.

"I thought—" Serge mumbles.

"Well, don't," the archaeologist growls back. "You're in a tent in sector K."

He jerks his thumb off to the left. Serge makes his way over the uneven ground in the direction the thumb indicates and eventually finds his tent, pitched in an uncordoned and neglected crater. The crater's shallow; the wind rushing across the upland swirls down into it, throwing handfuls of sand against the canvas in a way that seems intentional, malicious. Sitting inside, he wonders what to do. Unpack? There are no shelves or cupboards here; nothing but a thin and dirty mattress on the floor. Attend to his brief? He takes his notebook out and reads the two words written in it so far: *Méfie-toi*. Not much to go on. Slipping it back into his breast pocket, he leaves the tent and wanders the site for a while. He climbs to a high spot and gazes down over the excavations. The Qufti-chain, viewed from above, looks like a tail or ribbon lightly fluttering beneath a kite whose main frame is suggested by the posts and strings being laid out on the ground in intersecting triangles, the triangles' overlap allotting to each of the site's mounds and craters its own sector, or sub-sector. Falkiner's directing this pegging-out of station-marks, standing with the instruments he's brought down on the *Ani* and has lost no time in having unpacked. His body's shrunk by height and distance. His voice, too: Serge can see from the movements of his arms and shoulders that he's barking orders at the men who scurry around shifting the posts and paying out string, but these are silenced by the wind. If Falkiner's surveying, Serge wonders what *he*'s doing. *Über*-surveying: is that what Petrou would call it, after Alexander's *über*-Hellenism? Flat, unencumbered, plain, Macauley told him. He looks away from the site: to the north, the landscape flattens; to the south, it rises in ridges, plateaus, hillocks. Any of these spots could house a pylon. Taking his notebook out again, he writes, below the first two hyphenated words, a third one: *Arenow*.

That evening, a pot of stew is brought to his tent. After eating it, he wonders where the latrines are. Wandering around in search of them, he bumps into Alby.

"You in sector K?" the Antiquities man asks. "I'm in F. Windy, isn't it?"

"Where are the toilets?" Serge asks.

"Use a pot," Alby shrugs back. "They're everywhere."

The next morning Serge wanders around some more. He wanders down to the jetty. It looks firm enough to land the segments of a radio mast. Should he write that down? He'll remember it. He wanders back to the main site again, and follows the paths trodden between one hole and another, the lines made by the strings. It's an aimless wandering: he has to wait another day before the *Ani* sets back off to Cairo. Sometimes the paths split, or end, or double back on themselves; sometimes the strings angle him back to an intersection that he crossed ten minutes or a half-hour earlier, but he doesn't mind: it helps him pass the time. At around noon he finds himself descending into the long gash where Falkiner's tents are. Falkiner himself is absent; Serge passes unhindered through a tent-porchway to a chamber of tomb proper that's been turned into a living room: a desk, sofa and deckchair have been set up in it, and a carpet has been spread across the floor, its pattern strangely off-set by the decorations on the walls.

"Found your way here after all?" asks Laura, appearing in a doorway that leads further in. For the first time since he's met her, she's smiling—in a way that makes Serge feel embarrassed, as though found out, although what for he can't quite think. He tries to smile back.

"Come in," she says, rubbing her forehead again.

Her chamber has been turned into a kind of warehouse. All kinds of numbered objects lie around it—some crated, as though ready for dis-patch, some open, still awaiting processing. Some, like two wooden coffins covered on both outside and inside with inscriptions, are large, occupying a pallet each; others, like a set of headbands, necklaces and bracelets laid out on the floor in rows, are tiny; yet all seem to be accorded the same meticulous attention. This indiscriminate assiduous-ness has been applied regardless of age as well. Not all the objects are old: some, like a sardine-can with German writing on it, a scrap of newsprint, a wristwatch with a snapped strap and a leather boot with rusty cleats and a frayed lace, are clearly relatively modern—yet they, too, have been dusted down, laid out and numbered.

"I have to inventorise it all," says Laura, nodding towards two large ledgers lying face-open on her table.

"So it *was* newspapers I saw in those mounds," Serge says, "and not papyri."

"Could have been," she replies; "could equally have been papyri. It's an eclectic mish-mash around here. The newspaper that page came from is eighty-two years old, while other scraps we've found have headlines from six months ago. It's like that across all periods: the chambers have been gone through so many times that you get Fifth Dynasty, Late King-dom, Napoleonic and modern objects lying side by side. By noting where you found each you can date the various interventions, right back to the outset. Watch out."

Serge is running his hand over one of the two coffins.

"Why? Are they infectious?" he asks.

"No, delicate. The wood's rotting away, and the ink's fading. I have to copy the writing."

Serge lowers his face into the coffin: the texts are written in deep, blue-black ink that disappears in places into the dark mahogany, which, in turn, is full of holes.

"Ants," she explains. "It's funny: 'sarcophagus' means 'flesh-eating'—and now it's being eaten itself. Some of the objects we've found are in too delicate a state to be examined here. Pacorie takes a swab off them; then they get sealed and shipped back up to Cairo for examination."

"What are these flies made of?" Serge asks, pointing to a necklace that's composed of several plastic-looking insects all threaded together.

"Flies," she answers. "They *are* flies, preserved in resin. Necklaces of this type were fairly common. This one beside it's a mixture of ivory, carnelian and glaze."

She passes her hand over a set of beads strung in repeating sequences of white, gold and blue, with a red spacer-bar between them. Circular and domed, they look like tiny insulators made of porcelain or coloured glass.

"Look at all these scarabs!" Serge exclaims excitedly. There must be twenty or more of them. Their shapes, sizes and patterns are as varied as those of the ones he came across in the museum or the market—on top of which there's a detail that he hasn't seen before: two or three have, carved into their underside, not images or patterns, but whole sequences of words.

"Secrets of the heart," says Laura, noticing him peering in bemusement at the hieroglyphic phrases. "In New Kingdom burials, the deceased's unreported deeds, clandestine history and guilty conscience were confided to these things."

"And that's what's written on them, to be printed out after his death?" he asks.

"It's more complex than that," she answers. "What's engraved on them are spells to censor all these secrets, so they won't come out at judgement and weigh down the heart. It had to weigh less than a feather, or the soul was doomed."

"So the scarab *withholds* the vital information even as it records it? Even as it *prints*?"

"Exactly. They were often placed in the heart-cavity. This one," she continues, picking up a sparkling grey scarab carefully, "is made of basalt. And the one beside it is rough quartz."

"But it's got copper wound around it," Serge says, pointing with his little finger to a band circling the beetle's waist. "Why would some grave-robber or archaeologist wind copper round it, then leave it behind?"

"The copper would have been there from the start," she says. "The ancient Egyptians used it a lot. This bowl's copper; so's this ewer."

She flicks the latter with her finger; it rings out tight and clearly, like a tuning fork. Serge follows its vibrations round the chamber with his eye. The place looks less like a warehouse to him now, and more like the backstage area of the Empire Theatre where he visited Audrey. The anachronous medley of objects, their jumbled juxtaposition, seems as incongruous as the faux restaurant interiors, modern cars and Amazonian horse-heads. One of the objects in the room looks quite familiar: a shallow, open box in which a kind of circuit-board is fixed.

"Is that Isis's cohering set?" he asks, nodding at the thing. Straight metal strips divide its wood at regular intervals; above these, cut into the box's side, are notches, every fifth of which is larger than the four on either side.

"Professor Falkiner thinks that it's some kind of game," she answers. "You move up one side and down another, with the players starting at opposite ends. The notches are for counting. You can see the tenth and twenty-sixth lines are connected, which suggests that you could jump from one spot to another, like in Snakes and Ladders."

"So where are the dice?" he asks.

"They probably used knuckle-bones. A pair of these were found a few feet from the board—I think . . ." She steps back to the table and flips through the ledgers till she comes across a diagram. "Yes: right beside it."

"Wow, you really are forensic," Serge says, looking at a photograph pasted beside the diagram, confirming the positions, indicated by the latter, in which objects have been found. Beside each object in the photo there's a little stand-up card bearing a number—presumably the same one with which it's been labelled in its new location here in Laura's props-room.

"Oh, this is nothing," she replies. "You want to see forensics? Come with me."

She leads him through another doorway to a chamber to the side of hers. Pacorie's in here, chemistry set fully unpacked, tubes, slides and beakers laid out all around him.

"L'Homme Pylon," he says by way of greeting, "bienvenue." He has a ledger too, in which he's entering readings.

"He's scraped, scratched or rubbed at virtually all the objects in my room," Laura tells Serge. "The earth around them too; the walls, the floor, the lot."

Pacorie, faced with this accusation, shrugs. "Is necessary."

"And what have you found?" asks Serge.

"Gypsum, limestone, manganese, copper, calcite, the garnet, amethyst, red jasper—or, to state it in a mode more *scientifique*: Mn, SiO_2, Cu, $CaCO_3$, $CaSO_4$. *Surtout*, the C: the C is everywhere."

"The sea?" asks Serge.

"The letter: C."

"What's C?"

"*Carbon*: basic element of life."

Laura tugs at his sleeve, in a way that's familiar to him, though not from her. He follows her back to her chamber. At the back of this is a third opening, the only one he hasn't been through yet.

"What's behind there?" he asks.

"The part where all this stuff came from."

"Can we go in there?" he asks.

"No," she tells him. "Falkiner will be back soon." It's the first time she hasn't used the word *Professor* when talking about him—as though, inside the tomb, and perhaps only here, her allegiance and complicity were gravitating away from him and towards Serge. She's still holding his sleeve. Releasing it eventually, she says: "Come back in two hours, after lunch. He'll be out again then."

Serge returns to his tent, where he's served some more stew in a pot that looks just like the one he's using as a commode. He dozes after this, then wanders the site again, this time keenly aware of the plethora of buried objects it contains: he pictures coffins, boots, board-games and sardine tins lurking beneath him, particles shaken from the sand and plaster by each footstep trickling down across their surfaces. A rat scurries across the path in front of him, then disappears into a hole. Some of the tomb-openings have wasps' nests growing, mould-like, on their splintered hatches. He has to detour round a hovering cluster of them on his way back to see Laura.

He finds her busily transcribing lines of text from the coffins into one of her ledgers. The lines run in strips, like flypaper or film, each frame a single picture: bird, scythe, foot, ankh, eye, a pair of hands . . .

"What does it say?" he asks, peering over her shoulder.

"They're spells, for executing functions: opening the mouth so the deceased can eat, warding off crocodiles who want to devour his heart, things like that. All surfaces had these things written on them: amulets, masks, even bandages."

On the page facing the one onto which she's copying the strips are tables noting where these strips have come from: *outer coffin, right . . . outer coffin, left . . . ditto, foot . . . head . . . inner coffin, right . . . inner coffin, left . . . ditto, foot . . .* Below this, there's a register of objects, with columns for *grave, body, vases, coffin, beads.* The entries in this read like doctors' notes: *cut-up body . . . copper borer in bone . . . XLIII, 2 rolls of bandage . . . linen over left leg, head on box . . . linen . . . lion scarab . . . jasper scarab . . . linen . . . linen . . . linen . . .*

"You found bodies, then?" he asks.

"Mainly loose bones: these are everywhere, hundreds of them. Most of the intact bodies have been plundered or removed by expeditions. Royal and noble tombs get cleared out early on, due to the value of the objects in them. Middle-class ones are better: they tend to get passed over, and so end up less contaminated. I prefer them anyway."

"Why?"

"They're more interesting, more varied. From the Fourth Dynasty onwards, with the downsizing of the pharaohs' tombs, pools of skilled craftsmen were available to decorate the private monuments of anyone who could afford it . . ."

She's streaming information again—but the languor's gone, and the excitement's back. It excites Serge as well: not only what she's saying but how she's saying it, its strip-procession from her. He looks at her mouth. Its lips, coated by dust, are brown. Watching them move, he has the strange sensation that he's closing in on something: not just her, or information, but what lies *behind* these . . . Laura senses his excitement: her lips pinken beneath their dust-coat and quicken their pace:

"The decorators—artists, scribes—had greater freedom, more leeway to mix and match old texts, thereby creating new ones. A greater choice of subject matter, too. Look at this stele over here."

She leads him to a large, flat slab propped up against the wall. On it, a coloured vignette shows a man seated, in profile, at a table piled high with food. At his feet a dog lounges; musicians, acrobats and dancers entertain him; beneath him servants and craftsmen labour—bakers, perhaps, retrieving loaves from ovens, or perhaps carpenters sawing at waist-high beams, masons chipping and hammering at stone or butchers hacking away at meat; around them, further from the picture's central hearth, men work the fields and fish the marshes. All these figures—entertainers, tradesmen, farmers, pet—are drawn, like the main character, in profile. They interact with one another, and seem to be exchanging words—but in a silent, gestural language only.

"It's beautiful," says Serge.

"The colours?"

"No: the flatness."

"It's the autobiography of one of the people buried in the complex," she tells him. "His life, the characters in it, the world around them. Literature in its infancy. Here the scribe has put himself in, in the bottom corner. See that figure writing?"

"Yes," Serge answers. "What did you call this?"

"A stele. We found it just over here."

Pinching his sleeve again, she leads him through the doorway that she wouldn't let him go through earlier and, crouching down beside a large, square gap in the new chamber's wall through which a small, plastic-coated wire runs downwards into darkness, tells him:

"Stelae were placed one level up from the grave proper, as a kind of visual portal to it. They carried pictures of the deceased's old life to the underworld, and conveyed back up from there ones of the new life he was living—which, of course, was a better, more refined version of the old one."

"Two-way Crookes tubes," Serge murmurs; "death around the world."

"What?"

"Nothing. Where's the grave itself, then?"

"Down here," she says—and, like a rat, she's disappearing through the hole. She lowers herself feet-first, taking hold of Serge's arm to steady her descent. When she lets go, he climbs in too, and makes his way down a long, slanting shaft into whose lower surface footholds have been cut. The sides are moist, oily; the wire runs all the way down, unsecured. When Serge emerges from the bottom into a large room illuminated by electric lamps, he sees that it's the wire that's powering these; also, that his hands are blackened.

"Bitumen," says Laura, holding her black hands up too. "I hope you brought a change of clothes."

He looks around. The numbered markers that he saw in the photographs are still here, standing beside vacant spots. Others guard objects that haven't yet been hoisted to the upper chamber: alabaster dishes, copper pans, fragments of broken pottery.

"Don't move anything," she tells him.

"What are those?" he asks, pointing to three ebony statuettes.

"They're figures for the *ka*—the soul—to dwell in."

"They look like the same person, done in different sizes."

"They are: if one gets broken, the *ka* moves on to another; plus, they show the dead man in three periods of life—childhood, youth, age—so that he himself can relive all three, enjoying them simultaneously."

"And what's through there?" he asks her, nodding at another slab-shaped gap.

"Another chamber that we haven't processed yet. You want to see?"

"Yes," he says.

She picks up a zinc-carbon flashlight and disappears, rat-like again, into the new hole. This one leads to another downward-slanting shaft. He helps her steady herself, then follows her again. There's no electricity in this shaft, nor in the chamber onto which it opens. Laura's flashlight picks out random objects: more broken pottery, parts of a coffin, a tea-box with *Lipton* written on it . . .

"We'll do this tomb after we've cleared the one above," she says.

"Look: it goes on further!" Serge gasps, catching sight of yet another opening in the wall. The excitement's spreading in him, spurred on by the darkness, or the depth, or both.

"They all do: they continue endlessly. Which way do you want to go?"

She jumps her light from one wall to the next; each has a hole in it. Serge looks at one after another, then announces:

"This way."

They descend a little further, then the shaft turns sharply up. They climb it, then descend again. Sometimes the shaft runs flat. It feels like a sewer: slippery, with sides the texture of molasses. It smells like one too.

"Bat-dung," she tells him, holding his hand for balance.

"This one's a bordello," he says as the corridor opens up onto another chamber. Several coffins lie about here, overturned and empty; all around them are smashed pots and shreds of linen. An old metal lamp lies on the floor beside a pile of rubble.

"Looks like the one above has fallen into it," says Laura.

They press on, through chambers neither Falkiner and Laura nor, in most probability, anyone else will ever process, treading constantly over linen and ceramic fragments. Bones too: Serge steps on what feel like knee-joints, knuckles, shin-bones. Sometimes the corridor becomes so shallow that they have to crawl, dragging themselves forwards against whatever pitch-coated surfaces present themselves to their touch. Everything's written on: pottery, bandages, even the walls themselves. At one point, out of breath, they rest, still on their knees, inside a chamber so cluttered with piled-up objects that it makes the previous ones look like neatly kept households.

"Whose tomb is this?" Serge asks after a while.

"Who knows?" she says, pointing the light around. "It looks like twenty people's all collapsed together. Here's another stele."

This one, or what remains of it, shows two central figures, one male and one female, seated one behind the other, the woman whispering something into the man's ear.

" 'Ra-something, master of . . .' " reads Laura, narrowing her eyes; " 'his sister, his beloved, in his heart . . . words spoken by . . . do not . . .' "

"There's that scarab-god again," says Serge, pointing his finger at the image, just below the seated couple, of a man kneeling, arms raised, before a giant beetle mounted on a catafalque or platform.

" '. . . my heart of transformations,' " she continues reading, " 'who comes forth . . . who came forth from himself . . .' "

Her forehead's got black stains all over it. Her cheek too. Serge moves round behind her and, kneeling upright like her, watches as her flashlight moves across the stone, bringing its images and inscriptions into view, as though the metal object were itself projecting them.

" 'Meret-something,' " she reads slowly, " 'she who loves . . . who loves silence . . . he who is . . . who dies . . . who rests upon . . . upon his . . .' "

Her breath's getting shorter and shorter. So is his. Serge knows, and knows that Laura knows, and that she knows he knows, that it's not the lack of air that's causing it, nor the fragmentary nature of the inscriptions she's reading: he can smell, above the dung and bitumen, excitement emanating from her flesh too. His chest is almost touching her back. He leans slightly forwards, and makes contact. She tenses, then tilts her head back, towards his face; her lips continue moving in short bursts, but no more words come from them. He kisses her neck; she wraps her hand around his head, and pulls it down across her shoulders. He starts taking off her clothes, then his. Peeling away his sock, he's aware of a small tickling sensation on his ankle. Then he's in her, his hands sliding down her back while hers grab hold of debris, bitumen and bones. His knee slips on some object, whether organic or not he can't tell; then his hands, too, fall to the floor and find there other hands, not only hers. It feels like an orgy: as though the two of them, their bodies, had become multiplied into a mass of limbs, discarded wrappings and excreta of a thousand couplings, a thousand deaths. She drops the flashlight at some point; it flickers against the wall, then, just before their final gasps spill out and echo round the rooms and corridors, goes off. They crawl around on hands and knees afterwards feeling for it, for their clothes, each other . . .

Somehow, they manage to find their way back up to the surface. Laura stays in her chamber; Serge steps out into the daylight. He climbs to the spot he surveyed the landscape from earlier, and looks down on the site again. For some reason, he recalls Pollard's warning about fake antiquities, and the mad thought flashes through his mind that this whole cemetery might somehow be artificial, phoney as a dud 10-piastre coin. His ankle's itching. His clothes are smeared with black. Looking out across the wider landscape's ridges and plateaus again, he takes his notebook out once more and writes in it: *Here as good a place as any.* Before closing it again, he crosses the word *Arenow* out and writes, in its place, *Am not.*

iii

The journey back to Cairo takes much less time: they're travelling with the flow. The river seems more concrete now, a moving belt that carries the *Ani* instead of shunting it. Now that it's no longer rushing past him, Serge can see the individual silt clusters floating in the water's mass; huge clods as well sometimes, being flushed downstream as though the land were voiding itself with a giant, continental enema. He's alone with the crew now, the sole European. Fragments of his earlier conversations with the others play across his mind as the *dahabia* passes landmarks he vaguely recognises from the outward voyage—but, since he's moving in the wrong direction, these fragments play themselves out backwards, words and gestures scrambled through reversal. Serge scratches his continually itching ankle as he tries to reconstruct their phrases from the plash and creak, their positions and movements from angles of the boom and tiller or the sunlight on the water . . .

Boulaq, when they arrive there, seems reversed too somehow, not quite right: as though, in approaching it from the wrong side, they'd turned its quayside, warehouses and tugs into negatives of themselves. Pollard, who meets Serge off the boat, also seems wrong.

"Didn't your parting go on the other side?" Serge asks, looking at his hair.

"My what? Not got your land-legs yet?"

Serge is stumbling, his left arm lowered right down to his ankle, which he's scratching violently now, digging his nails in, drawing blood. This isn't the only reason he's stumbling: he feels dazed and disoriented, as though seasick, although he senses that it's something deeper than seasickness that's making him feel this way. Pollard's talking on and on, assailing him with information that doesn't make much sense, as though its logic were reversed as well:

". . . might opt for the direct transmission system . . . still to be decided . . . general feeling you've done excellently though . . . Macauley asked me to pass on . . ."

"How does he know how well I've done? I haven't reported back yet."

". . . leave brought forwards . . . back to Blighty and all that . . . Port Said tomorrow . . . report can be completed in your own time . . ."

"*My* leave?" asks Serge.

Pollard nods.

"But it wasn't due for . . ."

Pollard starts explaining something, but Serge can't listen properly: the movement of the taxi into which his colleague's bundled him is disorienting him further. They head straight for his apartment, where he finds his trunk already packed. He spends a fitful, sweaty night there, then is picked up in the morning and put on a train to Port Said.

"You've got a nasty cysthair," says the man sharing his compartment as Serge scratches at his now much-inflamed ankle.

"A nasty what?" asks Serge.

"A nasty cyst, there," the man repeats, more slowly. "Ought to get it looked at."

Serge looks at the man instead.

"You're an optician, right?" he asks him.

"Not at all," the other answers guardedly. He begins to tell Serge what it is he does, but Serge ignores the content of his speech, trying all the while to place his accent. That he can't do so isn't due to any socio-logical failing on his part, but rather to a growing acoustic strangeness overtaking him: all dialogues and tones have sounded foreign since he left the *Ani,* as though his aural apparatus had been thrown off-kilter by the land's vibrations. Port Said assaults his ears when he arrives: porters and lemonade-sellers haggling for custom, ships' representatives calling out the names of liners as they round up passengers, water-busses sound-ing their horns as they ply the harbour. Serge is escorted, by somebody or other, to the Island and Far East Line's *Borromeo,* on whose deck a gag-gle of tourists, businessmen and civil servants argue in cacophony with stewards over hold and cabin baggage, cabin size and cabin allocation. One lady is repeatedly complaining at being given the wrong one. Serge, surrendering both his cases, is led to his own, where he immediately lies down, passing the next few hours in a state between waking and sleep. At some point the *Borromeo*'s engines start up, and the whole room begins to shake. A little later, the huge ship starts moving. Dragging him-self from his berth, Serge steps out on deck to watch the land dwindle away. The city's lights appear to flicker on and off, as though signalling, Pharos-like, across the water. The ship's wake runs backwards like an inverted vapour trail, its parallels nearing each other as their distance from the stern increases. He wonders if they converge at some point—at the horizon, wherever that is, or perhaps just beyond it. Conversations are taking place around him: someone, leaning on the railings, is pro-nouncing the "Said" of the disappearing city's name "said," as in "he said, she said . . ."

Supper is called, but Serge skips it. Lying on his berth, sweating, he becomes aware of his own body in a way in which he hasn't been since adolescence. His limbs are heavy, gangly; they don't seem like part of him—at least not parts that fall beneath his mind's control, but ones jolted and twitched instead by some manipulating hand located else-where. The engine noise sounds in his chest. It seems to carry conversa-tions from other parts of the vessel: the deck, perhaps, or possibly the dining room, or maybe even those of its past passengers, still humming through its metal girders, resonating in the enclosed air of its corridors and cabins, shafts and vents. Their cadences rise and fall with the ship's motion, with such synchronicity that it seems to Serge that he's rising and falling not so much above the ocean per se as on and into *them:* the cadences themselves, their peaks and troughs . . .

When he falls properly asleep, he dreams of insects moving around a chessboard that may or may not be the sea. At times it seems more like a gridded carpet than a chessboard. The insects stagger about ponderously, stupidly, reacting with aggression towards other insects when these cross their paths: rearing up, waving their tentacles threateningly as antennae quiver and contract, and so on. Despite the unintelligent, blind nature of the creatures' movement, there's a will at work behind them, calculating and announcing moves, dictating their trajectories across the board. The presence of this will gives the whole scene an air of ritual. Above the board a voice intones, with a rhythm as steady as a galley drummer's beat, "*K4, K4, K4 . . .*" After a while the woven mesh of sea turns into desert: an enormous stretch of it, all parched and cracked, across which figures stumble—multitudes of them, whole armies, linked up hand-in-hand, wave after wave, heading towards a demarcated compound. Falkiner's inside the compound, fiddling with an urn, his station-marked geometries forming the supporting struts and girders of some kind of sandbox . . .

Serge wakes up briefly. His berth's drenched in sweat. Looking around the cabin, he sees nothing special: just a cupboard and a chair, his untouched trunk. The single porthole gives onto a night that's lit up by a full, bright moon. The sky's a kind of silvery-black—an odd combination that, again, gives him the sense of having pitched up in a photographic negative. Turning away from the reversed image, he falls straight back into a lucid dream, once more of insects—only this time, all the insects have combined into a single, giant one from whose perspective, and from within whose body, he surveys this new dream's landscape. In effect, he *is* the insect. His gangly, mutinous limbs have grown into long feelers that jab and scrape at the air. What's more, the air presents back to these feelers surfaces with which contact is to be made, ones that *solicit* contact: plates, sockets, holes. As parts of him alight on and plug into these, space itself starts to jolt and crackle into action, and Serge finds himself connected to everywhere, to all imaginable places. Signals hurtle through the sky, through time, like particles or flecks of matter, visible and solid. Each of his feelers has now found its corresponding touch-point, and the overall shape formed by this coupling, its architecture, has become apparent: it's a giant, tentacular wireless set, an insect-radio mounted on a plinth or altar. Serge is the votary kneeling down before it, arms stretched out to touch it; he's also the set itself—he's *both*. Twitching and shifting in his sleep, he fiddles with himself, nudging his way through the dial—and picks up, through the background thrum and general clutter of the conversations taking place all over, particular voices coming from some station that's located in a cabin close at hand: one neighbouring his own, or two away, or possibly lying one deck above or below his and then one cabin along. They're special voices, saying *important things*. There's music coming from this nearby cabin-station too, but Serge can't quite hear its melody: it, like the special voices' words, is just beyond the range of hearing. He can tell, though, from the rhythm, the solemnity and grandeur of both words and music, that they form part of a ceremony of such splendour and magnificence that, to it, the ritualised game of chess he witnessed earlier bore the same relation as a canapé does to a banquet, a prelude to a symphony or a quick sketch to a fully executed masterpiece in oil: the ceremony is the climax of the process he's embarked upon, the main event.

"That's the place to be," he says aloud—and, in doing so, wakes himself up. It's morning. The engine noise is still going. The ship's rising and falling as before. He feels slightly better; climbing from his berth, he digs a dressing gown out of his trunk and, slipping it on, makes his way to the *Borromeo*'s baths. These are located near the ship's stern: two rows of wooden shacks each of which opens straight onto the deck. There's a queue to use them. Men read papers and nod at one another gruffly as they wait. Women queue on the far side. A young, honeymooning couple wave to one another from their segregated spots; the lady who was complaining earlier looks out to sea indignantly, clasping her towelling robe tightly around her shoulders. Crewmen change the water between bathers, sloshing from buckets as they swing these across the deck. The bath itself is filled with hot sea-water, cooked in the ship's bowels and piped in through a tap; what the staff are replacing is the bowl of fresh water that rests above this on a shelf. Both have traces of engine oil in them. Stretched out in the tub when it's his turn, Serge watches the petroleum and coal-tar swirl and coalesce across the water's surface; then he shifts his gaze down to his ankle, which is suppurating. *Flesh-eating,* Laura told him: lying on his back quite still, ignoring the impatient tapping on the door, he pictures himself as a dead man in a sarcophagus, swathed in spells and imprecations, heart replaced with secret writing and censorious seals. The soap has a logo embossed on its surface; it has tar on it as well. Serge feels more dirty after he's washed than before, as though his labours, like those of a dung-beetle, had soiled rather than purified him.

Breakfast consists of blocks of bacon, fried bread, black pudding and mushrooms. They all look the same: dark lumps of matter. They taste the same as well, all giving off the flavour that, in vapour form, pervades the whole ship: a compound of decayed funguses, hot engine oil and onions. The indignant lady's at it again, complaining to the stewards that she hasn't been allotted the right table. The stewards try to relocate her, concocting a story about mixed-up or badly copied seating manifests, which they attempt to sell, with profuse apologies, to the family at the table the complainer covets. These people grudgingly move, although not to the complainer's table, which is too small to accommodate them: they're re-seated at a third one, which necessitates a new eviction, a new relocation. Pushing his plate away half-eaten, Serge leaves the dining room and skirts a game of deck quoits being played outside. Pausing for a while, he stares at the patterned markings and the poles rising above them; then, feeling fever taking hold of him once more, heads back to his cabin.

Lying on his berth, he sweats. The sweat, mixing with the tar-deposit left on his skin from his bath, turns black. That's what he thinks is happening, at least: it's possible that the sweat came out of him black in the first place. *Mela chole:* he hears, amidst the engine's rumble and the room's higher-pitched rattling, Dr. Filip's thin, electric voice talking about black meat. He hears a lot of things: chants of the Versoie Day School children as they reel off their pronunciation exercises, footsteps marching along country roads, the whirr and clack of film projectors or motorised curtains. It seems that these are welling upwards, from the bottom of the sea—and that the sea itself is black, oily and dense. Closing his eyes, he pictures it as shellac, and the *Borromeo*'s prow as a gramophone needle, bobbing as it rides the contours of a disc. After a while, the image grows so strong in his mind that he becomes convinced that there's a Berliner just outside his cabin: one deposited by someone, for some reason, in the corridor beside his door. He can clearly hear it playing, repeating variations of the same phrase:

Inking the centre
Inking the centre of the country
Inking the centre of

These words loop a few times, then give over to a single syllable, repeated:

kod, kod, kod, kod . . .

—a word, or non-word, that itself eventually mutates, changing its provenance and status until it finally resolves itself as a knocking on the cabin's door.

"Who is it?" Serge calls out, or thinks he does.

"*Thod, thod, thod, thod . . .*" a voice calls back. The door swings open, and a steward enters.

"Bodner?" Serge asks.

The steward says something, but it doesn't make much sense. His voice trips over itself, stuttering.

"Bring the Berlin inner," Serge says. "In, I mean."

"The what's the what, sir?" the steward enquires, holding some kind of clipboard in his hand.

"The ink set," Serge replies.

The steward momentarily retreats, returning behind a trolley on whose tray large, black machine parts lie. The parts, while different shapes and sizes, have a uniform look: Serge can tell that they all belong to a single, larger contraption. The steward runs his finger down his clipboard's columns until he finds the entry that he's looking for and, tapping his fingertip twice against the spot where the pertinent paragraph commences, tells Serge:

"It's inset inset."

"What's that?" Serge asks him.

"It's in sections," the steward repeats, without moving his lips.

Serge tries to ask him what the thing is, but his lips won't move either. None of him will move—not willingly, at least. It's by virtue of the gangly, mutinous movement willed from elsewhere he experienced earlier

303

that he finds himself, after the steward's disappeared again, crawling across the floor and, taking hold of each machine part with his feelers, reassembling the contraption. Segments slot together with an automated ease: he knows right where to put them, and they know right where to go. Pretty soon he has the whole thing up and running, in its full arched, columned, knobbed and needled glory: it's an even better version of the wireless set he merged with last night—an improved model, Mark II. As he hits the first clear frequency a voice spills from it and announces, in the manner of a call-sign:

"Incest-Radio."

Lubricating the dial with his sweat, Serge sets to work, first capturing, then moving around, the cabin-stations he was tuned into last night, the station-chambers. It's a matter of laying hold of each, feeling for its parameters, its walls, then lifting it up intact and relocating it wholesale: the room, and the conversation taking place in it. Parts of each spill in transit, trickling into other ones, distorting and corrupting their own conversations and adding to the general clatter—but Serge knows that, in methodically capturing and relocating one after the other, he'll eventually unearth the one he's looking for, the special chamber. He can feel its music growing closer, its melody gaining form; its voices, too, becoming clearer, more precise. At the same time, commensurate with this drawing-near and sharpening, corresponding to it with a perfect technological alignment, a part-to-part reciprocity, he can feel excitement and desire growing in him, driven to a pitch by the knowledge that nothing is, has been or ever will be more important than the successful execution of the task in which he's now engrossed. Finally, whether after minutes or hours he can't tell, it happens: the chamber itself looms into view and opens up to him, and he finds himself bathed in its noise and signal—not just the transmitted noise and signal, picked up at a distance, but the *source* noise, the *source* signal, at their very point of origin—as he stands right at the ceremony's heart, its main participant.

The ceremony is either a coronation or a marriage—or, more properly described, a combination of the two. The décor is regal: jewel-encrusted birds set upon boughs of gilded trees while peacocks roam a petal-strewn floor below them, their fanned-out, diamond-studded tails displaying large suns as they brush over amber-coloured blocks of camphor delicately spun around by filigrees of twisted gold. Serge and his bride stand on a raised podium. The couple wear, wrapped around their heads, black ribbons that have smudged their foreheads in the manner called for by the ceremony's custom. To the side of the podium a steward stands wearing the ibis-mask of Thoth, holding a set of towels or tablets, copy orders or reports. Behind the steward stretches Versoie's Mosaic Garden, stables dilapidated, path all overgrown, the ruins of the main house visible beyond its collapsed wall. Next to him, transformed into a towel-robed priestess, aerodynamic purple and black triangles running backwards from her eyes, stands the ship's indignant lady. Behind these two, just off the podium, seated at front-row tables over which they lean excitedly, are journalists: they thrash incessantly at typewriters, hammering out sheets of copy that are torn from their machines' rollers the moment each page is filled, handed to scurrying messengers and whisked off to Fleet Street to be typeset alongside insurance ads, printed on huge, groaning presses, bundled and dispatched to cities all around the world and scoured in secret rooms for keywords and acrostics. Since Serge and his bride have commandeered the typewriters' ribbons for their headgear, the pages are all blank—but this doesn't seem to worry anyone: they're hammered and handed out, transferred, typeset, printed and pored over nonetheless. Opposite the journalists, on the podium's far side, musicians play, vibrating as they do so. Behind these, and all around, handmaidens—androgynous children of both sexes—hold black circles aloft as they chant, in unison:

That in black ink
That in black ink
That in black ink my love

In front of Serge and his betrothed a male priest stands, canvas or papier-mâché wings extending outwards from broad shoulders. He, too, pronounces words, mumbling in liturgical tones long strings of blessing that, through their iteration, bring about the ceremony's goal. The exact form of each word can't be made out above the chanting of the hermaphroditic handmaidens and the *clickety-clack* of the reporters' Coronas, nor is it meant to be: like all liturgical oratory, it runs from his mouth and slips by in a smooth and constant thread. This turn of phrase, this figure of speech, "a smooth and constant thread" (and Serge can hear it too, this phrase, these *very* words, running alongside or behind or, perhaps, still further *within* the chanting and intoning and the rest, issuing as though from a room not separated from this one but lying rather somehow concurrent or convergent with it: words being reeled off like the radio commentary at a boxing match) is far from metaphorical: a silken thread is *actually* running from the priest's mouth, streaming over Serge's and his bride's shoulders and the shoulders of the handmaidens, the branches of the trees and the fragrant camphor blocks before it falls to the confettied floor and gathers round the gliding peacocks' feet. Parts of its script ring clear: the part (for example) about the "tick of time" that, at some juncture in the recent past, ceremonially bit him, or the associated, aptly reflexive two-word fragment "ticker-tape." The hand-maidens continue chanting, modifying their refrain's sequence as their voices, somehow dull and jubilant at the same time, rise in pitch and volume:

That in black ink
That in black ink
My love may still shine bright

Serge can feel this love, too, not in some abstract way but literally: physically *feel* it—see it as well, materialised in the camphor and the thread, the branches and the feathers, the gold filigree and, most of all, the black typewriter ribbons. It's in the texture of the air, which has a crinkled feel, like crêpe. It's in his transformed and transforming body. Two of the handmaidens step forwards and drape a garland on the pylon rising from his waist. Glancing down, he sees that the garland's made of dead flowers—and the knowledge hits him in this instant that the chil-dren are dead too, that the whole kingdom over which he and his new wife are being anointed is negative. It's negative, again, in the strict pho-tographic sense: a reversed template from which endless correct, right-way-round copies can be printed, but that itself is destined to be held back in abeyance, out of view, withdrawn—a fact that makes this one moment of revelation he's being granted all the more exceptional, all the more sacred, as though he'd suddenly been given access to the darkroom of all history. Chemical odours waft across the podium as the priest turns to bride and groom and pronounces their names. These are both long, and full of compound parts: Serge's is "Ra-Osram-Iris-K4-CQD"; his bride's is "CY-Hep-Sofia-SZGY." Crowds, thronging around the stage from further back, shuffling and stumbling forwards across squares extending to infinity, whole hordes of them, wave their feelers in the air in celebration. Time flattens as it rushes backwards, ticker-taping too: this is a send-off, a departure—only this time, Serge is on the boat, not the jetty . . .

A sudden whistle pierces the air: it's a reveille, a gathering-call. Everything's coming to a head, converging: the lines, angles and dimensions of the room, the gazes of handmaidens, priests, attendants, journalists and insect-populace alike. All these are now directed towards the veil covering the face of Serge's bride. The music, chanting, intoning and typing have all been suspended in anticipation of the fabric being lifted. Sophie does this now, peeling the gauze away and gazing straight at him. There's no need for her to ask him if he recognises her. Her face is blank—a featureless oval of the texture and off-white colour of a fluoroscope screen—which for some reason makes it all the more instantly recognisable. It has folds in it, creases and indentations. Images kink and distend as, accompanied by the familiar sound of whirring, they start playing across its surface: grainy and jumpy, they show siblings passing through an orchard, running down the neatly ordered rows between its trees. The trees themselves—their bark, leaves and fruit—are a corroded colour. The siblings are as well. The whole scene's flat, like film. Without unflattening, it rotates round until it's being shown from above, in plan view. Then it flickers out, and gives back over to the map-contours of Sophie's otherwise blank face. These, in turn, direct Serge's gaze downwards, to her hands, which rest above a vat of apples that are slowly fermenting. Picking a much-worm-drilled one from near the pile's top, she proffers it towards him . . .

It's not clear whether he's meant to take the apple or not. The contours of Sophie's face morph to form a mouth, which opens, in an equally ambiguous way: it seems at first that it's going to bite the apple; then that it's him into which the teeth are about to be sunk. But both these impressions turn out to be wrong: it soon becomes apparent that the mouth has opened in order to speak. Sophie's going to say the word that will complete the ceremony, bring about its climax, sealing his and her anointment, their ascendancy and union—and that will, at the same time, deliver to the crowd the proclamation that they've come to hear, transforming, unifying and redeeming them, redeeming everything. The word is welling, not so much in Sophie's lungs and thorax as in space itself, roaring across it like a giant wave, loudening as it approaches.

Then it arrives, rupturing the air as it breaks across the podium: it's a burst of static—a static that contains all messages ever sent, and all words ever spoken; it combines all times and places too, scrunching these together as it swallows them into its crackling, booming mass, a mass expanding with the strength and speed of an explosion of galactic proportions, a solar flare. The static rushes over the whole crowd, and roars through Serge's body, making his limbs and chest contract and shiver with convulsions. Sweat, or seed, or sediment, spills from him. Everything is spilling: as the chamber's walls are blown away, rows of box files spring open on ministry shelves, vomiting their contents; archives gush up from the ground like oil; glass cabinets shatter and erupt; bathtubs slosh and overflow; even graves are opening, the dead being catapulted back out of the earth . . .

The static comes at him again: a second burst, heading the other way, like an enormous echo or the backrush from the first explosion, air propelled out by its breath being sucked in again. This time it carries him along with it: he feels himself rushing backwards, through a black and endless void. He's merging with the void: seared, shot through, *carbonisé,* he's become the sea of ink, the distance between planets, the space across which signals travel. Like time itself, he's flattening, turning into carbon paper: the black smear between the sheets, the surface through which things repeat, CC themselves, but that will itself always remain black, and blank. Looking backwards as the sound-wave draws away from him, accelerating onwards, he sees things being duplicated in the expanse created by its passage: cats and phone-wires, cars and dancers, rivers. The orchard's been duplicated too: the siblings have stopped running through it and are sitting at a game-board. All these scenes and objects have been reproduced inwardly, as though injected through some kind of time-syringe into his stomach, in whose blackness they're suspended like small, lit-up screens, contained by the walls of a new syringe that frames them and injects them further inwards, again and again, the scenes and objects miniaturising more and more as they regress. Eventually, they become so small and distant that they dwindle. From where he is now, he can see the children in the orchard and their game-board shrinking, and the orchard itself shrinking, and the wires around it too: their edges all contracting to form a compound that itself shrinks until it's so small that it's no longer perceptible. Then the whole image fades away. The noise has faded too: only fragments of it are left, small residues, vague sonic smudges . . .

In the middle of the second night away from port, Dr. Martinov, an Island and Far East Line company doctor of some six years' standing (previously of the *Chakdina* and, before that, the *Aurora*), is summoned from his cabin to attend to a sick passenger. He finds the young man delirious, bathed in sweat and subject to a temperature so high as to be (in his opinion) unsurvivable. Quinine would be of little help: it's not malaria that's causing the fever, but rather a cyst on the patient's ankle that's become so infected that it's clearly poisoned his whole bloodstream.

"Tourist?" he asks the steward.

"Civil servant," the other replies. "He was muttering something about rooms being moved around."

The sick man, roused by these words, tries to speak.

"What's that?" asks Martinov.

The man, his eyes half-vacant, makes a great effort that results in no more than the word "dumb" issuing from his lips.

"Who's dumb?" asks Martinov.

The young man concentrates his face again and manages to say, beneath his breath:

"*Dummy chamber.*"

"Where?" Martinov asks.

"*Everywhere,*" replies the man. "*What's not?*"

"What's not what? Do you have a next of kin?"

The young man's eyes roll upwards and his face wrinkles into what looks like a smile. A kind of growl rises from his throat; he concentrates his facial muscles again, and manages to say:

"*It came through.*"

"Through what?"

"*Through me.*"

"What did?"

"*The call: I'm being called.*"

Dr. Martinov turns to the steward and instructs him:

"Go to the wireless room and ask them if anything's come in for him."

The steward leaves the cabin. While he waits for his return, Martinov pulls a chair up by the berth, and sits watching the young man's face. He's watched a lot of people die, but it's a little different each time. This man is struggling with something. Although his eyes are growing more and more empty and listless with every passing minute, the jaw seems rigidly determined, held in firm position; the lips, too, are taut and sculpted, as though trying to shape more words. With each outward breath, they form a small, thin parting, which makes the exhalation sound as a long, drawn-out *sssssss;* then, at each breath's end, after the failing lungs have emptied themselves but before they've thrown their engines into reverse and started the slow process of replenishing themselves again—in the short hiatus between exhaling and inhaling, the man's throat contracts three or four times in quick succession, making a repeated clicking sound, a set of quick-fire *c-c-c-c*'s. It does this every time, with a strange regularity: "*sssssss, c-c-c-c; sssssss, c-c-c-c; sssssss, c-c-c-c . . .*"

The wireless room is one deck down. It has two clocks on the wall: one showing Cairo time, one London. Beneath these, thin electric cables trail across the room's wooden panels, one leading to a lamp, another to a bell. A man sits below the wires with headphones on, facing the wall. To his right is a stack of paper and a stamp; to the right of these, nailed to the wall, a basket; above the basket, widening as it runs up to the ceiling, hangs a speaking tube. The room has no windows. The operator doesn't turn around as, in response to the steward's enquiry as to whether any telegrams have arrived for an S. Carrefax, he flicks through the basket and answers in the negative.

The steward leaves. As he passes the kitchen door on his way back to the stairs a Sudanese cook comes out and tips scraps from a bucket over the *Borromeo*'s stern. The steward pauses and watches the scraps bobbing in the churned-up water for a while. The moon's gone: only the ship's electric glow illuminates the wake, two white lines running backwards into darkness. When the stretch in which the scraps are bobbing fades from view, the steward turns away towards the staircase. The wake itself remains, etched out across the water's surface; then it fades as well, although no one is there to see it go.

ACKNOWLEDGMENTS

Many thanks to:

Louise Stern, for her animated lectures on deaf education; Jane Lewty, for her insights into radio and modernism; Penny McCarthy, for Spenserian guidance; Cathie Shipton, for chemical advice; Sam Crosfield, for his horticultural expertise; Aleksander Kolkowski, who knows everything there is to know about early recording equipment; Markéta Baňková, for finding me a perfect spa town; Edward Bottoms, for helping to disinter the Architectural Association's history; Steven Connor, for his reading list on séances; Marko Daniel, for images of *Arsenura armida* and Marconi operators' cabins; Charles Burney, for Egyptological wisdom; Alex Bowler, for his sharp line-editing; Dan Franklin, for his confidence; Marty Asher and Sonny Mehta, for their commitment; and Melanie Jackson and Jonny Pegg, for their untiring support.